Psychic Seductions

by

Ella Jade

Nola Cross

Jacquie Underdown

Lacey Wolfe

Lisa Knight

Stephanie Beck

Ellen Cummins

Psychic Seductions

Always You: copyright © 2015, Ella Jade

A Hint of Heaven: copyright © 2015, Nola Cross

Cupid and Cupcakes: copyright © 2015, Jacquie Underdown

Psychic Set-Up: copyright © 2015, Lacey Wolfe

Something in the Water: copyright © 2015, Lisa Knight

Indigo Stars: copyright © 2015, Stephanie Beck

Taming Fury: copyright © 2015, Ellen Cummins

Edited by Pamela Tyner

Cover Art by Fantasia Frog Designs

ISBN: 978-1-944270-03-2

All rights are reserved. No part of this book may be used or reproduced without written permission, except in the case of brief quotations in articles and reviews. The unauthorized reproduction or distribution of this copyrighted work is illegal.

This book is a work of fiction and any resemblance to persons, living or dead, or places, events or locales is purely coincidental. The characters are productions of the author's imagination and used fictitiously.

Published in the United States of America by Beachwalk Press, Incorporated www.beachwalkpress.com

Always You / Ella Jade

Always You
by Ella Jade

Aurora Mills has moved back to her hometown after a messy divorce which has left her penniless. Her friend Clara offers her a job at their family's pub, and within days Aurora runs into Clara's older brother Caleb. Aurora has always been attracted to him—there's something about him that just draws her in.

Caleb Larson has spent the past few years coming to terms with the tragic deaths of his parents and struggling with the guilt of not being able to prevent it. His gift of premonitions should have allowed him to see their future. After Aurora returns to town, whenever he's in her presence, he can sense that they have a deep connection of some type. Then he has a powerful vision from the past, and he knows there's even more to his feelings than he thought. Can these two lost souls find peace in each other's arms?

Always You / Ella Jade

Prologue

The Larson siblings sat at the large, round wooden table overlooking the view of the river at Bank Street Cafe, laughing and chatting about their week. They had always been a tight-knit group, but their bond had strengthened with the tragic and sudden loss of their parents two years earlier. Caleb, Clara, Austin, and Matt met every Thursday night for dinner at their family-owned pub, without fail.

The patrons often stared and whispered as they observed the eccentric group. Some sympathized with their loss, but others were drawn to their good looks and charismatic personalities. Then there were those who had lived in the town for years, spanning generations, as the Larsons had. Their chattering wasn't as sympathetic or admiring. Those townspeople were curious about the uniqueness of the siblings.

They wanted to know if the rumors swirling around the community for decades about the family were true. Did they have a special blood coursing through their veins that gave them some supernatural powers or were they just odd? Could one of them see into the future or another one connect with the dead as people had heard? What about the rumors of telepathy or that one of them possessed a sixth sense?

Always You / Ella Jade

It was that type of gossip that forced the group to keep to themselves. Living with special talents created a burden for each of them. The less people they let into their lives, the easier living became.

On this particular Thursday evening, something was about to change everything for one of them.

Always You / Ella Jade

Chapter 1

Caleb Larson hurried into the pub, hung his black wool coat on the rack behind the hostess desk, and glanced around the crowded establishment. Business was booming. The bar area was full, there was a bit of a wait for a table, and the kitchen doors opened and closed constantly as the busy waitstaff went in and out. Not bad for a Thursday night in such a small town.

As money filled the till each night the return on his investment was inevitable. The restaurant had lost money for years, and he had considered selling it, but Clara, his younger sister, wouldn't hear of it. She had a point. Bank Street had been in their family for fifty years. Their grandparents bought the place and handed it down to their parents. When they were killed in a car accident, Caleb was left to deal with the struggling dive.

Clara promised that if he invested in the pub she would do everything in her power to make it work. From the looks of things she was holding up her end of the bargain. Business had never been better. He suspected Clara wanted to hold on to the place for sentimental reasons, but she had done what she had promised.

When he looked over at the table in the corner and saw his siblings laughing and teasing one another, he realized keeping the restaurant had been the right choice. Thursday nights proved to be the best therapy any of them could ask for. His sister said she had a good feeling, and Caleb never doubted *Clara the Clairvoyant*. He shook the snow out of his hair before joining them. Waving to a few patrons on his way over, he politely smiled, but didn't stop to make small talk.

"Haven't you guys eaten all day?" Clara stared at their two younger brothers as they finished off an order of buffalo wings. "You're going to put me in the red."

"You say that every week," Matt said. "I'm a growing boy."

"You're twenty." Austin, still dressed in his uniform, sipped his beer. He had joined the local police force right out of high school, and now, at twenty-two, he was a respected deputy in the small town just outside of Salem, Massachusetts. "I think you're done growing."

"What's your excuse?" Matt snapped back. "You ate just as many as I did."

"You topped the wings off before I even got here?" Caleb kissed Clara's head on his way to his seat by the window.

"That's what you get for being late." Austin laughed.

"Hey, Cal," Matt said. "I need a check for rent."

"What else is new?" Caleb sighed. Matt was wild and enjoying every second of his partying ways during his sophomore year at the local college. "My house is plenty big.

You could come back home with me."

"No way." His youngest brother looked horrified at the suggestion. "I'm having way too much fun."

"That's what I'm afraid of." Caleb squinted at the board above the bar to see what they had on tap this week. "Make sure the grades aren't slipping, or you'll be back home faster than I could write any check."

"I told you." Clara pointed at the youngest Larson. "College isn't a game."

"It's supposed to be fun," Matt reminded them. "Mom and Dad let you both live away. I'm not even at Harvard. I'm not costing half of what you guys did."

"Yeah, but Caleb is a hotshot attorney, and what is it you're going to be?" Austin pushed his empty glass away from him.

"Not a cop." Matt smirked as he teased his sibling.

"There's nothing wrong with being a cop," Caleb reminded his brother.

"Said the lawyer," Matt quipped back.

"That's enough." Clara stood. "Are we ready to order dinner? I'll put it in."

"Let's get another order of wings." Caleb looked down at the empty plate in the center of the table. "I need a beer too."

It had been a long week. He'd been preparing contracts and acquiring land for a new building in a nearby town. He was quickly becoming one of the top real estate attorneys in the area. He wasn't complaining, but between work, monitoring the pub, and keeping track of his siblings, there was little time for anything else.

"You can get the beer." Clara nodded toward the bar. "I'll get the wings."

"Anyone else need a drink from the..." Caleb stopped talking when he noticed a beautiful woman standing by the bar. She wore a tight fitting t-shirt that said *Bank Street* across her chest and had a tiny apron tied around her slender hips. Her long, dark hair fell over her shoulders and flowed down her back, stopping just above her waist. "Is that..." He ran his hand through his hair as he watched the attractive new waitress stumble and trip over the small step to get behind the bar. "Aurora Mills?"

"Yeah." Austin looked in Aurora's direction just as she composed herself, glancing around to see if anyone had noticed her clumsy moment. "She's still an accident waiting to happen."

"That's not nice," Clara scolded. "She just moved back to town and needed a job, so I hired her yesterday. I was going to tell you all tonight. She could use some support."

"Didn't she get married?" Caleb asked as he observed his sister's friend sweep the bar area.

He hadn't seen her in a few years. Of course, back then she

was just a kid. He was six years her senior and already off at Harvard when Clara and Aurora were in high school. He'd always found her endearing, even a bit of a damsel in distress at times, but tonight he saw her as a woman. Now that he was thirty-two, their six year age gap didn't seem so big.

"It didn't work out. That's why she could use some friends," Clara said. "The bum left her in debt and alone. She's staying with her parents while she figures things out. Life hasn't been easy for her these past few years."

"She's pretty hot," Matt said. "Think she's into younger guys?"

"No, I don't," Clara replied, then directed her next comment to Caleb. "She's been divorced for over a year. Kind of like you and..."

Caleb glared at his sister, daring her to go there. He had been broken up with Darcy, his longtime girlfriend, for over a year. She'd left him at one of the hardest points in his life. He was grieving over the loss of his parents and trying to keep his family together. Austin and Matt were only eighteen and twenty at the time of the accident and needed supervision. The restaurant had been in a shambles and he'd had to deal with the estate. Not to mention his own guilt about not *seeing* the accident before it had happened.

"I didn't say it." She shrugged.

"You thought it," Austin chimed in.

"We're not supposed to use our gifts on one another." Clara fisted her hands on her hips. "Remember?"

"You never follow that rule," Austin said. "You're always going on about that sixth sense of yours, telling us what we should and shouldn't do. I can't help it if I don't know how to tone down my telepathy. It's most active around you guys because I know you best."

"It's okay, Austin," Caleb said. "Sometimes we can't control it."

"Well, no worries about my gift. I think I lost it." Matt pushed his empty plate away. "I'm better off anyway. What good is it if I can't..." He shook his head. "Whatever. Why are we even discussing the things we're cursed with? I thought we were supposed to be forgetting about them."

Clara made eye contact with Caleb, but he didn't intervene. Their youngest brother had been able to communicate with spirits since he was a toddler. He'd been discouraged lately because their parents hadn't reached out to him. It wasn't unusual. Not every spirit came through. Maybe their parents just weren't ready. Or perhaps they knew it would be too hard for the living to move forward if they made an appearance now.

Caleb had been stressing for each of them to give 'normal' a try. Living a life with supernatural tendencies hadn't been working out for any of them lately. Matt was right. Having these extra gifts did feel like a curse at times.

"I'm going to go and get that beer. I'll get a refill for everyone else too."

As Caleb walked across the restaurant he couldn't help but detect a strange energy buzzing in the atmosphere. He was surprised Clara wasn't all over the vibe. It wasn't the usual mix of customers and employees talking and socializing. Something seemed different tonight. It was a peculiar feeling, he thought.

With each step he took toward the bar, the more familiar the sensation became, but he couldn't place where he had experienced it before. Had he come across this impression before or was it a manifestation of something else, someplace else?

The skin on the back of his neck tingled as a cool sheen of sweat covered his brow. His heart rate increased, but the usual premonition that would follow these occurrences had yet to happen. It was as if his psychic abilities were kicking into high gear, but he wasn't getting a clear picture. He tried to dismiss it. *Normal*, he reminded himself. He was supposed to be giving normal a shot.

Just as he approached the bar, Aurora came toward him, fell down the little step again, and smacked into him.

"Sorry." She steadied herself against his shoulders as he caught her arm. "I keep forgetting about that step."

"Aurora." He smirked when her creamy cheeks turned crimson. He recalled her quirky shyness when their eyes connected. "It's good to see you."

* * * *

Aurora tripped over that stupid step where the back of the bar began. That made four times today. She looked around the restaurant, hoping no one had noticed her slip-up, and she caught the gaze of Caleb and Austin Larson as they stared at her from their table. They looked as if they were laughing at her, but trying not to be obvious.

How embarrassing.

She tried to play it off as she grabbed a broom and swept the already spotless floor. She glanced in the direction of the Larsons again. She had always admired their close bond and the way they took care of each other.

Clara had been a good friend to her through the years. Even after they had a falling-out shortly before Aurora left town to follow her now ex-husband Michael. What a loser he turned out to be. Clara had tried to warn Aurora, but she was too in love to see the truth. Five years later, she was broke, her credit was ruined, and she was living back at home with her parents. She had to figure out what she was going to do with her life now that she was alone and starting over.

Clara offered her a job so she could get back on her feet. As she studied the Larsons she couldn't help but concentrate on Caleb. He'd aged rather nicely over the years. She'd been attracted to her friend's older brother ever since the first time he'd come home from Harvard. Who wouldn't be? He was smart, polite, and sexier than any guy she'd ever seen. All the girls in Spring Valley swooned over his thick brown hair, haunting green eyes, and full kissable lips.

She enjoyed sleepovers at their huge, old house when she was a teenager. It was filled with so much warmth and love. Her favorite times being there were when Caleb was home for breaks. He never paid her much attention during her awkward teenage years, but she was completely aware of him. He was the stuff fantasies were made of.

She'd spent hours daydreaming about him rescuing her from her uneventful life. But as a shy kid, he probably only saw her as his sister's clumsy, little friend. He was dating rich, gorgeous college women when she and Clara were busy doing one another's hair on a Friday night, watching movies, and eating popcorn. It was her freshman year of high school, and he was her first serious crush.

She smiled at the memories as she finished sweeping the floor. She leaned the broom in the corner, quickly turned around, and lost her footing on that silly little step she kept forgetting about. Only this time she couldn't pull off her stumble as casually as she had a few minutes ago. Before she could catch herself, she tripped right into Caleb, slamming into his hard, muscular chest. Of all the people to fall into.

"Sorry. I keep forgetting about that step." God, he's pure sin, she thought, trying to pretend her weakened limbs had nothing to do with the tall, dark, yummy man in front of her.

He held her as he wrapped his arm around her waist to steady her. "Aurora." The corner of his irresistible lips curved into a smile. "It's good to see you."

"Hi." Why did she have to be so uncoordinated?

"We'll have to do something about that step. We wouldn't want you to get hurt."

She couldn't pull her gaze away from his. There was something off in his eyes. They had always been her passage into his soul. Even as a young girl, she knew when she stared into his sparkling green eyes there was something special behind them. Today they didn't seem as vibrant as she remembered. Someone had hurt him. She recognized the sorrow because it mirrored her own.

When had she become so deep? Standing in front of him, she no longer felt like an awkward kid. Could he see her as a woman?

"Welcome back to Spring Valley." He released her from his hold. "It's been a few years."

"I'm surprised you remember me."

"You're not easy to forget." His smile oozed all of that Larson charm. How many of her uncoordinated childhood mishaps had he remembered?

"I guess not." Her cheeks heated up when she thought about all the times she had fallen or gotten injured growing up. "At least not when I practically fall into your arms."

"I'm glad I was here to assist."

Me too.

"I'm sorry for your loss. I wanted to come back for the funerals, but, well..." *I couldn't afford it. My idiot husband wouldn't let me.* Why was she babbling? "I called Clara."

"That was very kind. I'm sure she appreciated it."

"It must have been hard for you. I remember how close you all were."

When he looked down at his feet she realized how uncomfortable he was with this conversation. Of course, she thought. That was where his shimmer had gone. He was grieving the loss of his wonderful parents. She shouldn't have brought it up, but she didn't want to be rude and not offer her condolences.

"I mean, it was probably hard for all of you." She had imagined their reunion to go smoother. She wished she could be more sophisticated. More like the women she figured he was accustomed to. That wasn't her. It never would be. "The guys look great. They're all grown up and everything."

"Yeah." He nodded toward the bar. "I need to get their drinks and get back to dinner."

"Right." She wanted their meeting to last longer, but she didn't know what else to say. "I told Clara I'd do some inventory in the back." She lingered for a few seconds, but the silence between them became weird. "Enjoy your dinner." She turned and headed for the back room, focusing on not tripping over anything.

"Aurora," he called after her.

"Yeah?" She looked over her shoulder to find him leaning against the bar. She hadn't noticed just how delectable he looked in his custom-fit suit jacket, crisp white dress shirt, and dark blue tie.

"I'll see you around."

"Okay." Excitement filled her over the possibility of running into him again. Well, maybe not so literally next time, but she did look forward to seeing him, and soon. "That would be great."

She headed to the back, feeling invigorated and full of hope. The last year had been difficult. She'd cried more than she had smiled. Tonight, things seemed different. How could one brief instance with Caleb pull her out of her funk? It was silly, really. Maybe it wasn't even him. Perhaps on this night she was supposed to start the rest of her life. Whatever it was, she'd take it. Her mood was light, and for once she wasn't carrying the burdens that were constantly on her mind.

Picking up the list on Clara's desk, Aurora looked over what she needed to do. Clara had hired Aurora to be a server, but Aurora wasn't comfortable with that idea yet. The thought of carrying trays of food across a crowded room made her nervous. Instead, she'd asked if she could do odds and ends around the pub for now. Clara had graciously agreed.

"Beverage napkins," she mumbled to herself as she looked up at the tall shelves. She needed to stock the bar area with napkins, straws, and paper towels. All were on the very top. She peered up at the high shelves, hoping this didn't end badly.

As she pulled the step stool over to where she needed, she thought about Caleb. He'd always been a cute, intelligent college guy, but now, he was a man. A hot, sexy, muscular man. She hadn't thought about him much over the years. Their lives had taken them in different directions.

She was surprised when Clara told her he was single. She would have thought a catch like him would have been married with a couple of kids by now. Not that marriage was all that. She'd tried it and had failed miserably at it. That wasn't entirely her fault. Her ex was a cheating, free-spending idiot who had wasted years of her life. Every time she thought about the things she let him get away with, she wanted to vomit.

Never again.

So much for her new attitude. How had she let her rotten marriage seep into her positive thoughts? She climbed the stool, holding onto the metal shelving unit, but when she reached up to grab the box with the napkins she lost her footing and let go. It was too late to grip onto anything as she fell backward. In that split second, she was fully aware that she'd be hitting the concrete floor, and hard. She closed her eyes, waiting for the crash, but instead she landed securely in the strong hold of a solid body.

"Whoa," Caleb said as he cradled her in his arms. "Are you okay?"

"Yeah, I lost my balance." She draped her arms around his neck, trying to calm her racing heart.

"You have to be more..." He trailed off, no longer focused on her. Continuing to look through her with no expression on his face, his eyes were distant, almost as if he were someplace else.

"Caleb?" She stroked his cheek, brushing her hand along his stubble covered jaw. When she touched him, she felt calm and secure. Those were emotions she didn't experience often.

He closed his eyes and shook his head as he mumbled something incoherent.

"Is everything okay?" she asked as he opened his eyes.

"Yes, I'm sorry, it's just—" Before he could finish Clara came into the stockroom.

"Hey, there you are." She stopped in the doorway and stared at them for a second. "What's going on?"

"Nothing." Caleb set Aurora on her feet, holding her by her forearm to steady her. "Aurora had a mishap on the step stool, but I caught her before she hit the floor."

"Thank you, by the way." Two times in one night he had come to her rescue. So much for him seeing her as anything but the klutzy kid from the past.

"It wasn't a problem," he said. "I'm glad you didn't get hurt." When he let go of her arm, she couldn't help but notice he still didn't seem right.

"Are you sure you're okay? You zoned out for a bit."

"What?" Clara came into the room and looked her brother over. "What happened?"

"Nothing." It seemed like Caleb didn't want to make a big deal out of whatever had happened a few seconds ago. "I reacted to Aurora falling. I was afraid I wasn't going to catch her in time. I rushed to her quickly, and I guess I was just recovering once I caught her. Don't make this more than it is."

"Aurora," Clara said. "Could you go up front and help Leah seat customers? The dinner rush is in full force."

"Sure." She nodded. "Thanks again." She smiled at Caleb,

embarrassed that he had caught her two times in ten minutes. "See you around."

"I'm sure." He loosened his tie.

She pushed the hair from her eyes as she turned and hurried out of the room. She stopped in the hallway and leaned against the wall, trying to compose herself before heading up front.

Mortified didn't begin to describe how she felt in that moment. As awkward as their two brief encounters had been, she couldn't ignore how her heart rate increased when she was close to him, her palms became sweaty, and her breath caught in her throat when she talked to him. She'd never been so drawn to anyone before. When he caught her, there was a chemistry between them. An energy that pulled them together. And her curiosity had been piqued.

The Larsons had always been different, even a bit off one could say, and they usually did. She'd tried to ignore the rumors in town because Clara was such a good friend, but after looking into Caleb's eyes there was no denying he was unique. She intended to find out just how unique.

Chapter 2

Caleb sat on the edge of the desk, trying to clear his mind. He'd been hit with a powerful vision when he held Aurora. Visions were nothing new for him, but this one was different. It would take him a few minutes to process what he had seen and what it had meant.

"You had a premonition." His sister sat next to him. "I can see how it has drained you."

"More like a retrocognition." He'd always been able to see events before they happen. From as early as he could remember he'd been blessed, or cursed, as Matt would say, with the knowledge of what was coming next. The visions weren't always a hundred percent accurate, and most times they didn't mean anything to him at all.

"Something from the past?"

"Strange, huh?"

"Well, you've done it before. When you were younger, you could describe details of Mom and Dad's grandparents. You've seen events that had happened in our family history."

"It's true," he said. "I've had past visions before, but none have ever involved me."

"Wouldn't that be a memory, not a vision?"

"That's the thing." He pinched the bridge of his nose, trying to stave off a headache. "The vision was not of me in this life. I was in the past. I think. It was me, but it wasn't. I'm not making any sense."

"You saw yourself in a past life? What were you doing?"

"I was in the basement of my house." The family estate that he took over when his parents died. "It was dark, damp, and cold. There were candles, but I didn't see any lights."

"It was before electricity?"

"I think so."

"What triggered the vision?"

"It just came on when I intercepted Aurora's fall. When I touched her, I was hit with a powerful perception. I sensed it earlier by the bar. I thought a premonition was coming, but nothing happened so I dismissed it. I intended to come back to the table, but something drew me to the stockroom. It wasn't a premonition that led me here. It wasn't as if I had seen her fall, but I came back here anyway. I couldn't stop myself."

"Hmm..." Clara thought for a moment. "I wonder what she had to... Wait a minute." She pushed off the desk and paced the room. "You weren't alone in that past vision, were you?"

Clara the Clairvoyant.

"Aurora was there with you. That has to mean–"

"It doesn't have to mean anything." He stood firm, because

he didn't need his sister creating something that wasn't there. He didn't want her getting some false expectation about him and her friend. A set-up was the last thing he needed.

"Are you kidding me?"

"We knew each other in another life." He shrugged. "I'm sure many people have, but not everyone has the capacity to know such things. We're odd, remember?"

"I saw the way you were looking at her when I walked in here. There was a definite zest swirling between the two of you."

"A zest?" He laughed, but he could tell by the look on her face she wasn't going to drop this. Determination was her strong suit.

"She didn't belong with her ex-husband." His sister chewed on her thumbnail as she thought. That was never a good sign. "I told her that before she left town with him. He wasn't her forever guy."

"You said he was a loser. It's not a shock it didn't work out."

"It was more than him being a complete ass. When they were together, I didn't feel anything between them." She stopped pacing, but then she replaced her frantic movement around the room with the fidgeting of her hands. She was about to tell him something outrageous. He could sense it. "It's the same vibe I got, or didn't get, with you and Darcy. There was nothing there either."

"Clara," he warned. Too much had happened over the last two years. When Darcy left, he had shut down and let the grief of his parents' death take over, something he hadn't been able to do before because he was too busy taking care of everything and everyone else. He was finally moving forward and didn't like to discuss his ex.

"Hear me out," she said.

"Do I have a choice?"

"No, you don't."

"Well, then, by all means let it out." He sighed. "The faster you do, the faster I'll get that beer."

"I never thought Darcy was for you. Even without my sixth sense I could tell. I'm sorry you had to find out the hard way, but there was a reason things turned out the way they did."

"She found out we're a family of freaks and left. She couldn't deal with it. Most people can't."

"You're saying we're all destined to be alone?" Clara asked.

Caleb didn't really believe that. He'd already had a premonition of Austin and his high school sweetheart having children, but he hadn't shared that particular vision. He liked to let things play out, especially when it came to his family.

"Not alone, but maybe we just need to find people more like us." He rolled his eyes at the thought, because finding others with authentic gifts was no easy task. It seemed as if everyone these days claimed to have some sort of psychic ability. Those who could truly channel their gifts did so quietly. That didn't mean there weren't some who were more visible, but Caleb found those people to be few and far between.

He and Clara had been approached by the local police to assist in a few investigations. He didn't like exposing himself that way, but Austin had promised the guys at the station would keep it quiet. A couple of cases worked out, a few others didn't, but being psychic wasn't an exact science. It couldn't be forced.

"Maybe not more like us, but more tolerant of what we can do." Clara patted his shoulder.

"Right." He tried to laugh off the conversation. "Look how well that worked out with Darcy. I was with her for years, and when I told her what I was capable of she told me I needed a shrink."

"She was wrong."

"I couldn't blame her. I was dealing with so much. It put a strain on our relationship. I thought by reaching out, it would help me with the guilt of not being able to see that accident."

"That wasn't your fault."

Even if it wasn't his fault, he still had to live with the guilt of not being able to stop what had occurred that night.

"You tell us all the time that whatever path we're on is the one we're meant to take. You didn't have a premonition about their accident because you weren't supposed to. They wouldn't want you to carry that burden. You have to let it go."

"I'm trying." Clara was right. His parents wouldn't want him to carry the guilt. Rationally he knew that, but someplace deep inside he wished his parents were still there. That his gift could have been the reason they didn't take that car ride that night.

"For the record, Darcy was stupid for leaving you."

"She thought I was cracking under the pressure. It's better she left town thinking I was nuts. She would never have accepted us for who we are. We're different, and I can't change that." He was tired of trying to be someone he wasn't. "Let's go eat. I've had enough excitement for one night." He'd also had enough of this conversation. "The guys are waiting for us."

"I'm not going to let you dismiss what you saw."

"I think I should leave that vision where I found it."

"In the past?"

"Exactly."

"I don't agree with you."

What else is new?

"You don't have to." He placed his hand on the small of her back and guided her out to the dining room. "I don't want to discuss it any further."

Always You / Ella Jade

"I'll do all the talking then. I'm used to it. I have three moody brothers."

"What am I going to do with you?"

Caleb stopped and studied Aurora as she sat a young couple at a table by the window. It was as if everything stopped when he was in her presence. Her awkwardness suited her. She didn't hold the grace and poise he was used to. She wasn't as educated as the women he normally dated, and she didn't come from money. She was the complete opposite of what he had grown accustomed to. But when he looked at her, he saw a genuineness that he'd never found in another. Her personality was pleasing, natural and real. She gave off a calming sensation. One he could trust. Maybe he could even find a way to open up to her.

She glanced over and smiled at him before making her way back to the hostess stand. When he'd walked into the pub thirty minutes earlier, he had no idea anything was about to change, but after that vision there was no denying something was coming.

"Isn't she pretty?" Clara broke his musings.

"She's stunning." He couldn't take his gaze away from her. "That doesn't change anything."

"We'll see." Clara headed for their brothers. "You know as well as I do that if it's meant to be, then it will be."

He couldn't argue that.

Chapter 3

On Sunday evening, Caleb tried to concentrate on the contract in front of him. It was for a new client and he wanted to make sure everything was right, but he just wasn't into it. He'd busied himself with work all weekend, leaving little time for thoughts about his sight from the past. Now that the day was winding down and the house was still he couldn't focus on anything but that vision.

What did it mean? What was that strange energy he had experienced on Thursday night? Why was he drawn to a woman he hadn't seen in years? One he'd never really given much thought to when they were younger. Why now?

He tossed his pen on the desk and gave into the urge to go down to the basement. He had been avoiding it for three days. When he moved into the house he had renovated the entire estate, finishing off the basement and including a wine cellar. Obviously the house had changed through the years, but he knew where the vision took place. The property had been in his family for over a century. There was a rich history of people who had resided there. Ancestors with unique talents like those that he and his siblings possessed. It hadn't shocked him that he would receive a premonition of a past life, but he was surprised to learn that he had met up with Aurora in another time.

He wandered down the staircase to the basement, stopping by the archway that led to the wine cellar. It was beyond there that he'd find the place where his retrocognition occurred. He moved through the room, and even with that odd sensation flowing through him, he couldn't seem to stop himself. His heart rate increased with each step he took. A rush overtook him, heating his skin and warming his insides. When he closed his eyes, he saw Aurora's pale skin, piercing blue eyes, and full pink lips. Desire filled his veins when he thought about touching her, taking her in the tiny room behind the wine cellar. He *had* taken her there. He was certain of it.

Once he stepped inside the small space, it was as if he'd opened a portal to another era. The room triggered a vision. This time it was more vivid than the last. The musty room in the back of the cellar was damp and dimly lit with candles. It was a secret room, their secret room. Their connection was forbidden.

The apprehension in her eyes was clear, but her body betrayed her with each kiss. As he pushed her against the cement wall, he attacked her neck, her chest rising with each erratic breath she drew. Her corset was tight, allowing him a generous view of her luscious breasts. Lowering his lips, he skimmed the tops of her creamy mounds, trailing his tongue along them.

Indulging in her sweet taste.

Mine.

"Sir," she moaned in a breathless plea. "We can't."

"Why not?" He slithered his hands up her torso, running his fingers over her erect nipples. "I promise no one will find us here."

"I shouldn't allow you such liberties with my body."

"I'll only take what's offered." He slipped her dress from her shoulders, pushing it low enough to reveal her ivory-colored corset. "You will offer yourself to me, won't you?" He licked his lips, focusing on the lace that held her breasts in place. One tug of the string and she would be exposed. She'd be his for the taking. "What are you offering, my sweet girl?"

The ding of his cellphone stopped the vision more abruptly than he would have preferred.

Damn it! He reached in his pocket and pulled out his phone. A text message from Clara scrawled across the screen.

Need a ride. Can you come to the pub?

He replied, wondering where her car was. He didn't even know she was working tonight.

Be right there.

He glanced around the small room one last time before closing the door and heading upstairs. The people in his vision,

Always You / Ella Jade

whether they were him and Aurora in another life, didn't use names so it might be hard to research who they were. He got the feeling *he* was the owner of the home, much like he was today, and *she* was a servant because she had referred to him as "sir". There wasn't much dialogue to go on, but that wasn't anything new. He usually didn't hear voices in his premonitions. Normally he had to rely on sight and signs to help him figure out what was going on.

He had to put it out of his mind again. If he showed up at Banks with a vision fresh in his head, Clara would pick up on it, and he wasn't in the mood to discuss what he had seen with his sister. Some things should remain sacred.

* * * *

Ten minutes later Caleb parked his car in the small lot outside the pub. There were no other vehicles there, so he figured the place was done for the evening. Sundays had always been a slow night in town, so they usually closed after dinner. No sense making employees hang around if there weren't any customers. He used his key to let himself in, calling out to his sister when he entered.

"Hey." Aurora came out from the back, wearing tight black yoga pants and a t-shirt with the pub's logo on it. The tee was raised slightly, giving him a glimpse of the skin on her stomach. "I was just finishing up. Clara didn't mention you were stopping

Page 30

by when she asked me to close up."

"She isn't here?" *What is my sister up to?*

"Nah, she left about two hours ago." She giggled, and he liked the way it sounded. "I think she had a date with that cute guy who owns that landscaping business."

"Anthony?"

"Yeah, him. Didn't you graduate with him?"

"How did you remember that?" He sat down at the bar, wondering when his sister started dating Anthony Conti.

"I remember a lot about you." She smiled as she hung glasses above the bar. "I may have had a bit of a crush on you when I was a kid."

"Really?" That was news to him. He was already away at school when she began hanging out with Clara. "I didn't know that."

"It was a secret crush."

When she reached up to put away the last glass he saw even more of the skin on her stomach. His fingers itched to explore her. He imagined she would be soft and delicate like in his vision. Would her skin taste the same? Feel as smooth?

"Are you almost done?" He needed to clear his mind of these thoughts. No other vision had been as sharp as the one he'd experienced in the cellar. "I can walk you to your car."

"Umm, my car kinda died this morning. I think it's the

battery. Maybe I'll get it checked out when I get my first paycheck. Until then I'll be hoofing it." She turned out the lights behind the bar. "It's only a few blocks."

Clever, Clara. She never said who needed a ride in that text.

"It's twenty-five degrees out there."

He remembered Aurora spending a great deal of time at his parents' house. Come to think of it, she had spent many nights there. When he was in college, he never gave it much thought, but now he realized her parents weren't around much. Clara said Aurora liked being with their family. She didn't have any siblings. She probably had no one to come and pick her up.

"You're not walking," he said.

"The cold isn't too bad when you're walking fast." She tried to convince him, but he wasn't having it. "I'm used to having a crappy, unreliable car." She laughed and he admired how she could stay so upbeat given her circumstances. "Clara said you renovated the house. I bet it looks amazing."

"I'm glad it's finally finished."

"It always seemed perfect to me when I was growing up." She pulled on a lightweight coat, hardly suitable for winter weather. "The kitchen was my favorite. Your mom was such a good cook. I loved eating over there. You would all hang out and talk while she made dinner. The house was full of so much love. The vibe I got from being there would stay with me for days."

"It sounds like you have some great memories."

"I'm being insensitive," she said. "I just thought you'd like to know how much I appreciated being able to have those memories with your family. Your parents were good to me. I'm really sorry that I couldn't make the trip back here to properly pay my respects. I wanted to, but..."

The remorse in her voice overwhelmed him. He'd spent years with Darcy, but he didn't ever remember her mentioning any times she had shared with his parents, and there were many.

"You don't have to apologize. It's very generous of you to share your memories with me. It makes me feel good knowing you have such fond recollections of my parents. They adored you."

"They were good people. They raised four great kids. You all made them really proud. I'm sure they look down on you every Thursday night when you're eating together, laughing and living. It's infectious." She zipped up her jacket. "I wish I could have... Well, anyway, I better get going. Are you staying?"

"I'm driving you home."

"I'll be fine."

"You don't have a proper coat, or gloves for that matter." He looked her over. "Perhaps we can give you an advance on your paycheck so you can get yourself settled."

"That's not necessary. I can manage until Friday."

He hoped he hadn't offended her, but she didn't have a car or a coat. He wondered what else she was lacking. The urge to make sure she was taken care of was uncontrollable.

"I'll hit you up on that ride though. It's been a long day." She pulled her hair out of the back of her jacket as she headed for the door. "You'll be happy to know I didn't trip down that stupid step all day."

He laughed.

"What?" The smile on her face intensified as she looked at him.

"You're quite refreshing."

"Now there's a word no one has ever used to describe me."

"Hmm..." He tucked the stool under the bar. "What words would they use?"

"Let me see." She chuckled. "How about *clumsy*?"

"Yes, I can see that."

"Right?"

"What else?" He opened the front door for her. "I'm curious."

"I've been described as *curious* too. When I was a kid I swore I would travel the world. I wanted to see everything."

"And now?"

"I'd be happy with seeing the forty-six states I haven't visited in this country." She headed outside. "I'll get there.

Eventually."

"An optimist." He set the alarm and locked the pub up. "I like that."

"I try to be." She nodded as she walked to his car. "I can't go around being negative all the time. What would that accomplish?"

"Nothing." He opened the door to his car for her. "You have a positive energy that surrounds you." He hadn't meant to say that out loud, but there was something about her that made him feel comfortable.

"Clara says that too." She slipped into the front seat. "Cool ride."

"Thank you."

He waited as she buckled herself in. He had a hard time pulling his gaze away from her. Images of the two of them in another time dominated his every thought. The commotion going on inside his pants reminded him how much he had wanted her in that cellar. But now, standing just a few inches from her in their own time, he realized it wasn't the emotions in the vision that fueled his desires. It was much more, and he intended on exploring all this life had to offer the two of them.

"Is something wrong?" Her soft voice broke his revelation. "Did you forget something?"

"Nothing's wrong." He grinned. "I guess you could say I

remembered something."

"I hope it was something good."

"It has the potential to be very good."

Chapter 4

Aurora's parents' house wasn't far from the pub. They'd be there in less than ten minutes, but she didn't want the conversation to end. Caleb was more relaxed in her presence tonight. Whatever had been bothering him on Thursday seemed to fade into the background. He even smiled a few times, and that ignited a flame inside her. She liked seeing him happy. She wanted to believe she was the reason for his mood.

She took in his strong profile as he focused on the road. His chiseled jaw was covered with a dark dusting of stubble that extended under his chin. She spotted a tiny mole just below his right earlobe. She wanted to press her lips to it and breathe in his spicy scent. Being this close to him brought back so many memories from her youth. She never would have imagined him giving her a second thought when they were younger, but now the possibilities were endless.

"Do you like being back in Spring Valley?" he asked.

"I missed this old town. I didn't realize how much until I came back. It's hard to explain, but when I returned, things seemed to change for me."

"Clara told me you've had a hard time these past few months. Coming back here sounds like the right move for you."

"I hope so." She continued to stare at his profile, mesmerized by his presence. "I'm a firm believer in things happening for a reason. My time away from here served a purpose, even if I'm not exactly sure what that purpose was."

"Interesting."

"Don't mind me." She laughed. "I'm a bit kooky." She felt so at ease with him. Almost as if she could tell him anything and he would understand.

"I wouldn't say that." He turned onto her street. "I like to believe everything happens for a reason as well. It's something my family puts a lot of stock in. It hasn't steered us wrong yet."

"Your family is so spiritual. I loved that about you all. When I would walk into your house, I always felt a sense of belonging. Almost like I'd been there before."

"What do you mean?"

"I haven't thought about this in years." Why was she bringing it up now? He was going to think she had serious issues. "I told your mother once."

"What did she say?"

"She said I *did* belong there." Aurora smiled when she thought about Mrs. Larson. "She had such a beautiful soul. A soul like hers doesn't end, Caleb. You know that, right?"

When he didn't say anything she realized she'd overstepped again. Why couldn't she keep her mouth shut when it came to his parents?

"I'm sorry." As they approached her house, a sense of relief came over her. The sooner she got out of his car, the faster she could stop making a fool of herself. "I don't know why I'm feeling so nostalgic."

"You're entitled to your memories too. I can see how much of an impact my family had on you. I'm glad you're back."

"Me too."

"And you're right about my mother's soul. It didn't end with death."

"I don't know why I said that. It's just something I know in my heart."

"I get it. You have a very genuine spirit. I like that." He smiled, but didn't elaborate any further. "I'll have Austin come by tomorrow and take a look at your car."

"That's sweet of you." When he drove up her driveway, she unbuckled her seatbelt, turning so she could face him. She liked looking at him. "You don't think he'll mind?"

"Not at all. He loves tinkering with cars. He says it's therapeutic."

"I should try it. I could use some relaxation these days."

"I know what you mean."

"Maybe we could hang out or something?" *Did I just ask him out?* "I mean, if you have time."

"This week is hectic for me."

"Oh, I'm sure you're really busy with your job." Heat burned her cheeks, and now she wanted to bolt from the car. Why did she think she'd have a chance with the rich, charming, and good looking Caleb Larson? "I guess I'll see you around."

She had to stop acting like a babbling goofball around him. If things were meant to be between them, they'd have to take their own course. She'd have to be patient.

"I hope so," he said. "I was thinking Friday. Perhaps we could go to dinner?"

"Like a date?" She hadn't been this excited since... Well, she couldn't exactly remember when she'd had something to be excited about. Except the other night when she had seen Caleb for the first time in years.

"We can call it whatever you want."

"Date works." *I can't believe this! We're going on a date.*

"Okay." He flashed his perfect smile, and she wondered what he thought of her. Did he find her amusing?

"You can get my cell number from Clara. I'll have to ask to have the night off." Would Clara mind that Aurora was dating her brother?

"Something tells me she'll agree."

"Cool." She kissed his cheek, lingering for a second before pulling away. "Thanks for the ride home."

She turned to make her escape so she couldn't do something embarrassing. He might already think the kiss was too forward, but she couldn't seem to help herself. It was impulsive, but worth it to have her lips on him, even if for a fleeting moment.

"Wait." He took her hand, keeping her in the car.

She shifted her position so she was facing him again.

"I think we can do better than that." He leaned into her, taking her face between his hands, licking his lips as he focused on hers.

Shit! He's going to kiss me. Like really kiss me!

"Not that your kiss wasn't sweet, but..." He brushed his mouth along her jaw, slowly working his way to her lips. "I've been thinking about doing this since I caught you in the stockroom. Can I kiss you, Aurora?"

"Yeah." She'd waited years for a proper kiss from him. "Anyway you want."

"Like this," he spoke against her lips. "Slow, so I can savor you."

"Hmm..." She shivered as his words vibrated into her mouth. Maybe she wasn't just amusing to him. Maybe he could see her as a woman capable of being with him.

He tilted her face to the side, kissing her. Tender at first, but then, as he deepened their connection, so did the intensity. She tingled in places she hadn't felt anything in for so long. The fire in her belly spread lower until she had to squeeze her thighs together in an attempt to create some friction there to ease the warm ache.

Releasing her, he smoothed out her hair as he placed soft kisses across her lips. The heat of his mouth left an impression on hers. She darted her tongue out and ran it along her lips, tasting him, needing to remember everything about their first kiss. The one she had dreamed about for so long. The kiss she never thought she'd get to experience except in her wildest fantasies. It was totally worth the wait.

"Good night, Aurora," he whispered. "You've given me much to ponder."

"Don't think too hard." She reached for the door handle. "That always tends to screw things up."

"That's probably some of the best advice I've ever received."

"Who would have thought I could come up with something so useful?" In all the years she had known him, tonight was the most they'd ever talked to one another. And that kiss... How had she ever lived without those lips on hers?

"I have a feeling you're very useful."

She slipped out of the car, missing him when he pulled out of her driveway. She shoved her hands in her pocket, trying to stay warm in the frigid air. The skies were dark and the wind had turned bitter. A storm was brewing. She could feel it coming as she skipped up the path and made her way into the house. Closing the door behind her, she leaned against it and smiled.

Caleb Larson.

Friday was too far away...

* * * *

Caleb tried to quiet his mind as he lay in bed staring at the ceiling. The sound of the sleet pelting against the skylight above his bed gave him an uneasy feeling. The more he wanted to relax the more restless he became. There was only one thing on his mind.

Aurora.

How had she known to say such things about belonging in his house? She was more insightful than he would have thought. She had no idea how much her ramblings in his car had resonated with him. She called to him in ways he had never experienced. He'd been with Darcy for years and never once had a premonition about their future. Now he knew why. They were never meant to be.

He left the perceptions up to his sister. He never claimed to be able to see what was or wasn't meant to be. Sometimes his visions never came to fruition. They were tricky. If the subject of his premonition changed one tiny nuance in the course of their life, then the vision changed too. He tried not to put too much stock in what he saw because there were too many variables.

After sharing a kiss with Aurora, he couldn't deny there was a chemistry between them. Something more than physical. The vision of them in the past was too strong of a correlation to ignore. That had already happened. They'd crossed paths long before this life, and now the universe was setting them back in motion. He wasn't sure he liked knowing about their past connection. Why couldn't things play out naturally between them? His gift had ended his relationship with Darcy. How could he consider taking a chance with Aurora knowing they were being pulled together by forces out of his control?

Just as he closed his eyes that familiar sensation took over. His heart rate increased as everything else faded into the background. When a premonition was about to come on, nothing else existed in those few seconds.

He saw the street sign first. Harrow Lane. His place was two houses from the corner. A car slid on the icy road in the dark of night. The street lamp was out, making it difficult for the driver to see in the foggy air. In an instant a woman in the distance began to cross the street, but appeared to change her mind at the last second and turned toward the curb. The driver didn't see her.

Aurora!

The vision stopped too abruptly. Caleb couldn't see the outcome.

Hell.

He jumped out of bed and pulled on a pair of jeans. There was no telling when the events in his vision would occur, but there was another force at play. Something made him go outside on that raw night. He slipped on his sneakers and ran down the staircase at full speed. Ripping open the front door, he stepped out into the thick fog as the sleet pelted his face.

He could barely see the porch steps as he made his way down and to the corner of Harrow Lane. As he got closer to the end of the street, he saw a figure in the distance. A tall, slender woman stepped off the curb, but paused for just a moment. He had an advantage. He knew the car was coming. Running fast, pushing his legs as hard as he could, he reached for her arm just as the car swerved, narrowly missing them both as they tumbled to the street.

Aurora landed on his chest, her eyes wide with shock as she stared down at him. The driver of the car got out and ran around to check on them.

"Dear God, are you okay?" he asked, the panic in his voice evident.

"Are you?" Caleb asked Aurora.

She quickly nodded.

"We're fine," Caleb told the driver.

"It happened so fast," he said. "I could hardly see you until I was right on top of you."

"It's okay. It's a nasty night." Caleb pushed up, taking Aurora with him as he sat on the curb. "We're good."

"If you're sure?" The man looked at Aurora who hadn't said anything since hitting the ground. "I could call an ambulance."

"No," she said, her voice low and shaky. "I'm okay. Just a bit stunned. I'm sorry for the trouble."

"No trouble, miss," he said. "I'm relieved I didn't hit you."

"Me too." She looked at Caleb. "Thank you."

"You're an accident waiting to happen." He swept the hair from her eyes, silently thanking whatever god would listen for getting him there in time to save her. "I'm just happy I was here."

"How did you manage that?"

"Let's just say I was in the right place at the right time." He stood and extended his hand for her as the driver got back into his car. "We can go back to my place. You're freezing."

"I don't want to impose."

"Seriously?" He hooked her arm in his and led her down the street. "We're not arguing about this. I'll light a fire and you can explain what the hell you were doing out here at this time of night. In this weather."

"I couldn't sleep."

"So you wander the neighborhood on a foggy, sleeting night? Do you know how dangerous that is? What could have happened if I didn't..." He hurried up the porch steps, trying to get them in from the cold night air. "Haven't you ever heard of reading a book? Watching TV, maybe?"

"I was too restless for that."

Once they were inside, he pushed the large oak door shut and looked her over. Her long locks were damp and frizzing at the ends. Her teeth were chattering, and her lips held a hint of blue.

"How long were you out there?" he asked. "When were you going to knock?"

"Huh?"

"You don't really expect me to believe you were just taking a walk in an ice storm, do you?"

"I told you..." A hue of pink brightened her cheeks, but she was busted. "I couldn't settle down. I didn't mean to end up here."

"Hmm..."

"The place is stunning," she said, changing the subject. She looked around the main foyer. "You've completely renovated, but it still has that same cozy feeling."

"Do you still feel like you belong here?"

"More now than ever." She continued to take in the changes he had made. "I don't understand what's going on with me. You must think I'm very odd."

"Not at all. Quite the opposite." He reached toward her, but then dropped his hand to his side, trying to resist the urge to touch. What was it with always wanting to touch her? *Ah, screw it!* He tucked a stray hair behind her ear, and she shivered. "You're cold."

Every fiber of his being screamed out to tell her she had been here with him before. In another life. How could he do that without sending her running in the opposite direction? No matter how strong his instincts were to tell her, he had to wait. He couldn't risk ruining what was developing between them. Not until he was certain she would understand what he was capable of seeing.

"Your jacket is soaked." He reached out, meeting her eyes, asking for consent before he gently lowered the zipper on the lightweight coat hardly suitable for Massachusetts winters. "I'll toss it in the dryer." He removed it from her shoulders and headed down the hall to the laundry room. Placing her jacket in the dryer, he quickly came back to the foyer. "It shouldn't take long to dry."

"Thank you."

"You can put your boots and socks on that heater vent if you'd like." He pointed at the vent by the window. "It will help to dry them until I start a fire."

"I don't mean to be so much trouble." She reached down and unzipped her boots, taking them off and then peeling off her damp socks. "I don't know how I ended up here. I couldn't sleep and I kept thinking about... Well, what happened in your car."

He couldn't stop thinking about that kiss either. He couldn't blame her. Their time together a few hours earlier had left him edgy too.

"I know," he agreed. "I've been thinking about you all night." He kicked off his wet shoes by the front door, leaving him in his bare feet.

"No socks?" She looked amused as she glanced down at his feet.

"I was in bed. I didn't have much time to get dressed before I went outside."

"How did you know I'd be out there?"

"I just..." He took her arm in his hand, noticing the blood seeping through her shirt. "Your shoulder. You're bleeding."

"Huh?" She gazed down at the blood that stained her white shirt. "I think I hit the sidewalk when you pulled me out of the way of the car."

"I'm sorry. I didn't mean to hurt you." He hadn't meant to

bring her down so hard, but his only concern had been getting her to safety.

"Are you kidding? If you hadn't done what you did I'd be worrying about a lot more than a scraped shoulder."

"Come on." He guided her up the grand staircase. "I have some bandages and antiseptic upstairs."

Once inside the master bathroom, he opened the medicine cabinet and took out the supplies to clean her cut.

"I'm sure it's not that big of a deal." She placed her hand over where she was bleeding. "It doesn't even hurt. You don't have to go through all this trouble."

"Let's take a look." He picked her up and set her on the counter in an attempt to make her more comfortable. "Umm...I need to..." He reached for the buttons of her shirt, trying to focus on the task at hand. "We have to get this off."

Chapter 5

A rush of heat flowed through Aurora's system as Caleb unbuttoned her shirt. He was just caring for her, but that didn't stop her from craving him. Needing him to do what he looked so determined to do. He brushed his fingers along her neck before pushing the cold, wet garment from her shoulder.

"I'll get you something to wear when we're done." He inspected the wound. "It doesn't look so bad."

"I told you." She swallowed hard, trying to calm her aroused body.

"We still need to clean it." He took some gauze and carefully poured the antiseptic on it. "This might sting a bit."

"It's okay." She closed her eyes. "Just get it over with."

He pressed the cool gauze to her cut, taking his time, being tender with her. Once he had it cleaned out he placed a bandage over it. "All done."

"Thank you." She opened her eyes to find him staring into them.

"Why did you come here tonight?" He undid the last two buttons of her shirt, sliding it off and leaving her in a strapless, demi bra.

"I couldn't stay away."

"I'm glad you're here." He broke his gaze from hers, lowering his eyes as he trailed his fingers down her neck and over the tops of her breasts. "Your skin is as soft as I imagined it to be. I can't seem to stop myself."

"Your touch," she mumbled. "It's familiar."

"Is it?" He continued to explore her flesh, tracing his fingertips over her nipples, watching as they pebbled under his direction.

"It's difficult to explain." She wasn't sure what was making her talk so much. "It's not like we've ever been together before. There's nothing usual about this. Oh..." A moan escaped her lips when he moved his mouth along her neck. "It's like this is the way it's supposed to be."

"I know what you mean. I feel it too."

"You do?"

He nodded as he worked his way to her lips. "I want you more than I ever thought it was possible to want someone."

She guided his hands to the front clasp of her bra. "I've wanted you for as long as I can remember."

"Sorry it took me so long to catch up."

He pressed his lips to hers, wasting no time deepening their connection, eagerly manipulating her lips to part as he undid her bra. Moving his hands up her heated flesh, he kissed her hard, pinning her between his taut form and the cool tiles behind her.

The sound of his breathing in her ear made her frantic with need. Her pulse quickened when he dropped her bra to the floor.

"Caleb, I can't wait anymore." She twisted her fingers in his hair, scooting her backside so she could wrap her legs around his waist. The scratch of his shirt against her nipples kindled her desire for him. "I want to feel all of you."

"Soon," he whispered as he thrust his hips forward, pushing his hard length into her damp center. "I want to touch every inch of you." He kissed a path down her neck and over her breasts, swirling his tongue across her nipple. "You're so beautiful."

Sweeping her lips along his, she kissed the corner of his mouth as she reached for the hem of his shirt. He stepped back so she could lift it over his head.

"Hmm..." She smoothed her hands along his fit chest, delighting in the way his muscles flexed against her palms. How many days a week did he spend at the gym to achieve this perfection? She kissed his chest, flicking her tongue over his hard nipple, eliciting a low growl from him. His breathing picked up when she ran her hand over his crotch. He tightened his hold on her as she palmed him through his pants.

"We need to take this into the other room." Scooping her off the counter, he carried her into the bedroom, kissing her as he went. He set her on her feet, walking her back until her calves hit the bed frame. "Let's get these off," he said as he reached for the waistband of her pants.

Oh, shit... She quivered when he dropped to his knees, placing hot, opened-mouth kisses across her belly as he unbuttoned her jeans.

Looking up at her, he smirked as he lowered her zipper.

"I'm going to lose myself in you." He gripped her hips, sliding her pants down her legs and to her ankles. "All night long."

She steadied herself by holding onto his shoulders as he kissed her mound through her panties. Sliding his fingers inside the white silk, he moved the material aside, caressing her with long, slow licks. Dipping his tongue inside her slit, he teased her with only the tip. Her stomach tightened when he cupped her backside, drawing her closer to his face. Rocking her hips forward, she kept a steady pace with him. A heat engulfed her as she lost herself in a pleasure she didn't know possible.

"Ahh..." She stiffened her legs when he slipped his fingers inside her, setting a faster pace. "Caleb."

No one had ever made her feel so desired. With each action he drove her deeper into bliss until she could handle no more. On a soft sigh, she shuddered before letting go completely. With her release she experienced the purging she had been waiting for. One she wanted but didn't know how to give herself. All the negativity and hurt left her system, and when she opened her eyes and looked down all that surrounded her was Caleb. His warmth, kindness, and passion.

"Come here." He pulled her down to her knees. "I'm not done with you."

"I should hope not." She kissed him hard, tasting herself on his lips. "That was really something."

"I'm glad you liked it." He lifted her into his lap and thrust his pelvis forward, driving the bulge in his jeans into her saturated panties. "There's so much more."

"Not just tonight." She reached between them and unbuttoned his pants, lowering the zipper. "I need more than tonight."

"I wouldn't have started this with you if I didn't want more," he assured her. "I know this is happening fast, but we need to go with it."

"Yes..." she cried out as he continued to move his hips, hitting her hard where she needed him, ached for him to be. "Now, please."

He guided her onto the bed, sliding her panties down her legs and tossing them onto the floor.

"You're perfect." He took in her exposed form, taking his time before bringing his attention back to her face. "Perfection."

She got up on her knees and tugged down his pants. "I could say the same for you." She considered his hard length, imagining what it would be like to taste him. "Make love to me."

"With pleasure, sweetheart." He kicked off his jeans and boxers before reaching to fumble in the nightstand drawer. "Here's what we need." He held up a strip of foil packets, ripping one off with a seductive grin. "Probably more than one too." He tossed the extra condoms on the nightstand.

Licking her lips as he sheathed himself in the thin latex, she trembled in anticipation over finally getting to have the man she'd always dreamed about being with. She extended her hand and moved him to her, covering herself in his warmth.

"Sweet Aurora." He took her chin between his fingers. "I've thought about you for days. You're consuming my every thought." He kissed her slowly as she wrapped her legs around his waist. "I wouldn't have it any other way."

He took his length in his hand, running the tip along her entrance. With no more words, he shifted his position and thrust deep into her. Pulses of electricity coursed through her as he took her. That sense of familiarity came rushing to the surface, thrilling her and fueling her lust. It was as if she knew what was coming next and how phenomenal it was going to be. Her body burst with excitement as he pounded into her, groaning each time he pulled out and reentered her.

"More," she moaned.

* * * *

Caleb slipped from Aurora's tight hold and turned her over.

Arching her hips, he held her still as he entered her from behind. *Damn, this woman is incredible. A perfect fit.*

As he slammed into her, she grasped the comforter beneath her, screaming out her pleasure each time he thrust forward. The building in his stomach shot lower, intensifying when she clenched her slick heat around him. The more he gave, the more she wanted. He thrived off her raw desire for him.

"Aurora," he breathed out when he couldn't stop the inevitable. "I'm going to..." He lowered her onto the mattress, intertwined their fingers, and let his body take over as he cleared his mind and reveled in the pleasure that only she could give to him.

"Hmm..." She continued to move underneath him. "Caleb, I..." She quivered as he kissed the back of her neck, letting go as she sunk into the bed.

"Are you okay?" He trailed his hand down her spine in long strokes.

"Never been better." She twisted around and lay on her back, her hair a tangled mess as it fanned out behind her. "I'm spent." She laughed low. "In such a good way."

He took in her beauty, mesmerized by her voice, her scent, and the way that she stared back at him. Even without his gift, he would have found her. There was no denying she was meant to be his.

"This has been some night, huh?" She rubbed the back of his neck. "I never expected this to happen when I came out into the cold, nasty weather."

"Some things are meant to occur and we have no control over how we get here." He sprinkled her with kisses, covering her lips, jaw, and chin with his eager mouth. Her infectious giggle warmed his heart. "I'll be right back." He lifted himself off her, already missing her skin against his. "I need to get rid of this." He motioned toward the condom.

"Okay."

When she scooted up to the top of the bed he couldn't help but gawk over her round, little backside.

Adorable.

He quickly made his way to the bathroom to take care of things, so he could get back and hold her. He glanced at himself in the mirror, resolving that before they could move forward he needed to tell her who he was. It was the only way he could ensure a positive outcome. No more secrets. Not this time. Their souls were intertwined not only in the past, but in this life too. There was no turning back.

What they had just shared had been the single most satisfying experience of his life, he thought as he retrieved one of his t-shirts from his dresser drawer. Never had he felt such a connection to another before now. When they became one, he knew they were destined in any life in which they crossed paths. It was clearer than it ever had been. They would find one another over and over again. He didn't need a vision to tell him that. It was obvious to him. Now he had to explain it to her. In moderation.

He sat on the edge of the bed and handed her the shirt. "It's not that I don't want you naked, but it can get cold in here."

"I think we did a pretty good job of heating things up." She shot him a devious grin as she pulled the shirt over her head. He watched as her perfect breasts disappeared under the cotton. He'd be taking that shirt off again really soon.

"That stuff you said about being familiar..."

"You must think I'm a total whack job, huh?"

"No, I understand completely."

"You do?"

This conversation felt right. He had kept his secrets from Darcy, but he didn't want to keep anything from Aurora. He couldn't make the same mistakes with her.

"Whatever this is between us, whatever it has the potential to become..." He took her hand in his. "I can't start out with a lie. You may not understand what I have to say. You may not even believe me, but something in me is screaming out to tell you. Even if I'm wrong about how I think you'll react, I hope you can keep an open mind."

"Caleb, you can tell me anything." She looked at him with trusting eyes. In them he saw an openness he didn't often find in others. He sensed her longing for a future together in this life and the next...

"I believe that."

"What is it?"

"You've heard the ramblings in town about my family. You know they think we're different."

"You're all amazing, kind-hearted, and caring people. Most of those fools who gossip have no idea what they're saying. If they really knew you, they wouldn't say those things."

"They may not know what they're saying, but some of it's true." He cradled the side of her face in his hand. "We *are* different."

"I already know that." She turned into his touch. "I love how tender you are with me."

"You're easy to care for." He stroked her cheek with his thumb. "Do you want to know how I knew you were outside tonight?"

"Only if you want to tell me."

"I saw you."

"From a window?"

"In my mind." He waited for a reaction, but she didn't say anything as she looked at him with those trusting eyes.

"Sometimes I see things before they happen."

"Premonitions?"

"Yes, but I don't always know when they'll happen, if they happen at all. I saw you in the street, and I knew it was on my corner. It was foggy and sleeting. I wasn't sure it was tonight, but a force that I can't really explain pushed me to get to you. I had to get to you."

"You saw me before the car hit me?"

"The vision stopped before I could see the outcome, but because I had the premonition I saw where to find you. It was one of the strongest intuitions I've ever had." He would never forget the jolt of energy that flowed through him as he raced down the steps and out the door.

"I'm glad." She leaned forward and kissed him. "It's like having my very own superhero. Pretty cool."

"You're not freaked out?"

"Why would I be?" She was so matter-of-fact. Almost as if she had no problem accepting what he had just told her.

"I just admitted I can see into the future. That's not something you hear every day."

"Well, like you said, I've heard what people say about your family. I spent a lot of time in this house when I was growing up. There's a definite spark running through this place. I've always felt something good here. I've always suspected that this family was special."

"Really?"

"It goes back to that sense of feeling familiar. I told you I feel like I've been here before. I wish I could explain it, but I don't know how."

"That's because you have been." He might as well put it all out there. "My visions aren't always of the future. Sometime I can see instances from the past. Not necessarily my own until a few days ago."

"What did you see?"

"Us—well, I think it was us, but it was a long time ago. Before we were even alive."

"So it wasn't us?"

He sensed her confusion. Hell, he'd had the vision and he was confused. "It was like a past life kind of thing."

"Okay, I think. Go on."

At least she was keeping an open mind. "We were here at the house, in the cellar. We were...*together*."

"Like a couple."

"Sort of." He thought back to the couple in the cellar—what they had shared, what they had meant to one another. "We were rather intimate."

"We were doing it? You had a vision of us doing it?"

"Not exactly, but we were close. It was a past life. I haven't done much research on that so I don't know how it works, but I do believe whoever they were, they somehow have a link to us."

"Reincarnation?"

"Maybe." He hadn't given it much thought, but he was intrigued that she considered the possibility. "I'm sure Clara's trying to find a way to figure it out."

"She's extremely intuitive, isn't she? I always felt she was 'in the know' about certain things. She had a way of keeping me out of trouble when we were growing up. I wish I would have listened to her about..."

"Your ex-husband?"

"Clara knew it wouldn't work out between us, but I didn't listen to her. I thought I knew better."

"Hey." He lifted her chin so he could look into her eyes. "We all have to find our own way. I tell my brothers and sister that all the time. Just because we have perception doesn't mean we can't let things play out. Clara was just looking after you, but you had to follow your heart, and that's okay."

"Do you always follow your heart?"

"I haven't had many opportunities to." He gently kissed her lips. "But I fully intend to now."

"Do you think there is any way we can research your vision? Can you figure out who we were back then?"

"You'd want to do that?" He liked that idea, but it was even more appealing now that she had suggested it.

"It would be really cool to discover who we were in a past life. How many times do you think we've found one another through the centuries? Do you think you'll get any more visions?"

"I'm not sure."

"Do you normally embrace your gift?"

"Sometimes."

"Don't you like being unique?"

"You mean 'strange'?"

"There's nothing strange about you, Caleb." She pressed her palm to his cheek. "I think you're amazing. Anyone who has ever made you feel wrong about who you are isn't worth your time."

"It's almost like you know." This was new territory for him. The Larsons didn't freely share who they were with outsiders. Caleb had only done it one other time, and that didn't go so well. Except if he hadn't told Darcy the truth, and she hadn't left him, he'd never be here with Aurora. The only woman he was meant to be with.

"It's not hard to figure out that someone hurt you. Made you feel less for being who you are."

"I have a feeling we have a lot in common when it comes to past relationships."

"I don't want to talk about that tonight. There's no need to pollute what we have with the garbage of our past."

"I like the way you think." He kissed her softly, taking his time, wanting her to feel how much he wanted her. "You're really not at all freaked out by what I've told you?"

"You just told me we've been together before. If that's not a sign that we're soul mates, then I don't know what is. When you kissed me earlier tonight, there was something between us. Something wonderful. Not just physical, but a deeper connection. I would never admit anything like this to you if I didn't think the universe was at play here."

"Something very special is at play." For the first time in his life he had found acceptance and understanding outside of his family. "There are so many things I want to tell you, but I want to do it in moderation. My world is different and takes getting used to, but if you can remain open I want to share my heritage with you. Together, I think, we might be able to find out what our relationship in the past means."

"It means we were destined to find each other in this life and the one after this." She smiled. "I'm certain of it. I belong here, Caleb. For the first time in my life, I know that's true."

"How did I not see you before?" he asked. She had spent years in his house, interacting with his family, practically right under his feet.

"Maybe it wasn't our time before."

"This is definitely our time." He lay down, pulling her on top of him. "I've been waiting a long time for you."

"I'm right here." She straddled his hips, rubbing her bare center along his hard shaft. "I want you to make me feel like you did before. I need you to fill my mind, body, and soul."

"And your heart, Aurora." He reached for the foil packet on the dresser. "I want your heart."

"It's yours."

"There are so many things I want to tell you. I need to tell you." He finally felt safe enough to share his secrets. There wasn't a doubt in his mind that Aurora would fully accept him for who he was. "But first we have more pressing issues."

"Give me that." She took the condom from him. "I got this."

When she leaned down to kiss him, his heart rate increased. He closed his eyes, blocking out everything around him. This wasn't exactly the most opportune time to have a premonition, but he didn't have any control over it.

When Aurora walked down a long, rose petal covered aisle adorned with white candles, Caleb lost his breath. Her beaming smile lit the way as she came toward him. His brothers were standing by his side, and Clara was waiting at the altar for Aurora to stand next to her. Soft classical music played in the background as his bride took her place beside him. She handed her bouquet to his sister before facing him. He took her hands in his and whispered, "I love you."

"Caleb..." He heard her voice in the distance. "Caleb, are you okay?" She shook his shoulders, bringing him back into their reality. He'd always come back to her.

"I couldn't be better." He smiled. "You have no idea."

"Did you have another glimpse into our past?"

"Not the past." He gripped her hips, memorizing the small glimpse into their future. The urge to be inside her was too overwhelming to talk.

"Tell me."

"I will, princess, but first we need to be one."

"That must have been some premonition." She giggled as he flipped her onto her back. "I can't wait to hear all about it."

"I can't wait to live it." He took her face between his hands, enthusiastic about the possibility of a new life. "With you."

About Ella Jade

Ella Jade has been writing for as long as she can remember. As a child, she often had a notebook and pen with her, and now as an adult, the laptop is never far. The plots and dialogue have always played out in her head, but she never knew what to do with them. That all changed when she discovered the eBook industry. She started penning novels at a rapid pace and now she can't be stopped.

Ella resides in New Jersey with her husband and two boys. When she's not chasing after her kids, she's busy creating sexy, domineering men and the strong women who know how to challenge them in and out of the bedroom. She hopes you'll get lost in her words.

Ella's Website:
www.authorellajade.com
Reader eMail:
ellajade818@gmail.com

A Hint of Heaven

by Nola Cross

Firefighter Jake Manley is a no-nonsense kind of guy. So when his little sister goes to see pet psychic Carrie Westfield, he lets the beautiful medium know he's got a watchful eye on her. But somehow she does seem to know more than she should, including painful secrets from his past. When the helpful spirit of his boyhood dog shows up, things get even stranger, making him question everything he thought was true. Can Jake accept that life doesn't end with death and let go of the guilt he's carried all these years? More importantly, can he let Carrie Westfield into his heart?

Dedication

For Muffin

Chapter 1

The impression of a cold, wet nose woke Carrie Westfield first thing Wednesday morning. She turned over, squinted at the clock, and groaned as she pulled the sheet up over her head.

"You must be my ten o'clock," she muttered into her pillow. "Go away and come back later, will you please?"

If she covered her ears, she could almost imagine she didn't hear the high-pitched canine whine.

"I know you're anxious, but your person isn't here yet. There's nothing I can do for you until she arrives. *Please* come back at ten."

Carrie lay motionless, hoping the dog-spirit would do as she asked, but more impressions began seeping into her consciousness: the dog was small, brown. Maybe a Yorkie? Then the image of a mug of hot chocolate popped into her mind.

"Cocoa?" she whispered, and the little animal yipped joyfully. Carrie couldn't help but chuckle. Finally relinquishing any hope of another hour's sleep, she shoved the warm covers away and sat up. "Okay. Okay, Cocoa. You can hang out with me this morning, I guess. Not that I'll be doing anything very exciting."

Half an hour later, showered and dressed, Carrie puttered

around her apartment, coffee cup in hand, straightening pillows, dusting bookshelves, putting things to rights for her first appointment of the day. She preferred to meet with her clients here in her own home, where deep cozy recliners, golden lamplight, and vanilla candles created a friendly ambiance. Making people comfortable was important when you were inviting them to rub elbows with the spirit world.

While she moved around the room, Cocoa's spirit followed her, his energy fading and then brightening again. It wasn't unusual for the lost pet she was supposed to connect with to show up in advance of the appointment time. At least now she was sure her client wouldn't be disappointed.

The little dog had a sweet, upbeat aura. It was no wonder the owner—a woman named Brenda—had broken down and cried on the phone when she'd called to make the appointment. People got very attached to their pets, and rightly so. The animal spirits Carrie had met as a pet psychic medium were often a cut above the everyday humans she had contact with.

"As evidenced by you, Mike Miller, you two-timing creep," she said aloud, giving her wrinkled couch cushion a firm karate chop.

Gosh, she hadn't thought about her ex in weeks. Why would that rat-bastard suddenly take up residence in her head? Last she'd heard he was cohabitating with his barely-legal, blonde

Pilates instructor across town. Too bad Carrie's psychic abilities hadn't extended to knowing he'd been cheating on her with a long string of women.

Determined to regain a positive mind-set, she walked to her front window and intentionally refocused her attention outside. From her small rental house in southwest Portland, she was lucky enough to have a partial view of Mt. Hood. This April morning the snow-covered mountain was lost in the clouds, but the quiet street and well-kept homes of her neighborhood made a peaceful scene. The grass sparkled with dew and pink dogwood blossoms made splashes of springy color here and there. As she took several cleansing breaths, calming her thoughts, a large black SUV pulled up to the curb out front.

Carrie glanced at her watch and frowned. It was still half an hour before Cocoa's owner was due. She stepped behind the drapes so she could observe without being seen, and watched as the car door opened and a big man in an overcoat got out.

Maybe he was there to see one of her neighbors?

No, he stopped in the street and looked straight at her house, then came around to the sidewalk and started up her flagstone path, his arms swinging as if he were on a mission from God.

Damn it! The last thing I need this morning is a verbal duel with another church missionary. Members of the local congregation had been stopping by at least once a week for the last few months, leaving their tracts and interrupting her mornings with their unflagging efforts at converting her. Apparently the church believed psychics of any kind were doomed to eternal damnation, and pet psychics were especially damned.

Determined to nip this visit in the bud, Carrie went to the front door and pulled it open as the man neared the steps to her porch.

"Good morning," she said in a firm voice. "You might as well turn around right now. I don't have time to talk with you today." She crossed her arms over her chest and gave the man her best steely-eyed glare.

He froze mid-stride, his handsome face a study in surprise.

Oh my. This evangelist was far-and-away the best looking one to show up on her doorstep. His dark hair was shorter than she normally preferred, but his eyes were the color of cognac, his jaw nicely chiseled, his neck and shoulders as burly as a Clydesdale's. The local congregation must finally be sending in the big guns in an all-out effort to save her soul.

"What?" His nostrils flared self-righteously. She didn't remember the other missionaries ever scowling like that.

"I said you'll have to leave. I have clients coming shortly."

"That's exactly what I'm here to talk to you about, Miss Westfield. You *are* Carrie Westfield, aren't you?"

The man had recovered his aplomb and was now mirroring her defensive stance. Between the meaty arms resting against his massive chest and his remarkable height, he made quite an imposing figure. Carrie's heart skipped a beat.

"You know darn well who I am. You folks have been harassing me long enough."

Another puzzled look flashed across his face, but he quickly regained his composure. Taking three long strides, he arrived on her top stair, just a foot or two from where she stood. The guy was so big and scary Carrie couldn't help but take a quick step backward.

"Listen, Miss, I don't know who you think I am, but I haven't even begun to harass you yet."

Was that a threat? Carrie felt a tingle of real alarm as the man narrowed his eyes and shoved a blunt finger into her face.

"I'm here to give you fair warning. My sister Brenda may be gullible, but I'm no fool. I'll be keeping my eye on you today."

"Brenda? My ten o'clock client?"

"That's right. She's so torn up over the death of her dog—"

"Cocoa."

"Yeah, that's right. And don't pretend you got his name by using your supposed psychic powers. I'm sure Brenda told you when she called."

"Actually, I make it a practice not to ask for any details up front."

"Oh, come on. Don't give me that line. All you quacks have your ways of extracting information."

Carrie's cheeks flared with heat. "Are you calling me a charlatan?"

"That pretty much sums up my opinion, yeah."

Now it was her turn to take a step forward and stab his chest with her finger.

"*You* are not my client, sir. Therefore, it is not of the least importance whether you believe in what I do or not. For those with open minds, I provide an important service for which I never apologize."

"Whatever," he said dismissively. "Just be aware that I've got buddies down at the precinct. If I so much as suspect that you're attempting to bilk my sister for future appointments, I'll have fraud charges brought against you in a heartbeat."

"Just try it." Carrie stuck her chin out and met the big man's belligerent stare with one of her own. It was at moments like this she was glad her father had stayed with the Portland police force, but she wasn't about to tell the angry stranger that he was the deputy police chief. If this guy was serious about making trouble for her, she'd play the Dad card when she really needed it.

"I'll be back at ten with Brenda," he ground out. "Watch

yourself, sister."

* * * *

Jake Manley took the flagstone steps three at a time down to the street, his blood roaring through his body like a three-alarm blaze. Just who did Carrie Westfield think she was coming at him like that when he'd barely set foot on her porch? His intention had been to give the woman a polite but firm warning, to let this so-called psychic know she wasn't dealing with a couple of dumb rubes with deep pockets. As it was, he hadn't even gotten a word out before she'd attacked him. She'd had no call to do that.

And what was the deal with her being so young and fresh-faced? Weren't psychics supposed to be crepe-skinned crones with too much eye makeup and a bunch of purple scarves draped around their shrunken shoulders?

He reached his SUV and yanked the door open. Giving in to temptation, he lifted his gaze once more to Carrie Westfield's cute little house. Sure enough, the pretty brunette was standing in the front window again, hands on her curvy hips, giving him the evil eye.

An odd, fiery jolt zigged through his gut. *Danger.* It was a good thing Brenda had him to take care of her. He didn't trust this woman as far as he could throw her.

Thirty minutes later, he pulled up once more outside the

same house and shut off the engine. Beside him, Brenda noisily blew her nose.

"It's so nice of you to drive me, Jake. But really, there's no need for you to come in with me. This stuff is probably boring and silly for someone like you." She dabbed at her eyes with a soggy tissue, smudges of mascara making dark streaks down her cheeks. She'd been crying since he picked her up, but now she gave him a watery smile.

Ah, hell. He liked dogs as well as the next guy, but it had been over six months now since Cocoa had eaten those damn chocolate bars. How long was Brenda going to keep mourning him? And more important, was seeing Carrie Westfield going to make things any better? He hoped it would, he really did, because if the psychic made Brenda any sadder, he'd make sure she was exposed for the fraud she was.

"I told you, Bren. I'm here for you." He gave her shoulder a playful punch before they got out of the car and went up the walk.

The psychic opened the door with a wary expression. For a moment her gaze met his and the air sizzled between them, then she turned toward Brenda and smiled. Her already-lovely face was further transformed by the radiance of that smile, and Jake registered an unsettling surge of attraction in the region below his belt. *Damn.* Muddying the waters with an ill-advised case of the hots for this woman was the last thing he needed.

"Good morning," she said. "You must be Brenda. Welcome to my home. I'm so glad you made the decision to come see me."

"Thank you," Brenda said. "This is my brother Jake. I hope it's all right I brought him along for moral support."

"Of course."

The woman motioned them into a warm, light-filled living room. Jake took in the cushy, geometric-print couch and matching chairs with surprise. He'd expected something darker, creepier, a setting designed to draw unsuspecting clients into a web of clever lies. But here, fragrant white candles flickered on the wide mantel and fresh cut daffodils filled a vase on the crowded bookshelf. Over the fireplace hung a large portrait of a gray and white cat. So far, everything seemed innocent enough.

"Would you like a cup of tea? I have Oolong or orange mint."

"Oolong, please," Brenda said. "Maybe a splash of milk?"

"Sure. And you, sir?" The woman turned her jade-green eyes on him.

"Nothing for me, thanks." *Shit.* The polite words came out like butter, like he was visiting his great-aunt Clara, not on the trail of a gorgeous con artist. He squinted one eye at her, letting her know he was still on guard.

A Hint of Heaven / Nola Cross

Her brows lifted and she smiled again. "Okay then. Brenda, why don't you go ahead and sit down at the table by the bookcase. I'll be right back with your drink. Sir, you can sit on the couch over there if you'd like to observe."

Jake lowered himself into one of the plump recliners. After a moment or two the woman returned with a steaming cup for his sister, and sat down at the table across from her. He noticed then that there were several mysterious items in a shallow brass bowl on the table and a micro-recorder lying next to it.

As he watched, Carrie Westfield picked up a bundle of herbs from the bowl and lit them on fire. His entire body tensed. As a firefighter, he was super-sensitive to the smell of burning vegetation. This stuff had an odd, musty odor. The woman blew out the flame, leaving a thin column of blue smoke curling toward the ceiling. She picked up a long, black feather and fanned the smoke toward Brenda.

Now she closed her eyes and murmured, "We ask today that we be assisted by our guides and angels. As we walk with them, let only light surround us. Amen."

Oh hell. He might have known she'd start spouting all kinds of New Age mumbo jumbo. He barely had time for that thought when she took a chunk of white quartz from the bowl and handed it to Brenda.

"If you'll hold this crystal while we talk, it will help the spirits to focus their energy."

His fingers dug deep into the soft upholstery of the chair arms. It took everything in his power not to leap up and bat the rock out of his sister's hand. Couldn't she see what a bunch of hokum this was?

But Brenda seemed to be taking it all at face value, the poor girl. At least she'd stopped crying, thank God.

"First, I'll explain a little bit about how I work. I've been given the gift of communication with our animal friends who have passed over. The spirits of these animals remain very much alive in a non-physical dimension. When they are willing to come forward, I begin to receive impressions from them, signs and symbols that I've learned to interpret in a certain way, almost like dialogue."

Brenda nodded, her eyes glued to Carrie Westfield's face.

"Sometimes, like today, an animal friend will make itself known to me even before the owner comes for the appointment." She gave Brenda another beatific smile. "There's been a little brown dog named Cocoa following me around all morning. Is that by any chance who you're here to talk with?"

Brenda gasped. "Yes!" Fresh tears sprang to her eyes. "How did you know his name?"

"He told me. He also told me he really misses you."

"Oh!"

A Hint of Heaven / Nola Cross

Jake groaned inwardly, his blood pressure inching upward. It didn't take a psychic to know what grieving people wanted to hear.

"And he misses the little blue ball you used to throw for him."

"That was our favorite game."

Good guess. All dogs love to play ball.

"And he's very sorry he got into your bottom drawer and ate your chocolate stash."

"But that was my fault," Brenda said. "I should have kept it up out of his reach."

"He says no. He says he knew better and ate it anyway."

Wait a minute. How did she— Jake scowled. Brenda must have told the woman about the chocolate. And about where she usually kept it. That was the only logical explanation.

"He's showing me a park bench with something like a brass plaque."

"That's right! I donated a new bench to Burlingame Park in Cocoa's name."

"He says whenever you sit on that bench he's right there beside you."

"Really?" Now his sister started bawling in earnest, her slim shoulders shaking. Carrie reached out and put her hand over Brenda's.

"Our animal friends remain with us in spirit. Cocoa will be there to greet you years from now when you make your own transition." She handed Brenda a fresh tissue.

Jake fumed. He wasn't sure how this woman could have known about that park bench, but one thing was for sure, she was a master at manipulating people into believing what she wanted them to hear.

* * * *

While Cocoa ran happy circles around the legs of Brenda's chair, Carrie closed her eyes again and sat quietly, allowing her client to regain control at her own pace. But now she began to get a sense of another animal waiting in the shadows. It was another dog. A border collie maybe?

"Belle?" she whispered as an impression of the animal's name came to her.

Across the room, Brenda's uptight brother shifted suddenly in his chair. When she snuck a peek at him he was staring at her with an even darker scowl on his face, his gold eyes practically throwing sparks. Meanwhile the black and white dog had stepped forward and was anxiously awaiting her turn to communicate.

"There's another dog here now named Belle. Does that sound familiar?"

Brenda looked puzzled. "No."

"She is saying she tried her best. She didn't want to let her boys down. But the fire was just too big."

Jake sprang from his chair as if he'd been shot from a cannon.

"I'm going to wait in the car, Bren," he barked and strode to the door.

Brenda started as he slammed the door behind him. "You'll have to excuse my brother. He's not into this stuff."

"I can tell," Carrie said, relieved to feel the energy in the room begin to lighten. At the same moment the big, angry man had left the house, Belle the dog had also disappeared.

Chapter 2

Carrie saw two other clients that day besides Brenda Manley. Even though she really loved the work she did, and even though she always scheduled at least an hour break between appointments, by four o'clock she could feel her energy waning.

After closing her front door for the final time, she wandered into the kitchen and opened the fridge, hoping to be inspired to prepare a real dinner. Nothing looked particularly edible, so she grabbed a cup of lemon yogurt. It was quick and easy. Maybe tomorrow she would feel more like cooking a proper meal.

Taking her yogurt and spoon with her, she walked to the back of the house where her small, informal family room was furnished with a slightly dog-eared couch, an old TV, and her favorite over-stuffed reading chair. She sank down into the chair and peeled the seal off the yogurt. She had just dipped her spoon into the creamy stuff when someone began pounding on the front door. Her heart leapt into her throat. Who could that be, and where did they procure a battering ram?

Had she locked the door? Where the heck had she left her cellphone?

Carrie approached the front door cautiously and peered out the peephole. *Of course!* Brenda Manley's brother Jake stood there, nostrils flaring, his big shoulders bunched with tension. Should she pretend she wasn't home? She bit her lip, hand on the knob. Probably he had seen her last client leave and knew darn well she was there. No doubt he'd just keep pounding. She straightened her spine and opened the door.

"Hello again." She pasted on a smile, hoping to disarm him.

His brows drew together. "Here's what I want to know. What are your sources, Miss Westfield? How did you know about my dog Belle? Her name was never published in the newspaper stories."

"You're not going to like my answer, Mr. Manley."

"Try me." He planted his fists on his waist.

"Would you like to come in first? Maybe sit down?" By now her heart had settled back into its normal rhythm, and she began to get inklings of something else beneath his belligerence. Sadness? Confusion?

"I don't need to sit down," he growled, brushing past her into the room. "What I need is to know who told you the name of my dog. Brenda couldn't have known. Belle died before she was even born."

Carrie shut the door and turned to face him. "Belle told me."

He flinched like he'd been punched. "I don't want to hear that crap. I want the truth, and I want it now. How did you know about Belle?" His face contorted, the veins standing out on his forehead, and his fists were balled tight as he stood like a pugilist in the middle of her usually-serene living room.

A ripple of primal fear moved down Carrie's spine. Jake Manley was a big guy, and he was really pissed. What if he decided to get physical? Forcing herself to remain calm, she crossed to the couch and sat down facing him, her hands clasped in her lap.

"Well," he said, "I'm waiting." He crossed his arms over his chest. The defensive stance seemed to be his favorite.

"Here's the truth, Mr. Manley. About five years ago, my cat, Muffin, died." Her gaze went to the framed portrait over the fireplace, and she smiled. "Muffin and I had a very strong connection in life, and apparently that connection survived his death. After a couple of weeks, I began receiving communications from him."

The big man snorted, but she noticed his fists had unclenched.

"It wasn't very long before he let me know there were other deceased pets waiting to talk with their owners. I was amazed to find that I could receive communications from them as well."

"So you hung out your shingle and started selling this crap to poor, unsuspecting pet owners."

Fresh anger bubbled up inside her, making her cheeks flare

with heat. "I perform a useful service to people who have no alternative."

"Yeah, right. And these dead pets just show up and start talking to you when their owners walk into your house?"

"Basically, yes. Somehow they sense that I can help them talk with their loved ones. They send me mental pictures and sounds—impressions—that I've learned to translate. Sometimes they arrive early for the appointment, like what happened this morning with Cocoa." She softened her voice. "And sometimes they show up for people who aren't really my clients, like your Belle did. She was so glad to finally have the chance to speak to you, by the way."

All the fight seemed to drain away as he turned wordlessly and slumped into one of the chairs opposite her. She watched as the anger sloughed off, leaving unmistakable pain in his golden eyes.

Touched by his vulnerability much more than she expected to be, she leaned forward and asked, "Can I help in any way?"

He stared at her. "I can't believe I'm about to ask this, but is she here now? Is Belle here?"

Carrie closed her eyes, letting her mind clear. Almost immediately the eager border collie came forward, the energy of her spirit clear and joyful.

Carrie grinned. "Yes, she's here. She's showing me a small

flock of chickens. Does that make sense to you?"

"We had chickens when I was a boy. She loved to herd them around."

"Border collies do that," she said.

"But that doesn't prove anything," he hastily added. "Lots of people have chickens."

"I suppose that's true." She waited.

"What else does she say?" he prodded.

"Are you requesting a reading, Mr. Manley?"

"Oh, I get it. You want money. I might have known," he sneered.

"No, I don't care about your money. This will be my treat. I just want to be clear about what you're asking. I wouldn't want you to get upset about anything I might tell you."

"I won't get upset. Just tell me what she says."

"All right." Suddenly Carrie's head filled with a dark swath of flame and smoke. The impression was so real she coughed, unwittingly throwing her hands up to protect her face. In the vision, the flames seemed to be raging out of control in some kind of narrow hallway. "She's showing me a fire. It seems like a house fire, a serious one."

He stared, his face losing color, but she barely noticed. The images in her head were more compelling than any reading she had ever done.

"Now she's showing me a picture of a little boy. He's maybe two years old. He's in a crib, wearing pajamas." Suddenly she realized what she was seeing. "Oh, no! He's down that hallway, isn't he, girl?" Tears pushed against the back of her eyes. "She's telling me she's sorry. She tried her best, but she couldn't get to that little boy."

The horror of the situation overtook Carrie and she began to cry. When she looked up again, his stricken eyes glistened with tears as well.

"How could you know about that?" he whispered. "That was twenty-eight years ago."

* * * *

It all came rushing back to him—the smells, the god-awful heat, the naked fear. He'd been just six years old, playing in the backyard with his dog while his mother hung out the wash and his baby brother Jeff napped upstairs. They said later that wiring in the old fan in Jeff's room must have overheated and sparked. What he remembered most vividly was looking up and seeing white smoke boiling from the bedroom window. His mother saw it too. She began to scream. Belle barked twice and headed for the open back door. By the time Jake could follow her, she had disappeared into the wall of smoke wafting down the staircase.

"Come back! Come back, girl!" he'd called, stumbling up the stairs. He choked but kept going, pulling himself up by the banister. He had to find Belle.

The closer he got to the top of the stairs, the thicker the smoke, the hotter the air. Breathing was like pulling shards of glass into his lungs. The flames crackled, wooden beams above him hissed in warning and then split apart, crashing onto the hallway floor. Far away, Belle barked one last time.

"I'm coming, girl," he'd screamed, and that was all he remembered.

He woke up later that day in the hospital in bandages, half the hair singed from his head. His mother slumped beside his bed, her eyes red-rimmed, her clothes covered in soot. She had clung to him, weeping inconsolably. His dad had hugged him hard too. "Don't blame yourself, son. You tried your best to save your brother. You're a hero to me."

"Was it your family home that burned?" Carrie Westfield asked now, jerking him back to the present. When he focused again on her face, her teary green eyes were soft with compassion.

He nodded.

"And the little boy?"

"My baby brother. Jeff. Two years old."

Suddenly he couldn't sit any longer. He stood and walked to the window, letting his gaze flick over the distant skyline of downtown Portland. Thoughts caromed through his head like errant billiard balls. What was going on here? How could this woman know what she knew? His plan had been to never think about that horrible day again. That was going to be a little difficult if Carrie Westfield—and apparently Belle—insisted on stirring up the past.

But he couldn't blame her, could he? He'd asked for this. And she'd warned him that he might hear something he'd rather not.

He turned back to her. The last rays of the sunset streamed in the window behind him, crossed his shoulders, and cast a pale orange glow over the couch where the woman sat. Her eyes sparkled with it and her soft, curvy body seemed lit from within. He really noticed her again: all that rich, cocoa-colored hair around her shoulders, the way her white sweater clung in just the right places.

"Are you all right?" she asked.

He realized he'd been staring. He shook his head, running one hand through his hair. It was a lot to take in in one fell swoop.

He paced to the end of the room and turned back. "So let me get this straight. My dog Belle, who's been dead since that fire almost thirty years ago, is now some kind of a ghost dog? And she's been hanging out all this time, waiting to tell me she did her best to save my brother?"

It sounded so crazy when he said it out loud.

"That's pretty much it. She felt terrible about not being able to get to him in time. But of course they are both fine now. She wants you to know that. In fact, they're together on the other side."

His head spun. "Okay. Okay. Wait a minute. Belle is with Jeff?"

"Yes, that's right. It's not unusual to be greeted by a beloved pet when you cross over. In this case, they crossed over together."

Deep in his chest, something began to loosen and lift away, something he hadn't consciously known was there. It was as if he could suddenly breathe again, after all these years. It was nuts, he knew it, but he felt like this woman had somehow set him free.

She seemed so sure about all of this. For the first time, he admitted to himself how much he wanted to believe that everything she told him was true.

But his dog coming back from the dead? Really? He could just imagine the reaction of the guys at the firehouse if they knew he was sitting here today, talking to a supposed psychic, and seriously considering the possibility of communication with dead pets. He'd never hear the end of their ribbing. Every firehouse had a favorite superstition or two, but the guys he worked with were a pretty pragmatic bunch.

He'd always thought *he* was pretty pragmatic himself. So why did he feel this unexplained pull toward believing her?

She sat forward on the couch, her sun-kissed cleavage suddenly visible at the neckline of her sweater, and he had his answer. *Of course!* Carrie Westfield was a total hottie. And he hadn't gotten laid in weeks. His neglected libido must be coloring his judgment. A profound sense of relief washed over him, and he felt his shoulders relax, his arm muscles uncoil. *This* he could deal with.

He smiled at her. "Well, you tell a pretty convincing story, but I'm not buying. I don't know who you had to con to get your inside information, and I don't care. As long as you don't take any more appointments from my sister, I won't make trouble for you. Are we agreed?"

Her perfect brows shot up and she stood to face him, her cheeks flushed. "Your sister is an adult. Whether she wants to see me again is hardly your concern."

He took several steps toward her, leaving only the breadth of the coffee table between them. From here he could smell her soft floral perfume and see every golden glint in her hair, every emerald striation in her amazing eyes. His body betrayed him, tightening against the zipper of his jeans.

Oh yeah, I need to get laid bad.

Before he could change his mind, he thrust his finger toward her lovely face. "I thought you understood, Miss Westfield. I'm *making* it my concern."

Chapter 3

Brenda Manley took a sip of her tea and let out a long, shuddering breath as she blotted her eyes with a tissue. "It's great of you to give me another reading, Carrie. I was so nervous the first time with my brother here that I forgot to ask half my questions. I'm so glad Cocoa was willing to visit with us again."

Carrie smiled at the young woman. "Cocoa is such a bright little guy. He's happy to come. He's showing me a red collar and leash now."

"Yes, he loved going for walks. The park was our favorite place."

"He's showing me water, some kind of small fountain."

"Uh-huh. They have a special drinking fountain there. It's built close to the ground, just for dogs."

"He says his happiest moments were when you two played together at the park."

Brenda seemed to hesitate then asked in a whisper, "He didn't suffer, did he? At the end?"

Carrie smiled at the dog's avid response. "Hardly. He says those chocolate bars were the best thing he ever ate. He felt a twinge or two, and then he just fell asleep."

"Oh, I'm so glad." New tears leaked down Brenda's cheeks.

"He seems to be fading now. He's saying goodbye."

"Really? Okay. Goodbye, Cocoa. I love you." Brenda blew her nose loudly and managed a watery smile.

After waiting a moment to make sure the little dog was really gone, Carrie said, "I guess that's all for now. I hope that was helpful."

"It certainly was. I haven't been able to think about anything else since our first reading two weeks ago. It's so great to know that my little sweetie is doing okay. But I still miss him."

"I'm sorry we didn't get to cover more last time."

"Yeah. It was hard with Jake here. Sometimes he can come across like a jerk, but really, he's just trying to protect me."

"From what?" Carrie couldn't stop herself from asking.

Brenda shrugged. "Bad stuff in general, I guess. We had a major tragedy in our family before I was born, and I think he's just hypersensitive about keeping his kid sister safe."

Remembering what she knew about the horrific fire and the death of their baby brother, Carrie nodded. That would make sense.

"Between you and me," the other woman went on, "I think he's trying to keep the whole world safe. I think that's why he became a firefighter."

Jake Manley was a firefighter? That made even more sense.

He was obviously trying to atone somehow for Jeff's death. The fact that he'd only been a six-year-old boy and would never be expected to rush into a raging inferno didn't mean he'd escape the experience without deep feelings of survivor guilt. Children often had unrealistic expectations of themselves.

Carrie felt a rush of compassion for the big, grumpy man. Knowing what she knew now she could almost excuse his bad behavior. Almost.

* * * *

The first time it happened, Jake thought it was his imagination. Or maybe he was overtired. Or needed his hearing checked. The crew was working a controlled burn in an industrial section of town, a century-old warehouse that needed to come down to make way for a new one. The exercise provided an invaluable training opportunity for the two new recruits in their unit, and so far everything was going like clockwork. The hose crew was pushing the fire into the central zone, keeping the high ceilings wet, but everyone knew the collapse of the old timber-and-composite roof was imminent.

A four-block area around the building had been cleared of spectators, so when Jake heard the excited barking of a dog it flustered him. The sound seemed to come from the rear of the building. Had a stray wandered into the fire zone?

He keyed his radio. "Cap'n, Manley here. I thought I heard

a dog barking. Do we have animals in the area?"

"Negative. The area's been cleared."

He scowled. There it was again. Far away but distinct, a dog going crazy. He glanced around. None of the rest of the crew seemed to have heard it. They continued to work the fire as if nothing unusual had occurred. But he couldn't let it go, couldn't take the chance that a creature might be in danger somewhere.

"Cap'n, Manley again. I'm going to do a perimeter check."

"Go ahead. Be careful. This roof is about to go."

Jake began to make his way through the smoke-filled building. He had taken only a dozen steps when the air was split by an ungodly roar, and he turned to see a section of flaming ceiling timbers crash to the floor right where he'd been standing. He sprinted away, his spine tingling. If he hadn't moved toward the sound of the barking dog, he would have been crushed by those fiery beams.

At the time, it hadn't crossed his mind that anything supernatural had happened. He was just one lucky son-of-a-bitch. And the barking dog was no doubt some noisy, flesh-and-blood neighborhood pet that had treed a squirrel somewhere nearby. But a complete check of the area revealed no animals of any kind, and none of the crew had observed a dog anywhere near the warehouse.

It wasn't until a small house fire a few days later that he

began to suspect something else was going on. He was going in through the back door when he saw an ethereal shape from the corner of his eye, no more than a quick flash of black and white. When he turned to look, whatever it was had disappeared. He took his mask off and cleaned the glass and went back to work. A few minutes later, in the smoke-filled kitchen, it happened again, and this time he got a better look before the image dissolved into the haze. It was definitely a dog.

A dog that looked exactly like Belle.

This is crazy. Shaken to his core, Jake stumbled out onto the porch and ripped off his mask. He checked the glass again for soot, but it was still clean. Despite the heat inside his heavy firesuit, goosebumps popped up all over his body. His belly gave a queasy roll. What the hell was going on?

There was only one person who could give him the answer.

* * * *

This time, when the pounding started on her front door, Carrie knew right away who it had to be. The dog, Belle, had been flitting in and out of her consciousness all day, so it was no surprise when she found Jake Manley looming on her porch in the evening darkness.

"Hello, Miss Westfield. Sorry to disturb you."

"My phone number is posted on my website, Mr. Manley. You can always call ahead to let me know you'll be stopping by." She softened her words with a smile.

"You're right. I should have called. My apologies."

Whoa. It was a new, unexpected version of Jake Manley who stood there tonight, his stance humbled, his wet hair slicked back as if he'd just gotten out of the shower. The faint scent of sandalwood soap made her toes curl with unexpected pleasure.

"Would you like to come in?" She stepped aside and held the door wide.

"Thanks, but it looks like I'm interrupting your dinner again." He gestured toward the cup of strawberry yogurt in her hand.

Carrie laughed. "Yeah, I keep thinking I'll learn to cook, but yogurt is just too easy at the end of a long day."

"Well, then..." He hesitated, looking uncertain for the first time since she'd met him.

"Yes?"

"Maybe you'd let me buy you a real dinner?"

"Pardon me?" The invitation was so unexpected she wasn't sure she'd heard him correctly.

He grinned, loosing a cloud of butterflies in Carrie's belly. "This is twice now I've interrupted your dinner. I think I probably owe you a meal. Maybe we could go someplace quiet where we can talk?"

"All right." The words tumbled out before she could stop

them.

Wait a minute. Did she really want to be stuck across some restaurant table from this guy? He was being perfectly civil at the moment, but what if he went sideways on her again?

"If you promise to behave," she added.

His smile widened. "I guess I deserve that."

The butterflies swooped and dove in a dizzying rush. The man needed to smile like that more often. He was absolutely gorgeous when he did.

"I'll get my coat," she said, turning away to hide the warm color she knew was staining her cheeks.

His SUV was huge, which was a good thing. There was plenty of space separating them in the dark interior. She told him how to get to the restaurant and then sat back as the quiet streets of her residential neighborhood gave way to the bright lights and traffic of the old highway.

She glanced over a time or two to check out his profile, and once he turned his head at the same time, catching her looking. They exchanged nervous smiles. Why had she accepted his invitation, anyway? This evening had disaster written all over it.

Ten minutes later they were seated in a quiet corner booth at Los Dos Perros, an upscale taqueria not far from Carrie's house. It was one of her favorite places to eat.

"I hope you'll like the food here," she said, slipping her

jacket off her shoulders. As she did so, her arm brushed against his and an unmistakable sizzle moved through her body. Maybe taking the booth wasn't such a great idea. Surreptitiously, she scooted down the bench seat, putting a few more inches between them. He didn't seem to notice, his eyes focused on the extensive menu.

"How are the fish tacos?" he asked.

"Everything's delicious." She picked up her menu and attempted to read it. The words seemed to writhe on the laminated page like rebellious worms. What was wrong with her? Why couldn't she concentrate? He shifted in his seat and a whiff of sandalwood made her pulse leap.

"What are you having?" he asked.

She felt his expectant gaze, and the butterflies executed a return performance as she let her eyes meet his. For several seconds she stared into his face, feeling a prickly heat rise in her neck. He looked back at her, unblinking, the corner of his mouth twitching slightly with the hint of a smile.

"Hmm?"

"What are you having?"

"Oh. Yes. Well, I usually have the taco salad."

He nodded. "Beef or chicken?"

"Ground beef."

A moment later their waiter appeared at his shoulder and

Jake gave their order, adding a margarita to the short list. "I have the next three days off," he told her. "How about you, Carrie? Something to drink?"

She rarely indulged in alcohol. It seemed to cloud her psychic senses. But tonight she suddenly felt a tad reckless. Maybe it was the fact that her first name sounded so perfect coming from his expressive lips. "I'll have a margarita as well. On the rocks, please."

Promising herself she'd stop at one, Carrie handed her menu to the waiter and took a corn chip from the basket in the middle of the table. Jake did the same.

"This bean dip is great," he said.

"Try the salsa verde. They make everything from scratch here," she told him. "The owners emigrated from Mexico only ten years ago. Jorge, the cook, used to be head chef at an exclusive resort on the Mexican Riviera. Cabo San Lucas I believe it was."

"Really?" His brows rose politely.

Oh God. I sound like some kind of babbling tour guide.

"Yep."

Awkward silence fell between them, broken only by the sound of their crunching and the lively strains of piped-in Mariachi music from behind the bar. Then they both reached for a chip at the same time, their knuckles colliding with an audible pop above the basket.

"Ow!" Carrie pulled her hand back and rubbed at the sore finger.

"Are you okay?" Before she realized his intent, he reached over and grabbed her hand. "Which knuckle is it?"

Flustered, she attempted to tug her hand free. "It's fine now. Really." What wasn't fine were the waves of sexual excitement rippling through her. And the waiter hadn't even brought their drinks yet. Knowing her own propensity to get handsy when she got tipsy, this did not bode well.

"Now, now," Jake teased. "I'm trained as an EMT, Miss Westfield. Don't you think I should be the one to decide how fine you are?"

Their gazes met once more, and the light moment quickly evolved into something more potent. All the breath left her body as his eyes darkened and his thumb made slow circles over the sensitive skin on the back of her hand.

"You've had a lot of experience with knuckle trauma?" she murmured, unable to tear her gaze from his face.

He nodded, a twinkle in his eye now. "I have a framed certificate that says so. Someday I'll show it to you."

"I'll look forward to that."

What the heck was going on there? Were they really flirting with each other? How was it that she was actually beginning to *like* this guy?

Just then the waiter came back with their drinks. Grateful and disappointed at the same time, Carrie pulled her hand free. As the first icy splash of citrus and tequila went down her throat, she struggled to gather her wits.

"You said earlier that you wanted to go somewhere where we'd be able to talk. Was there something in particular you wanted to talk about?"

"Actually, yes." His eyes shifted as he set his glass down, took a deep breath, and blew it out slowly. After several more seconds he gave her a bleak smile. "I don't really know where to start."

"Start anywhere," she encouraged, her curiosity fully piqued.

"Okay. Here it is. You remember how you heard from my boyhood dog, Belle? Well, I think I've been seeing and hearing her myself."

Goosebumps broke out on Carrie's arms. "Really? When?"

"On the job. When I'm working a fire. I guess I never told you I'm a firefighter." He shoved his hand through his hair and chuckled. "I can't believe I'm telling you this."

"No, it's fine. Go ahead."

"The first time it happened I just thought I could hear a dog barking somewhere nearby. But the area had been cleared beforehand, and the thing is, no one else on the crew heard it and no one saw a dog."

"Uh-huh."

"What made it even spookier was if I hadn't moved toward the sound to check it out, I would have been seriously injured by falling debris. It was like she knew and was trying to warn me."

"Wow." More tingles crawled over Carrie's skin. For the first time, she could picture him engaged in the dangerous work of his profession. Her heart squeezed in her chest.

"The next time, I actually saw her." He gave an unsteady laugh. "At least I think I did. It was crazy. I kept seeing this black and white shape out of the corner of my eye. It was kind of like the way Belle used to herd us kids around when we were small, keeping track of us. Keeping us safe." He picked up his glass and took a gulp. "But whenever I turned to look directly at this thing, this ghost dog shape, it wasn't really there."

She nodded, remembering how alarming it had been when Muffin first began communicating with her. Nothing can really prepare a person for those first surreal moments.

"So level with me, Carrie. Am I losing it?"

His beautiful eyes were so haunted, her first impulse was to comfort him. And so it felt natural to cover his big hand with hers. His skin was rough and warm and perfect.

"No. Far from it."

"Why is this happening all of a sudden, out of nowhere?"

She shrugged. "Probably because you opened yourself to it by coming to see me."

He was quiet for a moment, letting that sink in. Meanwhile, their food arrived. They both picked up their forks.

"You should feel lucky. Not everyone has this gift, you know." She loaded her fork with salad and smiled at him.

"Right now it feels more like a liability. It's distracting me from my work."

"You'll get used to it."

"Maybe." He scowled as he picked up his taco and took a bite.

Chapter 4

Carrie was right, the food was delicious, but Jake barely noticed. Between the disturbing news that he'd apparently developed a strange new hidden talent, and the distracting presence of the beautiful woman who sat across from him, there could easily have been wallpaper paste in the tacos.

You'll get used to it she'd said. But what if he didn't *want* to get used to it? What if he wanted things to go back to the way they were before Brenda got a wild hair to see a pet psychic?

In days past, he could always trust his senses to tell reality from his imagination. Not that he'd *imagined* Belle's presence exactly. At least he'd established that much. She was as real as a ghost dog could be.

"Let's talk about something else. What about you, Carrie? What were your first psychic experiences like?"

She looked up from her salad, her jade eyes dancing. "You really wanna know?"

"I do. Were you freaked out, or did you take it all in stride?"

She chuckled. "Oh, I was freaked out for sure. I had heard about psychic mediums, and I even kinda believed in them, but I never dreamed it would happen to me. I've always been level-headed, and talking to dead animals seemed pretty far out there."

"And the crystal and sage and that New Age prayer you said during the reading? Those aren't far out there?"

She shrugged. "I find them useful for setting a positive mood. I've developed my own style over time." She told him then how she'd struggled at first to know what to do with the communications from her cat. Finally she had made her own appointment with a well-known psychic medium, and the woman had taken Carrie under her wing, guiding her in developing and fine-tuning her abilities. "Madam Marie, she called herself. I miss her." Carrie smiled fondly.

"She died?"

"Uh-huh. Two years ago. It's a shame I can only communicate with animals. I'd love to check in with her." Her eyes glistened with moisture, and she dabbed at them with her napkin. "Sorry."

"No problem. What did you do before you started doing readings?"

"I was a third grade teacher. In fact, I kept teaching until last year when my client load became such that I could no longer do readings part time. Now I'm working full time at it and booked out weeks in advance."

"Do you miss teaching?"

"I do sometimes, yes. But I feel like I was meant for a higher calling."

For a moment he was tempted to bait her. Talking to dead pets was a high calling? But then he remembered the difference it seemed to make for his sister, and decided to let it go.

"Well, I don't plan to give up my career as a firefighter any time soon."

"I don't blame you. After what you experienced as a boy, it was a natural choice for you to make."

It was then that he almost told her everything. The dark secret he'd been bottling up for twenty-eight years. If anyone would understand, Carrie Westfield surely would. But something kept him silent.

They talked for hours there in the low-lit booth, nursing their drinks and nibbling at their meals. He found out that she had grown up in a small coastal town in California, that Paul McCartney was her favorite musician, that she was a registered Independent who most often voted Democrat. They weren't so different after all.

The more they talked, the more he felt drawn to her. Not just the gorgeous physical package, but her personality too, her quick mind. Her penchant for laughter.

It hit him a little before ten o'clock, just as the waiter let them know the place was about to close: *This is what I've been missing.*

He'd told himself for years that casual dating was all he was cut out for. No strings. Plenty of hot, uncomplicated sex. He'd been blessed with the kind of good looks that made the latter an easy thing to obtain, and it had suited him. Now, for the first time, he realized he was no longer satisfied with the idea of leaving a woman's bed as quickly as possible in the morning.

He grinned to himself as he helped Carrie into her coat. Of course, first he'd have to get *in* to this woman's bed.

* * * *

As he pulled up next to her curb, Carrie's heart was going like a race horse. This was happening way too fast. In the space of three hours, Jake Manley had gone from being an abrasive, overbearing stranger to a man who was far too appealing for her comfort.

Wasn't this exactly the way it had happened with Mike? She'd been sucked in almost immediately by his good looks and charm, believed everything he told her, and only wised up three months later when she'd stumbled onto him with Miss Pilates. In bed together!

Annoyed at herself for allowing thoughts of her ex to intrude on the lovely evening, Carrie turned toward Jake. "Thanks again for dinner," she said. "I can see myself to the door."

"Nonsense. I'll walk you."

Before she could object, he was out of the car and coming

around to her side. It figured that a man who made his living rescuing people would be the type of guy who made sure a girl got safely into her house. A lot of guys these days had dropped those old-fashioned manners, but Carrie decided she rather liked the idea of being pampered for one night. After the way Mike had treated her, she deserved to be with a man like Jake, didn't she?

Whoa! Her imagination had just hop-scotched several steps ahead of reality. It wasn't like she and the hunky firefighter were embarking on a real relationship. Sure, they'd had a wonderful evening together, and she'd been surprised at how easy he was to talk to and laugh with. But he'd only invited her out to discuss his questions about seeing Belle. It would be silly to imagine anything beyond that.

Besides, her battered heart wasn't ready to risk anything serious with another man any time soon. Was it?

As they went up the steps toward the porch, Jake's fingers brushed possessively against her lower back and a warm, treacherous sensation began there and spread over her whole body. By the time they stood facing each other under the porch light, she was sure her cheeks must be an embarrassing rose color.

"Thanks again," she murmured, fishing in her purse for her keys.

"And thank *you* for your reassurances, Carrie. I was afraid I was going around the bend there for a while."

See? The man had simply wanted her professional advice. He was lucky she wasn't billing him for her time. She did her best to smile as she looked up at him.

"Oh, you'll be fine, Jake. It sounds to me like Belle simply wanted to touch base and let you know that she and your brother are okay. Chances are she'll just kind of fade away now."

He chuckled. "That would be good. I need to be able to concentrate when I'm on the job."

She stuck the key into the lock and pushed the door partway open before glancing up at him again. "Best of luck to you, Jake."

His brows shot up. "What? No offer of coffee? Not even a goodnight kiss?"

He said it in a teasing tone, but she could see in his face that he was honestly surprised, maybe even disappointed. Her head swam with confusion. What did Jake Manley want from her?

Then he chased any doubt from her mind. Placing his hands on her shoulders, he turned her to face him again. "I've been anticipating our first kiss for the last hour."

"You have?"

He stood at least six feet tall, and his broad shoulders and muscular neck made her hyper-aware of his masculinity. She wasn't a particularly small woman, but standing next to him, looking up into the rugged planes of his face and his fierce, dark eyes, she suddenly felt utterly feminine. Her breath caught as he pulled her close, her breasts pressing into his chest, and tilted her chin up with one finger. Her knees trembled.

"You have the most amazing eyes," he whispered in the moment before his mouth came down on hers.

Jake's lips were firm and warm, and they moved against hers without hesitation, as if the two of them had kissed a thousand times. The faint scent of sandalwood still clung to his skin, and it rose around her, drawing her into its exotic spell. Her thundering heart crowded her throat, and she grabbed hold of his upper arms and hung on for dear life.

He didn't use his tongue at first; his clever mouth pressed close, then moved lightly away, nipping and nuzzling, inviting her to play. She sighed and kissed him back, tasting remnants of tequila and lime on his lips. It was a heady combination. A cool, spring breeze swirled across the porch right then, ruffling their clothes as if suggesting they'd be more comfortable indoors.

Carrie pulled back and stared up into his face. His ragged breath told her he was just as affected as she was. His eyes flashed and his nostrils flared slightly as he waited for her to speak. She could hardly believe what she was about to say. "Would you like to come inside?"

Chapter 5

"I think I have a bottle of wine," she said. "I might even have a beer in the back of the fridge from the last time my dad stopped by."

Jake stepped past her as she closed the front door. He waited while she hung her purse on the nearby coat rack, his gaze drawn to the smooth fall of her hair. When she began taking off her jacket, he moved up close behind her, lifted the jacket from her shoulders, and hung it next to her purse.

Before she could step away, he pulled her back against his body and swept her hair to one side, baring the creamy skin at the back of her neck. "A cold beer would be great," he said as he pressed his lips to that hidden spot. He breathed in the scent of her shampoo, a smell that reminded him of a sunny meadow.

She gasped softly and he felt a long, slow shudder run through her. Emboldened by her response, he turned her to face him.

"But what I really want is to kiss you again."

"Oh." She gave a nervous little laugh but didn't move away. Instead, she tilted her head up and looked straight at him, eyes wide. Her ripe lips were slightly parted, waiting to be tasted.

Suddenly it was all too much, the curve of that mouth, the

scent of her hair, the proximity of her soft, womanly body. When he kissed her this time, a primitive urgency rose inside him. Almost before he knew what he was doing, he'd backed her up against the door and taken her mouth, pressing his hips into hers, letting her feel the hard evidence of her effect on him. She whimpered and let her lips go slack, allowing him in. He thrust inside, his tongue swirling and tasting. His hands moved down her body, molding to the warm indentation of her waist, splaying on her rounded hips. She whimpered again and moved her tongue against his, encouraging him.

From some other part of his brain, the hazy thought came that he should stop and check with her. Was he moving too fast? Was she okay with this? But all the signals she was giving him seemed to indicate she liked what he was doing. Besides, even a short conversation would mean taking his mouth from her delectable lips, and that was the last thing he wanted right now.

He deepened the kiss, losing himself in the smell and taste of her, in the tiny sounds of excitement coming from her throat. She moved against him, fitting her lush body perfectly to his muscled one, and his cock hardened even more. It was like they were exactly made for each other, made to have sex. Hot, gratifying, immediate sex.

He pulled back and stared down at her. "Carrie." His voice broke with urgency.

Her eyes were closed, her lovely cheeks flushed, her swollen lips the color of Cabernet. "Hmm?"

And that was when he heard the thumping sound.

At first he thought it was his own heartbeat galloping along, or perhaps hers. But the sound seemed to be coming from somewhere behind him and down low. He glanced over his shoulder and saw nothing.

"Do you hear that?"

"Hear what?" Her perfect brows vee'd downward but she kept her eyes closed.

"You don't hear that thumping sound?"

The sound faded away and then began again. An odd, cool sensation crept up the back of his neck as an image floated into his mind's eye. It was Belle, clear as day, sitting at attention and looking inordinately pleased, her wagging tail bumping softly on Carrie's hardwood floor.

* * * *

An hour later Carrie was sitting on her couch, her gaze focused on the tiny, blinking flashers on the radio towers in the West Hills. The night sky in that direction glowed with the reflected light of downtown, and above that a thin crescent moon dangled like a silver ornament.

"Or more like God's toenail," she murmured, and took another long sip of wine. That's what her dad had called that kind of moon when she was a kid. Thinking about her dad made her think about Jake once more, and that embarrassing cloud of confusion settled on her all over again. What the heck had happened?

One minute she'd been swooning in the man's arms, fully aroused and ready to take him by the hand and lead him down the hallway to her bed. The next minute he'd pushed her away like she had some kind of contagious disease. He'd mentioned something about a sound he heard, but then instead of explaining himself he'd simply said goodnight and left. It was the strangest end to a date she'd ever experienced.

Maybe even stranger than finding Mike with the blonde Pilates goddess.

Maybe she was lucky Jake had taken a powder. The last thing she needed was another guy who didn't know what he wanted.

As she drained the last drops from her glass, she felt the impression of soft fur against her legs.

"Muffin?" It had been a couple of weeks since her old cat friend had last visited. Carrie set her glass down and closed her eyes, and immediately felt the energetic presence of her cat as it jumped into her lap and curled up. "I wish you were really here," she whispered, "in your beautiful cat body, so I could touch you one more time."

The cat-spirit began to purr, sending Carrie impressions that felt like memories: times they had played together with that ratty catnip mouse, cuddling on the couch on rainy days, the way he liked to "help" her grade papers on the kitchen table. She realized that he was trying to comfort her with those warm mental pictures. Maybe it was the wine—or perhaps the poignant overview of their times together—that brought tears to her eyes. He'd been gone for five years and she'd thought she was over missing him, but tonight she would have given anything to have him back in physical form for just an hour or so.

Swiping at her wet eyes, Carrie got up and went to the kitchen, Muffin in tow. She put the empty wine bottle in the recycling bin and rinsed out her glass. As she tidied up, the quiet click of dog claws began following her around the room. Another visitor!

Carrie stood still and closed her eyes, and in the next instant, the spirit of Belle the dog appeared. Tongue lolling happily, she sat at Carrie's feet and wagged her tail, thumping it softly on the floor. Suddenly that sound registered in Carrie's mind and understanding dawned.

"You were here earlier, weren't you, girl?"

The thumping got louder, confirming her suspicions. But why hadn't she picked up on Belle's presence herself? Was she too distracted by Jake's arousing kisses? That must have been it.

Now a host of impressions filtered into her mind, pictures of herself and Jake in a torrid embrace as seen from a dog's eye view. It seemed that Belle approved of the brief flights of passion they'd shared.

Carrie laughed. "Thanks for the vote of confidence, girl, but I don't think it's going to happen. I'm afraid your boy Jake isn't ready to be around someone like me."

The dog-spirit continued to grin at her.

"In fact, I don't think he's ready to be around you either. Maybe you should leave him be for a bit. You're kind of freaking him out."

Thump, thump, thump. Apparently Belle didn't see it her way.

* * * *

The next morning, Jake rattled around his empty apartment like a marble in a pinball machine. He was restless as hell, and it had to be Carrie Westfield's fault. Normally he enjoyed his days off to the fullest. Sometimes that meant simply doing his laundry or maybe catching an afternoon movie with a buddy. Sometimes he and his dad went fishing. But today nothing seemed to suit him. All he could think about was the way he'd catapulted out of Carrie's house last night in the middle of the hottest make-out session he could ever remember having.

What the hell? He'd acted like some dumbass school boy.

And over what? Another visit from the supposed ghost of his dead dog? In the stark light of day, the idea seemed absurd. This had to be in his imagination. It had to be.

And he hadn't ever imagined anything like this before he'd met the gorgeous psychic. It was obviously all her fault.

He scowled as he slapped together some bread and ham slices, slathering on way too much mayo. Today, he didn't care how many grams of unhealthy fats he might be eating. He just wanted to forget the woman and all the odd trappings she came with.

But holy crap, the chemistry between them had been potent. Thinking about it now brought an enthusiastic rise from his cock. Swearing under his breath, he tore off a big bite of sandwich, wolfed it down, and dialed his dad's number.

An hour later they were settled on the bank of the Willamette River in the older man's favorite secret fishing spot. They baited their hooks, cast their lines, and waited, a comfortable silence falling between them. Finally, Jake spoke without taking his eyes from the broad expanse of dark green water.

"You remember that dog we had when I was a kid? Belle?"

"The one who died in the fire? Sure I remember her. Damn fine dog."

Jake let a few moments tick by, unsure of how to proceed.

"Why'd you bring up Belle?" his dad finally asked.

"No reason really. I was just thinking about her the other day."

"She was great with you kids. It's a shame we lost her."

"Uh-huh."

Neither of them mentioned the loss of his baby brother, Jeff, but the unspoken acknowledgement hung heavy in the spring air. A few moments later the older man reeled in a beautiful twenty-pound spring Chinook.

"You ever think about life after death, Dad? Do you think there's something after this?"

His father looked up from cleaning the salmon, tossed the wad of guts into the river, and sat back on his heels, looking thoughtful. "I suppose so. I guess we'll all find out for sure one of these days."

"Yeah. I guess you're right." Jake chuckled softly. He let a minute pass while the older man rinsed his catch and his hands. "What about communicating with the spirits of the dead? Do you think that's possible?"

Now his father turned and stared at him, squinting in the sunlight. "What's up with all these questions today? You okay, son?"

"I'm fine. I just want to know what you think about that—communicating with spirits."

"Well, I've never thought much about it myself, but your grandmother would have plenty to say about it if she were here today."

"Grandma June?" His father's mother had passed away when Jake was about ten. He barely remembered her.

His father put the cleaned fish into a Styrofoam cooler and closed the lid then set about baiting his hook again. "Yep. She always claimed she could hear your grandpa talking to her from heaven. Matter of fact, she used to give readings for people when I was a boy. Not sure why she stopped doing that."

A chill ran down Jake's back. His own grandmother had been a psychic medium? Why had he never heard about this before? And more importantly, was it possible that the ability to communicate with the dead had been passed on to him?

* * * *

Later that week, Jake's engine company was called out to a residential fire. The bottom floors of a three-story townhouse were almost completely engulfed in flames when his crew arrived at the scene. Smoke wafted from the open third floor windows into the night sky.

The first engine company already had a large-caliber hose line with good striking power run, and were blitzing the main body of the fire, attempting to prevent it from spreading horizontally to neighboring units. But because this was a newer building, made from light-weight materials and trusses that would collapse in minutes, an interior attack on the stairwell to the third floor was untenable.

Time was of the essence. Jake jumped off the truck before it even came to a stop.

"We've got a life hazard on the top floor. A seven-year-old boy. Window on the right," the supervising chief yelled in Jake's ear. "We're deploying the ground ladder."

Jake nodded, the familiar flutter of apprehension in his gut. He knew the nervous sensation would fade as soon as he went into action. As two of his buddies unhooked the ladder from the engine and rushed past him to position it against the side of the burning building, Jake shrugged into a Zetex entry suit, adjusted the hood and neck shroud, and turned on the oxygen. By the time he was suited up, the ladder was in place.

There was rarely a question about who would go into a burning building if Jake was on duty. He was always the first to suit up. Now, as he gripped the rails of the ladder and clambered up as quickly as the suit would allow, his body thrummed with adrenalin. *This* was why he was a firefighter, for this rush, for the personal satisfaction of making the critical difference between life and death. Fire was the enemy, and his courage and skill were the most effective weapons of combat.

Jake reached the window and threw his leg over the sill. His heart rate skyrocketed as he stepped into the small smoke-filled room and attempted to get his bearings. Even with the suit on, he could feel the heat from the inferno below. There was very little time left. Where the hell was the kid's bed? The darkness and haze made it almost impossible to make out shapes of furniture.

He switched on the headlamp and swept it back and forth, but the light barely penetrated the thick smoke. He'd have to rely more on what he could feel. Quickly, he worked his way along the outside wall until he ran into what he thought was a dresser. He skirted it and went on to the corner. Nothing.

Along the next wall was something like a low toy chest and a pile of wooden building blocks that slid beneath his boots. He nearly lost his footing, then righted himself and took another step. Something hit him at knee level. He reached out and felt the give of mattress and blankets. The bed! Frantically, Jake patted down the entire surface of the twin-sized bed. It was empty.

His belly lurched. *The kid must be hiding.* It was a nightmare scenario. If the little boy was hiding somewhere on the third floor, chances were small that Jake would find him in time. He wasn't even sure how many rooms were up there.

He threw himself to his knees and ran his arm along under the bed, hoping to encounter the huddled softness of a small body. But only a stuffed animal of some kind lay there in the darkness. Cursing, he staggered to his feet again.

Then, clear as day, somewhere off to his left, a dog barked twice. Sharp, commanding barks.

Belle! Who else could it be?

Jake stumbled toward the sound, making his way through a doorway and into a short hall. The smoke wasn't as thick there, and the beam from the headlamp showed two other doorways, both open, and what appeared to be a small linen closet.

Where is he, girl?

He peered into one of the open doors. The bathroom. He walked in and flung the shower curtain aside. Nothing.

Belle? Belle, are you really here? Help me!

He ran back out into the hall. The other doorway led to a second bedroom, larger than the first. He could make out a neatly made queen-size bed. Apparently, the parents had not yet retired for the night. No doubt they had been on the first floor when they discovered the fire but were unable to make it up the stairs to their child. Hopefully, they were safe outside.

But where was their boy? Under their bed? In their closet? It was common for a child to seek the safety of his parents.

Jake started into the room. At that moment the floor just ahead of him gave way with a terrifying whoosh, swallowing the bed. A tower of flames leaped through the opening. He reeled backward. The entry suit did its job, protecting him from the frying heat, but just barely. His heart plummeted as he plunged back toward the hallway again and pulled the bedroom door closed behind him.

He had failed.

But there was no time left to digest that horrible realization. He had to get out of there himself, and there were only seconds to spare before the rest of the floor fell through.

Then he heard Belle whine. He whirled around. Now there was a definite scratching noise from the area of the linen closet, as if a dog were trying to dig through the cabinet door. Jake rushed forward and pulled the small door open. His light cut through the smoke, revealing the little boy in pajamas curled up inside. In an instant he'd scooped up the small, limp form and made his way down the hall toward the window he'd first come in. Behind him, the fire roared like a hungry giant, devouring the floor he'd just walked on.

He felt his way through the small bedroom again and arrived at the open window. There, at the top of the ladder, one of his crew members waited. As Jake handed the boy through, he looked down into the little face. The boy's eyes were still closed, and he seemed unresponsive. Had Jake been in time? A few seconds later he turned and followed his buddy down the ladder, his knees shaking with exhaustion.

Chapter 6

Carrie watched from the window as Jake's big SUV nudged up to her curb. The headlights winked out and his door opened. She turned away, her heart beating an erratic tattoo on her breastbone. At least this time he'd called first to ask if he could come over. And he'd offered to pay her usual reading fee, which, of course, she'd refused.

Questions tumbled through her mind as she waited for him. It had been almost three weeks since he'd run out her front door like the devil was after him. There hadn't been a peep out of him in all that time. She figured she'd heard the last of him.

Had she been disappointed by his silence? She smiled at herself. Try as she might to convince herself otherwise, her pulse had leaped every time someone knocked on her door. There was *something* between them. She wasn't sure what it was, but it surely didn't feel as if things were finished.

Did he feel the same way?

She heard his footsteps on the porch. When she opened the door, his large frame filled the doorway and a thrill coursed through her body, a visceral response she hadn't expected.

"Hello, Carrie." His smile seemed strained, his voice clipped.

"Hello, Jake. Come on in. Would you like some yogurt? I was about to open a cup for myself."

He chuckled at her little joke. "Maybe later." He strode to one of the recliners and sat down without removing his coat. Obviously he didn't intend to stay long. A twinge of disappointment nicked her. She sat down across from him.

"How have you been? How's Brenda?"

"She's fine. Myself, I'm not so sure about." He pushed his hand through his hair and stared off into space for a moment. Then he focused on her face again. Even though there was nothing sexual about his gaze, being the object of his attention did crazy things to her insides.

"Want to talk about it?" she prompted, feeling the color rise in her cheeks.

He sighed. "A lot has happened since the last time I was here." He rambled on for several minutes, telling her first about the discovery that his grandmother had been a psychic medium and ending with the story of Belle helping him rescue the little boy from the fire.

"Is the boy all right?" she asked, fully caught up in his narrative.

He nodded. "He is. He spent a couple of days in the hospital for smoke inhalation, but he'll be okay."

"You saved his life," she breathed, feeling her heart swell.

What would it be like to make that kind of difference?

He looked down, studying the backs of his hands, and nodded. "Yeah. I get to do that sometimes if everyone is lucky." Then he looked up again. "This time it was Belle who did the heavy lifting. She told me right where the kid was."

"That's wonderful."

"I guess so, yes. Thing is, she's showed up at two fires since then. Each time she made the critical difference between someone being fine or someone being hurt." He shook his head. "I'm starting to rely on her. That's bad, because I'm usually a team player, and I can't tell anyone on my crew about her. They'd laugh me out of town."

He looked so bleak she wanted to reach out and caress his face, smooth away the frown lines on his broad brow. Her heart began to skip like a scratched vinyl record. She was in dangerous territory here. The man had come to seek her help and advice, not to repair her pitiful sex life.

"You'll figure it out," she offered.

"There's something else." He stood up suddenly and strode to the window, shoving his hands deep into his coat pockets. Carrie waited, watching the tension bunch in his shoulders. Finally, he turned. "It's something I've never told anyone. Something I've carried with me since I was a kid."

"What is it?" she asked when he'd been silent for a full

minute.

"That fire that killed Jeff. And Belle. Everyone said I was some kind of hero. They all thought I ran into the house to save Jeff. That was the headline in the local newspaper. But the truth is I just wanted to save my dog. Belle was all I was thinking about." He turned miserable eyes on her. "I've been trying to make up for that ever since. It's why I became a firefighter I guess."

This time she did go to him, unable to stand the pain in his gaze. She stopped just shy of touching him and looked up into his face. "You were just a little boy, Jake."

"I should have thought about my baby brother first."

"There was nothing you could have done, even if you had tried to help him."

She couldn't stop her hand from traveling up his chest and settling on the curve of his jaw. His stubbled cheek felt rough beneath her fingers as she stroked him there.

He stared at her for a moment, digesting her words, then caught her wrist and pressed a kiss to the palm of her hand. "You know, I never thought of that. Crazy, right? I've always just flogged myself for thinking first about my dog. And all this time…it wouldn't have made any difference." His voice trailed away and his eyes closed. "Thank you, Carrie."

"You're welcome," she whispered.

In the next breath he groaned and reached for her, and she melted into the heat of his embrace. Their kiss was wild and passionate, searing away her inhibitions.

"I want you, Carrie," he growled.

"Yes." Her blood thundered in her ears.

He lifted her as if she weighed nothing and started through the house. She pointed toward the hallway and her bedroom door. In only a few strides he had laid her on the bed and began unbuttoning his coat. Her fingers went to the buttons of her blouse.

"No." He reached out and stilled her hands. "Let me undress you."

She gave a nervous giggle, trying to remember which pair of panties she was wearing. Hopefully they weren't the ones with the little rip on the side. And then she stopped worrying about it because he was on his knees on the bed, straddling her body, kissing her again. His lips were merciless, possessing her mouth fully, his tongue promising untold erotic delights.

His big hand stroked across her chest and Carrie completely lost track of her breath. Somehow he worked her buttons loose without breaking the kiss, and she felt his fingers at the front-close clasp of her bra. In no time it came open and he reached in and freed her breasts.

"Oh!" She sighed against his lips as his big, rough thumb

coasted over one nipple. The sensitive nub tingled and grew erect, sending an arrow of excitement straight to her core.

"Nice," he whispered, giving her other breast the same treatment. Then he ducked his head and drew one pulsing tip into his mouth. Carrie moaned and tangled her fingers into his dark hair, holding him against her naked flesh as he plundered her with his mouth.

She was nothing but sensation. Every other consideration shrank into the background as her whole body woke and responded to the touch of his lips and hands. Her slacks and panties disappeared like magic, and now she felt his fingers at the apex of her thighs, stroking, caressing, opening her to his command.

Through heavy lids she stared up at him. "What about you? I want to feel your skin against me."

He stood back for a moment and shucked out of his shirt and pants, leaving his boxers on. She had a quick impression of muscled shoulders and chiseled pecs before he rejoined her on the bed. As his fingers found their home once more in the flowering heat between her legs, she grasped his shoulders and hung on, lost in the heady wilderness of his kisses.

Jake teased and titillated, bringing her to the very brink and then moving away. Carrie's head spun, her body aching with unfulfilled desire. Finally, she begged him, her breath ragged,

"Take me."

"Yes, ma'am." He eased back, a happy grin on his face. "Hold that thought."

She watched as he fished a condom from his jeans pocket then stepped out of his boxers, revealing the impressive extent of his own arousal. She swallowed hard. Next time *she'd* be the one rolling the condom down his erection.

He rose above her again, prodded her gently open, and filled her with the hot steel of his cock. The rhythm of his thrusts drew cries from deep within her even before she came. They were joined, rocking, thrusting, tasting, finding their way to fulfillment. And then everything shattered around her, bathing her in stars. Just as she came back to earth, his body tensed above her and he groaned her name. In another moment he lay quietly across her body, his breath slowing.

"Amazing," he managed, repositioning himself alongside her.

"Uh-hmm." She nodded, her hand idly stroking his shoulder. Now that she could think straight again, she realized that the skin she was touching felt different somehow. She traced her fingers back and forth across the uneven ridges.

"It's a burn scar," he murmured, his voice already sleepy.

She pulled her hand away. "Oh! I'm sorry. Does it hurt?"

He rolled against her, his hand coming to rest on her belly.

His breath was warm on her cheek. "No. It's an old, old scar."

"From when you were six?"

"Uh-huh."

Later, as he lay sleeping on his side, she was able to get a better look at the rough patch of silvery skin. Its uneven margins were about the area of a man's hand. On a small boy's back, the large burn must have been horribly painful. She snuggled close and pressed a kiss into his hair, her heart opening to the wounded boy and the special man he'd become.

* * * *

They made love two more times that night, using up the small supply of condoms Jake carried in his jeans. Each time he held Carrie in his arms, he felt the rightness of her presence there. And each time he thrust into the sweet depths of her beautiful body, he felt the timelessness of their connection. Something big was going on, that was for sure; some indelible link between them was being forged.

He waited for the usual fear to rise in him, the usual urge to run for the hills. But as morning light filtered into the room, his only plan was to run to the drugstore for more condoms. He grinned at the thought. He couldn't wait to make love to her again.

As they sat an hour later at her kitchen table, drinking coffee and eating eggs and toast, she smiled across at him. Her amazing eyes sparkled like green gems and her robe gapped open a bit, exposing the creamy curve of one breast. His cock stirred. He really needed to head over to the drugstore posthaste. He hoped she'd still be wearing the sexy robe when he got back; he had all kinds of ideas about taking it off her.

Suddenly, she turned her head toward the kitchen door. Her smile widened. "Belle?"

Jake scowled. He didn't hear a thing. "Is she here?"

Carrie nodded. "Yes. Don't you feel her?"

Jake sorted through his thoughts, struggling to open himself to the spirit of his old friend, but nothing registered.

After a moment, her face grew sober. She turned toward him again. "I'm sorry, Jake. She's telling me she's come to say goodbye."

"Goodbye?" It should have been good news. It would resolve his issues on the job, not to mention relieving him of doubts about his own sanity. So why did it feel so much like a punch to the gut? "Are you sure?"

She nodded, her eyes glistening. "I'm afraid so. Turns out there was another reason Belle came back, besides letting you know that she and Jeff are okay."

He looked into her eyes and knew in an instant what it was. "She wanted me to find you, didn't she?"

"I think so, yes. She's very happy that we're together." She looked down, her cheeks pink. "What do you think?"

He got up and went around the table, pulling her to her feet. Her lush body molded right to his. She felt so right in his arms it was like they were one person. "Tell her thank you," he said, kissing Carrie's lovely mouth. "Thank you, and goodbye."

About Nola Cross

I've always, always wanted to be a writer. It's funny—and kind of sad—to look back and see how "real life" has gotten in the way of those dreams. It's only in recent years that I've consistently carved out the time and energy to get any serious writing done.

For a while I penned erotic fiction under a pseudonym. I have to admit it was fun to explore my "darker side". But now I am hearing the call of my heart: to write bigger stories that focus on emotion, loss, spirit, and the power of true love; stories I hope my readers will relate to and want to read more than once. Small town America is my favorite fictional setting.

I live in a funky, comfortable fixer-upper on three wooded acres in the foothills of the Cascade Mountains, in southwest Washington state. My husband and I run a family business together in a small town nearby, a town very similar to the ones I write about. Our younger son works with us too. At home, four fine cats and a collie dog act as my muses. And three years ago we welcomed our first grandchild, darling Ona Mae. I am so blessed!

I love to connect with my readers and other authors. Please feel free to email me, friend me on Facebook, or follow me on

Twitter.

Nola's Website:

www.nolacross.com

Reader eMail:

nolacross@gmail.com

Cupid and Cupcakes

by Jacquie Underdown

In a snowy, sleepy town is a quaint cupcake shop. People travel from miles away to visit this sugar-scented store because they think it's magical. They're not entirely wrong. But it isn't the shop, or the cupcakes it sells, that's magical…it's the owner.

Penny loves her little store, but people don't visit *Cupid and Cupcakes* solely for her cakes. They have an ulterior motive—they're seeking love. Penny is a matchmaker, a modern-day cupid, and she's great at it. Never wrong. Unfortunately, Penny's gift doesn't work where her own love life is concerned. That is until Jonathon reappears in her life. He's her best friend's brother, utterly wrong for her, and completely off-limits. Or is he?

Dedication

For cupcake lovers

Acknowledgements

Thanks to Pamela at Beachwalk Press Inc. for all your hard work in making *Cupid and Cupcakes* a published reality. Thank you to all the wonderful anthology contributing authors—my story sits proudly next to yours. Thank you to my family for showing me each day how lucky I am to love you all. And thank you, readers, for your continued support and belief in love.

Cupid and Cupcakes / Jacquie Underdown

Chapter 1

Penny smoothed her flour-dusted apron and peered up at the clock on the wall. Her lips twitched into a grin. Eleven AM and she had a match already. She could feel it. A gentle warmth in her heart, like she was eating home-cooked chicken soup in a wood-fire heated house on a winter's day. The sensation spread and her nose tickled like the lightest of feathers was brushing over the tip. Her lips plumped and warmed as though they'd been kissed long and hard.

The vision came, swirling and swishing through her mind. A flash of rose hued images. Of smiles and hand holding and faces pressed together lovingly.

The girl standing in front of the counter, pointing to a raspberry and macadamia nut cupcake topped with vanilla icing and fruit coulee was the star of her thoughts. Penny smiled as she reached into the glass cabinet and retrieved the cupcake with tongs. She dotingly slid it onto a pretty rose plate and reached behind for a plastic skewer, also pink, topped with a heart. She slipped it into the center of the cupcake and presented it on the counter.

The girl's brown eyes widened, and Penny saw her how her lover would see her—adoringly. She had long blonde hair rushing down her back in golden cascades. Her face was round, punctuated by a cute button nose spattered with pale freckles. She was full-bodied and short. Stunning. Everything her match didn't even realize he would love with all his soul. Penny smiled wide. She never tired of this.

"Coffee and cupcake is on me."

The girl grinned and her cheeks flushed as bright as the raspberry atop her cupcake. A hush fell across the store, followed by excited mumbling and flickering glances. "Who will be the lucky man? He must be in the store right now," they whispered among themselves.

Penny knew who he was already. He was the tall, broad man with dark hair and intensely blue eyes standing at the back of the store. Gorgeous. Why couldn't she find a man like that for herself? She lowered her gaze and carefully avoided looking at the customers until they were at the counter making their orders. She wasn't giving him away without some excited anticipation first.

People flocked to *Cupid and Cupcakes* from miles away, but mostly it was residents from this sleepy, wintery town of Somerset, New Hampshire. From the moment Penny opened her doors, there was a line extending down the street. Some were waiting to sample a lemon drop cupcake topped with sweet cream cheese, or vanilla-bean coconut cupcake with coconut lime frosting. Or perhaps they wanted a rich chocolate mud or a red velvet. But that's not where the focus should rest, because all of Penny's customers were there for something more than the cupcakes. They had an ulterior motive to satisfying their sweet tooth. They were there to find love.

Within five minutes the dark-haired man stood at the counter and ordered a lemon meringue cupcake. Penny took it out of the cabinet and slid it onto a plate. She found the matching colored skewer with a heart on top. All the customers gasped. She slipped it into the yellow, gooey center and placed the plate on the countertop before meeting his kind blue gaze. His eyes widened, and he cast a glance at Blondie waiting at the coffee bar. She was holding her breath. Then he looked back at Penny and cracked a shy smile.

"Coffee and cupcake are on me," she said, finishing with a wink.

The rest of the customers clapped and cheered as he walked to the bar to have coffee and cupcakes with his soul mate.

Cupid and Cupcakes was where love was made. Love, the emotion, not the act. Each person standing in line thought this place was magical, with its pale pink walls and sugary sweet scent. They were not entirely wrong. But it wasn't Penny's shop that was magical—she was. Well, perhaps magical wasn't the right word. She was more like a love maker. Or more accurately,

Cupid and Cupcakes / Jacquie Underdown

a love finder. A modern-day cupid if you will. And she was never wrong. Never.

Chapter 2

Penny's cellphone rang from her apron pocket. She pulled her hands out of the hot, soapy water, slipped off her rubber gloves, and checked the caller ID.

She answered with a cheery, "Mom."

"I haven't called at an inconvenient time, have I?"

She glanced around at the few dishes left and the dirty benches she still needed to wipe over before she was finished for the day, and shook her head. "Nope. Not at all."

"Good. Good," Mom said with her slightly anxious, high-pitched tone. "I was just calling to see if I need to set another place at the table on Good Friday for Paul?"

Penny sighed. "Who told you?"

There was a brief silence before her mother asked, "Told me what?"

Penny marched across the tiles, headed to the front section of the shop, and gazed out through the window at the row of shops lining the street—a butcher's, a deli, a gift shop. "Don't play all innocent. Who told you?"

"I ran into Paul's Aunt Betty at the doctor's this morning. She said you two broke up. I don't understand why. He was a nice man and…"

Penny held her breath, waiting for what she knew was going to be said.

"Before you know it, you'll be thirty years old—"

"Yeah, yeah. I've heard this speech before." At least a dozen times. Her thirtieth birthday, which was still quite a few years away mind you, was freaking her mother out, as though it was the cut-off date for any woman hoping to find love—particularly her poor, loveless, hopeless-at-relationships-despite-being-super-great-at-others' daughter. "I can't help who I love and don't love. I'm not going to force myself to stay with someone—"

"I want grandchildren, Penny. Keep going this way and you may find you miss out altogether."

Penny pressed her thumb and finger to her forehead and closed her eyes. *Deep breaths, Penny. Deep breaths.* "Well, thanks for calling, Mom, but if I don't keep on with this cleaning I'll never get out of here." No use arguing with Mom. She'd tried, it was a losing battle.

"Fine," Mom said brusquely. "I just don't understand how someone who can *find* love for so many others can be so hopeless when it comes to finding love for herself."

Penny bit back an angry groan and collected her voice after a deep breath. "Like I've said a thousand times before—I don't make the rules. I don't even think I'm capable of seeing who my

love match is. I'm totally blind in that department and have to operate like normal people do. Is that so hard to understand?"
Silence for a heartbeat, two, three. "Yes, it is."
Of course it is. "Well, you better try harder, because it is what it is. I can't change that. Anyway, I better go. I'll talk to you at Easter. Love you. Bye." Penny stamped her feet and groaned at the ceiling as she hung up the phone. Her beautiful, unjudging, non-critical, ceiling.

A loud knock at the glass door broke her from her contemplation and growing anger. She turned, expecting to see a customer who didn't respect her closing times. But when she saw the tall, broad man wearing jeans, a woolen suede jacket and a beanie, she was met with familiarity. An enormous hiking bag was slung over his shoulders and he was grinning widely as he waved.

Jonathon. Or more officially—her best friend's brother.

She narrowed her eyes and contemplated not letting him in. Despite not seeing him for over five years, Penny's dislike for this spoiled, bratty man stirred strongly. Her feelings must have shown on her face because he frowned and knocked again, tentatively this time.

She dropped her cell into her apron, went to the door, and unlocked the latch. He pushed through, bringing cold, blustery wind with him along with a swirl of leaves. Penny looked down at the mess on the tiles. He was lucky she hadn't yet swept and mopped.

"Penny," he said, his green eyes shining bright and with genuine amiability.

"Jon?" She eyed his backpack, then the two big dimples in his cheeks as he smiled. She didn't remember him having dimples. He looked a little more…of a man, thicker, taller, than the last time she'd seen him. Which was when? After he finished college. He would have been twenty-two, twenty-three perhaps. "What are you doing here? I thought you were in…" She had no idea where he was. She frankly hadn't cared.

"Last stop—Tibet."

"And what, you're home now and thought you'd drop by your sister's friend's cupcake shop?" Oh dear, that came out a little…bitchy. She was never bitchy, but she was still wound up from the phone call with Mom and couldn't stop picturing that mocking, scathing scowl that Jonathon would cast whenever his little sister or Penny entered his precious space. And now he had the nerve to enter *her* space and expect her to be nice.

He grinned—not mockingly, but rather…what? *Regretfully? Bashfully?* "Jessie hasn't told you that I'm going to be staying with you guys for a while?"

Her heart stopped beating as she sucked in a horrified gasp. "No. No, she hasn't. Not at all. Not one word. What? Why are you staying with us?"

He took off his beanie and stuffed it into a pocket at the side of his backpack before ruffling his hands through his dark, thick hair. "She said she got the all-clear from you. That I was to drop in here to grab the key."

Penny crossed her arms over her chest and took a step back. "What key? To where?"

He looked up to the ceiling, indicating the upstairs apartment that she shared with his sister, her best friend, Jessie. "The apartment."

"But you…detest our very presence." She stifled an eye roll at how childish that sounded. But she did clearly remember him saying that to her face. To Jessie's face.

He winced, along with that certain something that kept framing his features—bashfulness, definitely bashfulness. "I'm not a ratty college kid anymore, Pen…"

Pen? Did he seriously call me Pen? It was always Pen-*nay* with the ending emphasized as though she had the most ridiculous name ever.

"I've grown up a little. A lot, in fact."

She straightened her apron and rolled her shoulders back.

Of course. Goodness, she was being ridiculous. Over five years had passed. He was a man now. She was a woman. She ran her own business. Made good money. She wasn't some unconfident, gangly teenager stepping quietly around him, hoping he wouldn't notice her. Lifting her chin high, she called for calm civility.

"I apologize." Those words burned on her tongue, but she persisted. "I shouldn't have dredged up the past."

Penny turned from him and strode into the backroom that still smelled strongly of caramelized sugar, vanilla, and chocolate—she would never tire of those delicious scents—and grabbed the keys off the hook. She shimmied the back door key off and spun around to make her way back to him, but she hit something hard. And warm. Jonathon's chest. With her chest.

He caught her around the waist with two big hands and looked down into her eyes, his face mere inches from hers. She could smell him—laundry detergent, salt, and an unmistakable maleness that dizzied her. His warmth penetrated her. Not a bad feeling, all in all.

"Are you okay?" he asked.

Penny stared into his green eyes, familiar yet unfamiliar. She'd never been this close to him. Seen him this…much. She was drifting closer, wanting to drown herself in his dominating stature.

What the hell am I doing? She shook her head and took a step back, out of his arms. This was Jonathon. Her archenemy. Her best friend's brother. She needed to keep that in mind.

"I'm fine," she said, holding the key up in front of her. He held out his palm and she dropped it into his hand, making doubly certain not to touch his warm skin. She'd been closer this minute than she ever wanted, no use getting closer. "It's the backdoor key. Just head out around the back and there are stairs leading up to the door."

"Thanks, Pen. I appreciate it. I don't expect to be in your hair for more than a couple of months."

"A couple of months?" she queried, much more of a shriek than she would have liked.

He arched a brow. "Um, yeah. I hope that's okay."

Grown-ups at play here, Penny. You're not a teenager anymore. She attempted a smile, but her lips felt as tight as a band. "Um, sure. I guess that's fine."

He grinned, his deep dimples appearing, and nodded. But instead of turning and walking out the door to leave Penny to get on with her closing duties, he peered around the shop.

"This is a gorgeous little place you have here."

"Thank you."

His attention landed on the wall of photographs. Photographs of smiling couples. All her *Cupid and Cupcakes* success stories. "Ahhh, and these are your love matches," he said, eyes widening as he went to inspect them closer.

"Yes."

"Are you for real? Does it really work?"

She was used to skeptics. They no longer bothered her. Penny knew in every corner of her soul that she was legit. That's all that mattered. She took a deep breath and chased away the imminent scowl on her lips. "Of course. I'm not some charlatan."

He faced her and held his hands up. "I never said you were. It's just…so, um…I don't know…unusual." He rubbed his face with his hand and smiled. "You never spoke about it as a teenager."

She hadn't even known about her psychic abilities until she was sixteen. And they had frightened the hell out of her. She wasn't going to tell the world all about it. Especially not Jonathon, so he could go and tattle to his college friends and taunt her.

She still remembered his girlfriend with her snide comments and mocking remarks when Penny's breasts decided they wanted to fit into DD cups, rather than the more manageable C cup they were the summer before. "Starting young with the silicon, aren't we?" And Jonathon had laughed right along with her, even though he knew it wasn't true. Penny spent the next few months trying to hide them with extra-tight bras and baggy shirts. So imagine if they knew of her special ability while she was vulnerable and still trying to come to grips with it herself.

No, the only person she told was Jessie, because she trusted her unequivocally. Still did. Although, trusting Jessie didn't mean she couldn't be upset with her that very moment for bringing Jonathon into her life, her home, for a couple of months, without even asking how she would feel about it.

"No. I didn't speak about it. And that was my choice," she said.

"Of course. That was definitely your right." He peered back up at the expansive wall of pictures she'd been collecting since opening the doors four years ago. "Um, do you control who you see…" His voice had changed, as though he was trying to sound nonchalant, but failing severely. "Do you choose who you make a love match for?"

He turned and lowered his eyes, avoiding her gaze. She tried not to smile. If she read between the lines, he was wondering if she could find a love match for him. Interesting. Did he want her to? Or was he simply curious?

"No. It happens all of its own accord, without any warning, and I don't have the ability to control it."

He nodded and forced a tight smile. Penny couldn't hide her knowing grin.

He wiped his hands on his jeans and looked around the room. "So do you need some help finishing here?"

She shook her head quickly. It was bad enough he was

going to be living in her apartment for the next few months, she was not bringing him into her professional life too. "Thanks, but I'll be fine. I'm nearly finished anyway."

"You sure?"

"Yep. Perfectly sure."

"I guess I'll see you later then."

She nodded. "Yep."

Penny let him out through the front door and locked it behind him. She watched as he walked away, his toned ass filling out those jeans perfectly. She closed her eyes, berating herself for even looking at his ass, let alone thinking how great it appeared in those Levi's.

Fine. Fine. No denying it was fun watching him leave. Didn't mean she had to like the man.

Cupid and Cupcakes / Jacquie Underdown

Chapter 3

Penny marched to the kitchen where Jessie was frying ground beef and chopped onions in a pan. Jonathon was in the shower, out of earshot.

"Why didn't you tell me your brother was going to be staying with us?" Her voice was a little harsher than she intended.

Jessie looked at her, her eyes widening, as Penny stood beside her at the stove. "Are you upset about it?"

Penny shrugged and softened her voice. "A little. Yes."

Jessie's eyebrows arched high. "It won't be for long. A couple of months..."

"I just wish you'd told me about it first, instead of having to learn about it from Jon when he turned up on my doorstep."

Jessie rested the wooden spoon on the edge of the pan and turned to face her fully. "I forgot. I'd remember to talk to you about it while at work, and then I'd forget by the time I got home. Honestly, Pen, I didn't think you'd mind. I thought you'd be okay with it."

"But it's Jonathon. Awful, nasty, Jonathon. He was our worst nightmare."

"When we were kids. He's grown up. We've grown up.

He's actually civil with me now," she finished with a giggle.

Another reminder of Penny's inability to let go of the past. But how Jonathon had been was the only Jonathon she knew. Perhaps he had changed though. It had been more than five years. She owed it to Jessie to at least give him a chance.

"You're right. I'm sorry. I'm being silly. I just find it so difficult to forget how mean he was to me. To us."

"Typical hormonal big brother. I used to give him his fair share of torment too."

Penny shrugged. "I guess."

"Remember when we hacked his Facebook account and typed all those messages on his timeline?"

She'd forgotten about that. A giggle broke through. "We wrote some really embarrassing stuff."

Jessie laughed. "He was so angry with us. He chased me around the living room, threatening to break my laptop."

She giggled with her. "And remember when we put strawberry jam inside his gym shoes?"

Jessie's shoulders shook with laughter. "Yes. Oh my God, I thought he was going to kill me when he found out."

"We did do some terrible things, didn't we?"

Jessie nodded. "And he did some terrible things to us too. We were young. That's what brothers and sisters do."

Penny sighed. "Okay. Point made. I promise to give this

arrangement a go."

Jessie looked at Penny with her green eyes. Eyes very similar to Jonathon's. "Thank you."

"Well," she said, glancing down at her sugar-crusted clothes, "I'm going to get changed before dinner is ready."

Jessie smiled and flicked her long brown hair behind her shoulder. "Sure. This should be ready in fifteen."

Penny had started up the hall to her room when the bathroom door opened and plumes of steam rolled out, followed by Jonathon. Dressed only in a towel. She stopped dead in her tracks. His hair was wet and hanging loosely around his ears and neck. Goodness, Jonathon had definitely grown up. His skin was tanned and taut; the muscles in his chest, arms, and shoulders thieved her attention. The way his towel hung loosely on his hips, barely covering what was hidden underneath, made her heart beat faster. He was…hot. Jonathon was hot. This couldn't be right.

Whoa, back up, Penny. You cannot be perving on your best friend's brother. That had to cross a billion best friend boundaries. Uncrossable boundaries. This was Jonathon. Ratty, bratty, sexy-as-hell Jonathon.

She closed her eyes and took a few deep breaths.

"Everything okay, Pen?" came his deep voice. Deeper than she remembered it being. It sizzled through her veins, igniting her insides. Her belly squeezed just hearing his voice.

Penny opened her eyes and made certain she looked only at his face. Not at that delectable body. If the front of him was that good, she could only imagine what his back and ass...*oh dear God*. She couldn't help but look—he was so strong and toned.

Eyes, Penny, his eyes. She forced her gaze to find his face again and swallowed hard. "Absolutely fine. Just a dizzy spell. I think I'm tired."

He strode to her, reached out, and held her elbow. She tried not to breathe in the scent of bubbles and clean, male flesh, or revel in the warmth pouring from him, coaxing her own skin.

"You sure? You look a little pale."

Penny forced a smile. "I'm fine. Once I get out of these clothes and into something more comfortable..." *Oh, dear, did I seriously just say that?* Now she was picturing herself naked and Jonathon naked. Both naked...together. *Breathe, Penny, breathe.* "I mean, I smell like my cupcake shop still..."

He grinned. "You smell delicious."

Her eyes widened.

"When am I going to get to try one of your cupcakes?"

Was that a euphemism? Of course not. He was being completely literal here. She blinked and watched a droplet of water run down the side of his face, down his stubbled, square jaw. *Talk, Penny.* "Um...tomorrow. Come downstairs tomorrow and I'll give you a taste…of, um, my cupcake." She shook her head. "I mean, *a* cupcake."

He nodded and grinned again, those flashing dimples carving lines in his cheeks. "Look forward to it." He released her elbow and headed to his room.

Penny sucked in a deep breath and continued to her own room.

It was Jonathon. Yes, she found him attractive. Very attractive. Any warm-blooded female would. But it meant absolutely nothing.

1. because he's Jonathon.

2. he's Jessie's brother.

3. …um.

What was she talking about again?

Chapter 4

Penny wound spaghetti around her fork and shoved it into her mouth. Jessie was a great cook, no doubt about it. She handled the savory, Penny took charge of the sweet. It worked well.

"So, any matches today?" Jessie asked from across the small, round dinner table. Jonathon sat in the chair between them. His head flicked up and his green eyes widened.

She grinned and nodded. "Three. I had barely a match in almost a month, then all of a sudden I get three in one day."

"Oh, my goodness. You watch, tomorrow you'll be flooded with customers."

"Hmm, I did worry about that. I might go in earlier and prepare a little more stock than usual."

"What does that mean though?" asked Jonathon.

She lowered her fork to her plate. "What does *what* mean?"

"Three love matches? I don't think I understand the process. How it all works."

Jessie lowered her fork too and took a swallow of her red wine before answering for Penny. "Penny gets visions about the lovers if they are in close proximity to each other and to her. So if two people happen to be standing in her shop and they are destined to be together, she will see that in her mind. Pictures, right, Pen?"

She nodded. "Yep. A movie reel of their life plays out in an instant in my mind. I sense the connection, physically and emotionally, and can pinpoint exactly who they belong to. After a vision, I understand the intensity of their love for each other as though they are my own emotions."

Jonathon sat forward in his chair and leaned closer to her. "How do you let them know? Do you just announce it to the room?"

Penny grinned. "No. Jessie actually came up with a lovely way of handling it. I'll put a certain colored skewer in their cupcake, which indicates they have a love match in the room. It helps to build atmosphere and excitement. When the other half of the pair orders their cupcake, I place the same colored skewer in theirs. And I give the two of them their cupcakes on the house, plus beverages of their choice, so they can take a break to get to know each other. Because, some of the time, these people are complete strangers before they enter my shop."

He arched a brow. "Really? Strangers?"

She nodded. "Two out of the three couples today wouldn't have even known the other person existed."

"It's kind of amazing really," he said, before shoveling a forkful of spaghetti into his mouth.

Penny laughed. "It is."

"I'm surprised the media haven't caught on and started stalking you."

"Many charlatans have come before me, making it difficult for most people to believe my gift is real. A good thing really. Means I'm left alone."

"Now she needs to hurry up and find my love match before I'm forced to adopt a houseful of cats and spend the rest of my days alone," said Jessie with a teasing grin.

"That makes two of us, Jessie."

"And don't forget me," Jonathon said. They looked up at him. "Hey, I'm older than both of you, I should get special treatment."

Cupid and Cupcakes / Jacquie Underdown

Chapter 5

Penny enjoyed her usual morning routine of mixing batters and baking tray upon tray of cupcakes. Today, she increased the batch sizes, adjusting the flour, sugar, eggs, and butter measurements accordingly, in case she was inundated with customers after yesterday's match-making successes. While the cakes baked and cooled, she prepared frostings, buttercreams and ganaches of all flavors and colors. Soon enough, the aromas of sweet chocolate, honey, and toasted coconut filled her shop, complimented by the sharp scent of fresh raspberry and lime.

Penny pumped the music up louder than she would have it during opening hours, and sang along as she decorated the hundreds of tiny cakes. This was her favorite time of the day—the solitude and doing what she loved to do best.

But five minutes before opening, her barista called to say she wouldn't be in—her son had fallen off his bunk bed and had a concussion. No worries. Penny had a backup. Except, when she tried to call her backup—multiple times—there was no answer. So she went to plan C, only to be told by plan C that he was in Canada rock climbing on some obscurely named mountain. Surely it was much too cold to be mountain climbing? So much more pleasant in her little shop with all its warmth and yummy goodness.

Already, there was a line of customers, dressed in hats, mittens, scarves, and big, warm jackets. Snow fell like frosted baby powder on the sidewalk and roads. She couldn't make them wait any longer out there. Perhaps, she could just close the beverage bar for the day? Say the coffee machine needed repairs? But the customers would be disappointed. It was the perfect, frosty day for a hot drink.

Penny drew in calming breaths as she strode to the front door and unlatched the lock. The bubbling excitement she usually possessed was replaced by slightly trembling hands and a racing heart. She counted backward from five and opened the door with a smile.

The laughter, chatter, and cold bodies ambled inside. The first customer tapped on the counter, indicating she would like an apple crumble cupcake and…a large cappuccino. So from that very first order, she fell further and further behind until the line of customers was down the street and around the corner. And there was no love-matching happening. Slowly, the expectation that usually floated around the store fizzled. People were annoyed by the time they made it to the counter.

Penny didn't want that. That's not what *Cupid and Cupcakes* was all about!

A familiar face poked up above the crowd. Jonathon. When

she met his eyes, he frowned, then pushed through the line toward the counter, removing his beanie, gloves, and scarf.

Who does he think he is, pushing to the front of the line? Just because he was Jessie's brother, it did not entitle him to be so rude. He continued through to stand behind the counter with her.

Penny opened her mouth to growl at him, but he spoke first. "I saw the line from upstairs, and I came to see if you needed help."

She pressed her lips together as she looked at his concerned expression. Guilt settled in her belly for being so presumptuous. He was there to help her, not force himself to the front of the line for service.

"I'm drowning," Penny said, on the verge of tears by this stage.

He peered out at the disillusioned customers and their frowns. "I can see that."

"My barista didn't show," she said.

"Ahh, well, if there's one thing I know how to do, it's make coffee."

Before she could object, he jogged out the back, grabbed a clean apron from the rack, washed his hands, and started on the long list of coffee orders blinking on the computer screen. The immediate whooshing sound of the milk frothing and the beans grinding was blessed comfort to her—and for the customers as they reached for their warm cups of coffee, one after the other.

Within the hour, calm crept through the shop again. Everything was under control. Penny grinned widely as she looked up at the next customer with his strong, square jaw and trendy black-framed glasses. He set his brown eyes on her and asked for a double-chocolate cupcake. Before he'd even finished saying his order, a familiar warm fuzzy feeling began in her chest. Her fingers tingled, and her lips had that kiss-bruised sensation. She stepped back two paces as the physical effects compounded to the point that she had to lean against the bench. The visions were like a blur of color seen from a fast moving car. One couple, two couples. A double match. This had never happened before. Ever. Images of smiles, stolen kisses, fingers touching, bodies pressed together, flickered through her mind. They slowed and eventually stopped altogether. She realized her eyes were clenched shut.

Penny opened her eyes and wiped her hands on her apron.

"Are you okay?" the man asked, brow furrowed, when she peered up at him again. She glanced across at Jonathon, who had stopped and was watching her too.

She nodded, composing herself with deep breaths. "Yes. Fine. I have a, ah…a double match."

The man's eyes widened. "A double match?"

She nodded.

He grinned and spun to face the other customers waiting in the shop. "There's a double love match," he announced.

All the customers cheered and murmured, the buzz in the room intensifying. "There's a double match, there's a double match, there's a double match," was whispered over and over.

Penny reached into the cabinet with her tongs, found the requested cake, and slid it onto a plate. She slipped a blue skewer through the thick swirl of chocolate buttercream, into the center of the cake.

"Cupcake and coffee are on me," she said, handing the man his plate.

Jonathon hooted and clapped. The rest of the customers joined in. She pressed her hands to her hips, threw her head back and laughed loudly, overcome by the intensely blissful atmosphere. She took a moment to peer out over her little shop, all the customers smiling, laughing, and yahooing. How lucky was she?

* * * *

When the final customer left, Penny locked the door behind her and leaned against it, exhausted. That was the busiest trade she'd ever experienced.

Jonathon laughed. "Big day." Not a question, a factual statement.

Cupid and Cupcakes / Jacquie Underdown

Penny nodded and strode toward the coffee bar where he was starting to flush out the espresso machine. "Thank you so much for helping me. You're an absolute godsend."

He lifted an already-poured cup of coffee and handed it to her.

She sighed with relief. "Perhaps 'angel' is a more fitting description."

He laughed and took a sip of the coffee he'd made for himself. "Come on, let's go take a seat for five minutes before we start cleaning up here."

She shook her head. "No, you don't have to stay and clean up."

He arched a brow. "I do, and I am. No arguments about it."

They took a seat at the stools in the back room against a bench where Penny did her paperwork. She sipped her coffee and relished being seated. They didn't have a chance to have a break today and she could feel it in her aching legs and feet.

"All that study at college, to get your degree in…in…"

"International Human Rights Law," he said.

She nodded. "Right. Hang on. Wait. You studied law?"

He grinned, his deep dimples flashing. "Yep."

She didn't know that, nor had she expected it. "All that study to become a human rights lawyer, and you spend your days making coffee."

He shrugged. "I've spent most of my career working pro-bono. It doesn't pay the bills. Pulling coffee does. I've worked in coffee shops all over the world."

"I didn't realize you were studying law. No wonder you were such an edgy college student. That's a lot of pressure."

He took a swallow from his cup and set his green eyes on hers. "Yes, a lot of pressure. A hell of a lot of work too. But I've wanted to do something in human rights since I was fourteen and learned about slavery and human trafficking. I didn't want to let anyone down."

Penny opened her mouth, but nothing came out. Did she pay any attention to this guy at all when she was younger? Apparently not. Okay, so being a human rights lawyer was admirable. Particularly the fact he'd been working pro-bono for most of his career. And helping her out today was a really sweet thing to do. But he was still annoying Jonathon. Wasn't he? Either way, she was more than grateful for his help and he deserved to hear it.

"Thank you again. Your coffee-making skills were very much needed today."

He lowered his gaze as he smiled slightly.

"So you're home now. Are you planning on staying, or are you heading off overseas again?"

He looked at her, his expression serious. "I'm here to stay.

Hoping to get some local hours up my sleeve and perhaps open my own practice sometime soon."

She nodded. "A sound plan."

"It's just so good to be home. I've spent the last six months sleeping on a rolled out mat on the floor in bone-shatteringly cold temperatures. The weather here feels like summer in comparison."

"And I bet your bed feels like heaven."

He laughed. "Very close. I had the best night's sleep. Cozy and so, so soft."

Penny was silent for a moment as she recalled the way she'd treated him yesterday when he turned up on her doorstep. Guilt twisted in her stomach, because he actually was a genuinely nice guy and she had treated him as though he were the opposite.

After a sip of coffee, she mustered the courage to say, "I apologize for being so rude when you showed up here yesterday—"

He lifted his hand to stop her. "Please, Pen. Don't apologize. I understand. I was a downright prick to you girls. I won't deny it."

A small smile touched her lips. "And Jessie reminded me that we weren't so nice to you either. It went both ways."

He grinned widely. "Yes, there were definitely moments I

wanted to strangle you both."

She held out her hand to him. "Friends?"

He nodded and took her hand in his, shaking it firmly. "Of course. Friends."

Penny ignored the shot of tingly warmth that spread from her fingers and up her arm. They were friends, sure, but there was no use getting carried away.

Chapter 6

Penny packaged six leftover cupcakes into a pale pink takeout box, all different flavors, before she locked up for the night. She was halfway up the back stairs, with Jonathon two paces behind her, when Jessie called to say she was going out for drinks with her work colleagues and would be home late.

After ending the call, Penny shoved her cell back in her bag, opened the door, and asked Jonathon, "Takeout for dinner?"

He nodded. "Pizza?"

"That'll do it."

She placed her bag and the box of cupcakes on the kitchen bench and felt like collapsing where she stood. Her eyes were heavy-lidded, her limbs like weights. She was usually tired when she got home from work, but this was ridiculous.

"I think that double match took it out of me," Penny said. "Then to have another match less than an hour later…what a day."

"You know tomorrow's going to be just as busy?"

She sighed and flopped onto a stool. "Yep."

Jonathon frowned. "Go run yourself a bath and relax for a bit. I'll order the pizza."

She wasn't about to argue with him.

****

Dressed in her pajamas, Penny ate pepperoni pizza with Jonathon in front of the television.

"It was amazing watching you in action today," he said as he gathered another slice from the box, then took a big bite.

She peered at him. "What do you mean?"

He met her eyes. "The visions. The matches. It was unlike anything I've ever seen. The joy your gift brings...it's remarkable."

Penny grinned, warmth creeping up her face. "Thank you."

"I could literally see the physical changes as they were happening."

She arched a brow. "You could? How so?"

He took another bite and chewed it before answering. "Your cheeks flush."

She lowered her pizza to her plate and pressed her palms to her cheeks, hiding them.

"And your lips—" he said, running his finger across his bottom lip. "—plump and redden."

Her gaze fell to his lips, long and full. A kissable mouth. Very kissable.

"This look transforms your features…"

"What kind of look?"

He shook his head. "I'm not really sure, but perhaps, it's a look of…love."

She smiled. "You're probably right. That's what I see in my visions. Beautiful love."

"You're lucky."

Penny ran her finger over the edge of her plate. "You think so?"

He nodded. "It could be worse. Haven't you seen all those movies about people who see death and destruction?"

She laughed. "My life's not some silly movie."

"No, it's not. It's one hundred percent real and completely amazing. A successful business. I never knew… I didn't realize…" He stopped and took a bite of pizza. She waited for him to finish his mouthful. "Despite you spending nearly every weekend at our house, I really didn't know you, Pen."

"It does seem that way, doesn't it?"

His lips curled upward bashfully, and he looked away. "Can I admit why I didn't give you the time of day?"

She nodded when he met her gaze again. "Um, okay."

"Because right now I feel foolish and mean for acting the way I did—"

"Just tell me."

He peered into her eyes, his gaze sliding to her lips. "I had a massive crush on you, Pen. On my little sister's best friend. If I didn't avoid you, I probably would've kissed you, at the least, and that goes against all kinds of happy-family rules."

Penny couldn't speak for a moment as that sunk in. Her heart raced, and her cheeks warmed. Jonathon, who she thought had absolutely detested her, had a crush on her. Was he for real?

"I was four years older. That seems like nothing now, but at that age, it felt…wrong," he continued.

"I would never have even guessed at that."

He shrugged and grinned. "No. That's how I intended it to be."

She shook her head, eyes narrowing. "But you were so…mean sometimes."

His smile was replaced by a frown. "Yes, and I'm sorry."

"We were kids," she said, waving his apology away. "And besides, if you had tried to kiss me, I would've punched you in the nose."

Jonathon laughed loudly. "I definitely sensed that."

"But thanks for telling me. It explains a lot."

She didn't hear his response, because the strangest sensations found her. Familiar, wonderful, and utterly scary sensations. Her chest grew warm, her mind muzzy. Penny's fingers and toes tingled. No. No. This could not be happening. It was only her and Jonathon in the room. This couldn't be right. The images flooded her mind, beautifully intimate images of warm embraces and fervent kisses. Penny and…Jonathon. The adoration and love in those green eyes unstitched her completely. Such intensity. She gasped, covering her mouth with her palm.

When she peered at Jonathon, his eyes were full of concern and something else? Knowing, perhaps.

Could it be true that this man was her soul mate? Jonathon was Penny's love match?

She stood quickly, her plate and pizza falling off her lap onto the floor. No way. This could not be.

She opened her mouth to speak, but nothing came out. She needed time, space, lots and lots of space, to think this through, the repercussions of such a revelation. Without a word, she rushed away, up the hall, into her room, and slammed the door behind her.

Chapter 7

Penny sat on the end of her bed, shaking out her hands. Nervous energy swarmed her veins, making her heart rate gallop. Her breaths were short. How long she had waited until Cupid's arrow hit her, and now that it had, she was wishing it hadn't. It should not be this way. It simply should not.

Jonathon.

Jonathon?

Penny and Jonathon?

Too complicated.

Completely wrong.

She scrubbed her hands over her face and groaned. He was Jessie's brother. Jonathon had said it himself, that broke so many happy-family rules.

Perhaps she'd made a mistake?

The fog cleared slightly and she sat up straighter. *Yes, that's it. I made a mistake.*

But she was never wrong. Never. Always one hundred percent, utterly, absolutely, right.

Penny flopped back against the mattress and pulled a pillow over her face. She shouldn't feel this way. She should be…deliriously happy, not plain old delirious. Is this how her matches felt initially—confused, incredulous, unhappy?

A knock sounded at her bedroom door.

"Who is it?" she said, force of habit. She knew exactly who it was. The only other person in the apartment.

"Can I come in please?"

She shook her head. "That's not a good idea. I'm not feeling well."

The door clicked open and Jonathon stepped inside. Penny pulled the pillow off her face and sat up slowly. He sat beside her on the bed. She smoothed her hair behind her ears and straightened her pajama top. All this time she couldn't look at him.

"Penny," he said gently with his deep, caring voice.

She eventually raised her eyes and looked into his, as though it was the first time she'd done so, because she was now looking with the knowledge that he was her match. Her perfect pair. Her…soul mate. Could it be true?

His deep green eyes were full of warmth and compassion. Penny had seen those same eyes in her vision, but filled with more. Filled with love. So much love. For her. She shook her head and drew in a deep breath.

"Want to talk about it?" he asked.

"No," she said quickly. "I can't."

He sighed, shoulders slumping. "Pen?"

Penny looked at him again, her gaze wandering to his lips. She pressed a finger to her own; the memories from her vision, of his mouth on hers, lingered. His strong, broad shoulders. Long, muscled arms. A thousand embraces. His chest pressed to hers.

"Pen?"

His voice snapped her out of her reverie.

"I know what happened. I know how you look when it happens. You saw us, didn't you?"

It felt like minutes before she could gather strength and voice to answer. "Yes."

A long exhale from Jonathon.

"But I could be wrong." She finally looked at his face again. "I have to be wrong. You...you're Jonathon."

He grinned. "Yes. I've been Jonathon for almost thirty years now."

"This is not the time for jokes."

He sighed. "Then what is it time for, Pen? Freaking out? Refuting what you saw? Making me feel like I'm not good enough for you? Worthy enough?"

She shook her head. "No. Yes. Of course not. I'm...shocked. Aren't you?" She pressed her hand to her chest, her shoulders rolling forward. "And I don't feel it. I mean I saw it, the affection and intimacy. The love. But I don't..."

"You don't feel it?"

"Should I?"

He shrugged. "I don't know how this all works. You're the expert here. What have your matches told you?"

What had Penny's matches said to her? When did they know with all their heart that she had identified their perfect match? She straightened up and peered at his lips. When they kissed. That was what all of them said. When they shared their first kiss, it all fell into place. Penny needed to kiss Jonathon to prove that in this one instance she was absolutely wrong about who her love match was.

"Kiss me," she said quickly.

"What?"

"Kiss me. My matches all say the same thing—the first kiss is when they know it's real."

His eyes widened. "You want me to kiss you?"

"Yes. And we'll know then that I've made a mistake."

His smile fell away. "Right. A mistake." He reached for her and stroked a finger down her face. A tingling warmth followed his touch. "Or the truth," he said, his face nearing hers.

Penny peered into his eyes. "Truth?"

He moved closer. "A love match."

She simply had to get this over with, then she'd know for sure.

His lips pressed against hers, warm and gentle. Her eyelids drifted closed, and she waited for it to feel bad, forced. Awkward even, like she knew it would. His fingers wound around the hair at her nape, and prickled warmth fanned across her flesh. Lips parting, he slanted his mouth over hers. Heat. Tenderness.

Penny's muscles twitched when he held her waist, deep need pulsing in the pit of her belly. She'd come this far, and, to know for sure, she'd have to give this kiss some time. And besides, it wasn't so bad, the warmth from his body encompassing her, his scent. His tongue penetrating her mouth, soft and probing. He tasted…so good. Hot sparks of want darted through her.

She pressed her hand to his cheek, feeling the day's stubble under her fingers, holding him just right, and slid her tongue against his. Penny bit back a moan as he pulled her closer and deepened their kiss, his tongue tasting her, lips moving with hers. She couldn't deny that Jonathon could kiss. Remarkably well.

But there was no use getting carried away. Surely the crackle and spark was about to fizzle. In the meantime, there was no harm enjoying herself. Jonathon's breathing deepened; her heart beat fast and her flesh burned. His lips met Penny's more firmly, and his chest pressed harder against hers, flooding her with his body's heat. She had to touch him. If this was going to end soon, terribly, then she wasn't missing the opportunity to feel those muscles.

Her fingers crept under his shirt at his taut waist, then over his muscled back. Pressed firmer, more eagerly, higher up his spine, down again. Better than she had imagined, strong, hard, and so wonderfully hot.

Penny was lost then, in the moment, illuminated from the inside, scorching under his delicious intensity. Her back found the mattress, Jonathon nestled beside her, his mouth never leaving her. Oh boy, she was a tangled mess of bliss and didn't want this moment to end. It felt too good. So right. His kiss contained everything she'd ever yearned for. He leaned over her, his hand gliding over her thigh, up to her waist, pulling her tighter to him. And all the while he kissed her—deep and lush.

She didn't care that this was Jonathon. She wanted him, regardless. Because of that. And more. She wanted more. So damn much more. Penny wanted all of him—his heat and muscle, his body crushed against hers, flesh on flesh. Everything. All.

She was too scared to stop now, in case all this emotion and feeling fled. In case it ended and they went back to before, when she didn't care and didn't want him. She yanked his shirt, pulling him on top of her. He straddled her—big, strong dominance—and she gasped, rolling her hips to meet his hard length. Damn clothes. Damn time. She wanted him now. Right now.

She wanted to tell him, but was too scared to talk. She didn't want all this to vanish under a cloud of dissolved lust. Penny rolled her hips again, needing to feel his hard cock and know it was for her. That he felt the same.

"Oh, Pen," he groaned, his warm breath tingly against her ear. "This is truth."

His words echoed through her entire body, setting everything right. All those years of seeking and longing for that certain someone that would click like a puzzle piece with all that she was. "Yes," she breathed, as his mouth crashed against hers again. His lips trailed down her jaw to her neck. He sucked her flesh into his mouth, and she sighed.

"I've wanted to do this for so long," he said, half growl, half whisper. "I want to taste every part of you."

"Yes," Penny said again, a long hiss from between her lips, incapable of anything else when she had a man like Jonathon on top of her.

A knock came at the door—three soft raps. Her eyes snapped open, and she pushed Jonathon off her. It had to be Jessie. Home early.

"Penny, are you asleep?" came Jessie's whisper.

Penny sat up, pulling down her rumpled clothes and smoothing her hair. She wasn't ready for Jessie to know anything about this yet. She needed time. Though, convinced now that her vision had been correct, she had to come to terms with this in her own mind. All in all, Jonathon was still Jessie's brother.

Penny lurched from the bed, opened the door a little, so Jessie couldn't see Jonathon sitting on the bed, and slipped out into the hall, shutting the door behind her.

"You're home early," she said. Her lips were tingly and plump. Her face felt warm.

Jessie narrowed her eyes. "Everything okay?"

She nodded quickly, running her hands over her hair in case she'd missed any tangled tufts. "Yep. Fine."

Jessie looked up and down the hall. "Where's Jonathon?"

Penny avoided meeting her eyes and started down the hall toward the living room. "Um. Not sure. Maybe he just popped into the bathroom."

Jessie nodded.

They made it to the living room. The pizza was still on the coffee table. Penny's plate had been picked up off the floor and was resting beside the box.

"You want a piece?"

Jessie shook her head. "Thanks, but I've already eaten. So how did your day end up? Busy?"

"Ridiculous. And my barista didn't show. It was chaos until

Cupid and Cupcakes / Jacquie Underdown

Jonathon stopped by and helped out for the rest of the day." She told her the entire story, about the huge line and how Jonathon had cleared it out in no time.

"He's so much more pleasant now that he's developed some maturity."

Oh, yes. So much more pleasant. And his maturity...his big, hard maturity. Arousal shot through her. She shook her head, chasing away that thought. Not in front of Jessie.

"I could say the same about you," Jonathon said, striding into the room.

Jessie laughed. "Hardly."

He sat on the couch, in the only free spot left, which was directly beside Penny. Her body buzzed, being in close proximity again after what had happened in her bedroom. She glanced at him from the corner of her eye. He was, now that she was willing to accept and admit it, unbelievably sexy. Those gorgeous dimples, his long, broad, body. The square line of his stubbled jaw. Those lips. Such kissable lips. Jonathon smiled at her, reminding her she was daydreaming.

"Um...so..." She couldn't form a sentence.

Jessie peered at her, waiting for her to finish. But she didn't. Jonathon jumped in. "I still haven't tasted your cupcakes yet," he said.

No. He'd definitely not done that...yet.

Cupid and Cupcakes / Jacquie Underdown

He grinned cheekily.

Penny rested her piece of pizza on a plate and stood. She grabbed the box she'd brought home from work out of the kitchen, and carried it back to the living room. Sitting down, her leg brushing against his, she said, "I guess these are the least you deserve after all your help today."

She opened the box.

Jonathon peered inside. "Hell, yeah."

"Your pick?"

He reached in the box and pulled out a peanut butter cupcake with salted caramel drizzle and peanut buttercream. Pulling back the paper patty tin, he took a big bite, closed his eyes, and groaned as he chewed. She'd heard that sound before and it stirred lust in her belly.

"I'm in heaven," he said.

Penny watched his mouth as he chewed, a glint of caramel on his lips. She wanted to lean over and suck that sweetness right off them. Her breaths were shallow. She stood and held the box out to Jessie. "Here you go, Jess. Your pick."

Jessie took the box from her.

"I'm going to take a shower and hop into bed." A really cold shower.

Jessie looked at her pajamas. "Haven't you already had one?"

"Um. Yep. But I need another. I spilled pizza down my shirt earlier." And she strode away.

"Good night," Jessie said.

"Good night," Jonathon said with a chuckle.

Chapter 8

Penny wasn't getting any sleep tonight. Not after the revelation. Not while Jonathon was in the next room. Best first-kiss of her life and now all she wanted was to do it again, and again, and again. She yearned for his touch, strength, and heat, so much so that a throbbing ache had found its way between her legs.

She grinned in the darkness as she lay against the bed, the blankets pulled up over her. Who would have ever guessed it? Of all the people on the planet, she was to end up with Jonathon.

How would Mom feel about Penny finding her soul mate? A part of her didn't want to tell her that it had finally happened, that she had foreseen her own romantic future. Not for a while anyway. Let her stew for a little longer, for all the times she'd been impatient.

But more importantly, how would Jessie feel about this? They'd been best friends since Penny was nine years old. Jessie's family was like an adopted second family to her. In reflection, she had even detested Jonathon like a disgruntled sibling might.

Would Jonathon and Penny easily overcome that type of relationship? She grinned again and clenched her thighs together.

They'd had no trouble earlier, and by his own admission, he'd thought of her as more than a bratty friend of the family anyway.

She remembered his words at her ear, his hot breath against her skin. "I've wanted to do this for so long." Had he truly been attracted to her since she was a teenager? She was oblivious to it all. Too caught up in her own life.

Something stirred inside—a tightening across her chest. Regret? Regret for not opening herself up earlier to the possibility that this hardworking, compassionate, sexy-as-hell guy could be The One. They could have been kissing like they did today for years. No need for an endless stream of bad relationships.

Penny shook her head. No. There was a reason the vision only came to her today. Now was the right time. When they were both older, and, as Jessie said, more mature. There needed to be life experience, independence, and emotional growth before this could ever work between them. That's why she had never seen her own love match. She wasn't ready for love. Certainly not with Jonathon.

That's it. She couldn't lay in bed any longer without him there with her. She pushed back the covers and pressed her feet to the floor. Her heart was drumming in her ears, but she wasn't giving herself an excuse to back out. She crept to the door, opening it quietly, so as not to wake Jessie, and snuck down the darkened hall to Jonathon's room.

With renewed indecision, she stood outside his door for a long moment. Should she go in there? Or was it too risky with Jessie sleeping close by? What was she going to say once she was in there? He could be sound asleep and not in the mood to be awakened.

But all the answers to all those questions weren't as bad as spending the long, cold night alone in her room without him. She pulled on the handle and opened the door of the dark room. It creaked so loudly, she anticipated sirens and alarms to start ringing and Jessie to come running out of her room with a baseball bat at the ready. She held her breath and waited, but nothing happened.

Penny slipped into the room, trying to quieten her hastened breath that seemed like a roar against the silence. She closed the door quietly behind her, another creak sounded out, then she tiptoed toward Jonathon's bed. The moon crept through the cracks of the curtains, illuminating his big frame and her way. The bedding was pulled down to his waist, and his defined chest covered by a light spattering of hair was on full, glorious display.

She heard the rustling of sheets and froze.

"Pen?" came his deep voice.

"I can't sleep," she whispered.

He rolled on his side, resting on his elbow, and pulled the

blankets back in invitation. "Neither can I."

Her stomach tightened and warmed as anticipation of feeling his body against her swept through her. Was he naked under there? *God, I hope so.* She was thrumming all over just thinking about it.

She crawled onto the bed and laid beside him, not yet touching, though she could feel his heat like he was fire and she was kindle ready to be set alight. Penny peered at his face, covered in a beautiful play of shadow and light. His hair was messy and his eyes shone.

"Why can't you sleep?" she asked as he pulled the sheets over them, enclosing her with him. She fought the urge to press against his chest.

A small grin touched his lips. "I keep thinking of you."

She nodded. "Me too." He had consumed every thought.

He rested a hand on her chest and she struggled to breathe. Her heart beat fast under his palm. "Do you feel it now, Pen?"

She knew what he meant—the possibility of love, the beginnings of love. "Yes," she whispered.

Jonathon smiled. "Me too. Though, in a way, I think I always have." He pressed his lips to hers. She didn't resist. This was what she yearned for—bodily contact, luscious intimacy, with him. Only Jonathon.

All her blood scattered to her breasts, belly, and lower,

between her thighs. She wanted him in every way physically possible.

"Are you still…exhausted?" he asked with a raised brow.

Hell no. She was rejuvenated. Buzzing. She shook her head. "Not at all."

He grinned in the darkness, and the crackling lust sparking between them intensified. His hand slipped down her shoulder, over her swollen breast. Penny's nipple zinged, like it was struck with electricity, as fingers roamed across the delicate surface. Lower, his hand swept, under her pajama top to her waist, down her belly, leaving a burning trail in its wake.

"I want to see you naked, Pen," he said.

She nearly whimpered as his husky request hit her directly between her thighs. Her belly pulled tight. Oh, how easily she'd transitioned from seeing him only as her best friend's big brother. How effortlessly he'd become a much-wanted imminent lover.

"This isn't…weird for you?" she whispered.

Fingers at her pajama top, he began undoing the buttons. "Not one bit," he said. Another button. Another. Her breaths were coming hard, her chest rising and falling. "I've wanted you for so long." The last button. Slowly he opened her top, exposing her bare breasts and pebbled nipples. He peeled it off her shoulders. "All the way," he said, his voice hoarse.

Penny lifted her body to remove her top completely. His gaze drifted to her chest. He palmed a breast, her nipple tingling from the friction.

"You're so damn beautiful, Pen."

Her cheeks warmed. The way he looked at her as though he could cover her in cream and devour her whole made her feel sexy. His finger and thumb gently pulled at her nipple. Her eyes closed, and a raspy moan left her throat.

"You like that?" he whispered.

"Yes," she hissed as he replaced his fingers with his warm, wet mouth. His tongue flicked over her nipple before he sucked it between his lips. "Yesssss."

Penny gripped his hair and arched her back; her breast pushed further into his mouth. He was greedy, caressing, sucking, and licking until her body was deliciously engorged with desire.

"Need you," she managed to say, though barely.

Jonathon released the nipple he was working on and peered into her eyes. "Tell me what you want," he whispered as his hand dipped under her pajama bottoms, her panties.

She gasped when he landed right where she needed him most. She gripped his broad shoulders and bucked compulsively against his hand. Her hyperaware body was so utterly sensitive to his touch, completely needy. He ran his fingers along the length of her slick sex, and she groaned when he circled over her clit.

"Tell me," he said again, so hoarse his words sounded like more of a croak. It was good to know she wasn't the only one about to fall apart.

She rolled toward him, needing his body against her, bare chest against his. Penny felt it then, his long length against her belly. He was completely naked, as rigid as rock, and very...big. She swallowed hard as she reached for his cock and gripped.

He groaned.

She was going to tell him what she needed, complete with hand gestures. Gripping the base of his cock, she stroked all the way up to the tight head. "I want this in me." With each breathless word, she stroked his length. And with each stroke, he rocked his pelvis, pushing his cock between her tight grasp. He continued to finger her clit until she could barely think, let alone speak. "Over and over and over again. Deep and powerful."

A rumble sounded in his chest. He pulled at the waistband of her pajama bottoms. "Take. These. Off. While I grab a condom."

Penny rolled out of the bed and pulled the bottoms down her legs until they dropped to the floor, and she stepped out of them. Then her panties. Jonathon scrummaged through his backpack and pulled a condom out of a pocket. She headed back to the bed, but he put his hand up.

"Wait, please."

She stopped.

He took a seat directly in front of her. His eyes roamed over her body, down to the apex between her thighs.

"Perfect," he whispered. Raising his eyes, he met her gaze and wet his lips with his tongue. "I want to taste you first."

Penny's breath caught in her throat. Her heart raced.

He held his hands out. "Come here."

She took a slow step forward. He gripped her hips and pulled her closer, motioning her to stand astride him. Once she did, she was opened wide for him.

"I can smell your arousal," he said, his face but inches from her. He pressed a kiss to her mound and looked up at her, while his lips lingered against her flesh. "Fuck, you're so gorgeous."

Penny gripped his shoulders, her legs suddenly weak. He turned her on; she could feel it like a deep pulsing base in her sex. Right where she wanted his tongue.

With a hand on her ass, he tapped his shoulder with the other. "Put your foot here."

She opened her mouth to protest, but he was already lifting her leg and positioning her foot before she could find any words. A guttural groan streamed from him when he looked at her, spread wide open, at perfect height for his mouth. She felt so utterly sexy. Desired.

He pushed her lips apart with his fingers and licked firmly along the length of her. The single leg keeping her standing trembled. Again, his tongue worked along her sex to her clit.

"You taste so fucking good," he whispered, never taking his lips off her.

The tip of his tongue flickered over the engorged nub. Penny's head rolled back and she sighed. She gripped the hair at his nape and cradled his face with her other hand, needing to hold on, wanting him closer. His intensity increased, licking and sucking, feeding his tongue inside her.

Pleasure shook her low, a deep throbbing ache. Who would have guessed that Jessie's big brother was so damn good with his tongue? As he sucked on her clit, she bucked against his mouth, desperate for more, unable to do anything else as she chased the stars.

"Jon, so damn good," she tried to say, but it came out weak and distorted.

She felt him chuckle; the vibration only deepened the sensation.

Jonathon was insistent, hitting the spot just right, over and over. The precipice zoomed into focus, too soon, not soon enough. Her thighs tightened, breaths rasped from her throat, and her entire body burned and thrummed. She pushed against his mouth as her orgasm slammed into her. She gripped his shoulder and bit down on her bottom lip to stifle the loud moan trapped in her throat. He held tight, sucking and licking at her clit, holding her against his mouth as she bucked. Pulses and pulses of pleasure pounded Penny, stealing her strength, replacing it with a warm, tingling lightness.

She drifted slowly back to earth, trying to catch her breath and still her galloping heart.

"Oh my God," she whispered as she lowered her foot from his shoulder. Her legs were weak; she thought she might drop to the floor.

His features were loose with arousal as he peered up at Penny, his eyes filled with something more primal—an animal hunger. Her gaze dropped to his lap. His cock was thick, long and iron stiff. It brushed against his belly as he sat there. Just seeing it, the head glistening under the slice of moonlight shining across the room, stirred her anew. She wanted him deep inside her.

Penny leaned over, her face nearing his. He held her breasts, squeezing them together until they touched. His thumbs grazed the nipples. Heat flamed between them. A piercing current of lust. His eyes held fast to hers. Anticipating. Her fingers swept up his muscled arms until they rested at his strong jaw, where she cupped his face. Nearer still until her lips met his. She lingered there, breathing him in.

She backed away a fraction to look at his handsome face, into those lush green eyes. Their lips met again, with more force. She opened his mouth and her tongue met his, silken, warm. Her belly tugged with the sensation. Jonathon tilted his head to seek more from her mouth. The quietest of purrs vibrated in Penny's throat. She deepened the kiss, tasting, wanting.

His tongue penetrated her mouth as his lips moved with her, demanding more. She gripped his cock and slid her hand up and down the steely length. He moaned against her mouth and the guttural sound stung her low, fuelling her desire more. She wanted him to feel what she had just felt—the intensity of pleasure. And she wanted him to take her there again.

She pushed at his chest, and he fell back against the mattress. Fumbling for the condom, he ripped the packet with his teeth and rolled it onto his dick. She climbed onto the bed, up his body until she sat astride his lap. His erection sat snug against her sex, right where it belonged. Every part fit. Every move was right. They were meant to be together. There was no longer any denying that.

He pressed his palm against Penny's heart as she peered down at his gorgeous face. "Can you feel it, Pen?"

She rested her hand on top of his and waited for some heartbeats to pass before she answered. "So much. Right in here."

"Me too."

She pressed up on her knees and directed his cock to her entrance. He gripped her hips and guided her down onto his length.

"Oh yeah," he growled, as she took him all the way.

She moved against him, long and slow, feeding him in and out. The pressure began to mount and she rocked quicker, a beautiful rhythm as he rolled his pelvis to meet her; to inch that little bit deeper. Already the distant hum of an orgasm sounded in her body. She wanted to go slow, but the desire to come and to make him come was stronger.

Jonathon caressed her breasts, lightly rolling her nipples between his fingers. Penny's back arched, her head lolled back as sensation unfurled in her body, sought every slope and nook. She thrust harder, her clit pushing against his pelvis. Jonathon's breathing was labored, his eyes closing when his pleasure heightened. She wanted to give him everything. Make him come so hard.

Her pace quickened, she took him a little deeper, harder. A luscious ache started low, the beginning of an orgasm. "I'm going to come again," she breathed, working against him, igniting the sensation further, willing it to find her.

"Come," he said, his neck straining as he fought his own

release. He bucked up into her, his breaths sounding like faint growls. "Come," he said again.

And that was enough to undo her completely. She clenched around his length as waves struck her low and deep then spread through her body. Only Jonathon's long grunt and jerky movements beneath her as he came hard brought her back to earth. Grounded her in the room again.

Penny draped over him and rested her head against his chest until their breathing slowed. Until she could bring herself to remove him from inside her. She rolled onto the mattress beside him and nestled against his shoulder. His arm holding her to him, she cuddled in close and closed her eyes, thinking only of the sound of his rhythmic breathing and the rightness she felt.

Chapter 9

A knock on the door snapped Penny out of a beautiful dream. Before she had even realized where he was, whose room she was in, the door creaked open.

Jessie spoke, "I'm heading off to work early, do you think you could…" Her voice broke off when their eyes met. "Penny?" she shrieked.

Penny started to sit up, but remembered she was stark naked, so she stayed where she was and pulled the blankets up to her chin.

"What the hell is going on here?"

"Um," she managed.

Jessie took a step into the room and pressed her hands to her hips. "I thought you were upset about him staying here, and now I find you in his bed. Oh God, you're both naked under there, aren't you?"

Penny couldn't speak. Her mouth was flapping open and shut.

"He's my brother," Jessie shrieked. "She's my best friend," she directed at Jonathon, who looked just as stunned as Jessie was. "You're like a big brother to her."

He gave a cheeky smile. "I wouldn't call this arrangement

at all brotherly."

"Yuck! Jonathon. You do not say things like that around me."

He sat up, making certain the blankets didn't go lower than his waist. "Well, sis, I think you're just going to have to get used to that."

Jessie shook her head. "What the hell happened here? One minute you're enemies, and now you're sl—sleeping with each other."

Penny sighed and closed her eyes. For a little while longer, she had wanted to keep things between her and Jonathon a secret, but it seemed she didn't have that freedom. She peered back up at Jessie's frantic eyes. "Jonathon's my love match," she said quickly.

Jessie's eyes widened. "What?"

"Last night I had a vision. It was about me this time. Jonathon is my love match."

She shook her head. "No. There must be a mistake."

"I'm never wrong," Penny said.

"She's never wrong," Jonathon added.

Jessie's lips twisted. "My brother is your love match?" She said *brother* as though it left a foul taste in her mouth.

Penny nodded. "Yes. I know it's hard to believe—hell, I didn't believe it myself either—but he is."

"He is?"

Again Penny nodded.

"Yes, Jessie. I know this is right," said Jonathon, his eyes softening as he gazed down at Penny.

"Oh my God," Jessie said, each word enflamed with disbelief. "My brother is your love match. You really, really, really owe me now. I expect my own love match by the end of the week," she said as she strode out of the room and shut the door behind her. Penny smiled as she heard her mumbling all the way down the hall.

Jonathon looked at Penny and laughed. "Well, that went better than I anticipated."

She laughed with him. "No tears. No screaming. A lot of screeching, but it could've been so much worse. She actually seemed okay with it by the end, don't you think?"

With a shrug, he said, "Yeah. I think she was." He glanced at his watch, then down at her. "What time are you heading downstairs to open?"

"About eight."

He grinned. "Good. We can squeeze in a shower together before we leave."

She arched a brow. "We?"

"Yeah. I quite enjoyed myself yesterday. And last night. I thought it only right we do both again."

Penny giggled as warmth crept over her cheeks. She wasn't about to argue with logic.

Chapter 10

So this was how Penny's love matches felt when she told them who their soul mate was. Nervous, curious, then altogether besotted, blissful, and overjoyed. She never knew what it felt like to be in the process of falling in love. Completely underrated in her opinion.

She took the photo she had printed earlier and stuck it to the wall with a pin so it could sit among all the other smiling couples. Penny peered at her happy face pressed lovingly against Jonathon's. The mere sight of him made her heart race.

Jonathon grabbed her hips as he placed a gentle kiss on the back of her neck. "We look good up there."

She nodded and spun to face him. "Yep."

"So your mom is coming in later today?" he asked.

"About two-thirty. I said I was having a special celebration day and she needed to stop by the shop to check it out. She'll be so surprised when she sees this photo."

"And happy, I hope."

Penny laughed. "She'll be very happy."

He grinned wide. "Good."

Jonathon released her from his grasp, and they strode over to the glass cabinets filled with an array of cupcakes Penny had spent the morning cooking. The shop already smelled like rich delicious coffee and caramel sweetness.

"The celebration cakes look amazing," he said, eyeing the new cakes she put out specifically for today. Vanilla cupcakes in the shape of a heart with strawberry pink frosting. One word was written in red icing on each cupcake and together it spelled out *The matchmaker has met her match.*

"Yeah. Not too bad at all," she agreed.

"So are we ready to do this?"

She smiled and nodded. "Yep. Let's open up."

Jonathon followed her to the front door. She unlocked the latch and pulled on the handle, a natural, wide grin on her lips. "Good morning," she said to the customers as they pooled inside her shop. "We're having a special celebration today. All cakes are half price."

"What's going on?" they asked excitedly. Then they saw the sign hanging on the back wall with the same words that were on the celebration cupcakes. "What does that mean?"

Jonathon pointed to the photo of them both on the wall and the customers' eyes widened as it all clicked into place—Cupid had been struck by her own arrow.

"He's your match?" one lady asked.

Jonathon swept Penny into his arms, dipped her, and planted a lingering kiss on her lips.

The customers burst into cheer and applause. They laughed and offered their congratulations because, finally, the matchmaker had met her match.

About Jacquie Underdown

Jacquie resides in rural Victoria, Australia. On permanent hiatus from a profession she doesn't love, she now spends her time wrapped up in her imagination, creating characters and exploring alternative realities.

Jacquie has a business degree, has studied post-graduate Writing, Editing and Publishing at The University of Queensland, and is currently finishing her research dissertation as a student of the Master of Letters program at Central Queensland University. She is an author of a number of digitally published novels, novellas, and short stories that are emotionally driven and possess unique themes beyond the constraints of the physical universe.

Jacquie's Website:
www.jacquieunderdown.com
Reader eMail:
authoraire@hotmail.com

Psychic Set-Up

by Lacey Wolfe

During a drunken night of self-wallowing over his failed love life, Parker Evans wanders into *Psychic Set-Up* to see what a matchmaking psychic can do for him. But once he meets the luscious psychic he's not interested in anyone else.

Willow Webb is an aura reader who plays matchmaker for a living. While she has tremendous success matching up others, her own love life is nonexistent. Men aren't able to handle being involved with a woman who can read their every emotion. But she finds herself drawn to her handsome new client. When it comes time to match him up, will she do her job or keep him for herself?

Chapter 1

Parker Evans stared at the glowing sign in the dusk of the evening. *Psychic Set-Up.* Psychic, his ass. Would a psychic have told him that his ex-girlfriend had been screwing his best friend? Who did these people think they were predicting someone's future? But this was worse. Whoever was inside that building seemed to think they could play matchmaker as well.

Parker rolled his eyes and tossed the beer bottle into a trash can. He'd had too much to drink tonight. He was supposed to be walking it off, as the bartender had suggested, but he couldn't bring himself to walk past the building.

Psychic Set-Up wasn't a new business. It had been around for a few years, but it wasn't until now that the place bothered him so much. Could this so-called matchmaker help him find true love? Because he sure as hell did a crap ass job finding it himself. He needed a new best friend now too.

He approached the door and read the hours. It was closing in the next fifteen minutes. What the hell, he had nothing to lose. He'd go in and see what this full-of-shit psychic had to say about his life. He tugged the wooden door open and entered, a bell dinging loudly above his head.

"Hello," he called out.

The clink of high heels echoed on the floor, and a beautiful, curvy woman pulled a velvet curtain back. She smiled, her ice blue eyes making him feel welcome.

"Good evening. How can I help you?"

Parker's gaze flowed over her body. She wasn't thin by any means. Her breasts were large and her hips wide, but she stood before him with such confidence he found himself attracted to her.

"I came to learn more about this matchmaking of yours."

"Sure. Come on in." She pulled the curtain back more and stepped to the side for him to enter. "Have a seat in front of my desk."

He did as she asked, and as she passed him to go to her chair, he stared at her curvy ass in the dark green skirt. God, did this woman know what kind of body she'd been blessed with?

He rubbed his temple and sighed. Coming there was a bad idea. He'd drank too much at the bar. He should be home on the couch, getting ready to pass out, instead of sitting there ogling this woman.

"Let's start with a simple question. What's your name?" She held a pen to a piece of paper.

He chuckled. "You're psychic, you should know that."

She grinned as though she heard that a lot. "I'm not a mind reader."

Here he thought psychics were supposed to know the answer to everything. "How about you tell me what powers you possess?"

She set the pen down and leaned back in her chair. "All right. I can see auras."

"Auras." What the hell was that?

"Yes. I see colors around you. They can tell me your emotions, as well as if you have any illness or conditions in your body." She picked the pen back up and tapped it on the desk. "The way this works is, I get to know you. We go out a few times, in a professional way, and I get to interact with you and see how you react to things by your aura. I then match you up to someone that will work for you."

"So right now you see colors around me?"

She nodded. "Yes, but I don't see them all the time, unless I focus in."

What a joke. "What do you see?"

She stared hard at him, her eyes slightly squinted. "You've got some blacks and a lemon color coming off you right now."

"And they mean…"

"Lemon means you're dealing with a loss, and black is negative, unforgiving."

He let out an exasperated sigh, unable to believe his ears. Was this woman for real?

"Are you interested in my matchmaking services? I sense you've got a broken heart, and I really think I can help. I have a good track record. In fact, there have been several marriages that resulted from my skills."

Parker's interest was piqued, even though he hated to admit it. What the heck did he have to lose by letting her learn his aura? His own track record of dating hadn't gone well. "Sure."

"Good. So let's start with your name."

He leaned back in the chair and rubbed his thighs. "Parker Evans, and what is yours?"

"Willow Webb."

Willow Webb. He was going to take dating advice from a woman with the craziest name he'd ever heard. He'd definitely had too much to drink.

* * * *

Willow locked the door to the shop and then headed up to her studio apartment that sat above it. As she climbed the steps, she couldn't brush Parker from her mind. He had a damaged soul. Someone had hurt him badly. His breath had reeked of beer as he attempted to mask the pain. Hopefully the time he'd spent at Psychic Set-Up had sobered him up a bit. She'd call him in the morning to see if he was still interested in her services and go from there.

In her apartment, her black cat, Chester, greeted her.

"Hey, sweet baby." She scooped the furball up in her arms, and he purred instantly. "I bet you're hungry. I didn't get a chance to come up and check your bowl today."

The bowl was never empty, but her cat was peculiar about the level of food. If Chester could see any of the ceramic dish, then he demanded she add more food. She topped the dish off with a fresh layer of food before raiding her fridge. Not only had she not had a chance to check on Chester today, but she hadn't eaten herself. Which might not be a bad thing. She could stand to lose a few pounds.

Parker had actually made her feel self-conscious with the way he'd stared at her. She worried the skirt she'd worn had been too tight and he was eyeing her rolls.

She plopped down at the kitchen table and ate her leftover Chinese food. Chester sat in the chair next to her and stared at her. "Just one piece of chicken, got it? One of these days the vet is gonna catch me feeding you."

The cat happily ate the chicken she'd given him then bounced away without a care in the world. She wished she could feel the same way as him, because Parker was still front and center in her mind. She didn't understand why she couldn't stop thinking about him.

Those deep green eyes, perfectly chiseled nose, not to mention his dark, almost black hair. He was hot, but he wasn't the first hot guy to walk through her doors. She'd set plenty of them up, but something inside her wanted Parker to herself.

It had to be his aura and the sadness that emitted off him. She'd given up on dating long ago. Men never liked a woman who could always read their emotions. She was destined to live alone in her tiny studio with Chester.

Chapter 2

"Good afternoon, Mr. Evans." Willow approached the handsome gentleman who waited for her outside the restaurant they'd agreed to meet at for their first professional 'date'.

"Call me Parker. After all, this is a date."

She grinned. "Sort of."

Parker opened the door, waiting for her to go inside first. He was a gentleman, at least. She walked to the hostess then stood back to see if he was a take-control kind of guy or if he wanted her to be in charge. Her personal preference was a man who spoke up.

"Hi, how many?" the cheerful woman asked.

She hesitated for a moment, but it didn't seem as though Parker was going to answer. Just as she was about to speak, she heard him.

"Two, and a booth please," he said.

A man who knew where he wanted to sit. "Do you care where in the restaurant they place us?"

"If they put us near the kitchen or bathrooms, I'll ask to be moved."

The hostess led them to the center of the dining area and to a booth. Willow waited again to see how Parker felt. He nodded and scooted into his side. She sat.

She stared at him. He appeared happier today. Silver and gold radiated off him, meaning he was in a more positive mood, but black was still there as well.

A waitress approached their table, holding a pen to a pad. "I'm Ariana, and I'll be your server today. Can I start you off with something to drink and an appetizer?"

"Just water for me, no lemon." Parker didn't look up from the menu.

Willow moistened her lips. "The same."

"Did you want an appetizer? Maybe some mozzarella sticks?" Ariana asked.

Willow glanced at Parker, and he shook his head. The server turned on her heel and strutted off.

"I hope you didn't want anything. Sorry. I should have asked." He still didn't make eye contact, which made her think he was nervous.

"It's fine." She glanced down at her menu and scanned the sandwich selection. After a few minutes of silence, she looked back up at him. "So, what are you thinking?"

He shook his head slightly. "I'm leaning toward a burger and fries. You?"

"The club sandwich with fries."

Now to wait and see just how much of a take-charge kind of

guy he was. Would he order her meal or sit back and let her do it?

Ariana returned, setting their drinks on the table. "Do you need a few more minutes?"

Willow and Parker shared an exchange with their eyes, before he turned his attention to the waitress. "I'm gonna get the All-American burger, hold the mayo, with fries as a side."

"Okay." The perky waitress smiled.

They each gazed at her and Willow relayed her order. "Club sandwich, with mayo, and a side of fries." Folding the menu, she handed it to the waitress.

"I'll have your order out soon."

Parker rubbed his palms together. "I feel like I'm on a job interview with you. It's like you're studying everything I'm doing."

He'd picked up on that. Usually she wasn't as nervous as she was today, but something about him had her on edge. "I apologize. My goal is for this to feel casual. Like lunch between two friends."

"It doesn't feel that way at all."

She sat straight, wondering why she was acting so differently with him. She was more worried if he did things *she* liked than what a potential match might like. This wasn't about her, and she needed to remember that. Parker wasn't at all interested in her. He most likely wanted a tall blonde with big boobs. She had the big boobs, but the complete opposite of the rest.

"Have you had a good day so far?" she asked as she placed her straw in her glass.

"I've had an okay day. My boss is on my case about an assignment. Guess I should have done a working lunch."

"It's good you got away. It's important to have a life away from work. What do you do for a living?"

"I'm a stockbroker." He snickered and crossed his arms. "I do my best to have a life outside of work, but it's hard. I'm sure you experience that, right?"

She cocked her head to the side and bit her lip. She really didn't have much of a life away from setting people up. Sure, at least to her neighbors, it probably looked like she dated a lot...and was bisexual. "I can't think of the last time I did something that was for me."

"How about this." He sat forward and placed his fists on the table. "On our next 'date' we do something you like."

Their next date. She really liked the sound of that, and the fact he wanted to do something she liked. When was the last time she did something she enjoyed?

But she couldn't. "That's not how this works."

A dimple formed in his cheek. "One thing you'll quickly

learn about me is that I like to make sure the woman I'm seeing is happy. Right now, you're the one I'm involved with."

A shiver tore down her spine. "I'll have to think about it."

"When will our next date be?"

Her stomach fluttered. He made her feel as though he was interested in her, and she couldn't think straight. "Um, I'll have to check my calendar."

He shook his head. "I like to be spontaneous." His smile lit up his handsome face, and she could tell he had something he really wanted to say.

"Do tell."

"Tonight."

"Tonight what?"

"I want to get together tonight. How about this...I surprise you."

She found herself grinning as her heart picked up in pace. "I don't know, Parker."

"Come on, you're the one who needs to get to know me. I want to show you just what kind of man I am."

She took a deep breath and nodded. The more she got to know him, the more she worried she was going to fall for this man.

* * * *

Parker guided Willow across the parking lot later that

evening.

"Is the blindfold really necessary?" she asked.

"It is. I told you it was a surprise, and I meant it. I love to do things for others." In his experience, women loved surprises. His ex only liked the kind that came in jewelry boxes though.

Something about Willow told him she liked the greater things in life than platinum and diamonds.

"Okay, we're just about there."

Sounds of laughter and screams circled them. He untied the blindfold and stuffed it in his pocket.

Willow's gorgeous blue eyes widened with shock. "The carnival."

"Yeah. I thought it would be a fun place for you to get to know me."

She gazed at him. "You've definitely surprised me a lot today. The night you came into my shop, I thought you'd be one of those grouchy men. You smile more than I thought and are laid-back."

He shrugged. "I like fun. Maybe a bit too much. My exes have complained that I'm not serious enough."

"Serious is for work."

And that he was, but when he was away from the office, he liked to pretend that side of him didn't exist. "Ready to go in?"

She nodded. "I haven't been to the carnival since I was a

teen."

He placed a hand on her lower back, liking the way it felt so natural. "You're in for a real treat, because I intend to take you on every single ride."

Chapter 3

Willow stared up at the ride called Tilt-a-Twist, and it looked insane. The people spun around while an arm brought them from side to side. She'd gone on many rides with Parker so far, but this one scared her.

"How about it?" he asked.

Her stomach tightened. "I don't know."

He chuckled. "Don't be scared. Say, what color aura are you right now?"

"Probably a murky brown."

He grinned. "How about me?"

"A brilliant red color. I can see your passion tonight."

The woman she set him up with was going to be lucky. He was a good catch—personality and good looks.

"All right, I won't make you ride this one. Let's do the Ferris wheel."

"That I can do."

Parker touched her lower back again, and a cool shiver swept through her. His touch affected her in a way she didn't expect. It was electrifying.

The line was short, and before long they were sitting in the small, enclosed silver box—just the two of them. Willow stared across at the handsome man. He'd brought her there tonight to make her loosen up and have a good time. And she had. *Parker is perfect. He shouldn't need my services. Any woman would love to go out with him.*

As the ride began, she asked, "Why do you need to be set-up?"

"Tired of getting a broken heart."

She licked her bottom lip. "Recent?"

He nodded.

"Tell me about it."

"I don't think so. How is that going to help you find me a woman?"

She wasn't sure it would, but she really wanted to know so she could find the woman who had hurt him and smack her across the forehead. "I don't know. Just curious."

He rubbed his chin before leaning against the side of the box. "Her name was Leila, and she was someone I really liked. I thought we were on the same page, but I was wrong."

That was a story she heard often from clients. "How so?"

"She was using me to get to my best friend. She weaved her way in, causing problems with Ty and his girlfriend. All this took place while I worked. She was young though, still in college, and her parents were paying the way. I did the crazy man thing and wanted someone younger."

Considering he was pushing forty, a girl in college was pretty young. "I'm sorry."

"Losing the girl doesn't hurt nearly as much as losing my friend. That's the real betrayal and pain."

"I'd imagine so. How long were you friends?"

He huffed. "Since sixth grade."

Ouch.

The ride stopped, giving every person a chance to be stuck at the top. When she was growing up, not everyone got to be stopped at the top. Nowadays, everyone got to do everything or it wasn't fair.

"What about you?" he asked.

"What about me?"

"You've got a man in your life, I'm sure."

She smiled, not saying anything. She typically did not delve into her personal life with a client. They didn't need to know her, she just needed to know them.

"Tell me about him. How does he feel about your work? He must not be the jealous type."

She imagined a boyfriend would have a hard time with her job. Especially on a night like tonight, when she was sitting close to a sexy man whose aftershave made her panties wet.

"I don't have a boyfriend." *Shit. Why did I confess that?*

"Now I'm surprised. As beautiful as you are, I can't believe no one has snatched you up."

Beautiful? She had at least thirty pounds to lose to be beautiful in a man like Parker's eyes. Sure, she knew it wasn't all about weight, but she'd let herself go the last few years. "You're quite the smooth talker."

He grinned. "I only speak the truth, and you, my lady, are stunning and captivating."

His expression was serious, and she couldn't find anything in it that told her he was kidding. His aura was showing passion. Before she could stop herself, she slid a hand around his neck and brought her lips to his.

Parker wrapped a hand around her waist, deepening the kiss. She moaned in response, relishing in how good it felt to kiss someone. It had been so long since she'd had this kind of interaction. Tonight this man had shown her so many things in life she'd forgotten about. This kiss, this breathtaking, make-her-knees-weak kiss, was one of them.

She pulled back and placed a finger over her swollen lips. "I'm so sorry. I'm embarrassed."

He caressed her cheek. "Don't be."

During their kiss, the ride had moved and now they sat at the top. Could this damn wheel hurry the hell up? She needed to leave. Tomorrow she'd refund his money and apologize for not being professional.

"Willow."

"Yes." She gazed out at the night sky, not really registering what she saw.

"Look at me."

She couldn't.

"That kiss was good. I enjoyed it. I think it was a perfect end to our evening."

She tried not to smile, but this man had a way with her. She glanced at him. "I appreciate you saying that. You showed me a very nice time tonight."

He cleared his throat. "Perhaps it won't be the last."

Her breath caught. There was no way he actually liked her, was there?

* * * *

A light knock sounded on Parker's office door. He glanced up at his secretary standing there with a bright pink envelope.

"This just came for you, Mr. Evans." She set it on his desk. "I'm gonna head to lunch early, if that's okay."

"Sure. Enjoy. Close the door when you leave please."

He'd come in this morning to a mess, and he planned to work through lunch. He rubbed between his eyebrows, wishing he could magically transport back to last night, when this hell hole was the last thing on his mind. It was time for a new job. He was sick of being the one to always clean up his boss's messes.

Grabbing the envelope, he flipped it over. It was from Willow. He leaned back in his chair, thinking back to last night when he'd dropped her off at her office.

"You've been quiet since the kiss," he said as he turned the engine off.

She sighed. "I crossed a line tonight."

He didn't feel as though she had. In fact, her kiss had been one of the best in his life. Okay, the best. "You didn't. That was the beauty of it. You did what felt right. We only get one life to live, why spend it always trying to be proper?"

"Because I have a reputation to keep."

She was being silly. "We're adults."

"You're correct, we are. I let my feelings get the best of me."

Was it possible she liked him? As more than a client? He wasn't going to push it. Instead, he'd find a way to see her again. "When will we be doing this fake date thing again?"

She pushed her door open and climbed out. He stared at her round ass in those form-fitting blue jeans. She leaned down, giving him a quick glimpse down her blouse. "I'll be in touch, Mr. Evans."

She closed the door and hurried away.

Psychic Set-Up / Lacey Wolfe

He was worried at first she would drop him as a client. He got the feeling she didn't date—ever. Which was a shame. She was a sensuous woman who would one day make a man very happy. He wanted it to be him.

Parker didn't want her to find him someone. As far as he was concerned, he'd found the woman he desired in a way he'd never expected.

Opening the envelope, he pulled out the contents. The first thing was a check made out to him for the same amount he'd given her for her services. He then unfolded the paper.

Parker,

I want to apologize yet again for not being professional. You paid me to be that way and kissing you was not in your plans. For that reason, I am refunding your money. I would still like to help find you a match. I've included a profile of a woman I think is perfect for you. Please have a look, and if you're interested, I would love to set up a date for the two of you. She's already agreed to a date.

I look forward to hearing from you.

Best regards,

Willow Webb

She'd refunded his money and found him a date. He

dropped the letter on his desk, not even glancing at the profile of the woman. He wasn't interested. In fact, at this very moment he was pissed as feelings of rejection flooded through him.

Chapter 4

"Ouch." Willow sat up from the couch where she'd been trying to nap, but her cat Chester had taken a playful bite of her nose. She lightly pushed the cat away. "What's the matter with you? Do you see me biting you when you're asleep?"

She'd closed the shop early today, one of the perks of being the owner. She had no scheduled appointments, and most everything she needed to do was paperwork, which she could do from the comfort of her living room.

If she was going to get any work done, it was best she make a pot of coffee. As she got the machine ready to brew, the phone on her counter rang. It was her work line.

"Psychic Set-up, Willow speaking."

"Hi, Willow. It's Ashley Hall. I'm calling to tell you that Ray and I are getting married!"

She smiled. "You are? This is fantastic news." And quick. They'd only been on their first date two months ago. However, they were both at a point in their lives where they were ready to settle down.

Ray was very high-strung whenever she read his aura, and Ashley was laid-back. She'd taken a bit of a risk with the two, but it had paid off.

"We have the wedding set in a month. Will you be able to come?"

"I wouldn't miss it."

"I've been telling everyone I know about your services. There is no better matchmaker than you."

"Thank you for the compliment. I can't wait to hang your wedding photo up on my wall."

Ashley squealed. "I can't wait to wear a white dress!"

"You'll be stunning with your skin complexion." Ashley had the most beautiful olive-toned skin.

"Be on the lookout for a wedding invitation. I just might hand deliver it."

"If you do, we'll get lunch."

Ashley chuckled. "Sounds like a plan. We'll talk soon."

"We will. And congrats again."

She set the phone down and leaned against the counter. She loved hearing from her clients when they found true love. Even better, she loved having been a part of it. It made her job worth it.

The coffee pot beeped, and she poured herself a cup and headed into the living room. Her laptop was still on, the way she'd left it before her nap. Chester was curled up in a tight ball, snoozing in a small spot of sunlight.

"I should bite your nose."

Psychic Set-Up / Lacey Wolfe

She stared at the spreadsheet open on her laptop. Profit was up in the shop, which was a good thing. She really needed to hire some help, but that was hard to do when not everyone off the streets could read auras. Maybe her cousin, who also saw auras, would come work with her. She'd have to call her, but for now she needed to do her favorite thing...play matchmaker.

She had several clients who were ready to be paired. John was a total sweetie pie with a shy side. *Nothing like Parker.* She shook her head, trying to push him from her mind. She entered John's information into her database and began to scroll through the matches. Tiffany was a definite no. She often spoke before she thought, and John was too sensitive for that. Perhaps Abbie. She'd have to pull up her file and study her aura readings again to see if she was a good fit.

Parker came back to her mind, front and center, with his dark hair and mesmerizing eyes. Then the toe-curling kiss. She couldn't even imagine what it would be like to do other things with him. She'd probably orgasm the moment he touched her. It had been that long since she'd been with a man. She hated to admit it, but it'd been five years since she'd had sex with anything other than plastic toys.

She walked to her bedroom and stood in front of the full-length mirror. Parker had said she was beautiful. She ran her fingers through her hair that she'd straightened that morning. She had nice hair. If she had to choose another feature about herself she liked, it would be her nose. It was the right size for her face.

Her cheeks were full, but if she lost a little weight, that would change. When Parker looked at her, he didn't seem to see the same person she did. It was much easier for her to find flaws in her appearance than anything she liked.

She grunted and started to leave the room just as the phone on the counter rang again. Maybe it was someone else with good news...she could use it.

"Psychic Set-Up, this is Willow."

"It's Parker. I stopped by to talk, but it looks like you're closed."

His voice caused her nipples to harden. "Oh. Yeah, sorry. I didn't have any appointments, so I came up to my loft."

"Oh, do you live in the space above?"

Say no and get off the phone. "I do."

"Perfect. Can I come up?"

"Well, I don't usually mix business with my home life. I've never had a client up here before. Can you just make an appointment?"

"Willow. I'd like to see you. Please buzz me up."

Letting him up here was exactly what she shouldn't do, but damn it, she really wanted to. "All right." She disconnected the call, went to the door to her loft, and hit the button to let him in downstairs.

****

The door to Willow's home opened and she greeted him with a smile. Parker's gaze traveled over her body, taking in the turquoise dress she wore. It cinched in tightly at her waist, but was loose everywhere else. He itched to peel it off. He was addicted to this woman, and her kiss had put a spell on him. Yet she had no idea.

"What brings you by? Did you get a chance to look at Brandy's profile?"

He followed her in. "She's not right for me."

She stopped and turned to him, then pointed at a chair in the living room. "Can I get you coffee?"

"I'm good."

She sat in what looked like her usual spot with all the things around it. "How come you didn't like Brandy?"

She wasn't you, but he wasn't about to say that. "I don't like the name."

She raised an eyebrow. "I never thought you would be someone who judged a person by their name. Any other names you dislike?"

"It isn't really about the name. Look, I'm not cashing the check you sent. I asked you to find me a woman, and you did."

She lifted her mug. "Not one you like yet."

"You."

She froze a moment then lowered the mug. "Parker, I'm not an option."

"Why?"

"I don't date."

"Why?"

She groaned. "I just don't. Could you imagine being my boyfriend?"

He could. As he glanced around her tiny space, he could see them making breakfast together in the kitchen on Saturday mornings. Spending Friday nights on the couch, cuddled up together watching their weekly shows off the DVR.

"And how frustrating it would be for me to see your aura. You'd never be able to hide anything from me," she added.

"I have nothing to hide. I'm an open book. That's how relationships are supposed to be."

"Plus." She rubbed her thighs. "You just got out of a relationship. I don't want to be your rebound girl."

Since meeting Willow, his ex and friend were a thing of the past. It felt like it happened years ago, not two weeks ago. That's what she did for him—healed his heart. "You wouldn't be. I don't even believe in rebound stuff. I believe in fate, and I would think you do too."

She clasped her hands together. "Yes, fate is something I

believe in."

"All right then. I believe I walked into your shop to meet you."

"Parker, you can't say things like that to me."

"Why not?"

She rubbed her forehead. "Because I can't handle it. I've not been with a man in years. A relationship even longer. No one has shown any interest in me, until you."

She hadn't been with a man, as in sex, in years? That was insane…and so was the fact that she hadn't been on a date of her own either.

"Let me change that."

"No."

He resisted the urge to grunt. Instead, he stood and went to her.

"What are you doing?"

"I'm gonna make love to you." He held his hand out to her.

"Excuse me?"

It was insane of him to ask such a thing, but Willow needed this. Someone—and it was him—needed to reassure her that she was a woman. "I'm going to take you to your bedroom and show you how fucking sexy you are. How much I want you."

She shook her head. "You're insane."

"No, I'm not. Stop resisting. I know you want to. That kiss

was so hot between us. I've never experienced such a pull to someone as I do to you."

She stared at him, and he could tell she was running all kinds of scenarios through her head. As he held his hand out, he began to wonder if she was going to turn him down, which would suck. He'd put it all out there, much more than he had before.

The truth was he'd never had so much confidence in himself as he did with Willow. She brought out a side of him that he'd never experienced before. A side he liked.

"What do you say?"

She took his hand and stood. "I can't believe I'm saying this, but yes."

His wish was going to come true. He was going to peel that dress off of her slowly.

Chapter 5

Willow couldn't believe she was going to do this, but it was obvious the man wanted her—at least one time. As he'd stood there, his gaze locked on hers, she realized she'd be a fool not to let a man as handsome as Parker have his way with her. His touch on her skin, his lips on hers as he slipped inside of her. God, she wanted him—bad.

The awkwardness set in as they stared at one another. Taking a deep breath, she debated bolting.

"Uh, so, how are we going to do this?" she asked.

He chuckled and wrapped his arms around her, putting her at ease. "The right way. I'm going to seduce you until you're pleading for me to be buried deep in you."

"Oh." She liked the sound of that.

He brought his mouth to hers, kissing her in a slow, sensual way. Her lips parted and his tongue mingled with hers. Sighing, excitement built within her. Was it too early to beg?

He walked her backward until her legs hit the bed. His lips trailed down her neck as he worked the buttons on her dress. He was smooth, and she liked it.

Her last encounter had been with a man she'd met at a bar. They'd shut the lights off and took their own clothes off. No foreplay. Just sex.

He took her chin between his fingers. "Hey, stay with me."

She smiled, staring at his eyes, which were dark with passion. There was nowhere else she wanted to be than in his arms. "Gladly."

She didn't want to think about her past sexual experiences. Parker was going to blow those out of the water.

He slipped her dress down her shoulders and sucked on the skin at the base of her neck. She moaned and wiggled, her panties already wet. In one swift move, the dress pooled around her ankles.

"You're the most beautiful woman I've ever laid my eyes on, Willow."

She crossed her arms over her stomach, but he pushed her arms apart, not allowing her to cover up. She laid back on the bed, and he climbed between her legs.

"Kiss me," she whispered.

He winked and licked her cleavage as he rolled her nipples under the lace cups of her bra. A cool shiver swept through her as he caressed her stomach just above her panty line.

She grabbed his face and brought his lips to hers, passion flowing out of her with a force. He yanked her firm against him, his erection pressing into her through his slacks. Something primal took over, and she ripped at his shirt, not caring if she tore any buttons off. She tossed the shirt across the room, never breaking the kiss.

She propped up on her elbows, and he slipped a hand around her, unclasping her bra. Once it was off, he grabbed her breasts, pushing them together and pinching her nipples. If there was one thing she couldn't do for herself these last five years, it was this. The skin-to-skin contact and the touch from someone else.

"I'm ready." She broke the connection to begin working his pants off.

Before she could push them down, his finger dipped inside her panties and through her folds.

"You're wet."

Her cheeks warmed, because she wasn't sure that was a good thing.

He kissed her chin. "It's fucking hot. I can't wait to be inside of you."

"Please don't make me wait much longer."

He pressed a finger inside her and she arched. She was going to orgasm from such a little touch. She pushed his hand away so she didn't make a fool of herself.

"Not yet. I want you inside me when my release comes." She finished removing his pants and boxers, revealing his cock.

She wrapped her fingers around the thick base and stroked.

His breath caught and he grunted, pushing her hand away. "I'm in the same boat. How about we get this show on the road, and next time we'll add in the foreplay."

Next time. She liked the sound of that.

He yanked her panties off then knelt down to the floor, removing something from his pants. He stood before her with a condom in hand.

"Let me." She held her hand out.

He climbed on the bed and knelt above her. She took the packet and tore it open. She'd never put a condom on a guy before, but any excuse to touch him again would work. She placed the rubber at his tip, then slowly rolled it down with both hands.

"I'm gonna come if you keep toying with me." He placed his hand over hers and pulled it away.

"Should we get under the covers?" she asked.

"Hell no, I want to see every inch of you."

He spread her legs apart and licked his lips as he stared at her pussy. Before she had time to think about what she must look like down there, he thrust in, making her forget any thoughts.

"You're so tight," he whispered in her ear.

She nodded, because his thickness was stretching her as her body accommodated him. After a few slow thrusts, he picked up the pace. She pulled her knees to her side and wrapped her legs around his hips, deepening the movements.

She closed her eyes, relishing in how good this felt. His lips captured hers, making the moment even more perfect as they rocked their hips together. Her stomach tightened as her release built, and before she could stop it, it hit her. Breaking the kiss, she cried out. Every nerve in her body was on fire.

With one hard thrust, Parker joined her as he buried his face in the crook of her neck. After a few final pumps, he stilled on top of her. She was still heightened and energized from the release. Part of her wanted to go again.

She caressed his spine, enjoying the feel of him holding her. This was what it was like to have someone. To make love and still feel the need to be connected as one. She could stay in Parker's arms the rest of the day, without another care.

"Meoow." Chester hopped on the bed.

"Damn cat," she whispered. He had the worst timing.

Parker propped up on his elbows and glanced at Chester. "This is awkward." He reached over and pulled the side of the comforter up and over them before rolling off her. "Here, kitty, kitty."

"Don't be nice to him. He's been awful today. Bit me on the nose."

Chester sauntered up and stood on top of Parker. "I think he likes me."

"I thought the same thing." She chuckled.

"Will you let me take you to dinner tonight?" he asked, staring into her eyes as though he was searching for her soul.

It was hard for her to believe this man wanted anything more than sex. He'd get bored with her in no time. "No need for dinner. We were just scratching an itch."

"Uh-uh. You're not doing that. Trying to pretend what we have isn't real."

"We don't even know each other, so it's easy to pretend."

He sat up, and Chester jumped off the bed. "I thought us making love would show you I was serious about you."

"You can't be serious about me. You don't know me."

"Only because you won't let me. Look at me, Willow."

She did.

"I'm right here in front of your eyes. Are you just gonna let me slip away?"

"I don't even know if our auras work well together."

He groaned and tossed the covers aside, then searched for his clothes. "There is more to two people getting together than their auras. There is something called chemistry, and we have it."

He dressed quicker than she would've liked, but he didn't storm out of the room.

"I'm gonna do what it takes to show you that. Meet me at

the little bistro on Eighth Avenue at seven tonight."

"Okay."

He kissed her cheek. "I'll see you then."

* * * *

Parker had never been more nervous about a date. The more time he spent with Willow, the more he wanted to get to know her. Her favorite food, TV shows, how she liked her coffee. There was more behind this psychic woman than he'd thought when first meeting her.

She'd seemed mysterious before, but as he unfolded more layers about her, he found himself more intrigued. How could a woman like Willow have not been with a man in years? Sure, she wasn't model thin, but her curves were fucking sexy. Her breasts were large, her waist dipped in, and her hips were wide with thick thighs. She wouldn't be a woman walking around the pool in a string bikini, but he could see her in a sleek one piece with stilettos—which was much sexier.

He waited outside the entrance to the Italian place. Glancing at his watch, he took a deep breath. She was ten minutes late, or maybe she was already inside at a table.

He entered the quaint building and approached the hostess. "Excuse me, have you sat anyone waiting for another person?"

"I have." The young girl smiled. "Follow me."

He did and she stopped in front of a small table in the

corner. The woman sitting there looked vaguely familiar.

"Oh, I think—"

"Parker Evans?" the woman interrupted.

"Yes."

"Hi." She stood and tugged on her tight red dress. "Brandy Stenson."

Brandy Stenson? When the name registered, his eyes widened and his blood boiled. Willow had sent the girl from the application. Why the hell would she do that?

"Would you care to join me?" The young woman had a concerned expression.

Fine. If Willow really wanted him to go on a date with this woman, then he would. "Sure. I'd love to."

He pulled out his chair and sat. He'd been wrong about Willow. If she cared for him half as much as he did her, she never would've gone against his wishes and set him up with Brandy. She claimed to read auras, but apparently she had no idea what his meant.

Chapter 6

Willow smiled as she sat across from Ashley at the small sandwich shop next to Psychic Set-Up.

"And then he dropped down to one knee and inside the flower pot, on the stem of the daisy, was my ring." She held her hand out.

Willow admired the large diamond. Ray had done a very nice job picking it out. "It's gorgeous."

Ashley crumbled up the chip bag. "So what about you? Do you see marriage in your future?"

Willow patted her lips with a napkin. "No."

"How come? There has to be someone out there."

There is, or was, but she'd stupidly handed him off to another woman. She hadn't heard from him since, and that had been a week ago. She still didn't know what she was thinking when she'd done that. Every day that passed, she regretted it.

Oh right, her mind wouldn't let her out of matchmaking mode. She'd promised Brandy a date, and so far Parker had been the only man at all who might be a match for the woman. She let this other woman's needs come before hers. But it was more than that.

"I see you're lost in thought. Someone special?" Ashley

asked as she sipped her drink.

"It's weird to talk about me."

"It's good. You spend so much time listening to us clients go on and on about ourselves. Besides, we're friends now. You helped me, let me help you."

Willow smiled. "I suppose you have a point. It's this job that is messing with me."

"How so?"

She took a deep breath. "A man came in not long ago requesting my services. From the moment I met him, there was something about him that I liked, but I didn't think he'd ever like me. I mean, this guy is incredibly hot. A whole other league." And he shouldn't want anything to do with her abilities, but Parker didn't seem to mind them.

Ashley giggled. "You're silly. I'm sure you are the one way out of his league."

"Thank you for that." It meant a lot to her that her new friend had said that. "Well, we did two trial dates, and I kissed him."

Ashley's eyes widened, but she didn't say anything.

"I refunded his money, but he wouldn't give up. I gave him a possible match, and he still wanted me."

"Wow! That's so romantic." She placed a hand over her heart.

"Yes, I suppose it is." *And I'm a moron for screwing it up.* "Well, we had a little romp in the sheets, and he asked me to dinner after."

"That's wonderful, but why do I sense a *but*?"

Willow leaned back in her chair and pinched the bridge of her nose. "I sorta didn't show for the date and sent the woman I originally set him up with instead."

"You did what?"

Willow clenched her teeth together and scrunched her nose. She'd been a moron for sure. "I haven't heard from him since."

"Well, duh. That was pretty much a slap across his face. What are your plans to fix this?"

She shrugged, because she was clueless. She'd been wracking her brain for days. Aside from groveling at his feet, she had no idea. "I don't know if I can."

Ashley smirked. "You can always fix it."

"Any ideas? I might be good with matchmaking, but when it comes to relationships, I've got no clue."

"Hmm." She twisted her chin, then her eyes lit up. "I do."

* * * *

Parker made his way through the airport. He'd had to make a quick trip out of town to deal with a client his boss had pissed off. Parker was always cleaning up the messes, but the client was happy again and keeping his money with the company. Which made his boss very happy. Parker was ready to have a little fun and forget all about work. Take tomorrow off and make it an extended weekend.

Part of him wanted to go to Willow and show her once and for all how he felt. Yet he couldn't. If she'd had any desire to get to know him better and pursue a relationship, then she would have come to dinner. Not just had sex and flung him away like trash.

She'd made no contact with him. The date with Brandy had gone okay, but he'd told her he wasn't sure he'd see her again. The woman seemed to understand, because he really hadn't been into the date.

His phone buzzed like crazy in his pocket. He stopped to check it, taking a seat in a vacant chair. Email never ended—send one and twenty more came in. One stood out, and it was from Psychic Set-Up.

Mr. Evans,

At Psychic Set-Up, I strive to make a love match for my clients. I was sorry to hear that your last date didn't go well and you didn't discover the chemistry you were looking for. Rest assured, I won't rest until I find you your perfect match. A package will be delivered to your office early tomorrow. I hope this next candidate is the one.

Best regards,
Willow Webb

He chuckled, unable to contain it. She'd found him yet another woman. When he got into the office tomorrow, he'd email her and request she stop looking for a match for him. There was no perfect match for him, but there was a woman he was interested in. Problem was, she didn't seem to feel the same way. In fact, she insisted he find someone else.

Willow was a strange one.

* * * *

Parker trudged out of his boss's office. Instead of telling him he'd done a good job with the client, he'd been able to find a way to make Parker feel like he hadn't done his job correctly. As he closed his own office door and sank down in his chair, he knew it was time to look for a new job. With his experience and knowledge, he should be able to find something else. At the age of forty, he was tired of being talked down to like a naughty child.

A pink package sat on his desk. He already knew who it was from, and he wasn't in the mood to see who Willow had picked out for him now. He grabbed his office phone and dialed Psychic Set-Up.

"Psychic Set-Up, this is Willow speaking."

It was nice to hear her voice. "It's Parker."

"Hey. I was hoping to hear back from you today. Did you open your package?" Her voice was almost giddy. He couldn't remember ever hearing her so happy.

"No, I didn't, and I don't plan to. Please stop trying to set me up. I'm no longer interested in your services. Coming into your shop was a big mistake."

"Oh." Her voice cracked.

His secretary knocked on his door and pointed at her watch. He glanced at his planner. Shit, he had a meeting with a potential client he'd forgotten about. "I've got to go."

"Parker."

"Yes?"

"I can't make you open the package, but I really think you should."

He rolled his eyes. "I already told you, I don't care what's inside."

"I understand. Goodbye."

Before he could tell her bye, she'd already disconnected the call. Her voice had gone from ecstatic to what sounded like almost crying, and it made him feel awful. Perhaps he should open the package.

His secretary knocked on the door again with impatience. Whatever was inside would wait.

Chapter 7

"This is really strange," Cari, her newest client, said with a giggle.

"Just think of us as friends. I want to learn what you like." Willow grinned, trying to reassure Cari.

This was their first "date" at a restaurant. Willow needed to make it as comfortable as possible for Cari, but it was always a little odd at first.

"Typically with men, I wait to see if they are the take-charge type, but I want to ask you. When we go inside and we get to the hostess, do you mind telling her 'party of two' or do you prefer for the man to do that?"

Cari shrugged. "I don't care. I've never thought about that."

"Few people have a preference, I've learned." Parker had taken charge, just the way she'd wanted.

It was time to stop thinking about him. He'd made it clear this morning he was done with her. Her calendar had been cleared for the day in hopes they'd spend it together, but after he rejected her, she called Cari to get the ball rolling for her.

"I really don't mind speaking to the hostess, but I think men prefer to do it."

"Perfect. Let's go in."

They were seated within moments, and Cari went straight to her menu. When Willow was getting to know female clients, it was a bit different. They were on more of a friend level. All she did was study their aura. Cari's was very energetic. Willow already had a few ideas of matches for her.

"I'm starved." Cari closed her menu. "I'm getting a burger, loaded. You?"

A girl who wasn't afraid to eat what she wanted, that was another good quality. Willow was surprised how many men had told her they disliked a woman who always ordered a salad. "I think I'm gonna do the same. It looks really good, and sounds like heaven."

They gave the waitress their order.

"Tell me about your exes and why they weren't right, in your opinion."

Cari crossed her arms. "I need a man who can keep up, and I can't stand workaholics. When you're home, be home and forget about the job."

Parker was that way. Thinking back to their fun date at the carnival, she remembered his aura had been bright that night with happiness. He hadn't had a care in the world.

"Do you have a profession for a potential match you'd like to avoid?"

"Business men. Find me a MMA guy. That would be hot. I

could totally do that."

Willow laughed. Cari would be a good match for an energetic athlete. "Speaking of sports...how do you feel about them?"

"As long as it's not golf, I'm good. Golf is so boring. I love football."

"Do you watch the games on TV?"

"Yup. I love to tailgate too."

She certainly had several matches that were right. It wasn't always easy to find a sports-enthusiastic woman. All she needed to do was study how Cari reacted to situations, note her aura, and begin looking in the database.

"What do you think? Will I be a hard match? Many men like girly girls, and I'm far from that."

She lifted her glass of water the waitress had left on the table. "I think you'll be an easy match."

Setting people up was the highlight of her life. The smile on Cari's face, knowing there might be someone for her, was what Willow loved about this job. If only she could've been as open as Cari. Instead she'd pushed away the first man who really seemed to genuinely care about her.

* * * *

Parker's day had been nonstop, but he finally had time to close his office door and breathe. He sat at his desk and booted up his computer. He'd tackle a few emails and then head home.

The pink package Willow had sent caught his attention. She'd been awfully upset when he'd told her he didn't care what was inside. He supposed it wouldn't hurt to open it.

He peeled it open and found a handwritten note stapled to what he assumed was the profile for the match she'd found.

Parker,

I spent some time going over your file again and studying your aura. I believe I've found a woman you'd be interested in, and she finds you very desirable and sexy.

He stopped reading and rubbed his chin before continuing.

Please take a moment to look over the attached profile. I've cleared my schedule for the whole day, so if you'd like to spend some time with your match, she's ready.

Willow

His heart raced. He had a feeling he knew just whose profile he was going to see and how much of a fucking jerk he was. Taking a deep breath, he flipped the paper over to Willow's smiling face and a printout about her.

He closed his eyes and groaned. She'd cleared her day for

him, expecting him to see this and come to her. Fuck, if he'd just opened the package, he would've pretended to be sick and left for the day.

Instead, he'd told her he wasn't at all interested in who was inside the package.

This day had gone from bad to shit.

Chapter 8

"Yes, Chester, I'm coming."

The black cat kept smacking Willow's ankles then running toward the food bowl. Why had she picked out such a weird cat? Chester had so much personality she wondered if he was really a cat shifter. She wouldn't be surprised if, when she wasn't there, he shifted to become human, then shifted back to a cat as soon as he heard her footsteps on the stairs. She wouldn't put it past him.

She filled the food dish. "Now leave me alone. I've had a bad day. All I want to do it put on my sweatpants and a baggy shirt and curl up on the couch until I fall asleep wallowing in self-pity. Got it?"

Of course Chester ignored her as he buried his face in the food bowl. Perhaps she should get a dog since they were supposed to be man's best friend.

As she entered her bedroom, her cellphone in her back pocket beeped. She had a new text, which was odd. No one ever messaged her. She had no friends. No life.

Pulling the phone from her pants, she saw the text had come from a number not programmed in her phone.

Let me in, please.

That was odd. Who was here?

Who is this?

Your knight in shining armor.

She stared at the message, unsure if she should buzz whoever it was in. Her phone beeped a moment later.

It's Parker.

He must've opened the package since he now had her personal number. She darted to the mirror and checked her hair. Her makeup needed a serious touch-up, but there was no time. She hurried across the loft, pressed the button to let him in, and opened her door.

He walked up the stairwell, carrying a brown bag.

"Hey." He pushed his way inside.

"Hey." She followed him into her living room, and he plopped down, making himself comfortable. "What's in the bag?"

"Ice cream." He opened it and pulled out the carton and two spoons.

"I could go for some ice cream."

He patted the spot next to him and she sat. He opened the carton and handed her a spoon. "I'm sorry about earlier. I was cruel."

She scooped up some chocolate ice cream. "No, you weren't. I assume you hadn't opened the package."

"I hadn't." He ate a bite. "But I was still very rude to you.

My boss is horrible to me, and I think it's time I find a new job. I took my anger out on you."

"I'm sorry too. I never should've sent you on a date with someone else when you expected me."

"That was a pretty shitty thing to do."

"I know. I don't know how to not be on the job all the time. In my mind, I was breaking the rules. The truth is, it killed me while you were with Brandy. I kept thinking you'd take her to bed and like her more than me."

He scooped up more creamy goodness and fed it to her. "We barely know each other, but I feel something with you. I want to explore it. It just might be love for all we know."

"It just might be." She set her spoon down. "Which scares me."

"Why?"

"I'm good at matchmaking for others, but not for me."

His gaze held hers. "Willow, stop thinking about work. Look at me, really look at me. What is my aura telling you?"

She stared at him. The sadness she once saw had gone away. His aura read sincerity as well as passion. These were things he felt about her. She'd be a fool not to explore it. Looking at her hands, she could see her own aura was beginning to match his.

"Your aura tells me you're sincere."

"My aura can't lie."

She giggled. "No, it can't."

He caressed her cheek. "Then let's do this. Get to know each other. I really think we're gonna find everything we've been looking for."

"I think you're right." He was everything she'd been looking for.

She closed her eyes and inhaled his spicy scent then leaned forward until her lips found his. As soon as they were connected, her inner spirit felt as though it had become one with him. Her soul mingled with his.

He pulled away from the kiss. "I'd like to make love to you again. Only this time, more slowly."

"I want that too. I promise we can get dinner after, and I will be your date."

He chuckled. "Damn straight you'll be. I'm not interested in anyone else."

"Kiss me."

"Gladly."

She wasn't sure they'd make it to her bedroom. The couch would do for the plans she had for him. Never in her wildest fantasies did she think she'd ever land a guy like Parker, but even in her matchmaking database, he'd come up as her match.

Perhaps before long, she'd be hanging their wedding photo

on her wall of perfect matches.

About Lacey Wolfe

Lacey Wolfe has always had a passion for words, whether it's getting lost in a book or writing her own. Her goal as an author is to have a romance for everyone, whether it's sweet, sensual, or spicy. She's had several books on the Amazon best seller lists. When she isn't writing, she can be found running, talking to her pets, spending time with her family, or lost in some sort of craft. Oh, and she takes kindly to anyone who feeds her cookies.

Lacey lives in Georgia with her husband, son and daughter, their herd of cats and one black lab who rules the house.

Lacey's Website:
www.laceywolfe.com
Reader eMail:
laceywolfe@live.com

Something in the Water

by Lisa Knight

Kindergarten teacher Jill O'Halloran does her best to disregard the visions she sees in pools of still water, having learned from a young age that it wasn't something that happened to *normal* people. But when images of Darcy Albright in the throes of passion keep appearing, they prove too difficult to ignore. Jill can't understand why she's so drawn to Darcy. Sure he's gorgeous, but she doesn't *do* relationships.

When Darcy's ex-wife drops a bombshell, Jill discovers that he's all too familiar with futuristic visions. But is the prospect of learning more about the gift she's denied for so long worth the risk of falling for him?

Acknowledgements

Thank you to all the wonderful staff at Beachwalk Press.

Something in the Water / Lisa Knight

Chapter 1

Jill forced her tired arms through the water, finally reaching the wall of the swimming pool with a loud gasp for air as she struggled to catch her breath. This whole getting fit business was proving harder than she'd initially thought. Still, the four pounds she'd lost was great motivation to keep going, and there was no question that after the past two weeks of swimming laps at the local pool, she was lighter on her feet and sharper in her mind. Quite handy really, considering the daily drama in her job as a kindergarten teacher. Those five-year-olds could be tough.

She rested her head against the edge of the pool and stared up at the cloudless, blue sky, inhaling deeply to slow her racing heart. It was going to be another scorching day in Eau Claire, Wisconsin. Just what she needed after the feral way her class had behaved in yesterday's heat.

Jill glanced around at the empty water, wondering where the crowds were. Every other time she'd been here, there'd been at least five or six swimmers braving the early morning hour to fit in their laps of freestyle or backstroke. But for the moment she had the pool to herself, and it was heavenly.

Her mind raced with thoughts of all the things she had to do today. Get home, quick breakfast, shower and dress, get to

Something in the Water / Lisa Knight

school to prep for the first lesson. Oh, and there was that new student starting today. Jill squinted into the sky, trying to remember the new girl's name. Camilla? Carena? Something like that. Her mother had been on the phone at least five times over the past week, urging Jill to understand just how gifted her daughter was. Jill had merely rolled her eyes as she'd listened. At age thirty, she'd been teaching for seven years and had come to learn that every child has their own unique abilities. While she was certain little Carmen, or whatever her name was, was indeed special, she didn't appreciate the overbearing demands of her mother.

Feeling sufficiently recovered from her twenty-eight laps, Jill looked down into the clear pool, admiring the mirror-like reflection of the still water. The sun was warm on her bare shoulders, covered only by the thin straps of her bathing suit, and a lovely sense of peace settled within her. She closed her eyes and smiled softly as she enjoyed the calm, knowing it would inevitably evaporate all too soon.

Reluctantly, she opened her eyes, and the first thing she saw was the reflection of a man. He was staring at her, his eyes wide and a little menacing with his mouth set in a rather grim line. Jill spun around, ready to accuse the man behind her of being a creepy nut job. But she was alone. She flung her gaze back to the water, but all that remained were ripples from her frantic movements, rolling in soft waves toward the edges of the pool.

Her mind began to swirl with plausible explanations. Maybe light had decided to defy the laws of refraction. Or a bird flew overhead and the man she saw was simply its shadow. Perhaps an alien spaceship had crossed over the sun at the exact time she'd thought she'd seen the image in the water.

Then again, maybe this kind of thing had happened before. Perhaps she knew exactly what it meant but was trying to ignore it.

* * * *

Endeavoring to forget the events of the morning, Jill focused on her class of nineteen five-year-olds currently gluing coloring sheets into their art books. A tentative knock on the open classroom door caused her to look up, and in that same second the tin of coloring pencils she was holding slipped from her grasp. The sound of the crash on the wooden floor was horrendous, and the children squealed, jumping out of their seats in fright, then rushed to help pick up the mess.

With an inaudible curse she ignored the chaos, carefully stepping over pencils as they rolled precariously to every corner of the floor, and walked toward the door. Standing with his hand protectively on the shoulder of a young girl was the man she'd seen reflected in the water. She was sure of it. His eyes were exactly as she remembered—stern with the tiniest hint of charm—while his lips seemed unsure whether to smile or frown. His hair was a deep brown, almost black, and his complexion dark, as though he'd spent the last month on vacation somewhere luxurious.

Jill did her best to smile and swallowed back the nerves that suddenly made her feel like she was being strangled. "Can I help you?"

The man nodded, moving his hand from the girl's shoulder onto her back, gently urging her forward. "This is Caitlyn. She's starting school here today."

"Oh, of course. Yes, welcome!"

Jill instantly became all too aware of the rising noise level and bedlam in the classroom. The children were all out of their seats, giggling as they scooped up the fallen pencils, while three boys had deemed it a good time to stand on their desks and take their shirts off—again. There was a definite career in the stripper industry for those three.

She winced in apology. "Sorry about the commotion. It's not normally like this." She turned her attention back to the unruly room, clapping her hands. "All right everybody, settle down please." Utterly ignored, she spoke more forcefully. "One, two, three, eyes on me!"

Instantly, the children stopped and the room went silent.

"Impressive," the man mumbled.

Jill's lips twitched at the unexpected compliment, not certain whether he meant for her to hear it or not. "Back to your seats now, and continue with gluing your sheets please."

As the children moved to their desks, she turned again to the guests in the doorway.

"Sorry about that. Now, where were we? Oh yes, Caitlyn, welcome to Northwoods Elementary. I'm Miss O'Halloran."

The girl's head rose at a painstakingly slow pace, and Jill's heart went out to her. It must be difficult moving to a new school midway through the year, not knowing anyone. Her mother had mentioned some kind of trouble with her old class, but Jill tried not to read too much into that, preferring to see how things would turn out of their own accord.

When their gaze finally met, Jill was startled by the vibrant blue that stared back at her. She'd never seen such eyes on a child before. In fact, they were quickly overtaking Bradley Cooper's on the breathtaking scale.

She turned her open mouth into a genuine smile and was pleased when it was returned, albeit shyly, by little Caitlyn. A sigh escaped from the man next to them, as though he'd been holding his breath, anticipating a different response.

Jill looked at him, again remembering the image in the still water of the swimming pool. "I assume you're Caitlyn's father? I'm sorry, I don't know your name. I've only spoken to her mother over the phone."

A deep crease formed between his eyebrows. "Yeah, sorry about that. Sarah can be...intense. I'm Darcy Albright." He extended his hand for her to shake.

"A pleasure, Mr. Albright. I'm Jill O'Halloran." She had to force the words out, wanting nothing more than to blush and giggle like a teenager as her belly somersaulted madly over the smile that finally cracked his grumpy face. It transformed him. Sure, he'd been nice-looking before, in a Captain von Trapp kind of way, but with teeth now visible, he became extraordinary.

"Please, call me Darcy."

His handshake was strong, and her jaw dropped at the sight of a huge bicep bulging underneath his crisp, white t-shirt. Seeing him in this new light, she realized just how broad his shoulders were, and he had those lovely muscles at the base of his neck that she could never remember the name of but found so appealing.

A light sweat began to form between her breasts, and Jill reluctantly let go of Darcy's hold, taking a breath to ease the racing in her chest. She tucked her hair behind her ears, not that any strands had come loose from her long, straight ponytail, but rather she didn't seem to quite know what to do with her hands.

"Well." She coughed awkwardly. "Let's get you settled, Caitlyn."

Darcy bent down and kissed his daughter on the top of the head. "Have a great day, sweetheart. Mom will pick you up this afternoon." He lingered, kissing her softly again before lowering his voice to a whisper. "Please remember what we talked about."

Caitlyn nodded with great enthusiasm, suddenly losing her earlier shyness. "Don't worry, Daddy. There'll be no funny business, I promise!"

Jill raised her eyebrows in delight at the statement. She could just imagine the conversation between the two and had to bite her cheek to stop from laughing as Darcy's healthy tan became a shade of embarrassed red. He straightened and gave a curt nod before exiting the room without another word.

It was well into the afternoon before Jill had a chance to sit down and think about Darcy Albright. Caitlyn had settled in well, returning from the lunch break with her elbows linked with two other girls', looking happy and content. The children were currently resting on the floor with a fan blowing the air to cool them down. It wouldn't surprise her if one or two fell asleep. She wished she could do the same.

Stifling a yawn, Jill reached for the glass on her desk, conscious of keeping up her fluids in this hot weather. Her heart skipped a beat when Darcy's face reflected back from the water. He looked calm and relaxed, with a half-smile on his handsome mouth. In fact, it looked a little like he was... Oh dear God! She

Something in the Water / Lisa Knight

sat up stiffly in her seat, cheeks flaming with heat as her gaze darted over the room, desperately hoping nobody saw what she'd just witnessed. But of course no one had. She was the only person strange enough to see visions in water.

It had begun when she was about five or six years old. Pictures had started to appear in the bath, or in puddles left after rain. She hadn't known what it was at first, but it had never occurred to her to be frightened. That didn't come until later, when she told the foster parents who were caring for her at the time.

Jill had quickly learned that other people didn't think it was normal to see visions in pools of water. They thought it made her weird and was something that had to be beaten out of her...regularly. As she grew older and moved from foster home to foster home, she'd learned to keep her mouth firmly shut. Even once she'd found a safe place to live, with people who seemed to care about her, she never told another soul about her ability.

There wasn't all that much to tell anyway. It came in waves. She'd see glimpses of things for a few weeks or months, and then nothing for long stretches of time. It had been over a year since her last vision. Right around the time she'd got the job at Northwoods Elementary.

The thing was that every image she'd ever seen had ended

Something in the Water / Lisa Knight

up a reality, resulting in some kind of change in her life. The social worker who came to the door when she was eight to take her to a new home, her best friend Karen who she met on the first day of high school, the mailman who delivered her offer of a college scholarship, various school principals offering her teaching jobs. And today, Darcy Albright, on the verge of an orgasm.

At least she *thought* that's what it was. Her visions were always brief and not entirely clear. Mostly they were just people's faces, although sometimes she too appeared in the image. But what the hell did she know about men's orgasms? Maybe he'd been about to sneeze.

Feeling more than a little guilty, Jill took another peek into her glass of water. Oh yep, definitely an orgasm. He was enjoying it too. A slow, sexy smile began to take shape on his lips, lifting his flushed cheeks to transform his face in that surprising way she'd seen this morning. The man was utterly glorious.

As the vision faded she squirmed in her seat, decidedly hot and bothered by what she'd seen. Why on earth would Darcy Albright be the subject of her apparition? He was a married man. Why the hell was she seeing him in the throes of sex? It didn't make any sense. Perhaps for the first time in her life, her visualization did not apply directly to her.

Jill stared into the water again, but Darcy did not return, which was probably for the best. It was already going to be awkward enough facing him again. She closed her eyes, instantly swarmed by the picture of his face, smiling and peaceful after the intense release. Her breasts ached at the thought of such attention. It had been a long time since she'd had sex.

"Miss O'Halloran?"

Jill's eyes flew open.

Jayden Polson was standing at her desk, bare chested and clutching desperately to his crotch. "Can I please go to the bathroom?"

"Yes, quickly, off you go. And put your shirt back on. This is not a strip club!"

Chapter 2

Two days passed without another vision, despite Jill meticulously checking every drop of water she came across. She'd never chased images before and wasn't entirely sure why she was doing so now. Oh, all right...if she was totally honest, she knew exactly why she was doing it, and it was all due to the accidental—on purpose—discovery that Caitlyn's parents were happily divorced. Thus, Darcy Albright was single.

This knowledge had not helped her any, however, because he hadn't made another appearance at school. Thanks to Jill's careful questioning, she'd learned that Caitlyn spent various days of the week with her mother and the others with her dad. There didn't seem to be much routine to it, and so far her mom had been the one dropping in each morning and afternoon to collect her daughter.

She was quite a strange woman, with no real regard for boundaries, frequently asking a range of inappropriate, personal questions. It was as though she thought of Jill as her best friend, not the teacher of her five-year-old daughter, and certainly not the woman who wanted to get down and dirty with her ex-husband. Then again, Jill was keeping that information firmly to herself.

Something in the Water / Lisa Knight

By the end of the week, the wave of hot weather had finally reached its peak. Jill watched the rain falling outside her bedroom window, wondering what to wear to work and whether she might actually need a sweater. The week of high temperatures was unusual for Eau Claire at this time of year, but having lived in lots of places throughout her life, many of them unbearably hot, she wasn't too bothered by it. The cold was a different story, but her rented house was well insulated and the previous winter hadn't got to her badly enough to make her think about moving on...yet.

She was unable to swim this morning, thanks to a few streaks of lightning around, although that had disappeared without too much havoc and now the rain fell gently, watering the plants in her garden and soaking into the grass, which already looked greener as a result.

A pool of raindrops had collected on the hood of her car, and as Jill dashed past to get out of the weather, a crystal clear image of Darcy smiled at her. She stopped abruptly, skidding in her strappy sandals, eagerly backtracking in the hope of another glimpse. Sure enough, there he was. His smile turned to laughter, and he threw his head back in a look of sheer happiness that she never would have guessed him capable of. But when his head came forward, his face was serious. He ran a hand through his crop of thick, dark hair and his mouth slowly opened as though enjoying yet another mind-blowing orgasm.

"Oh Lordy," she muttered, getting into the car and forcing her thoughts toward neutral things like panda bears and Mt. Everest, in a futile attempt to dull her pent-up sexual frustration.

It didn't work. By the time the morning bell rang, Jill was just about ready to sit on a block of ice in order to cool the heat pooling in her downstairs region. She could barely concentrate and fumbled her way through polite hellos and information exchanges with parents in a state of agitation and discontent.

She'd just begun the day's class when a frazzled-looking Darcy appeared in the doorway, followed by Caitlyn, whose normally well-groomed appearance had been replaced with bed-head and a rumpled uniform. She smiled brilliantly and took her seat quietly, while Darcy eyed Jill from the back of the room, making it clear he needed a word.

With as deep a breath as her pumping chest could manage, she moved toward him, desperately failing in her attempt to not conjure up any dirty images. He stepped out into the corridor and she followed, keeping an ear on the unattended children, who so far were being kept busy with their reading activity.

There were creases around the edges of Darcy's eyes, and Jill wondered what had happened this morning to stress him out.

"I'm sorry she's late."

"It's fine, honestly. Is everything okay?"

He sighed, running a hand through his messy hair. "Um, yes, no. I don't really know."

His lips twitched as though deciding whether or not to smile, and surprisingly then broke into a grin. Jill had to cross one leg over the other and remind herself to close her mouth.

Standing in the empty hallway, Darcy proceeded to laugh. It was such a lovely sound, deep and hearty, right from the core of his belly. She got the feeling he didn't do it all that often, and now that it had slipped out he might not be able to stop.

It took a while, but eventually he did, clutching his stomach as though he'd damaged his abs with such a strenuous workout. Perhaps she ought to take a look and offer some medical attention.

"Oh, that feels better." His shoulders rose and fell as he recovered his breath. "I'm not sure what it is, but there's something about you that lets me...unwind."

It's probably all the times I've seen you—

"Would you like to have dinner with me tonight?"

Jill's eyes widened in surprise, then narrowed suspiciously as he swayed unsteadily, reaching blindly for the wall with one hand splayed to widen his chance of hitting something tangible.

"Oh my God. Darcy, are you *drunk*?" Jill whispered the final word, darting her eyes around nervously to ensure no one was in sight. Miraculously, her kindergartners were behaving like angels."

"No," he shot back defensively. "But I do feel a little weird."

Alarmed, she grabbed his arm above the elbow. Though evidently not too alarmed because she couldn't help but notice the hard muscle underneath his warm, tanned skin. There must be some serious weight lifting going into those babies. She held on tight to steady him, and also herself as it turned out, while he used the other hand to rub his forehead and temples.

For a moment neither one spoke. Jill subconsciously caressed her palm over Darcy's skin, watching him blink rapidly before shaking his head as if he were trying to shoo away whatever it was that he was feeling.

"Are you okay?" she asked, finally breaking the silence.

"Yeah, thanks. Just had a dizzy spell, but I'm fine now." His gaze turned downward to where she was still stroking his arm and a slow smirk lifted the corners of his mouth.

Jill dropped her hand, cursing the heat that suddenly spread into her cheeks.

"Did you eat breakfast?" She hoped it sounded helpful, not nosy.

Darcy shrugged. "Only a cup of tea. I'm probably just hungry." His eyes clouded over as though remembering something, and a slight crease appeared between his eyebrows.

But just as quickly it disappeared, and his smile returned. "So, about dinner tonight?"

She blinked warily, expecting him to retract his offer. Yet he remained silent, watching her curiously, waiting for her response. Her mind flashed with all the images she'd seen in the water, making her belly flip.

"Um." It wasn't a good idea. She knew that much for certain. Surely there was some kind of policy against dating the parent of a student. Not that she was going to 'date' Darcy. There was absolutely zero chance of that happening. So it was actually more like one tiny dinner. They both had to eat, right? She couldn't possibly get into trouble for that. "Okay."

"Great. How about we meet at Drew's…say seven o'clock?"

* * * *

The hours dragged by at a ridiculously slow pace, and Jill was a bundle of nerves when the time finally arrived to meet Darcy. 'Drew's' was a trendy little restaurant that had opened a few years ago. She'd been there a handful of times, but never on a date not that this was a date—and certainly never with anyone as gorgeous as Darcy.

In fact, it was bordering on a year since she'd been out with anyone of the male variety. She just wasn't good with men. Found it hard to trust them. Of course it all stemmed back to her childhood. It didn't take a shrink to figure that one out. Her own father was a horribly abusive man, beating her mother on a daily basis until the day he'd gone too far and killed her, then himself. Jill had been very young. Bits and pieces sometimes returned to her in nightmares, but she tried hard not to dwell on things for too long.

It was when she entered the foster care system that things really got bad. There it seemed every male viewed it as his right to lay down the law with a punch, a kick, or a slap on the face. Or often a combination of all three.

It was no surprise that she was now left with a tainted view of men. If only she could be a lesbian. Life would be so much easier. But after one quick attempt in college, that notion had been firmly squashed. It wasn't that she hated males. She was definitely attracted to them, found them charming and amusing. It was just the relationship part she had trouble with, so that's why she stuck with one-night stands. Anything more than that was asking for trouble.

She spotted Darcy from outside the restaurant, sitting on a stool by the bar, swiveling gently from side to side as though he too might be harboring a few nerves. The thought made the butterflies in her tummy stop their violent fluttering and take up a less intrusive mild flicker.

He glanced up as she pushed through the heavy glass door,

causing a tingling bell to announce her arrival. As he stood, a smile shaped his face into a look of happiness and relief at the same time, making her wonder if he'd been afraid she wouldn't show up. Surely no one had ever stood up a man as glorious as Darcy Albright?

"Hi, I'm so glad you're here." He leaned down and kissed her cheek, bringing the subtle scent of soap and shampoo, making heat gather in places that had been neglected for far too long.

Jill swallowed, humbled by the fact that he'd shaved and taken time to get ready for their date. Most guys she'd been with had barely managed to brush their teeth, let alone style their hair with actual *product*. Her liking Darcy scale went up ten points.

Their waiter was a young man in his early twenties with too much hair and a piercing through his lip that she found disturbing. How did he kiss with that thing in? As he led the way to their table in the far corner of the restaurant, she followed behind Darcy, utilizing the opportunity to study his butt, which in a pair of dark Levi's was round, firm, and nothing short of spectacular. That, and the fact that he had no piercings that she knew of, added another ten points to his scale. He was up to twenty.

The earlier dip in her nerves was evidently only temporary and now spiked back to full throttle as she sat down opposite

Darcy. She practically tore the menu from the waiter's hand, pretending to peruse its contents while she hid, taking in deep, shaky breaths, trying to settle the pounding in her chest.

"Anything you fancy?" His voice was low and smooth, reminding her of a television commercial from years ago where creamy, melted chocolate was poured all over a man's body.

She fought the urge to say 'yes thanks, I'd quite fancy you', instead blinking away the chocolaty image as she peeked over the top of her menu to find him smiling in that way she liked so much. "Um, maybe the angel hair pasta with shrimp?" The truth was she hadn't even looked at the options and hoped that dish was still available. It had been absolutely delicious the last time she'd been there.

"Great choice. I think I'll go for the beef with mashed potatoes. Want to share some bruschetta to start, and maybe a bottle of the house white?"

Jill nodded, all of a sudden hungry now that the idea of food was a reality.

Darcy sat back comfortably in his seat, resting his hands on the crisp, white tablecloth. "So, Miss O'Halloran…how was school today?"

She smiled at his formal use of her name. "Well, aside from a wobbly beginning where a father brought his daughter in late and then acted very oddly…it was great."

Darcy's face fell. "Hmm, sorry about that."

"What happened anyway?"

She watched his Adam's apple bob in his throat as he swallowed and a slight sweat broke out on his forehead. "Caitlyn was being difficult, and Sarah wasn't helping matters. She's very…different."

Jill widened her eyes in question, wanting more information.

Darcy started to fiddle with the tablecloth, taking his gaze with him. "Um, she's always been slightly weird, eccentric everyone said. It was kind of what attracted me to her in the first place. But then, things got a bit out of control, especially after Caitlyn was born."

What in the hell did that mean? Though by the look of Darcy's face she thought it wise not to pry any further. He'd gone rather pale and was drumming his fingers against the table so frantically there was a good chance it could topple over.

"How long were you married?"

His shoulders relaxed at the question. He was obviously relieved to be in safer territory. "Two years. Sarah became pregnant shortly after we met and we married pretty quickly." He shook his head. "I can see now how dumb it was, but at the time I wasn't listening to what anyone said."

Jill shrugged. "But it brought you Caitlyn."

Darcy's eyes lit up as he smiled. "It sure did. She's the best thing that's ever happen to me. Although I don't suppose you've noticed any…odd behavior from her at school?"

"No, why?"

"Oh, no reason. I'm glad she's settling in."

Jill stared at Darcy, trying to make sense of what was going on. All this talk about strange behaviors, yet he was the one currently on the top of her crazy list.

"Sorry," he said, meeting Jill's gaze. "I'm rambling on with nonsense. I suppose I'm a little nervous. I haven't dated in a long time."

"Really? What made you ask me out?"

"To be honest, I'm not sure. I hadn't planned it at all. I just went with what felt right. Thanks for saying yes."

Her laughter cleared the tension, and as Darcy joined in, Jill felt herself relax properly for the first time all evening. A happy demeanor suited him so well. It lifted his cheeks and enhanced his dark eyes so perfectly that they became the highlight of his handsome face. His hair was such a deep, luxurious brown. She quite fancied the idea of running her hands through the tousled waves, and quickly sat on them to stop any involuntary acts of violation.

She suddenly became very aware of the fact that she was staring at Darcy, with a high probability of possessing a dopey, adoring face. The thing that made her tummy flip multiple times though, was that he was watching her just as closely, and was most definitely sporting an expression of admiration. Okay, if she was totally truthful it was more than admiration. More like desire and lust mixed together. It was a lethal combination, sending a clear message directly to her groin. Jill crossed her legs and took a shaky breath.

There was a definite shift in the air, as though pent-up sexual energy had released its way to freedom and now danced around them in an invisible dust of glee. Her bra suddenly felt too tight. She glanced down, mortified to find her nipples straining, like two Hershey kisses, against the fabric of her white linen blouse. With a gasp, Jill's gaze flew to the opposite side of the table, but Darcy had already noticed.

She crossed her arms over her chest in an attempt to cover her body's shameful lack of discretion. But a second later she changed her mind, bringing her hands to her lap, worried that trying to hide the evidence would only make it all the more obvious. Daring a peek in Darcy's direction, Jill saw that his gaze was firmly planted in the area she'd been trying to conceal. Oh God.

"Here is your appetizer." The waiter's voice was so unexpected that Jill's heart leapt and she slid sideways, almost coming off her chair. "Sorry. Didn't mean to startle you." He placed the dish in the middle of the table with an amused grin, glancing back and forth at her and Darcy as though he knew full well what was going on between them.

She gave him an awkward smile as he departed then reached for a piece of bruschetta, hoping to hide her embarrassment behind the salty tomato bread. Heat from Darcy's hand touched her before anything else, and as their fingers accidently brushed against each other, a jolt of something very good traveled its way through her entire body.

She closed her eyes, momentarily swept up in whatever the hell was happening. She'd never felt such chemistry with a man before. Ever. It was an actual physical force that she had no control over. And it felt good. Damn good.

Despite wanting to leave the restaurant immediately and ravish his body, Jill remained in her seat, and she and Darcy enjoyed the rest of their meal while getting to know each other a little better. He chatted about his job as a project manager where he was currently working on the construction of a new military base just outside of town. She told him about the various teaching positions she'd had and how much she liked working at Northwoods Elementary.

All the while, the chemistry between them continued to build until Jill was convinced that if she scooped the air with her hand she'd receive an actual electric shock. By the time their plates were empty she and Darcy were giggling like teenagers. The bottle of wine they'd consumed had only helped their cause, and the way he kept brushing his fingers softly over hers was sending Jill slightly over the edge.

The pierced-lip waiter arrived again. "Can I interest you in any dessert or coffee?"

"No!" she and Darcy practically shouted in unison, making them both laugh.

The waiter rolled his eyes, and Jill was pretty sure she heard him mutter "gross" under his breath, followed by a much clearer, "I'll get you the check."

They left the restaurant in much the same way they'd come in—with Jill greatly admiring Darcy's butt as she walked behind him. Out on the street she crossed her arms over her chest, struck by how quiet it was away from the hustle and bustle of the busy restaurant. The night air was refreshingly cool, with the heat of the days earlier in the week long gone after the hours of steady rain today.

She'd thought it sensible to walk to the restaurant, given that she lived just a few blocks away. But now, striding through the parking lot with Darcy, Jill was hit with a wave of anxiety. What if he simply kissed her on the cheek and drove away? She'd be left standing there like an awkward fool.

He stopped at a sleek, black SUV and she followed suit,

Something in the Water / Lisa Knight

alarmed by the volume of her pounding heart. Without any words spoken, she was suddenly pushed against the side of the car. A huge hand protected the back of her head, holding her firmly in place while Darcy kissed her.

His mouth was hot, and his lips molded against hers with an expertise that left Jill breathless. A combination of relief and lust infiltrated her body, and she did her best to kiss him back without losing her senses, wanting to remember every detail, to savor each second. But as his tongue flicked inside her mouth, brushing eagerly over hers, she gave in to the delirium of the moment and let herself get washed away.

The sound of his moan brought her back to reality. No one had ever moaned from her kiss before and she smiled against his lips, feeling more alive than she had in a long time. Darcy's grip moved to her hips and he pulled her tightly against him, letting her know that he was feeling exactly the same way. His lips didn't leave hers for a second, but his hands continued to wander, one traveling upward into her hair and the other south, over the curves of her behind. Jill murmured a silent prayer of thanks for all those weeks of swimming, which had done wonders to tone her muscles.

"You're utterly beautiful," Darcy whispered, his mouth brushing softly against her lips with the words.

Jill knew she shouldn't fall for that. It was a trick taught at men's school to make women swoon. Yet he didn't make it sound cheesy or shallow. In fact, it sent her liking Darcy scale up about a hundred points.

"Would you mind giving me a ride home? It's not far, I walked here." Jill swallowed, trying to steady her voice. "Maybe you could stay for..." She couldn't finish the sentence, but still had a sense of relief at having managed the question she'd been thinking about asking all evening. Now that the words were out, she actually felt empowered. An emotion she'd never even come close to experiencing around a man before.

Darcy's lips traveled along the underside of her jaw, and Jill leaned her weight against the car, certain her legs were going to give way at any moment. "Yes." It was no more than a whisper against her ear, and her eyes closed as his mouth continued to journey over her skin, leaving her trembling.

The sound of the car unlocking made her jump, and Darcy chuckled as he held the passenger door open. With wobbly legs, Jill managed to climb inside and rested her head back against the seat, grinning into the darkness while she waited for Darcy to make his way around to the driver's side.

She uttered a silent prayer of thanks that she lived so close by, and after a few quick directions they were parked in the driveway of her house. Her stomach fluttered with nerves as she unclicked her seatbelt, taking a deep breath in the silence of the car.

"You know, we could just have coffee if you'd prefer..." Darcy's voice trailed off, and Jill stared at him as though he was speaking a foreign language. "Or not."

She launched herself across the car, suddenly finding the space between them far too distant. Darcy inhaled sharply as she crushed her lips against his and he fisted his hands in her hair, opening his mouth wider to accommodate her demands. He smelled so wonderful that for a moment she contemplated taking a bite out of his skin, but relented at the last second, running her tongue over his bottom lip before sucking it into her mouth.

He groaned and pulled her toward him, lifting her right off the seat and into his lap. Jill laughed at their awkwardness, then let out a mighty squeal as Darcy pulled on a lever and sent their chair flying backward. He was practically lying straight down and she maneuvered herself over him, finding his mouth again while he cupped his hands firmly on her behind.

Good things were happening to every part of her body, and she didn't care if neighbors were watching or if anyone could see through the car windows. Her driveway was relatively private and with no moon tonight it was really dark out there, but none of that even mattered as Darcy's hands moved to her breasts and he ran his fingers over her tight nipples.

Wanting more, she sat up on top of him and watched while

he undid the buttons of her blouse. She shrugged out of it, not caring in the slightest where it fell onto the floor of the car. Darcy ran a finger along each lacy top of her bra before scooping under the fabric where he skimmed her straining nipples again and again until she was panting uncontrollably.

With trembling fingers she tried to unfasten the buttons on his shirt, starting with the bottom one closest to her. But the damn things were so tiny and she was shaking so much that she gave up, tugging just a little to help it along. Buttons suddenly flew around the air and Jill gasped, realizing she'd just ripped his shirt open.

"I'm so sorry!"

"I'm not." His voice was deep and sexy, and she shuddered as he pulled her back down to him, merging their bare skin together.

There was a layer of black hair on his chest and she ran a hand over it, loving the soft tickle through her fingers. She continued down his chest along the trail of hair there too, leading down into his jeans. His breath was almost a hiss as she reached the front of his pants, and she kept her hand there, caressing all that lay beneath as Darcy's hips began to rock.

His hands slipped upward to unhook her bra and she was forced to bring her arms up to get it off completely. Jill utilized the moment to unbuckle Darcy's belt, followed by his jeans. She

Something in the Water / Lisa Knight

looped her fingers over the rim of his black boxers, enjoying the smile on his lips as he lifted his hips for her to pull everything down. It was a struggle in the confined space of the car, and they both laughed as he maneuvered one leg out, opting to leave the other with his pants bunched around his ankle.

Jill was wearing her favorite pencil skirt—gray with tiny pink flowers. It fell beautifully against her skin, that was, when she wasn't pinned up against a man in a car. Now, however, it stretched as far as it could as she straddled her legs across Darcy's hips, kissing him with the urgency the rest of her body felt.

With their mouths locked, he pulled her skirt up, tugging it over her thighs to expose her underwear. He ran one finger and then another over the exact spot that ached for his touch, and she writhed on top of him, desperate for more.

"Condom?" The word came out in an unsteady breath.

Darcy smiled against her lips and reached for his jeans, still attached to his leg, where he pulled a foil square from the pocket. She sat up while he put it on, nearly jumping out of her skin when her back hit the horn and it gave a loud blast.

Darcy laughed, pulling her skirt up and completely off over her head. With a smile, she lay down on his chest again, loving the way he ran his hands across her back and over the satin fabric of her underwear.

"This'll even things out for the shirt," he mumbled, trailing his tongue along her neck.

"What will?" Jill could barely focus on anything except having him. *Now.*

His reply was to rip her panties clean off, and she was suddenly naked against him. It sent a shock through her entire body, making her gasp. Darcy's gaze met hers, wide and unblinking, with the barest hint of a smile on his lips. She felt his hands on her hips and the heat from his body as he pressed against her, slowly and unassumingly.

But she'd had enough of slow and unassuming. She slapped her hands over his pecs and sank upon his entire length, loving the way his mouth opened and his eyes rolled back into his head. She began to move, shocked at how satisfying it was, how different to anything she'd experienced before.

Darcy sat up, cupping her butt with his hands as he took one breast in his mouth, gently biting her nipple. The sensation was overwhelming and she moaned, driving her hips harder against his until he filled her completely.

He tightened his grip on her butt and dropped his head back with a groan as a slight sweat broke on his forehead. Jill pushed him back so that he lay flat on the seat once more, and his lips curled into a smile as he pulled her down with him. He wrapped one arm around her waist while the other hand went into her hair, urging her mouth onto his where his breath was hot and urgent.

The windows fogged up from the heat of their breaths, and Jill was vaguely aware of various sounds flying out of her mouth. While she'd normally get embarrassed about things like that, right now she was far too preoccupied by the impending orgasm heading her way.

Her body was on fire. She'd never known sex could be this good and didn't want it to end. Darcy's abs flexed every time he pushed within her, and he had a look on his face that let her know she was doing everything right. It was enough to send her crumbling, and as waves rocked her body, she couldn't take her gaze off Darcy. He was a vision of pure bliss. Exactly how she'd seen him in the water.

Something in the Water / Lisa Knight

Chapter 3

Jill was awake but kept her eyes shut, trying not to move until she'd figured out whether or not Darcy was still in her bed. She strained her ears, listening for any sound of breathing, and gave a disappointed sigh when the room remained silent. She rolled over to where he'd been lying earlier. The quilt was pushed back and the sheets rumpled, but that was no surprise considering the vigorous workout they'd given the bed during the night.

After making it out of his car, they'd stumbled to the front door, where Jill had rummaged through her handbag trying to find the keys while Darcy stood behind, kissing her neck until everything became a blur. Finally inside, he'd pushed her against the door as it closed, pulling off the skirt she'd only just managed to get back on and cupping her breasts inside the linen shirt she hadn't bothered doing up.

She couldn't keep her hands off Darcy either and ran them over the smooth skin of his back, down his unzipped pants and over places that made him moan in that way she was really getting to like. They hadn't even made it to the bedroom.

After that, she'd brewed coffee, and they'd sat in the kitchen smiling at each other over the tops of their mugs like

Something in the Water / Lisa Knight

goofy teenagers. She then gave him a quick tour of her tiny house, ending upstairs in the bedroom where he'd made her come so many times she was practically hoarse from screaming his name.

Jill sat up now, wincing as she swung her legs off the bed. Her muscles were stiff, and it took a few attempts to actually lift off the bed and stand up. She peered out the window. Darcy's SUV was still in her driveway. Memories of last night flooded her mind, and she placed a hand over her tummy at the flip of delight that danced there.

The smell of coffee filtered into the room. Jill grabbed her robe, wrapping it around herself as she headed downstairs. Darcy stood in her kitchen, looking as delicious as the coffee he was brewing. He was wearing nothing but jeans, which hung loosely around his waist. His chest and feet were bare.

She stared at him, unable to fathom that such a gorgeous male was in her kitchen. Had she really spent the night with him? Had they really gone for round after round of glorious sex? Thank God he'd brought along a mother-load of condoms. Clever man.

Darcy turned to face her, smiling as he held out a mug of steaming coffee. "Good morning."

Jill blinked a few times, still trying to comprehend that all of this was real. She returned his smile and accepted the mug gratefully, taking a sip. "How did you know how I liked it?"

Darcy held his cup in two hands, making it look tiny. "I remembered from last night."

"Oh, right..."

"I remember *lots* of things from last night."

Heat rose up her neck and into her cheeks. She kept her eyes on the drink in front of her.

A soft chuckle left his throat and Darcy stepped toward her, lifting her chin up between his thumb and forefinger. "And it was all amazing."

She met his gaze. His brown eyes were wide and smiling, and she couldn't help but smile back, tipping her head forward to rest against his. Neither of them spoke as they stood in her kitchen, foreheads pressed together, grinning like two idiots with a huge secret.

"You smell good." He broke the silence, leaning in to kiss her softly on the lips.

His face was prickly from overnight growth, leaving dark stubble over his top lip and around his jaw. It was utterly sexy and the feel of it against her skin sent heat pooling south. Jill shook her head, shocked that after everything last night, she could still be turned on so readily this morning.

Jill jumped when Darcy's phone, which was on the kitchen

bench, began to vibrate, spinning over the smooth, stone surface as though it were alive.

"Ugh. I have to go, I'm late for work." He silenced the phone without answering the call, shoving it into the back pocket of his jeans. "I'm sorry to have to rush off."

"You work on Saturdays?"

Darcy scrunched his nose, looking rather adorable. "Yup. And I have Caitlyn for the weekend, so I won't get a chance to see you until Monday." He cocked his head. "I wish I didn't have to go."

Jill folded her arms across her chest. "Don't be silly, you have to work. It's fine."

He held her gaze, and she knew he was trying to figure out if she was okay with him leaving. Which, of course, she was. Wasn't she?

She forced a smile. "Come on, off you go. I don't want to be the reason you get sacked."

He opened his mouth as if to say something more, but then decided against it, kissing her on the cheek instead. "I'll see you later."

She nodded and watched Darcy move away. He took a quick gulp of coffee from the mug on the bench before scooping up his shirt and shoes that had been left scattered on the floor last night. Wrestling his arms through the sleeves of his shirt, he quickly realized there were no buttons to do up, and he flashed a grin as though recalling the exact moment she'd sent them flying through the interior of his car.

He headed toward the front door. Jill closed her eyes at the sound of it opening and then closing, trying to understand why she was overcome with a sudden urge to cry. She'd had men stay over before, but hadn't ever felt an inkling of sadness when they'd left. In fact, she'd been the one shooing them out without a thought of seeing them again.

But this felt different. The idea of spending a day with him made her feel a bit gooey inside. She chuckled softly, shaking off such a crazy notion. So she was disappointed that he'd had to leave. It didn't mean she was falling for him. She would never do anything so stupid.

* * * *

By Monday morning Jill had convinced herself that she and Darcy were a one-time thing, never to be repeated. He'd sent her a text on Saturday night, but she'd successfully avoided typing anything in reply, despite swiping her phone to read it every twenty minutes. Okay, ten.

Been thinking of you all day.

It could mean anything. He'd been thinking all day of ways to let her down gently. To let her know there was nothing between them. She knew how men worked, and there was no

Something in the Water / Lisa Knight

way she was going to lose the upper hand to one. She would be doing the dumping, thanks very much.

Standing in the kitchen clutching a glass of water, Jill felt an unhealthy dose of apprehension about going to work. Darcy would be dropping Caitlyn off at school, and she wasn't at all confident about seeing him again.

Would it really hurt to sleep with him just one more time? That hardly constituted a relationship. Did it? Normally, a one-night stand sent her off men for a while. But her night with Darcy seemed to have only increased her desire. She could still feel the warmth of his skin, the heat from his mouth, his body entwined with hers.

With a sigh, she glanced down into her glass, startled to see an image in the water. It had been days since she'd had a vision. Sarah, Darcy's ex-wife, was smiling, and then she winked at Jill as though they shared an important secret. *Oh no.* Had she found out about her and Darcy? She looked into the glass again. Sarah looked downright happy, smug even. Not like an ex-wife insanely jealous of her husband's new partner, er one-time partner. The thought was only slightly reassuring.

The image played on her mind all morning, and accompanied by her indecision about Darcy, Jill was feeling decidedly frazzled by the time she got to work. When the bell rang to signal the start of class, parents disbursed with final hugs and kisses for their kids. She scanned the room for what surely must be the millionth time, yet Darcy and Caitlyn were nowhere in sight. Perhaps he was avoiding her.

Jill settled the children, and as she turned to face the chalkboard every hair on the back of her neck stood on end, as though physically trying to reach something at the back of the room. *Darcy.* She spun around to find him watching her, an amused smirk turning up the corners of his kissable lips. His damp hair was jutting out in all directions. Obviously he hadn't had time to even run his hands through it to comb it down. But it only added to his appeal. The man was undeniably gorgeous.

"Great work, children. Keep coloring your trees and we'll add some pictures when I get back. Come in, Caitlyn, and get started."

Jill walked out of the room, Darcy following her, and in a similar scene to last Friday, they stood in the hallway outside the classroom.

"You know, you're getting quite a reputation for being late."

His nose crinkled in apology. "I promise it won't happen again." He kept his gaze on hers. "How are you?"

The warmth in his voice made it so much more than just a casual question, and for the briefest moment, all of Jill's fears dissipated. The concept of a future with Darcy trickled through her rocky barricade, filling her with an utterly foreign sense of pure pleasure.

She hadn't realized she was holding her breath and as he took a step closer air gushed from her lungs, bringing her back to reality. What the hell was she thinking? She didn't *do* relationships. But he looked so happy, and the memory of all that marvelous sex was still firmly in her mind. Perhaps just one more time would be all right.

"You haven't answered my question, but I take it from that smile that you're doing fine." He moved forward another step, standing close enough for Jill to catch the delicious scent of soap wafting from his skin. Her body tightened, conjuring images of him naked in the shower, and without permission from the sensible part of her brain, she leaned into his neck and inhaled deeply.

He was divine. Clean, earthy, and *manly* all at the same time. She ran the tip of her nose over his cheek, sighing in satisfaction as unshaven stubble bristled against her skin.

"What are you trying to do to me?" His voice was a soft whisper, and Jill felt the lift of his cheek as he smiled. She couldn't see his face but sensed his eyes were closed as he brushed his cheek along hers, stopping to kiss her gently on the lips.

He pulled back, evidently as disturbed as she by the fact that

Something in the Water / Lisa Knight

they could both easily rip each other's clothes off at that very moment and get down to business in the corridor of her work place. Not to mention there were twenty kindergarten students just feet away.

Jill's heart pounded frantically. No part of her was touching Darcy, yet his gaze had them locked tightly together, and she stared into the deep brown of his eyes, knowing something unspoken was passing between them. It was exhilarating, but at the same time, it scared the living daylights out of her.

It seemed like forever before he spoke. "Can I see you tonight?"

She nodded, not trusting herself to speak.

"My place, seven o'clock. I'll cook you dinner."

Jill watched him walk away, pressing her back hard against the wall to take the weight off her wobbly legs. Her eyes closed in disbelief. What the hell was she doing? This thing with Darcy was going to end badly, so why was she so incapable of staying away?

"Miss O'Halloran?"

Jill's eyes few open to find Caitlyn poking her head out into the hallway. She cursed under her breath, having momentarily forgotten that she was in charge of a class of five-year-olds, and pushed her weight off the wall to stand.

An enormous grin spread over Caitlyn's face. "I want to

show you my picture."

She held up the paper that Jill had given each student for the purpose of drawing a tree. But instead, Caitlyn had sketched a couple getting married. It was quite a good picture, really. The man had dark hair and was dressed in a gray suit. The bride was wearing a veil and a white dress, and holding a bunch of pink and purple flowers.

Jill sighed. "That's lovely, but what about the tree I asked you to do?"

"Oh, I finished that already. See?" She flipped the sheet of paper over to reveal a gorgeous, green tree, complete with a bird in a nest on one of the branches.

"Wow, Caitlyn, that's an excellent picture."

"It's you and Daddy."

"What?"

"Getting married. It's you and my daddy."

Jill held her breath. What exactly had Darcy's daughter just witnessed standing in that doorway? "Sweetie, why would you draw your father and I getting married?"

"Because I saw it in the water."

Everything stopped. Time. Movement. Sound. Jill simply stared at Caitlyn, her jaw hanging so low she could have licked the floor. But then, just as quickly, everything started again and a roar of noise rushed to her ears as her brain frantically called for possibilities to make sense of the words she'd just heard. Swallowing, she tried to quiet the commotion in her head as the child before her simply smiled and blinked innocently.

Finally she managed to speak. "What water?" It came out as a croak.

"All different kinds. The bath, my drink bottle, the bowl my dog drinks from. I saw it lots of times."

Jill's heart was in overdrive, surely about to pop out of her chest. "You can see things in water?"

"Mmm-hmm." Caitlyn nodded as though it was the most normal thing in the world. "I know you can too. My mom told me."

"Oh God." Her words were no more than a breathy whisper, and a prickle of fear edged its way to the pit of Jill's stomach. She didn't know whether to ask questions or run away and hide.

Without warning the degree of noise in the classroom reached a catastrophic level, and she had no choice but to dash inside and calm the children who were screaming excitably at the three boys who'd yet again stripped off their shirts and were parading around on the desktops.

Struggling to keep her cool, Jill managed to get everyone back into their seats, and she slumped down into her own chair, counting the minutes until the recess break. She couldn't help peeking intermittently in Caitlyn's direction while the words played relentlessly in her mind. *I know you can too. My mom told me.* A myriad of questions begged to be answered. How on earth did Sarah know such private information, and perhaps even more disturbing, what the hell else did she know?

Jill had never been so pleased to hear the recess bell, and as the children ran outside, squealing in delight for their morning play, a loud sigh of relief escaped her lungs. Opting not to join the other teachers, she remained in the classroom and sat at her desk, resting her elbows on the flimsy, cheap timber in a state of mild shock. She rubbed her fingers against the sides of her head, trying to ease the headache that was beginning to form.

"Miss O'Halloran?"

Leaving her head in her hands, Jill moved only her eyes upward to find Sarah Albright standing in her line of vision. "Oh shit." She closed her eyes again and dropped her head to the desk.

Sarah's laugh floated through the room. "I choose not to take offense to that."

"What are you doing here?" Jill's voice sounded like a booming echo between her elbows.

"I think it's time we talked."

The air was thick and hot in her hidey-hole but it was still with great reluctance that she raised her head. Out in the open, she blinked a few times and brushed wayward hair from her face.

Something in the Water / Lisa Knight

"Okay, talk away."

Sarah's eyes narrowed as she seemed to ponder what to say first. "Tell me about your scrying abilities."

"My what?"

"Your scrying abilities. I know you see visions in water."

"Huh? What are you… Wait, what?"

The impatient glare on Sarah's face made Jill feel like one of her own students about to get into deep trouble. But unexpectedly the scowl softened, as though she suddenly understood things a little more clearly. "Jill, do you have any idea what you are?"

Jill shook her head, not comprehending the morning's events at all.

"You *do* see things in water, right?"

Suddenly it was hard to catch her breath. It had been well over twenty years since she'd told anyone about the things she could see, and that had ended with two black eyes and a near concussion. She considered the woman before her, taking in her unruly, curly hair and eyes as blue as her daughter's. Could she trust her? Should she trust anyone with information that had only ever caused her suffering?

Yet Sarah wasn't looking at her in any kind of negative way. In fact, if the lines on her forehead were anything to go by, she was actually concerned for her.

Something in the Water / Lisa Knight

"I, uh…"

Sarah nodded in encouragement.

Jill swallowed, trying to prevent the dryness from completely taking over her throat. "Yes, I see things in water. How did you know?"

Sarah smiled, pulling up a chair to sit at the desk. "I've had a few visions of you."

"*You* have?" Recalling her own recent images of Darcy, Jill's eyes widened in panic. "Oh my God, doing what?"

"Teaching children, having visions yourself. Of course, I don't see the same things that you do, every scry is different."

Jill sat up in her chair. "So you're telling me that I'm not the only weirdo in the world that this happens to, and there's an actual name for this, this…thing?"

"Of course. We're scries, Jill. We see images from the future that will, in some way, have an impact on our lives. For some people it happens through a crystal ball, but for others, it's pools of water. Didn't your mother explain any of this to you?"

"My mother?" She pushed her chair away from the desk and stood up, taking a few steps while trying to process what was being said. "My mother died when I was very young. But what does this have to do with her?"

Sarah sat back, crossing one leg elegantly over the other. "Well, as far as I know, this trait is passed from mother to daughter."

Jill began to pace in earnest, crossing from one side of the room to the other in front of the large chalkboard. "So my mother was a…a scry?"

"Most likely, yes. How did she die?"

She stopped abruptly, giving Sarah a blank stare. "She was murdered, by my father."

Sarah's hair flew about as she shook her head. "How dreadful. I'm so sorry for you. Some men find it too hard to deal with."

Jill's mouth dropped open. "You think he killed her because of *that*?"

"Well, there's no way to know for sure, but it's a strong possibility. In my experience, men are put off by things they don't understand."

"Are you talking about Darcy?" She could still feel the heat of their connection this morning and couldn't imagine him ever rough handling a woman.

Sarah's head fell back as she laughed. "Not in the way you're thinking. No. He's not the violent type. But he does struggle a little with Caitlyn and my 'funny business' as he calls it."

"Is that why you got divorced?" It was an entirely inappropriate question, but by this point Jill didn't care.

Something in the Water / Lisa Knight

"Among other things. How are you two doing, by the way?"

Heat crept into Jill's cheeks. "So you know about us?"

Sarah's smile became a mischievous grin. "Know about you? Who do you think orchestrated the whole thing?"

Oh no. There it was—just as she'd seen it this morning in the water—the wink.

Chapter 4

Jill knocked on Darcy's front door that evening with a knot in her stomach and a head full of mixed emotions. The bombshell from Sarah had only strengthened her resolve to end things, yet the idea of not seeing him anymore left her with an emptiness she was struggling to comprehend.

He opened the door with a smile that took her breath away. His feet were bare, and he wore jeans with a black apron over his t-shirt stating *Dad's an awesome chef!* He was relaxed and happy, and her motivation to cut things off wavered considerably.

"Come on in," he offered, stretching his arm back in toward the house like they were on a game show.

Jill swallowed, wishing her mouth didn't feel like a sandpit, and stepped inside. Instantly, the most delicious aroma of frying onions and garlic surrounded her, and she turned to Darcy with wide eyes. "Yum, what's cooking?"

He led her into the kitchen, where the bench was scattered with bowls and utensils. Steam rose from a saucepan containing the onions and garlic, and Darcy gave it a stir. "We're having ravioli. I thought we could make it together."

She tried to hide her horror. "That's brave of you. I'm not

much of a cook."

He turned the heat off and went to the fridge, pulling out a ball of dough wrapped in plastic. "It's easy. I'll show you."

Holding her gaze, he proceeded to sprinkle flour over a plastic board sitting on the bench. Their lack of conversation should have felt awkward, but it was surprisingly comfortable, allowing her time to watch his biceps flex with each kneading movement of the dough. It was one of the sexiest things she'd ever witnessed.

"Now we roll it flat."

He picked up a wooden rolling pin, handing it to her with a lazy smile. Jill stepped into place at the bench and Darcy stood behind, bringing his arms around her to assist. He ran the tip of his nose along her neck and Jill inhaled sharply as tingles of desire scattered to every part of her body.

His hands covered hers, guiding the rolling pin over the dough while he planted kisses under her jaw and up to her ear. She let her head fall back against his shoulder and moaned softly as Darcy's flour-coated hands left hers, moving to her breasts where he cupped her gently and ran a finger over her hardened nipples.

Abandoning the dinner, she spun around to face him and his mouth instantly covered hers, hot and wanting. She ran her tongue over his, pulling him harder against her, smiling at the moan that sounded from his throat as their kiss deepened.

The level of desire she felt for Darcy was hard for Jill to fathom. Every ounce of her burned with a hunger she hadn't experienced before, and it was overwhelming. With her butt pressed against the stone bench, she tilted her head to the side, giving him room to kiss her neck and further down, in between her breasts as he unbuttoned her shirt.

She ran her hands through his thick, wavy hair and groaned in pleasure as he bit her nipple through the fabric of her bra. In a sensual haze, she glanced over the contents on the cluttered bench, her gaze landing on a bowl of water, where an image of Darcy stared back at her. It was very sobering.

"You're crying."

Darcy kissed his way upward over her neck until his face was level with hers. There was a hint of amusement in his eyes. "No, I'm not."

Jill gasped, covering her mouth with her hand as she leaned away from him.

Darcy's smirk dropped, replaced with a confused squint. "What's wrong?"

Her mind raced, desperately trying to understand. She'd thought he would be the one to hurt her, that was why she had to end this between them, whatever *this* was. But seeing him in the water, crying, it was clear that she was the one who was going to hurt him once the truth came out.

She struggled to find the right words as her vision became blurry with tears. "Darcy, I…"

He gently stroked her cheeks with his thumbs, brushing away the tears that fell. "Jill, honey, what is it?"

The affection in his voice only made her cry harder, and she let herself succumb to his tight embrace, sobbing into his apron-covered chest as he rubbed his palm in tender circles over her back.

When the tears finally stopped, Jill remained in his hold, knowing it would be for the last time. "Darcy…there are things you should know. Three things to be exact."

"Okay." His arms remained firmly around her.

She took a shaky breath, squeezing her eyes tightly shut to hide from her own embarrassment. "I've never had a proper relationship before. Not that I'm saying that's what this is, but…" She swallowed back the lump in her throat. "I feel things for you that I haven't…that I don't know what to do with. Anyway, it doesn't even matter because you're going to hate what I tell you next."

Darcy's grip around her lessened, but he kept his arms in place as he brought his face to meet hers. "There's so many things I want to ask about what you just said, but I'll wait until you've finished. What's the second thing?"

"Um, well, I had an interesting conversation with your ex-wife today."

"Oh Christ." It was a soft mutter, complete with eye roll, and this time he dropped his hold around her, taking a step back. "I can only imagine what she had to say. Did you tell her about us?"

"She already knew."

His lips flattened into a straight line, and he suddenly found the floor very interesting. "Right."

Jill inhaled slowly, not wanting to sound as nervous as she felt. "She said she gave you something to 'help us along.' Do you remember last week at school when you got dizzy?"

Darcy nodded, still focused on the ground.

"She'd made you a cup of tea before you brought Caitlyn to class?"

This time he looked up. "Yeah, she'd called me that morning, all distressed, and asked me to help with Caitlyn, who was being a little…five-year-old." He cocked his head. "She put something in my tea?"

Jill bit her top lip, uncertain how he was going to react. But he surprised her, laughing as he shook his head from side to side.

"I half-suspected. Sarah and her damn concoctions. It's not the first time she's done it to me, and even if I did believe in that mumbo jumbo…" His nose scrunched as he searched for the next words. "Is it really that bad? I mean, if that's what brought us together, maybe I should even thank her." He obviously registered the shock on her face and, with a grimace, continued. "Look, Jill, I know this must seem bizarre to you, but Sarah is…an unusual person. Please don't let her come between us."

Her shock was actually over how well he was taking the news. But she was curious about what he thought of Sarah's abilities. "In what way is she unusual?"

He held her gaze quizzically for a moment before looking at the ground again, running a hand nervously through his hair. "She, uh, has certain skills. Oh fuck it, you're going to think I'm crazy but…she has visions of the future. They come to her as pictures in pools of water. Caitlyn seemingly shares this gift as well." With a sigh of exasperation, he began to pace the kitchen floor.

Jill remained standing against the bench as Darcy marched out his frustration in front of her. She knew if she didn't tell him now there'd never be another chance, but it didn't stop her stomach from twisting anxiously. "The thing is…I see images in water too."

He stopped mid-step, keeping his back to her. She held her breath and waited, counting silently in her head. She'd reached thirty-one before Darcy slowly began to turn, and even from six feet away she could see the disbelief in his eyes.

Something in the Water / Lisa Knight

"You?" His voice cracked.

She hated hurting him, but thought he deserved to know the truth. "I've spent my whole life thinking I was some kind of a freak. It was actually Sarah who told me that my ability is a real thing. It even has a proper name! She explained so many things...and I've never had anyone do that before. As weird as this all is, I'm just so relieved I'm not the only one." Tears welled again and she let them fall, dripping down her cheeks onto her unbuttoned blouse.

"Have you had visions of me?" It was a simple enough question, but the words were full of angst.

Jill wished she could lie, but the way her cheeks were burning gave him his answer without her having to even speak.

"What was I doing?" He shoved his hands into the pockets of his jeans, taking a step forward to lessen the distance between them.

"Darcy, you don't—"

"What was I doing, Jill?"

"I really don't want to tell you."

He was standing close enough now for her to see the pulse beating steadily in his neck. His eyes were so dark, yet they held a hint of amusement, which surprised her. She blushed again, certain he must know her visions were somehow related to sex. Darcy glanced over her shoulder to the kitchen bench, still scattered with the makings of dinner. He reached for an empty drinking glass, flicked on the tap, and filled it with water, taking a big mouthful before bringing it between them.

"What do you see now?"

She stared at him incredulously, eyes narrowed, refusing to look down.

Darcy laughed. "It's okay. Go on, tell me."

She was mad that he was making light of the situation. Why wasn't he shouting and throwing things around the room in anger? He waved the glass under her nose and she gave into temptation, letting her eyes glimpse the water. Immediately she wished she hadn't. Heat rose up her neck and into her cheeks as well as all areas south of her belly button. Hiding out in the freezer became a tempting option.

"What was it?" Darcy's voice was all tease.

She shook her head, clamping her mouth tightly shut.

He laughed again, gently placing the glass back on the bench. "Hmm, let me see. Was it this?"

His index finger traced her lips, luring them out of hiding before he pressed his own against them. The tenderness of his kiss was astonishing. Jill closed her eyes, instinctively curling her body into his. She felt like they were crossing some kind of barrier, moving into new territory, and was all too aware that this was going to make it harder to end things. But then again, maybe she didn't want to end things.

Darcy's lips left hers and pressed softly onto her forehead. "Was that it?"

Her hands rubbed over his biceps, and with a smirk she dropped her head against his chest. "No."

"Hmm, maybe this then?" He kissed her neck, sending shivers of delight all the way to her core. Unhooking her bra, he slipped the straps over her shoulders, carefully removing it, along with her already unbuttoned blouse. He dipped his head and took her taut nipple in his mouth, flicking his tongue over it.

Jill moaned and let her head fall back as he took her other breast in his hand, working his thumb in unison with his tongue. Just as her legs reached total jelly consistency and she was at the point of near collapse, he stopped.

"That was it, wasn't it?" His head cocked to one side and his eyes were curious despite his confident smirk.

She couldn't help but laugh, shaking her head. "Nope."

Darcy closed his eyes and rubbed his fingers over his temples as though trying to loosen his brain in order to figure it out. Grinning, he opened them again, raising his eyebrows knowingly. His playfulness was a quality Jill hadn't expected, having been so serious the first time they'd met. It was another thing that simply made her like him more, and if she was totally honest with herself, she had to admit that she was falling for him.

It was during this thought that Darcy dropped to his knees and ducked his head under her long, flowing skirt, skimming his lips upward along her inner thigh. Jill gasped, losing control of any ability to think at all, and cried out as he tore apart yet another pair of her underwear. His mouth explored her, gently at first, and she moaned as his tongue traced every contour before penetrating her body in the most exquisite way.

She was dangerously close to falling over, writhing at his relentless affection, and had to support her weight on the bench with her elbows. Darcy ran his hand behind her right knee, lifting her leg to rest over his shoulder. The movement left her legs wider apart and cries flew from her mouth uncontrollably as she came hard and fast, almost knocking them both to the ground.

Without hesitating, Darcy scooped her up in his arms, carrying her as though she weighed no more than a child, and she snuggled against his chest, still panting and shaking from the intense orgasm. He moved through the kitchen and into his bedroom, removing her skirt as he lowered her onto the bed. The cool fabric of the duvet hit her naked back, quickly followed by the heat of Darcy as he hovered over her.

"That was it, wasn't it?"

It was more of a statement than a question, and Jill grinned, reaching to untie his apron. "Part of it. How about I show you the rest?"

She tugged the apron and then his t-shirt over his head before sliding off his jeans. Darcy's mouth locked onto hers, and she molded her hands over the smooth, firm mounds of his behind, arching her hips to meet his. She smiled at the moan that vibrated deep within his throat, and then proceeded to demonstrate *exactly* what she'd seen in the water.

It was close to an hour later before either of them spoke. Jill lay on her back in Darcy's bed, catching her breath and waiting for the air to cool her sweaty, naked skin. Darcy too was on his back, with one arm protectively around her shoulder, and she nestled in against him, happier than she'd felt in a very long time.

He kissed the top of her head. "Can I ask you something?"

"Sure."

"How is it that you've never had a relationship before?"

Jill bit her bottom lip, trying to come up with the right words. "Um, well…I have a little issue with trust."

Darcy shifted to the side so he was facing her, yet she remained on her back, horrified to feel tears so threateningly close.

"I had a shit childhood." She shrugged at the simple explanation, sitting up abruptly and wiping her wet cheeks. It had been years since she'd cried about her past, damn it.

He joined her sitting up, reaching for a blanket that had fallen off the edge of the bed and wrapped it around her shoulders. Jill smiled gratefully, pulling the multi-colored crochet tightly against herself.

"Do you want to talk about it?"

She looked into his wide, brown eyes, offering so much affection and support, and in that split second made the decision to tell him everything. There was nothing left out, from memories of her father's rage and her parents' terrible deaths, to the different foster homes and the many times she'd been abused.

"It wasn't all bad," she offered, concerned about the menacing scowl developing on Darcy's face. "There were some good people in the mix."

He brushed strands of hair away from her eyes. "I just hate the thought of you being mistreated. You must have been so frightened and lonely."

She nodded. "Yeah, I was, but I reached a point in my life when I decided that I wasn't going to be held back by all of that. I talked to a counselor a few times, but it really was just a choice I made to let go of it. I suppose the one issue that I still struggle with though is…men."

Darcy took hold of her hands, resting them on the bed between them. "You don't have to be alone anymore. We can work through this together. Do you think you want to try, with me?"

She stared at their joined hands, his so massive in contrast to hers. It would be all too easy for him to raise them to her head and deliver a hard blow. Yet as he rubbed his thumbs gently over her fingers she couldn't deny how safe and protected she felt. It was a foreign sensation. One that was going to take some getting used to.

"I'll need you to be patient, but yes, I want to try."

He brought her palm to his lips and kissed it softly. "I'm not sure what the future holds, although you do, so we're one step ahead there. But I can promise you this—I will never, ever hurt you in that way. I give you my word." He raised his right hand, holding up the three middle fingers. "Scout's honor."

Jill laughed. "You were a Boy Scout?"

"I still have the badges to prove it!"

His smile was so uplifting. She trailed her finger over his handsome cheek. "Darcy?"

He waited, watching her curiously.

"Do you really want to get involved with another scryer? I mean...it didn't exactly end well for you last time."

His eyes grew thoughtful. "It wasn't the 'seeing the future' part that I had an issue with. More that Sarah took her visions as gospel. You see, I think the future is *not* certain, and we can change our behavior or thoughts to make things happen differently. She didn't see it that way, and that's what we argued about."

"I feel like such a novice with this whole scrying thing. I hope you don't mind if I talk to Sarah more about it?"

Darcy kissed the top of her head. "Of course I don't mind. I can't even imagine what it must've been like for you growing up not understanding your gift. I'm so grateful that Caitlyn has her mom for that."

Jill's stomach let out a mighty growl, and she laughed. "I'm starving!"

"Me too, although I think the pasta dough will be rock hard by now. Fancy anything else?"

"Um…"

"Here, I know what to do." He stretched out his body, reaching for a glass of water on the shelf next to the bed. After taking a sip, he handed the glass to Jill. "What do you see?"

She eyed him curiously. "That's twice now that you've drunk from the water. Why do you do that?"

Darcy smiled. "It seems I know a lot more about scries than you do. If someone drinks from the water before you look into it, you'll have a vision about them."

"Really?"

He nodded. "Go ahead. Hopefully it will show what we're

going to eat for dinner."

She looked into the half-full glass and laughed at the image she viewed, so happy that she could finally enjoy and accept her gift for what it was, with this man who was going to be by her side. She handed the glass back to him with a shrug. "I guess it's not time to eat yet."

His eyes widened and he managed to put the water on the floor only seconds before she pushed him onto his back and climbed on top of him. Darcy slid the blanket off her shoulders and hurled it across the room, running his hands over her bare behind.

"You know, the future is not set in stone," he said. "We *do* have the choice to change it if you want to."

Jill smiled and pressed her lips against his. "Most definitely. But right now, let's choose to accept what I saw…just a little something in the water."

About Lisa Knight

I love writing all kinds of stories but romance is definitely my favorite. Curling up with my laptop on a cold winter's day is my idea of writing heaven, and if there's coffee and chocolate close by that's even better.

I am always on the lookout for story and character ideas and am inspired by everyday things like people doing their grocery shopping, having morning tea at the local café, or the beautiful 'welcome back' hugs and kisses at the arrivals gate at the airport. Makes me cry just thinking about it!

I live in Canberra with my husband, and whenever I can, I snatch time to write between being a mum to our three boys and my job as a social worker.

Lisa's Website:
www.facebook.com/lisaknightauthor

Reader eMail:
lisaknightauthor@gmail.com

Indigo Stars

by Stephanie Beck

Indigo's ability to create light with her mind was always a fun parlor trick, but since her cancer diagnosis, the parlor has closed for business. On the brink of major health failure, she can't help but wonder when her good luck ran out.

Dr. Lee Russell believes in healing by any means necessary. He uses his psychic powers in special cases when modern medicine just can't help. Indigo's case is special. She's like him, yet she wastes her gift creating stars. He heals her, but doesn't expect much, not until he gets sick himself and only Indy's touch can ease his pain. He's never seen himself as anything more than a healer, but to save his own life, Lee will have to mentor Indigo to reach beyond the stars and use her gift in ways she never imagined.

Chapter 1

Lights danced on the ceiling like tiny fairies listening to heavy metal. Sharp motions, not gentle or sweet. They rocked.

Indy smiled at the giggles coming from the next room. The kids loved when she attuned the lights to rocking hair bands. Who knew kids these days enjoyed hard-core metal?

Squeaky nurse shoes put an end to the fun. Indy cut the light and turned to her side as pain exploded through her abdomen.

The red button on her bed had become her challenge point. How long could she go between pushing the demon button that would call in the needle nurse? She couldn't keep an IV line in without major problems, and the pain patches only made her break out, so her pain management came in pills. Or, in extreme cases—and the one building in her gut definitely had the symptoms—a needle. She swore and slammed her hand on the button.

A muffled response came immediately. "Be right there, Miss Bravo."

Indy curled tighter into her ball, hoping the nurse grabbed a heating pad. Six months earlier Indy had been in Rio. She'd drank and partied until she'd tossed her cookies. But then she hadn't been able to stop throwing up. The constant nausea forced her to the hospital when she returned to the States. After a few scans, she'd been admitted, and hadn't left.

Squeaky shoes, the ever-present sign of nurses, brought her out of her pity party. If she thought too much about the last six months, she'd cry, and that would give her a headache. Enough ached at the moment.

"Miss Bravo, what can I do for you?" a nurse asked. The voice wasn't familiar. Indy sighed and turned.

The older woman in pink scrubs could have been a dozen other nurses, but the keychain around her wrist said she could get Indy what she needed.

"I need pain meds and a heat pack, please." She hated how weak and young she sounded. Some thought her a child in the wrong ward, but at twenty-seven she was an adult. One in pain.

"I can do that. I've been briefed on your unique allergies and needs. Would dairy help the medication settle well?"

"Thanks for not offering me ice cream to help the medicine go down." Indy revised her opinion of the nurse. She might look ordinary, but she was good. "Cheddar?"

"I saw cheddar in our fridge. I like ice cream, but I can see how it would get old in this situation." The nurse made a note on the computer and closed it down. "I'll return. Doctor Russell will be in shortly."

Indy would have sat up to get a better look at the nurse, but the pain increased. "Doctor visit at this time of night?"

"He's recently back to the States and making rounds. I'm his nurse. Be right back."

"Wait." Indy fought nausea. "What's your name?"

"Amanda. I'll return soon."

More squeaks, and then silence. Not enough silence happened in the oncology ward. Kids cried, adults cried, nurses chatted, doctors fussed and checked scans. Always something.

A little someone cried in the room across the hall. With the old school windows above the door, Indy could easily reflect some light through it and into the little one's room. She swallowed the bile rising and blinked at the door. As it had since she was a baby, light burst free. Instead of heavy metal this time, Indy imagined a lullaby.

Indy changed the sparks of light into stars, sweet little five-pointed friends to gently dance. The crying eased, replaced by quiet whimpers, and finally hiccupped breathing. For the moment she focused on the light, and she didn't remember the pain, but it waited for her. The squeaky shoes returned, and Indy cut the light.

She bit her lip to stop the moan. Nurse Amanda stepped in with her cart. "I apologize for the delay. We have admitting privileges, but they've changed a few systems. Here is your heat pack."

Nurse Amanda pried Indy's arms from her body and tucked in the extra warm pad. Indy wanted to burrow inside, anything to dull the pain.

"Easy, honey." Amanda worked rapidly and soon Indy swallowed pills. "Those will work quickly, but this will be faster."

A heartbeat later, Nurse Amanda put a bandage over where she'd inserted a needle and pain medication so quickly Indy barely felt it.

"If there were medals for nursing, you would win them all." Indy's words slurred, the instant influx in medication taking away some of her control along with most of the pain.

"Such a kind thing to say." Amanda fluffed her pillow and brought warm blankets from somewhere, probably heaven. "The doctor will be in soon, and we'll find a way to control this pain better. And then we'll get you healed."

She snorted. "Healed? I've been here six months and the cancer only grows. It's eating me. That's why I hurt so much—my body is eating itself."

Amanda brushed her hand through Indy's hair. When was the last time someone touched her for non-medical reasons? "Poor dear. I'm calling the masseuse right now. You've had a bath recently?"

"Showered yesterday."

"You need a bath." The nurse bustled to the bathroom and the sound of rushing water followed. "I'm adding salts and oils. Any other allergies?"

"Not to salts or oil." Indy sat up in bed, keeping the heating pad in place. "I can have a bath?"

"Of course. I'll help you. You'll soak until the masseuse comes, and then be ready for the doctor."

"The doctor or a hot date, one or the other." Indy swung her legs to the side of the bed, but didn't dare stand. Being stubborn got one a bruised ass and stitches.

The nurse was a picture of efficiency, yet she didn't seem rushed. When Amanda put her arm around her, Indy knew she'd be fine. Amanda helped her into the bath, and good to her word, salts and oils bubbled up. Tears burned Indy's eyes.

"Good, right?" Amanda coiled a towel and tucked it behind Indy's neck. "I'm grateful for medication, but the physical aspect can't be ignored. You'll feel so much better now, and be able to sleep. I'm going to fuss in your room if you don't mind. I won't be leaving you out of my sight in case you get drowsy."

Was that an accent? Indy closed her eyes and did as the nurse said, relaxing deeply into the water until her chin touched.

"Being short has its perks," Amanda said from the sink.

"Five feet two inches makes for trouble with cabinets, but bath time is always good. You're so special, Amanda."

"You are special, Indigo. You may have forgotten, but I know it. I'm going to purify your room. No falling asleep."

Purify? That didn't sound like hospital talk, but Indy would let Amanda do whatever she wanted. Did she like stars? Indy cracked an eyelid and projected stars onto the ceiling of the hospital room.

"Aren't those lovely. That doesn't tire you?" Amanda called.

"Nope." What had been in the shot? In the bath water? She didn't show her gift for strangers, let alone adult ones. "Feels good, actually."

"Excellent, then keep it up. Is that the extent of your gift?"

"Pretty much." Indy blinked, letting go of the illusion. "Pretty little."

"Didn't seem small to the kiddos in the next room. You rest. The masseuse will be here in ten minutes and the doctor will follow."

"Who is this doctor? Are you sure you're not washing me up and then tenderizing me for the Big Bad Wolf?" Indy snorted, tickled with herself. "What a picture."

"Those meds sure do work well, don't they?"

"Yep. Like a glove. No. Like a charm."

Her mind fuzzed, not completely to sleep, but to a different level of awake. Her ears buzzed, the dull tone so close to a drone she wanted to escape it, but that would have taken too much effort. Whatever Amanda was doing made no noise. She could have been going through all her stuff, playing her video games, chewing her gum. Indy didn't care.

"Hey, sunshine. Let's get you out of the bath before you're fully pruney. I have Bridget with me to help get you into bed."

She wrinkled her nose. "Nurse Bridget? Seriously?"

"Nope, Bridget the masseuse," a friendly voice emerged. "I've met Nurse Bridget, and I'm glad to not be her. I won't tell her either, she seems a little spiteful."

"A little? Really?" Her legs were rubber, hot rubber after the bath, so Amanda and Bridget did most of the work.

Indy laid face down on her bed, but it didn't smell like her bed. "What did you do to my bed?"

"Fresh sheets, good ones, washed in lavender," Amanda said. Someone patted a warm towel over Indy's body. "Isn't that nice? Now, a massage. Bridget, I trust you'll do a good job?"

"Of course, Nurse Amanda. I'll treat her like my own sister."

Indy wanted to be awake, but the moment Bridget's hands started working, she was out.

* * * *

Amanda dropped a file in front of him. Lee rubbed his eyes. He'd been back in the States for three hours when his nurse called him to the hospital. It was what they always did, but after two months in South America, exhaustion had caught him for the first time in his life.

"I have three candidates, two non-urgent, but one other." Amanda entered information on the computer. "Room six-twelve needs immediate attention."

He checked the chart. "Adult? Really? Amanda, you know I want to help—"

"You'll help this one. She's like you. Well, kind of."

He rubbed his forehead, a migraine building. Finding a nurse who understood his manner of healing had been an undertaking, but when Amanda entered his tiny office ten years ago, she'd taken charge. When they'd seen their first patient, a young girl with a horrific tumor, Amanda had noticed something wrong from the start. He had too, of course, but he'd always been able to see sickness in people. To heal them, though, required more from the patient.

The first test set had told him what he needed, and he'd followed enough protocol for Amanda to be comfortable. The mother had cried, but the little girl had looked to him and Amanda with confidence. He'd known he could heal her, and with Amanda at his side, he had. His psychic gift didn't do much for him, but it had given the little girl a second shot at life.

He'd stopped keeping track of all the names, too many to

count, and while in the States, Nurse Amanda was at his side. He trusted her more than he trusted himself sometimes.

"The poor thing is in so much pain. I called in a masseuse and they should be finishing up. You're going to like Indy, she's a character."

"Indy?" The name rang a bell.

"Yes. Indigo Bravo. What an interesting name, and she's an interesting young woman. I want her well so we can have coffee sometime. I don't meet many people I want to be around."

Lee tucked the file under his arm and headed for the room. The deeper into the children's ward he walked, the more he was pulled toward them. Children could be healed, because they believed they would be well. When he could get into a mind, he could use his gifts to heal the body. He didn't know how, just knew it worked. Some kids would do fine with traditional treatments, so he was careful not to do too much. If medical experts thought they didn't need to research any longer, they would stop. So, he couldn't do it all, but in his way he hoped he made the world better, at least for some.

A young woman with blonde hair hanging down her back crept out of the room. She carried a large brown bag and looked up to him with wonder in her eyes. He didn't need a psychic gift to see she'd been touched.

"You're going to see Indy?" she asked.

"Yes. She's well?"

"She's sleeping." The young woman blinked. "I'm sure she'll be happy to see you. Please let Amanda know I'm available any time."

"Thank you."

The woman hurried away, but glanced back several times before leaving the ward. What had she noticed about Indy? He strode in, the darkened room dim and calm—signs of Amanda.

"Not squeaky shoes," the tiny lump on the bed said. "Must be a doctor. What is the difference, do you suppose?"

"Dress shoes. When I worked in the ER, I squeaked like a nurse, but no longer have that distinction. I'm Doctor Lee Russell. Tell me about your last six months." He pulled up her computer file with treatment log.

"Well, I drank too much in Brazil and started tossing my cookies and couldn't stop. Since being admitted, I've had radiation and chemo for stomach cancer. It's spreading at a rate so alarming, my doctor stopped giving me numbers."

"I don't blame him." Lee winced at the rapid growth pattern before him. "Damn. How are you feeling?"

"Thanks to Amanda, I'm as close to okay as I've been since I got sick, but even after everything, including the morphine, I'm at about a four right now."

"By four, I'm sure you mean a seven on a normal person's

scale." Lee pulled the stool to the side of the bed. "Let's take a listen."

"Whoa, you're huge. Or are you a reasonable size, and you just seem big because I'm small?" Indy adjusted on the bed, her generic hospital gown not Amanda's style, but then, Amanda usually dealt with kids. "I know you."

He tucked his stethoscope prongs in his ears and pressed the scope to her belly through the gown. "I'm six foot four—perfectly reasonable. Where do you think you know me from?"

He didn't need the device to see, but it gave an action to his method. The scans he'd seen only represented part of the picture. The strands of cancer and tumors intertwined with Indy's muscles and veins, explaining the pain. Every breath strained the already hurt muscles, and every heartbeat inflamed the veins. Cutting it out meant cutting everything.

"Yeah. You were in Panama at the thing. You guys are so tall."

"Panama?" He looked away from her stomach and straight at her face. "You."

She grinned. "Surprise! We were never properly introduced at the Headcase Convention. I'm Indigo Bravo."

"You stole my cab." He looped his stethoscope around his neck, fishing for more memories of the young woman before him. "And if my memory is correct, you stole a few wallets and maybe an identity?"

She rolled her eyes. "Always with the exaggerations. I tried to share your cab. But you were grumpy and said no despite there being plenty of room, so yeah, I took your cab. I didn't steal anything from any of the attendees."

He adjusted the light over her bed, illuminating the room to the lowest setting to give his eyes a break from the darkness. "So what did you steal? Rumors starts somewhere."

She shrugged. "I found a box of money next to the hotel. I gave it to the police. Turns out it was marked by some mobster guy they were trying to catch, and they gave me half as a reward. See? No mega criminal stuff for me. Nope."

"But you walked away from Panama with mobster money?"

"Do you have any idea how much treatment costs?" She waved her hand, tiny and with the tips in chipped purple. "Anything I've taken has gone into this, and into the treatments. If this keeps up, I'm going to have to start selling my stuff."

He lowered her bed so that it was flat. "The good news is you shouldn't have to hawk your stuff. I can heal you, and you should be up and out of here within a week."

"Really?" She sat straight up. Lee reached out and caught her before she collapsed. Amanda was right about Indigo's pain.

"Yes, really, but it's not going to be without some trade-offs. I'll be honest, you have the most invasive, aggressive cancer I've ever seen. I can get rid of it, but I'm not sure how your body will react."

She nodded, her caramel-colored cheeks nearly white. "Will Nurse Amanda be able to stay? I like her."

"I like her too, and I think she'd have my head if I tried to reassign her."

"Is this your gift?" she whispered.

"Yep." He didn't bother locking the door. A locked door inspired more curiosity than one half-closed. He did, however, pull the privacy curtain.

"Does it hurt you?"

"No, not at all." He rolled his shoulders. "I'm like a laser beam. I see inside you and break up the tumor or cancer, but your body has to be strong enough to force the contaminants out. There's also an element of belief...you have to believe this can happen. And no, I don't understand why."

"A laser." She closed her eyes, her lips pulled so tightly premature lines etched into her skin. "I like it. I make light."

He rested his hands over her belly. The contact helped him focus and gave his patients a sense of something happening. "Lights, huh? I'd like a show when you're better."

He closed his eyes and pictured what he'd seen before. Gobs of cancerous cells, crowding and suffocating her stomach and spine. He detangled them from her spine, leaving them adrift. White blood cells attacked the mass in ways they hadn't been able to before. He continued, systematically releasing the intruders. Indy's body did the rest, containing and irradiating the tumors.

Indy whimpered, but he kept on. It hurt, it had to. That doctors had kept her alive so long was a testament of how far medicine had come in only fifteen years. He tackled a mass nearest her stomach. This time she gasped and grabbed his hand.

His powers didn't emerge from his hands, but her connection sparked...something. The cancer he'd been breaking up withered and died. The white cells swarmed, and the mass disappeared.

"That hurts," she gasped. "So bad."

"I bet." He allowed her to continue gripping his hand and focused on a smaller mass near her liver. He pried it from the organ, but didn't stop there. The focus changed the mass into a prune, and the blood cells got rid of it. Again. "This is amazing," he muttered, continuing until all the cancerous cells had been destroyed.

Would it be the same for someone else? Had his powers changed, or was it Indy?

"I'm going to call Amanda in now and have her take care of you."

"Don't leave me." Her grip turned iron, and for the first

time since he started, she opened her eyes. "Explain what you did."

Lee relaxed in his chair. "I looked inside your body and pried the cancer cells from the healthy ones. Once they were no longer part of your body, your white cells recognized them as invaders and attacked. That might sound simplistic, but it's the best way to explain. You're feeling rotten, because you're currently feverous and rapidly becoming dehydrated. Something else happened though. Are you a healer?"

She shook her head. "Not at all. I make light."

Her gaze flew to the ceiling. Snowflakes danced on the white tiles. Swirling in circles, they worked in harmony to create a ballet unlike anything he'd ever seen. His stress, exhaustion, everything melted as he watched the lights.

He forced his eyes closed and turned away from the bed. In an instant the fatigue and jet lag returned, full force. It was an illusion.

"Just lights, huh?" he asked, the icy coldness of his voice harsher than he'd anticipated.

"Yeah, why? Didn't you like them?" Innocence, and yet, she had to know.

"I did. Is trickery how you lulled the police in Panama into giving you money?" Psychic powers led to more headcases than happy endings. Indigo Bravo was another abuser of power. "I'll send Amanda in, and don't try that shit on her."

"What shit?" Indy sat up. "Are you saying my lights did something to you? Because if my lights did something to people I'd have finagled a better room. My gift is practically worthless, and easily replicated with most flashlights."

"Yeah, right." He turned and headed for the door.

"Yeah, I'm right." She threw something, but it landed to his left. He didn't look, just kept striding toward the door. "Thank you for curing me, even if you were an ass about it."

Lee closed the door behind him and leaned against it. For a second there, he'd felt back to the normal self he barely remembered. But it had been a lie. An illusion put on by a two-bit thief. He'd have to watch out for her.

Chapter 2

The lights shivered on the ceiling, no dancing for them, no, they'd come from nowhere and Indy couldn't control them. Just like Amanda couldn't control the pain coursing through Indy's body. The second Doctor Russell—the ass—left the room, her pain skyrocketed, and despite Amanda's tender care, it wasn't easing.

"The lights are back." Amanda's voice brightened, but when she looked up, she froze. "Those aren't like the others."

Indy wanted to answer, but her jaw chattered too violently. Her greatest fear had come true. She didn't have control, and couldn't grasp the reins.

"I'm going to call Doctor Russell." Amanda ran from the room, all signs of calm gone.

Indy focused on her lights, but for the first time in her life, she couldn't control them. They shivered in the corners, as if they too were afraid. Tears filled her eyes. Her only friends were gone.

"What's going on?" Doctor Russell sat beside her. If he'd been wearing nurse shoes, there was no way he could have snuck up on her. "I have two more patients I can heal tonight, but I can't if I'm babysitting a con-artist."

One by one, tears rolled down her cheeks, burning paths down her skin. She never cried, hated it. And she never cried in front of her enemies. Not that Doctor Russell was a nemesis, but he might be.

"The lights are gone." She lifted her hand, the appendage shaking without her permission. "See?"

Silence met her words. With him in the room, though, some of her pain eased. It was probably part of his power. Power he should be using to heal someone, not babysit her, as he'd said.

"You can go," she whispered, the last of her strength dwindling. "I'm not dying or anything."

"Yeah, you are." He took her hand and eased it back to the bed. "You don't see it, but I do. Your heart has weakened. What's bothering you?"

"My lights are gone." She pointed with her other hand. "They're all I have left."

"They're not gone." He took her second hand and tucked it with the other. "Obviously, as a doctor, my sight is better than yours, so I can see your lights. They are hiding though. What has you nervous?"

"I know I'm healed, but my body feels wrong. I don't know what's going on."

"I don't know either, but the cancer is gone. It happened differently than my other patients. I wonder if the rapid erosion is causing an adverse effect. I'll bet your body is in shock. Be right back."

"No." True panic threatened to choke her. "Don't leave again."

"Okay." He pressed the red button on her bed. "That'll get Amanda. You're in shock. We don't usually see reactions so severe, I didn't anticipate it. I'm not surprised Amanda missed it. Poor kid."

"Not a kid. I'm nearly thirty. You headcases are so damn big, it's like walking in a forest of redwoods."

He smiled. "I've noticed even the women are tall. Do your parents have gifts?"

"Not the mental kind, but they are the most generous people. They're in Ecuador."

"Vacation?"

"Deported. Well, not exactly. They returned home before getting the big D. They started off as students, fell in love, cut on classes, and worked illegally for almost twenty years."

"And not here to help?" He smiled at Amanda when she strode in. "Thanks for getting here so quickly. We need more warm blankets and dopamine when you get a chance."

"No can do on dopamine," Indigo said, almost sing-song. "Allergies. I hate to question your doctorness, but jeez."

"Thank goodness for nurses who read charts, right?"

Amanda hurried from the room and returned with the med cart. "But there are other things. She's in shock, isn't she? I've never seen it happen after your sessions."

* * * *

"Always a first for everything." His headache was gone again and damned if his mood hadn't changed. "Damn it. What are you doing?"

"Trying not to die. You?" Indigo kicked in bed and clenched her stomach. The hiding lights blinked out. Even with them gone, his head remained clear.

"I've got the medication ready and more blankets. I don't like this. She seemed to really calm with touch last time. Should I have the masseuse return?"

Lee took the syringe and plunged it into Indy's arm. She whimpered, but didn't turn to him, or open her eyes. He wanted to be grumpy, wanted to blame her for making him not angry. Control was what got him through life with an unexpected gift. Who else had manipulated him over the years? Who could in the future?

"That'll help." He tossed the syringe on the tray Amanda held. "I'll stay with her. Go check the others to see if they're having similar reactions."

"Of course." Amanda hurried again, the squeak Indy mentioned marking her path.

Indigo moaned and rocked. Lee rubbed her arm, especially where the needle had pierced. No blood emerged from the tiny hole, but heat radiated there. People with mental gifts often had physical quirks. His body hated metal and polyester. They all had their issues.

"This sucks." Her words slurred, the medication doing its job. Her heart rate also decreased to a reasonable rate.

"But you'll feel better soon." His positivity was more hope than confidence. He'd never seen a patient react like her, and yet, he could only be positive. No traces of doubt in his mind...what was wrong with him? "You have some kind of effect on me. I don't like it."

"I can't do a darn thing about it, and no one has ever noticed a difference around me before. The lights calm people, but I tend to piss them off. Sarcastic. Smarter than they think I should be. Eccentric. Eidetic memory. I whistle out of tune. Basically an irritant."

He snorted. "I've never heard anyone be called an irritant."

"Oh, I believe people have called you one. Bedside manner totally sucks. The medicine is working. The pain is easing up, and my chest might not explode."

"I can take my irritating self to the other room now." He removed his hands, but immediately wanted to touch her again. His head didn't start pounding, but something in the shared touch soothed him.

"No, please don't. You stopped and the anxiety returned." She reached behind her, not facing him, offering a hand. "Please?"

He took her hand and settled on the rolling stool. He wouldn't be able to stay seated long, but he would until she slept.

* * * *

"Lee." The whispered voice wasn't enough to wake him, but the shaking on his shoulder did.

He opened his eyes, immediately awake, and stared at Amanda, who hovered above him. "What's going on?"

His nurse smiled, the gentle kindness in her eyes one of the reasons he'd hired her. "I'm waking you up before the other doctors start rounds."

"Rounds? But they weren't coming until morning." He sat up but stopped halfway, a warm, soft lump stalling his efforts. "What happened?"

"I checked on the others—they're all progressing normally—and when I returned, you'd crawled in bed beside Indigo. Her stats were normal, and you were impossible to wake." Amanda shifted Indigo in the bed, freeing him, but also...depriving him?

He stood and fixed his shirt, wrinkled now with blood spots. "She bled a few times last night from previous poke places," Amanda said. "I think it's another way she expelled the cells? We need to do a few tests and make careful study, if she'll let us."

"I agree." He should have been annoyed at falling asleep, something he'd never done at work, but as he'd found before, he couldn't be angry near Indigo. The resting woman's color had returned, a bit pinker in her cheeks. The change brought life back to her face—a petite, lovely face he hoped to see smiling soon. What would it take to get Indigo Bravo to smile for him?

"Doctor Russell, are you okay?" Amanda laid her hand on his arm. "You're really...well, odd."

"I'm okay." He rolled his shoulders. "You said you knew she was like me from the start. How?"

"I felt it. And I saw the lights coming from her room. Then meeting her...the allergies, the toughness—honestly, she reminds me of you."

"She's a petty thief and half my size," Lee protested.

"She's independent, internalizes pain, tries to help others even when it hurts, and can't tolerate a standing IV. That's all you." Amanda clicked into the computer. "I'll get the paperwork finished and stall the rounding doctors so you can tidy up."

He needed to shower and change, but he'd have to endure question-and-answer time with Indigo's doctors. The other patients in the hospital would go into remission on their own.

The ones he'd helped would have died without intervention. As easy-going as the hospital administrators were about granting him privileges, and as much as the other doctors liked when he 'consulted,' he still had to face the music with answers other than "I looked into their bodies and freed the cancer cells".

"Any chance Nurse Amanda has another shot for me?" Indigo asked from the bed, where she'd curled back into a ball, tight and shivering.

"Seriously? You were fine." He sat on the bed again and pressed his fingers to her pulse. "Your pulse is going nuts. What the hell?" Under his fingers her heartbeat eased again. "We've got some connection, don't we? Hell."

She swatted his fingers. "Really? You're the one cursing about it? You walk away from me and you're fine. I'm the one who feels like she's going to die. Go ahead and go. I will take the shot and be fine. You said so."

"Fine." He spun and strode out of the room. Amanda stood in the hall, conferring with other doctors. "I'm going home. I'll be back around noon. Miss Bravo requested you."

"Lee, wait." Doctor Anderson chased him down. "Amanda said we have three patients with no signs of tumors or cancer. How? What the hell do you do, and how can we replicate it?"

"You can't replicate it. I've been studied, and there's no way to do it. I can't heal everyone on the floor, it's a by-case thing." He stopped at the elevator and hit the button. "You know all of this. All of you do, but every time I'm here, you pull the same crap. *Why? How?* I don't know, and I can't explain. All I can say is, you now have time to take on more patients."

Anderson frowned as the elevator pinged, doors opening. "Are you all right? You look... Honestly, you look sick."

"I'm fine. Believe it or not, working twenty-four hours straight for weeks on end will get to anyone. Even me." He entered the empty elevator and hit the close button. His head pounded so hard his eardrums shook. The further he got from the hospital floor, the worse it became.

The elevator pinged at the second floor. Two more to go, and he'd be able to get in his car, take a few headache pills, and drive home. Sleeping in his own bed would be enough, then he'd return, check his patients, and make plans to travel to California where he'd do it all again.

"Doctor? Are you all right?" Strong hands, seriously strong ones, wrapped around his biceps.

Lee forced his eyes open, the sudden sensitivity to light making even a sliver of opening painful. "Yeah. I gotta get home."

The elevator stopped again, but Lee no longer supported himself. His brain blanked white. So much for going home.

Chapter 3

Indy scratched her pencil across the white drawing paper Nurse Amanda got for her. She couldn't draw worth crap, not even after dozens of lessons, but she still enjoyed it. If she had to stay by Doctor Russell's side while he worked through an episode, she could at least draw pictures of him with exaggerated body parts. So far, ears were her favorite. She lifted her page and compared it with his pale face. Yep. Huge ears made for a hysterical Lee Russell.

He moaned and winced, like the moan hurt his ears. If he'd had a true mental meltdown, it probably did hurt. She'd only heard about the events secondhand, but from what she understood, a person with mental gifts who overused them ran the risk of an aneurism. The doctors had scanned Lee's brain, but no results yet.

Amanda had dragged Indy out of her dim, quiet cave and took her to his side. As much as Indy didn't understand why, her presence seemed to ease Lee. Not that he woke up, but his stats weren't falling.

His eyes twitched.

"Hey, quit moving or you'll ruin my drawing." Despite the words, she set down her notepad, more relieved to see his eyes open than she cared to admit. "Feeling okay?"

"If you're here, I should feel better," he grumbled. "I did before."

"I'm basically pure sunshine and morphine combined." She pulled his blanket higher on his chest when he shivered. "Which you know is not true. I don't have healing powers. That's your thing, but I think you may have overworked yourself."

He rubbed his eyes, no IV lines in his way, because Nurse Amanda had jumped in. Indy wished Nurse Amanda had been her nurse from the start.

"Overworked, yes, but not unreasonably so. I don't know what the hell happened." He relaxed against his pillow. "But my headache is gone. It eased when I was near you last time too. Leave."

"Wow. You are such a dick." She got up, amazed she'd even tried after the way he treated her. "I came here because Amanda thought it might help. I was here for her. Not for you. Have a nice life."

She spun, but he grabbed her arm before she could march away. His strong grip from earlier was much more limited now, but it was enough to make her pause.

"I apologize. I'm not usually like this, and I'm not sure what's affecting me so strongly. I'm sorry I left you earlier. I'm sorry I blamed you for what's happening in me. Obviously, I'm sick, but I shouldn't have taken my frustration out on you." He pushed himself up to his elbows, but no further.

She recognized pain, had lived it for so long, and no matter how much she wanted to stomp out and give him a taste of his own medicine, she couldn't. She sat back down in the chair and shifted his grip to her hand. "Does it help when you hold my hand?"

He relaxed against the bed again. "Yes. How are you?"

"Sluggish." She pushed her chair closer without releasing his hand. "My gut hurts and I have headaches, but the pain is lessening."

"Does being near me help?"

She took mental inventory of her aches and pains. "Maybe."

"Good." He closed his eyes, a lock of brown hair falling over his forehead. Not his eyes. He didn't strike her as the kind of guy who let his hair get too long, but he should. He probably had a standing appointment every few weeks to keep his shiny locks in check. Did she really know anything about him though?

He was large and used his gift to heal kids, and though he'd taken cranky out on her, he'd also apologized. She sighed and rested her chin on the bedrail. If they needed each other for the time being, she wished she knew more about him, but it really didn't make much of a difference.

"Feeling any better?" she asked after a long stretch of

silence. "I'm surprised the nurses aren't in here bugging you."

"I'm sure Amanda is running interference. The side you're sitting on is much better than the other. This is ridiculous. You swear you don't have healing power?"

"I swear." She looked up at the ceiling and thought of diamonds. As they exploded on top of each other, an idea grew. "That's the extent of my power, what you see up there. What do you think would happen if I got into bed with you and we let our bodies do what they want? I mean, obviously something beyond our conscious minds is working. Why not let our bodies lead and see what happens?"

He turned his head, a single eyebrow raised high. "Do you really think sex is the answer?"

She jerked her hand back, but returned it when he winced. "Sex? Who said anything about sex?" She considered her words and winced. "Yeah, never mind. I hear it now. I didn't intend to proposition you. I mean, you're kind of my type, but kind of not, and I don't really know you well and—"

"If not sex, then what?" Lee's jaw tightened. "I'm calmer with you here, but the headache is persisting."

"We cuddle." She climbed over the bedrail, her own pain flaring at the awkward movement. "For the love of everything holy, something has to help. I hate being brainless with the shots, and Amanda said they had to be really careful with what they gave you, so I can't imagine how you feel."

She settled to his side, stretching as long as her body allowed for the most contact. Immediately, her lingering aches subsided. She sighed at the same time he did. She wished she could see his face, but didn't dare move from her spot of comfort.

"Was that good for you?" she asked.

"Oh, baby." Pure bliss growled through the two little words, reminding her they were not having sex. No, just a medicinal cuddle. "That was like...nothing else. It has me wondering what would happen if we did have sex right now."

"We'd melt into pleasure puddles." Her words fumbled as exhaustion hit. "Would it be bad form for me to fall asleep?"

"No. Please do, then I can sleep too." His breathing softened and slowed, matching hers. "Thanks for this. I forgive you for taking my cab."

She rubbed his chest through the blanket and his gown. "I forgive you for being a total dick. Look at us, practically BFFs. Sleep."

He adjusted the blankets until they no longer separated them. Indy swallowed, unsure she wanted to be so intimate with a man she barely knew, but the few places they touched skin to skin were appropriate and felt amazing.

"Sleep." Lee's command, so weakly given, made it easy to

obey.

Chapter 4

Indy heard squeaky shoes followed by squabbling outside the door. She pried her eyes open, more human than she had been in months, and all because she was drooling on a giant heating pad. A moving heating pad. She groaned. She'd fallen asleep on Doctor Russell, and she couldn't be happier. He might have saved her life, and he was still breathing, so they'd dodged a bullet.

"That snake oil wielding hack is done, do you hear me? AnnMarie said he was in there with a patient. Is he sick? Is she sick? All I know is it's a huge breach of hospital policy, and he's done." The guy sounded pissed, but also excited. She'd accused Lee of being an ass, but her intuition said she was about to meet a real one.

"Doctor Fields, you're not comprehending the situation. If you'd listen—" Amanda's protest was cut short.

"I'm comprehending, as I'm sure you are. You're out of a job. Go pack up his office. I'll take care of this."

Indy shook Lee. His eyelids popped open, but sleepy haze remained. "Hey, I was dreaming we were in bed together. You're softer than you look. Heavier too. Smell really good."

"Aren't you sweet? Who is Doctor Fields?"

"Dick chief of medicine."

"And he'd like you fired?"

The haze lifted. "He'd love it. What's happening?"

The door flew open, stomps not squeaks. Indy pressed her lips near Lee's ear. "Do you trust me?"

"Kind of."

Fair enough. "Follow my lead."

"Doctor Russell, I'm sorry. I tried to stop them." Amanda hurried in beside an older, distinguished man in a gray suit. "How are you feeling? We're still waiting on the lab tests and CAT scan."

Indy pressed her finger over Lee's lips when he inhaled to speak. His eyebrow raised, the same one that seemed to ask the important questions. She winked and then took a breath so shaky her shoulders quivered.

"Is he going to die, Nurse Amanda?" Indy sat up, but didn't move away from the bed. "He just got back last night. I know it wasn't right for me to crawl in bed with him, but it had been so long, and I thought... He was so ill. I was afraid he'd die before I could tell him I love him."

Amanda's jaw dropped, but it was the chief of medicine Indy was worried about. She hated waterworks, but with pain such a close memory, was able to tap some. Her sinuses filled at the manufactured memories.

"No one is saying anything." She grabbed Lee's arm and held it to her chest. "Lee will get better, right?"

"Young lady, who are you? I was told you're a patient here. Which ward? Mental?" the chief demanded. He flipped the ends of his suit jacket and propped his fists on his hips.

"Oncology." Indy stroked Lee's arm, his skin surprisingly soft. "When my fiancé finally came home, and then got sick, I had to come. I'm sorry. This is my fault. Please don't take it out on Lee."

"Fiancé?" The older man snorted. "Like I'm going to believe Russell has a fiancée."

"Why wouldn't he?" Nurse Amanda demanded. "He's been traveling abroad while Indy has been dealing with her medical issues. He's lucky she forgave him. You should see the diamond he brought her."

Indy gasped and grinned down at Lee whose eyes were now open, even as he stayed still. "Ring or necklace?"

"Both." His word, barely a whisper, reminded her of how sick he really was. They needed to wrap up their game.

"You're the best, baby." She leaned close, like she'd kiss his lips. He raised his chin to meet her, but she dodged at the last second, pecking his cheek instead. She turned to the intruder. "The sweetest. Doctor—I'm sorry, I didn't catch your name?"

"Doctor Fields. Fiancé or not, this is highly inappropriate

and Russell knows it."

"He was unconscious when I crawled into his bed last night. This entire thing is my fault." She pushed up to her feet, wobbly after so long in bed. She reached for the bedrail, but Lee's hand caught her instead. His warm grasp instantly balanced her. "If anyone is to blame, it's me, and I don't know how you can punish me, but please do what you feel is right. I can transfer to another hospital, just please, don't take it out on Lee."

"That's not up to you." Doctor High and Mighty straightened his jacket. "If you would, please return to your room so I can speak with Doctor Russell."

Nurse Amanda stepped around the doctor and grabbed a fistful of papers from another nurse. "Test results." She slammed the stack into Doctor Fields's chest. "Do your job."

He scowled but opened the file. Indy sat on the bed again, stronger than the night before, but her body simply didn't have stamina. Once upon a time she'd loved running and playing soccer. She'd get back there.

Lee's warm hand stroked up and down her back. Did he need her? She turned to him and rubbed his temples. His eyes drifted closed. Whatever was in the files needed to say what was wrong with Lee.

"An aneurism? Seriously?" Doctor Fields approached and pulled out a penlight. "I need you to sit up."

"You're going to need to use the button to move the bed." Indy moved to the chair, but wasn't about to leave Lee with Doctor Feel Good.

He grunted but did as Indy said. After a few minutes of checks and scribbles, Doctor Fields tucked his pen back in his shirt. "You're a sick man. I'm upping your blood thinners, so easy on the physical contact. I want updated scans every hour until we get a normal one. Something for anxiety—I'll have to check against allergies. I don't want him here, it's too far from ICU. If he crashes again, I want him near the scanners."

"Yes, Doctor Fields. I'll take care of everything," Nurse Amanda said. Over the doctor's shoulder she caught Indy's eye and mouthed *thank you*.

Indy's claim of being his fiancée got her a little closeness, but once he was in ICU, the rules applied, and visits were cut short. Indy paced the small waiting room. He'd been slightly better when she'd been booted the last time. A little, as in, speaking and had sipped broth between brain scans. The head nurse of ICU had given her a stern lecture about sitting on Lee's bed, forbidding her from stretching out. Indy chewed her nail.

She could leave now—once she got an official discharge or even without it, if she wanted. Wasn't Lee in great hands? The best in the state? Someone else could be using her room, getting the care they needed. She switched thumbs, but the nail was already down to the quick.

"Hey, doing okay?"

Without the squeaky shoes, Nurse Amanda had been able to sneak up on her. Out of her scrubs and sneakers, the older woman looked like any other lady ready to run errands in jeans and a sweater. She'd let her hair down, and the long brown and gray strands brushed out across her shoulders. She offered Indy a familiar backpack.

"Oh, thank you. Did I get booted from my room?" Indy took her knapsack and dug through, her clothes and cellphone distracting her from nibbling on her fingers.

"Nope. Your primary wants to check you over before you're released tomorrow, but I thought you might like your bag."

"Thanks. Are you going home?"

"Not yet. I'm sitting here and waiting for news. I get out of practice when the doctor is traveling. Not skills-wise, but boy do my feet yell at me the first few shifts." She plopped on the plastic couch. "You're looking better, but still pale. Sit."

Refusing entered her mind, but Indy immediately rejected her usual response to authority and collapsed near Amanda. "This might have been the longest twenty-four hours I've had this year."

"This year?" Amanda tilted her head back and looked at the ceiling. "I know nothing about you, except the cancer, the lights, and Doctor Russell said something about you being a thief?"

"He forgave me. I stole his cab last year at a mind-ninja convention. To be fair, I would have shared, but he was grumpy." Indy frowned. "Has he been having headaches for long?"

Amanda nodded. "Yes, though he denies it. He says the healing he does doesn't affect him, and I think at first it didn't, but after almost fifteen years he's fatiguing."

"I've heard of that."

"From where? Is there really a mind, um, ninja convention?"

"Not really." Indy pulled the coffee table closer and put her feet up. "But a few times a year there are gatherings if you know where to find them. I don't go often, but I was in Panama when Lee was. People show off, bitch about problems, hook up—it's pretty much like a traveling salesman convention, only with weirdly brainy people."

Amanda lifted her feet and put them on the table. "So, tell me more. I just have to get my feet off the floor. Anyway, your gift includes some healing, and the amazing lights."

"No healing."

"Yes, you do have healing. I saw it. Doctor Russell's process changed with you, because your stuff messed with his. Then, when he was so sick, you being close helped. I actually don't like that you're away from him. I talked to the ICU staff, but I won't be able to get you in more until the night shift."

"Doctor Jackass's orders?"

Amanda sighed. "Doctor Fields isn't so bad, but he doesn't like miracles."

"Why?"

"Because they are unexplained and can't be reproduced."

"And everything about Lee is unexplainable and impossible to reproduce."

Amanda nodded. "Exactly. Doctor Fields works hard, and is a good chief of medicine. Lee respects him, even if they do butt heads. After third shift starts, we'll head in and see what you can do."

"I told you, I don't have any practical mental powers. The lights are it. Anything else has been...beyond my control." She shrugged. "Lee is right, I might be a thief. That's what my gift helps me with. I travel the world taking mediocre photos, drawing all-right pictures, and being bestowed large quantities of money, usually from mobsters and crooks."

Amanda sat up and put her feet on the floor. Indy waited for it, the condemnation. She didn't have many friends, because the people who usually were accepting of her financial reality were people she really didn't want to be with.

"Interesting. And how do you get the money?"

"I don't know, right time and place, I guess. I've never, like, planned anything. I'd be awful at that." She twisted the hem of her shirt, one of the few articles of clothing she had at the hospital, because she'd been more comfortable in sleepwear. "Like, this one time in Paris, I was walking by a bank and the guy in front of me dropped an envelope. I picked it up, followed him inside the bank, and tried to give it back. He disappeared and when I went to give it to the bank authorities, the lady at the teller window refused to talk to me. The guy walked by again, so I chased him down and tried to give him the envelope, but he refused and actually yelled for me to get away from him."

"Really?"

"Yep." She shrugged. "It was weird, even weirder when I found almost a million dollars inside. Before that, I was working for a delivery company in Texas. I found an old jar thing and took it to a museum. I would have donated it, but the curator insisted I take a huge check for it. I guess they were at the end of their spending year, and absolutely had to spend the money or their budget would be cut the next year."

"That's not stealing," Amanda said.

"It might be. Money I hadn't earned... Yeah, maybe not stealing. But the guy in Paris—"

"Also wasn't stealing if you tried to give it back. Indy, have you ever gone out of your way to maliciously take something?"

"No, but I also haven't ever worked other than when I get bored. I always have money."

"Sounds like another gift you have is being perpetually lucky, but you've never noticed. What's to say you've never noticed your healing power?" Amanda patted her knee. "What would it hurt to try?"

"I don't know, given that we're talking about Lee's brain, I'd think a lot could get hurt."

"We'll talk to Lee, and he'll get you through it. I'm confident if you have a gift, you'll only be able to use it for good." Amanda checked her watch. "Want to order a pizza?"

"If pizza could be Chinese food, I'd be in, and more receptive to try my mind skills."

Amanda pulled out a cellphone. "See, this is how I know you and Lee have this in common. You're basically the same people. Chinese it is."

Chapter 5

The night nurses worked on paperwork, checking in every two hours as stipulated, but Lee knew sleep was most important now, just like they did. The day and evening shifts had bothered him incessantly, for good reason, but the peace helped calm the storm brewing inside him. What was wrong? For as many people as he'd helped over the years, the ability to self-heal should have been included.

"Psst." The whisper from the doorway certainly wasn't a nurse. No squeaky shoes. Indy. Could it be? He pried open his eyes, the dim light assaulting him, but giving enough illumination to see her in the doorway with Amanda. "You okay?" she asked.

"No." The single word took far too much effort. He didn't bother with more.

Indy's warm fingertips brushed across his forehead. He moaned, the instant easing in pain disarming. Tears flooded his eyes, so he slammed his lids closed.

"See." Amanda's pointed voice didn't hurt his ears, even if the accusation made him wince. "You're a healer. Maybe a different kind, and maybe it came on later in your life, but you have power. See if you can take care of the aneurism."

"Wait, what?" Tears or not, Lee scowled at his nurse. "You want someone who may or may not have healing capabilities to go rooting around my brain? Are you nuts?"

Indy slapped his bicep. "Exactly what I said. Although, she did point out I'm exceptionally lucky, not a thief. You know, except for that cab incident. Every other time I've come into money was a fluke. Yay, right?"

Either the subject change, Indy's sweet scent—something new—or his faulty brain made following along difficult. "You still stole my cab."

"Yep. Total heartless thief. Told ya. Anyway, I'm hesitant to look in your head, because I've never done it and I have no proof it would help. I wish I could." She squeezed his arm. "Seriously."

"Thanks." He closed his eyes again. "I appreciate that."

The sound of fingertips against a keyboard from his left side, Amanda's side, said he'd get the answers he'd been asking for the last few hours. The nurses kept delaying, saying Doctor Fields would brief him in the morning. He should have known his nurse, even if she did get crazy ideas at times, would know what he wanted.

"She needs to try. Now."

"Amanda—"

"They thought it was a false tumor this morning when the

aneurism showed, but the scans cleared the false and confirmed a glioblastoma. You have a huge..." She stopped.

Lee sat up, even as lights exploded behind his eyes. "Hell."

"That's bad." Indy didn't have Amanda's cool delivery. "Lee, that's brain tumors they can't cure. I heard about them in oncology. When someone was admitted with one, it was morphine and comfort cares."

"I know." Anger, unreasonable because it masked fear, fear he hated the second it came, roared to life. "What are they giving me, Amanda?"

"All the right things." More clicking from the computer. "Fields has exploratory surgery scheduled first thing in the morning. He's called in...wow, he's called in the right guys. He's going aggressive, according to the notes."

"I'll still die. Shit." He rubbed his forehead, even though there was no pain there.

The beeping of his monitors filled the room, no more clicking from the computer. The sentence was written. What the hell had he done wrong? He stopped himself. That path would only lead to more anger, and he knew there was nothing he did or could have avoided to prevent the condition.

"I could try. If you tell me how, I swear I'll do only what you say." Indy's timid voice broke the partial silence.

"I appreciate it, but—"

"If she doesn't try right now, she's not going to get a chance." Amanda closed down the computer and returned to his side. "If you were any other patient, and this was me talking to you about how quickly you need to work on the patient, I'd grab you by the ear and get you to their room. I'd tell you, even if they didn't believe, even if they weren't receptive, that it was worth a try."

"Does belief matter?" Indy asked.

"It does. Unless the other person believes I can fix them, their mind stays closed, and therefore their body does too. That's why I usually help kids, because they honestly believe they'll be cured—they don't know any better. Adults, for all they say they want to be cured, are only open to certain things."

"And it worked with me because..."

He smiled, the memory of meeting her in Panama distancing him from the pain. "You're a headcase, right? Isn't that was you called us?"

"Yeah, we are, and that's why if there's something I can do, it will work. I swear I won't, um, you know, hurt you. More likely I'll just catch glimpses of your naughty past. Not that I'm psychic, but if I'm rooting around in your brain, I might as well get a show."

"Lee." Amanda took his hand. She rarely touched him. Where Indy's touch stole his pain, Amanda's brought him back to earth. He turned to her and found tears in her brown eyes. "If we don't at least try, I'm going to re-live tonight and wonder what I could have done. If you go for it, and it doesn't work, then I tried, and if you die, then it's not my fault."

He closed his eyes, needing to think. His parents loved him. He had no real friends—a few guys he enjoyed spending time with if he was in any given town. Women rarely tolerated his traveling and extended hours more than a week or two. Amanda, though, she'd been through everything with him. If he died, aside from his parents, Amanda would be the most affected.

"No other doctor is going to hire me." Amanda poked him. "I'm too confrontational."

He snorted. "Okay. I'll try, but you have to tell me you understand there's nothing you did, or could have done, to change this."

"I know there isn't anything. Thank you for trying. Tell her what to do and keep an open mind, damn it."

Indy poked him this time. "Seriously? You've got her cussing?"

"Close the door and curtains." Lee pressed the lowering button on the bed until he lay flat. The tumor threatening to kill him any minute didn't lend to peace in his mind, but at least the pain ebbed.

"Hey." Indy's tiny voice in his ear, and her breath on his

skin, set his nerves on end. Hypersensitive because of the tumor, the situation, or because it was Indy?

"Hmm?"

"Please believe in me. I make lights and I'm lucky. I don't see how either of those things qualifies me to help, but I want to." She looked to the ceiling.

He followed her gaze to the new lights on the ceiling. They exploded and sparkled, more than lights. Why had he thought her gift so slight? The lights moved in time, like a choreographed dance. They were art in motion, straight from Indy's mind.

"You'll do that, only in my head." He took the hand he held and put it on his forehead.

"You have nice hair." She stroked his head, her fingers little nodes of heaven. "What first?"

Her anxiety increased, her breathing faster, even as she tried to sound positive. He wrapped his arm around her waist, drawing her closer. "First you look at me and tell me you're happy to see me."

She laughed. "Okay. I'm happy to see you. You're my fiancé. I understand there are diamonds?"

"Excellent." He needed her tension lower. "I would buy you diamonds. The fiancé part, I'd have to wait on until I know you a little better. Or at least see you naked."

She giggled again. "Wow. What a charmer." She rested her

head on the pillow beside him. "As much as I like diamonds, I think I'd put the same two criteria on furthering our relationship. What's next?"

"Next, get in bed with me." Their touch connection could only be helpful in the process.

"I knew it," she muttered, but crawled beside him in the uncomfortable bed. "Guys always have an angle."

"Know many guys?" He hoped he sounded teasing instead of possessive, though the latter became more of a problem every time he saw her.

"Not as many as you'd think, being a modern, open-minded woman with a thirst for adventure." She settled beside him and joined him on the pillow, nose to nose. "What now?"

"Now, you think about brains." He closed his eyes, because every time he looked into hers, *really* looked, he forgot what he was doing.

"I bet you have a great brain," she said. "A nice big brain."

"With a glioblastoma over his right ear," Amanda said. "With spider aneurisms surrounding it."

"I would have made that sound way sexier." Indy sighed and rubbed her hands through his hair again. "Brains, on the right side over your ear."

"You might not see it." Lee flowed through his process, checking Indy. "But keep picturing it, maybe even spatially, or looking for an intruder. I'm checking you and your cancer is gone. Inflammation remains though, so you'll be tender for a while. Your body destroyed the cancer all at once. Must have been a shock, but it's pretty to see now."

"It's kind of oval-shaped, and gray, isn't it?" Indy's voice was so close, so tiny, but she wasn't talking about herself.

"Yeah, a glioblatoma would be an odd shape and different color than the rest. Did you find it?"

She swallowed so loudly he couldn't miss it.

He rubbed his hand up her back. "You're okay, Indy. Think about getting it away from the rest of my brain. Once it's away from the actual flesh, my body will get to work tearing it down."

"Or burn it," Amanda said. "I don't want anything floating in his brain if it doesn't have to."

"Burn it. Right." Indy's hands shook, but she didn't pull away.

"Or just think about it away from my brain." His 'usual' process had been different with her. He couldn't tell her exactly what to do. "Try a few things. You're not going to hurt me. I trust you."

Mental abilities singled a person out and made them unique, but also could lead to trust issues. The outside world laughed, or tried to exploit what it didn't understand. In the worse case, it tried to crush a person. Indy was so far out on a limb for him.

The last thing he wanted was for her to fear a fall.

"I don't want to hurt you."

Behind his closed eyes, stars swirled. During extreme exhaustion, he'd experienced flashing lights, but nothing like this. His breathing slowed, tension eased. This was Indy's gift. The lights would save him.

"I think I got it." Indy sighed. "But I don't know, Lee. It was there, and now it's gone. Does it hurt?"

His lips were numb, and the lights kept rolling around, tumbling over one another. He opened his mouth. At least he thought he opened his mouth.

"Amanda, what's going on?" Indy's sweet voice turned to panic.

The door handle jiggled, followed by pounding. Lee tried, but couldn't open his eyes. The lights kept twirling. He'd either get better, or he'd go out with a hell of a light show.

Chapter 6

Indy waited for someone to call security, but no one did. She stood near Lee's feet and kept her hand on his ankle. His touch had gotten her through the pain. She didn't know if he was experiencing any, but if he was, maybe she helped. The nurses checked the machines and manually assessed Lee's vitals, frowning at one another as they spouted numbers that sounded reasonable enough to Indy. Amanda had gone into work mode, assisting the two nurses by handing them things, but not interfering with the smooth dance the two executed.

"Call Doctor Fields," one of them said. "I want him double checking this, so he's not giving us hell later."

"Not the ER doctor?" the other nurse asked.

"Call Fields," Amanda seconded. "He won't believe it otherwise. Can you get him into a scan?"

"We can," the leading nurse nodded. "Good idea. Missy, call Fields, I'll call radiology, and we'll have new scans before the doctor arrives."

So much happened, and too quickly. Indy couldn't accompany Lee to the scan, so she paced outside the door.

How had she gotten wrapped up with the cantankerous doctor? She refused to think romantic feelings could have popped up, despite their teasing. Only fools fell in love with their doctors, and at the end of the day, that was the only real relationship Indy had with Lee. He was her physician and had helped her. If all went well, then she would have done the same for him, and they'd be even. Even, and able to go about their lives without being beholden.

The door opened. Indy jumped from where she'd been resting against the wall.

"How is he?" She grabbed his foot before they could wheel past her.

"He started waking in the machine. We need to get him back to ICU and better medicated." The same nurse from the ICU frowned at her. "You really shouldn't be touching him. Were you discharged?"

"It's fine." Indy walked alongside Lee's bed. "I'm fine. I'll go back to my room when Lee is in the clear. He's my fiancé."

The lie came easier each time she said it, and it kept her at his side as they waited for Doctor Fields. Indy wanted Lee to wake up, but his eyes remained closed. She did as he'd instructed before, picturing his brain and going in, and though she made it inside without any trouble, there was nothing out of the ordinary there. Maybe if she knew more about brains she could be more helpful.

The lights stayed low, so low her eyes strained. She looked

to the ceiling and set the lights free, snowflakes this time. As long as the nurses were busy with other patients, she could have her show.

Where would she go now? She'd told her parents she'd visit, and though she ached, she did feel better. Cancer free, or she would be once she had scans in the morning. She believed Lee when he said she was better.

She needed to return to her apartment and get back to the land of the living. The lights changed, more snowflakes. Maybe somewhere cold? Skiing? She hadn't skied in ages.

"Where'd my lights go?"

Lee's words, muffled and slurred, were beautiful to her ears. He blinked, his dark blue eyes starkly different, nearly white. She froze. "Um, Lee, can you see me?"

"I can. You're so lovely. I noticed before, but didn't say so. I might be an idiot."

"Might?" She waved her hand in front of him. "You see okay?"

He caught her hand. "Yeah, I told you. Why?"

"Your eyes are lighter. A lot lighter." She shifted onto the bed to look into his eyes. "They were dark blue, but now they're almost white."

"Really? Mirror?"

She looked around. "There's not one in here. Wait." She

fished out her cellphone and took a picture of him before turning it to him. "See?"

He blinked at the screen. "Huh. Definitely lighter. From the healing or the blastoma? I don't know. Don't care, really, because I'm okay."

"You just know?" She put her phone back in her pocket.

He held out his hand for her. She took it and relaxed. "I think I do. The tests will confirm, like yours will today. It's a crazy thing, huh?"

"Pure insanity." She wanted to sit on the bed beside him, but they were strangers despite everything they'd experienced together, and neither of them was in pain. "I'm scheduled for tests and scans at eight AM, and then I'm heading home if I get the all clear."

"And where is home?"

"Seattle. I keep a small apartment here, but I travel so much I don't use it often." She wrinkled her nose. "Might be stale after being closed up so long."

"Then what?" He closed his eyes. "The headache was gone even before you took my hand."

She couldn't resist, she half-sat on the bed and brushed his hair from his forehead. The pain lines remained, but they were relaxed. The lines might stay, but she hoped they never engaged again. "Feels weird, doesn't it?"

"Odd, but good. What are you up to after settling at home?" He found her hand again, even with his eyes closed.

"I think I'll head to Ecuador to see my parents. I have other family there as well."

"And then?"

"Then I don't know. Why don't you ask what you want to ask?"

He shifted and opened his eyes. The lack of color would take some getting used to, but it was a small price to pay to have him well. "When will I see you again? I have a few diamonds to buy, and there was talk of commitment."

She could shut him down with a shrug, like she'd been playing a part, but as much as it may have started as an act, it didn't feel like one anymore. "Twenty-four hours ago you didn't like me."

"I was misinformed." He kissed her palm. "I'm a quick learner. And I'm joking about the commitment. I want to get to know you outside hospital walls. I still might end up finding you irritating."

She smirked. "Yeah, likewise. I'm going to go, but I hope we reconnect. I think I would like you, you know, like you said, outside hospital walls."

Nurses and doctors convened in the hall, marking their time. Time to make the break, but it didn't feel right. Her lips couldn't find a smile, and Lee also frowned. She looked into his eyes, ones that had looked inside of her and cured her cancer.

"There's bound to be a headcase convention in the next few months." She ran her hand through his hair again, because she couldn't stop herself. "How about we have coffee?"

He snagged her hand and pressed it to his cheek. "Coffee it is, but only if you get Amanda's cellphone number before you leave. Doesn't have to be mine, and you don't have to give her yours, just be able to get a hold of her, okay?"

"Okay."

The doctors and nurses continued to talk, and despite needing to leave, and having a moment that allowed for a clean break, Indy stayed. If this was goodbye, and the moment she was away from him the growing feelings she had stopped, that had to be okay. She didn't want to have a healing love affair that ended when the prescription expired. But when would she have another moment like this? Cuddled up with a man she liked, respected, and even if it was situational, kind of loved?

She leaned closer, and the lines around his eyes appeared again, but this time, ones of pleasure. Only he wasn't laughing. They stared at each other as their lips touched. Indy stroked his cheek, the stubble there prickly, and she'd bet, out of character. Just lips, nothing more, but something deep inside cried to never leave this man's side.

Throat-clearing from the door silenced the cry. She pulled away, slowly, even as Lee's arms tried to hold her closer.

"I'll see you soon." She stroked his brow again, but had to let go. "Thanks for everything."

"You will see me soon." He freed her, and kept eye contact, even as she shuffled toward the door. "Thank you."

She bumped into someone. Doctor Fields caught her and shook his head. "Hell, another one. Ms. Bravo, you're scheduled for testing."

"I know. Take good care of him." Tears burned her eyes for reasons she couldn't give life to. She hurried out of ICU. She had to get her life back before she could think about including Lee.

Chapter 7

Three months later

Another scan and he'd be inducted into the frequent scanner's club. Lee rubbed the back of his head, his hair longer than it should be, but growing it out had become a half-hearted plan. Taking a break from his rounds to get another scan at Doctor Fields's command hadn't been on his list, but following Fields's orders was part of getting Lee working again.

"Clear again, I'll be damned." Fields waited near Amanda at the nurse's station.

Lee didn't need permanent office space, he just needed a place to drop his stuff and collect whatever information Amanda had for him while he was in any given hospital. His nurse gave him two thumbs-up behind the chief's back. She pointed to the patient floor and headed that way. There were patients to see before he left on his midnight flight to Nevada.

"Yeah, it's a miracle."

Fields shook his head. "I don't like that word. Whatever you do...why can't we all do it?"

"I don't know." Discussing mental and psychic abilities never happened with Fields. The other doctor didn't want to believe, and probably never would. "Being on the receiving end of it this time really opened my eyes to how difficult it is to be in an impossible situation. Thanks for taking good care of me."

Fields froze in flipping through the papers.

"I mean it." Lee picked up his own clipboard. "If I had to be as sick as I was anywhere in the world, I'm thankful it was here with you watching out for me."

"The hard cases are the worst. I'm glad you pulled through."

"I've had enough hard cases to know sometimes you can't win."

"I'm glad we won this time. Let me know when you're back in town, and I'll approve your privileges. Is it all right if I contact you with any, um, special cases?"

Progress. Lee held out his hand and Fields shook it. "Call Amanda. She knows how to reach me."

Lee left Fields at the desk, but the man's voice followed him. "What happened to your fiancée?"

It was Lee's turn to stop. He glanced over his shoulder. "I'm heading out to see her this weekend." At least he hoped he'd get to see her.

Fields nodded. "She's good for you. Have a nice time."

Lee finished his rounds in record time, his extended stay in Seattle lending to healing in him and others. He left the hospital and headed for the parking lot.

Amanda waited at his car, a tote at her feet. "You are not leaving without saying goodbye."

"You're not planning on coming with me, are you? This isn't a hospital—just a personal trip to Vegas. After that I'll be in Boston for work."

"I know." She lifted the bag. "This is for Indy. The nurses had a box in the office of notebooks and things she left lying around—including an envelope stuffed with cash. Seriously, I bet it's not even hers, but something the universe dropped in her box."

He took the tote. "I'm not sure I'll see her."

"You will." Amanda stepped away from the driver's door. "You let your hair grow out—you look like a hippy, by the way—and you said it, the headcase convention is where you saw her last time. She'll be there."

"Has she called?"

Amanda shook her head. "She'll be there. Tell her I said hi."

"I will." He unlocked his car. "Is your ticket set for Boston?"

"I'm leaving tonight. I could use a few fun days on the east coast. I'll be ready when you arrive. And if Indy is with you, that would be great."

He opened his door and leaned on it. "You seem to think

this is going to work in my favor."

"If by 'in your favor' you mean you and Indy fall madly in love and make beautiful babies for me to spoil, then yes, I do think it will work out. You have to believe before these things work."

"These things?"

"Oh, Lee...so good with work." Amanda squeezed his arm. "Put your focus on what you want with Indy and then go for it. Be happy. And I want to be an auntie. I plan on going by Auntie Amanda."

Somewhere along the line, he'd needed someone to watch out for him. The universe had sent Amanda. She'd become a guardian angel on more than one occasion.

"I'll do my best." He patted her hand and slid into the driver's seat. "Happy thoughts, prayers, voodoo, whatever you've got, get it going now."

Amanda gave him two thumbs-up. If all went well, maybe he and Indy could find what his nurse said they both needed.

Chapter 8

Of all the people in the world, Indy loved her parents most, but at the moment, leaving them to wander in the Las Vegas airport tempted her beyond belief. Her head pounded, not due to any illness, just crazy. Crazy caused by her parents who hadn't visited the US since they'd left. The amount of paperwork she'd had to do to get them to the States contributed to the headache as well, but they were there, and would have a nice vacation.

If they would move their butts.

"Mama," Indy called when her mother stopped in front of another glitzy airport shop. "There is an entire city of gaudy, ugly things for you to buy outside the doors."

Her mother waved, a classic movement for *I'll only be a moment*. A bullshit gesture that almost guaranteed they'd spend the bulk of their vacation in the airport shops if Indy didn't do something.

She cleared her throat. "Papa, the buffet changes from breakfast to dinner soon. If you want to hit the magic time, we have to go now."

Her father, rail-slim as he'd been her entire life, ate like a man starved. His body metabolized food at an intense rate, one that her own worked at for the moment, though eventually she'd have to stop eating as much or she'd be more like her soft, cozy mother.

"Time to go." Her father took her mother's arm and steered her toward the door.

Indy led the way. The rental car people had their comfortable commercial ride ready. She would have preferred something sporty, but with the way her parents shopped, they needed the space, and the backseat.

She drove to the hotel, mind racing as her heart thumped to catch up. Lee might be at the headcase convention. When she'd left the hospital, he'd been on the mend, as had she. She'd flown to Ecuador, where she'd spent three months regaining strength.

What would he think of her now? She hadn't put on much weight, but her caramel skin had darkened in the sun, and her cheeks were fuller. Her mental abilities had increased exponentially, and during her time in Ecuador she'd healed people. When ash from a volcano had left numerous children with breathing problems, she'd helped some of the poorest by gently removing the ash and tar from their systems. It all whirled together, giving her purpose—something she'd always craved but could never direct.

She pulled into the parking ramp. She looked forward to making lots of money off the casino slots during the headcase convention. It never failed to tickle her when they met in places where money was at play. From now on, her winnings would fund a life of service.

"We need to eat," her father said after she checked them into their adjoining rooms. "You too, Indigo."

Her stomach growled. "I bet I'll out-eat you."

She led the way, enjoying showing her parents this different side of the world. Now that they traveled legally, they could do more.

Passing the front desk again gave her a moment to scope out headcases. Her parents knew about the lights, and healing—they thought it was a gift, but didn't know that's why they were in Vegas. They also didn't know about Lee. If nothing panned out, she didn't want them to be upset.

She craned her neck as they walked through the lobby. Was the guy with long hair familiar? The brown curls were, but Lee's hair hadn't been so long last time she'd seen him.

"Come along," her mother said. "You gawk at people."

Indy ignored her mother and kept craning until she found the right angle—and person. "Lee."

The single word, even over the crowd, caught his attention. His eyes, still unnaturally light, focused straight on her, the pure pleasure in them telling her everything. He'd missed her. Abandoning her parents, she ran to him.

Lee set down his bags, arms open wide by the time she

made it to him. The best things happened when you dove in, and Lee's embrace was the best ever. She pressed her face to his neck, inhaling the scent she'd wished she'd been able to take with her.

The long nights alone, remembering him, hadn't done the man justice.

"Who is this?" Her mother's voice shattered her moment.

"Parents?" Lee asked, the word rumbling against her ear.

"Yep." She pulled away, but clung to his side. "Papa, Mom, this is Lee Russell. He was my doctor."

"Come to lunch," her father said. "We'll hear more."

Her mother's eyes narrowed. "Doctor care, huh?"

Indy couldn't separate from Lee, even for the sake of getting her mother off her back. "He's someone I've missed. Lee, will you join us for lunch? We're eating at the buffet—my father's favorite."

"Thank you for the invitation. Let me check in and drop my stuff off, and I'll join you." He pulled out his phone. "Put your number in, so I can find you."

The 'later' was there in the sentence unspoken. She dialed her number and called herself. When her phone rang, she hung up, and handed Lee's phone back to him. "There ya go. Now you'll always be able to find me—us."

As much as she hated it, she followed her parents instead of

Lee. Out of the corner of her eye, she saw Lee walk by another of the space's exits.

"I'll be right back. Start without me." She waved to her parents and all but ran to the second door. A path cleared, her lucky streak shining again.

She made it out the large door in time to see Lee turn left. She ran again, seeing just his foot this time when he turned another corner.

"Lee! Wait up."

Surely he heard her, but when Indy turned the next corner, it was to an empty hall. She tiptoed down the hall, hoping for a feeling, a niggle of direction. The first door on her right opened, and before she could turn, hands grabbed her and pulled her into the room.

* * * *

Lee closed the door and locked it. Ready to explain the quick grab and apologize, he turned Indy in his arms, only to be attacked with kisses.

"I can't believe you're here," she panted between kisses. "I wanted you to be here."

"I feel the same way." Not sure how far she wanted to go, Lee stayed standing by the door. If this was his greeting, he couldn't ask for a better one.

"Bed." Indy grabbed him around the waist. "Now."

She'd asked for better. Lee lifted her off her feet, easily enough, and carried her to bed. The silky comforter billowed around her body, until he moved it aside and took its place.

"So much nicer than the hospital." She sighed against his lips. "Take your pants off."

He pulled back and raised his eyebrow. "Are we in a hurry?"

"I can't believe your eyebrow asked me a question." She grabbed his belt and tugged. "Yes, we're in a hurry. Haven't we waited long enough?"

When she put it that way, he had to agree. He pushed to his feet and stripped out of his clothes. From her cocoon on the bed, Indy did the same, tossing aside her cute sundress and making quick work of her bra and panties. He'd see them next time, and enjoy stripping them from her beautiful body.

He stopped. "I don't have protection."

Indy rolled to her side and dug in the gift basket on the nightstand. "Headcase con, remember? They always have... Aha, here we go."

She pulled out a box of condoms and ripped it open. He'd never been so grateful for the convention hosts. He might have to start donating more money to the cause. Indy tore open a single condom. He reached for it, but she shook her head.

"We might as well get acquainted, don't you think?" She sat

up at the edge of the bed and crooked her finger. "If you trust me, of course."

Naturally, she had to challenge him. Could he be any luckier? Lee stepped closer, not stopping until his feet were planted between hers.

"Wow." She stroked the head of his penis before starting with the condom. "Lovely to meet you face to face."

He ran his hand through her hair, the silky strands warm and soft. "You did warn me, didn't you?"

She cupped his balls and stroked his cock. "About being eccentric and irritating? Which one am I being now?"

He let his head fall back and didn't even attempt to stop the moan building in his throat. Sex hadn't been on the table in so long, and no one tempted him like Indy. She stroked him again, long and firm, but this time, ending with a tug. His eyes flew open.

She grinned and scooted back on the bed, still gripping his penis. "Come on, you. Let's get started, before you finish."

"Now that was the sarcasm I expected." He followed her onto the bed. Her knee demanded a kiss, and as much as she wanted to get started, he wanted to explore.

He stroked the inside of her knee, the softest skin he'd ever felt. Her legs fell open a fraction of an inch, inviting him higher. With every kiss to her thigh, the sassy things she'd been saying turned to gasps. He glanced up after a nip to her inner thigh, so close to her center. The smile on her face was too bright, too tense. He stopped and rested his elbows on either thigh.

"What's wrong?" he asked.

"Nothing. You're just really close, and I'm just really...close."

"Quick trigger?" He brushed his fingers over her labia. "So, what does this do?"

She grabbed him by his shoulder, her grip stronger than he would have thought.

"You can find out next time. Hurry." She tugged at him, drawing him up, but he held firm at her breasts. "Seriously?"

"Yes, seriously." He circled her nipple with his tongue. The already hard nub protruded further, and he wrapped his lips around it.

She moaned and hit his shoulder. "Come on."

He let go of one, but couldn't move on without greeting the other. He gave her second nipple the same treatment, massaging her breast, the light handfuls the perfect compliment for her body.

Indy grabbed him by his armpits, and pulled. He released his prize, although he planned to get well acquainted with her breasts soon, and moved until he lay over her. She wrapped her legs around his waist. As much as he wanted to play, he followed her lead and plunged in. Despite Indy's bold command, both had to stop for a moment when they were truly joined.

Every good feeling he'd experienced with her so far couldn't hold a candle to the intense pleasure coursing through him. Something more than physical nerves was at play, and with every motion, every thrust and retreat, the feeling grew. He didn't have to look up to see the stars on the ceiling, they were in Indy's eyes as orgasm approached.

She bit her lip, but he couldn't have that. He kissed her, letting loose her lips for a better purpose. She moaned into his mouth, the pleasured groan tangling with his own as his body drove toward release. Her abdominals quivered under his, the tight muscles of her body betraying her pleasure. Having given her pleasure, he wanted a taste of his own. He thrust harder, faster, urgency in each delivery.

Indy clawed at his back, her strength showing again as she tried to crawl inside of him. She planted her feet on the bed and thrust against him, meeting him press for press while their tongues battled. Who was in charge of this? Was either of them holding the reins?

Orgasm, hot and hard, surged through him, the release almost painful after the intense, quick build up. Indy smacked his butt, shocking him from the cerebral loop his pleasure censors caught in, and bringing him back to the beautiful, loving woman who'd delivered a blow to not only his body, but to his heart. Lee fell to his elbow and rocked to his back, taking Indy along, so he could see her with the lights overhead. He swallowed hard, never wanting the moment to end.

She smiled and ran her fingers through his hair. She kissed him deeply, all soft and sweet, but that something extra remained. This is what they were supposed to have. Hadn't they both outrun death to get here?

* * * *

Indy rolled to her back, bent her elbow, and held up her hand. Without a word, probably because he was panting like he'd finished a race, Lee mimicked her action and clasped her hand.

"Glad you found me." She propped up to see his face. "I missed you way more than is reasonable."

"Same here." He wiped his forehead on his pillow. "Seeing you again with your parents wasn't quite what I imagined."

"They wanted to come to the States, and this seemed like a safe trip. I'm sure they're happy having dinner right now." The explosive reunion faded, and yet, her pleasure remained. "So. What's next?"

He chuckled. "Well, I could use a nap, but instead I'll shower and join your parents for lunch and try my best to not look like I just had amazing sex with their daughter."

"Good luck. My mom will know. Papa won't care until it's so obvious he can't ignore it. After?"

"After, I don't know. I'm scheduled to be in Boston Tuesday. If you want, you could come with me. I'd really like it if you came with me."

She tucked a strand of hair behind his ear. "I love the longer hair. I want to go, but I think, before I can do real good, I need to enroll in medical school."

"Has your gift increased?"

She looked to the ceiling, letting loose her lights. They were more powerful than ever. Even in the daylight of the hotel room, they glowed brighter than the filtered sun.

"Magnificent. They were dancing in your eyes earlier."

"Really? And yeah, the healing is there, but if I understand the body better, I can help others more effectively." The unease and self-doubt she so rarely indulged in scrambled to life. "I was going to ask your thoughts about med school. I have a bachelors with plenty of emphasis on science, but I don't know if it's the right choice."

Lee caught her by the waist and rolled her onto his body until she sat up. Her first instinct was to cover her breasts, but he wasn't looking at them, he was looking at her face.

"I'm only going to encourage you to do what you want. If you're looking for someone to tell you *no*, or to tell you *yes*, you're not going to find him here. I will, however, say you have a unique understanding of the human body, and with your gift, you could do amazing things."

"I should...if I want. What about if I need a letter of recommendation or maybe a tutor?" She traced her finger down his cheek.

"You've got it, sweetheart." He caught her hand and kissed her finger. "Would you consider doing some hands-on learning between classes?"

Her heartbeat skyrocketed. "Not sure if you mean with patients or in the bedroom."

Lee took her hands and held them to his bare chest. "Both. I don't want to put an end date on what's starting here."

In the way life had dealt with her, in terms of luck, and cause and effect, Indy saw Lee as her prize after a long, hard battle with illness. He made her feel again, and through him, new doors opened. Walking beside them with him and finding what was in store: adventure, healing, a new career...love. She wanted it all.

"No sense wasting time." She kissed him hard on the mouth, pulling away before his tongue could convince her to stay. "Time to get started. Don't worry, I'll be gentle."

About Stephanie Beck

Even before she understood what all the thrusting meant, Stephanie Beck loved reading romance. When the stories didn't end the way she wanted, writing her own was the perfect solution. From ridiculous humor to erotica, Stephanie loves being transported within a story. When she's not elbow deep in words, her husband and three children command her attention. After they are sleeping she knits or bakes cookies…or squeezes in more writing.

Stephanie's Website:
www.stephaniebeck.net
Reader eMail:
stephaniebeckauthor@gmail.com

Taming Fury

by Ellen Cummins

Holly is a mind-moving Fury who electrifies all human flesh she touches. Even her own family has sent her packing. She moves things with her mind, manipulating fire with the flick of her finger, but she burns for the one thing that has never been an option for her—love.

When she catches sight of the handsome man helping her new neighbor move in she longs to take a chance and introduce herself…to pretend to be normal just once. It could easily end in disaster, but surprisingly, when she shakes his hand, no mind-blowing electrocution follows, and she begins to hope. But it turns out that her touch has affected Jacob in a way she never imagined, and it will change his life forever.

Dedication

To my husband Robby. Thanks for putting up with me and my "room of requirements" and for always keeping the home fires burning.

Acknowledgements

Thank you, Pamela Tyner, for editing me like a beast. I learn so much from you.

Taming Fury / Ellen Cummins

Chapter 1

Holly stepped out of the car, and the cold rain pelted her hot, bare shoulders, making spiraling trails of steam drift into the air around her. Her fingers hurt like hell. She balled her hands into fists, wishing away the curse that kept her from interacting with the world.

They called her a Fury—a mind mover—but her family called her an expert at being an outcast. Growing up in a home void of compassion was a time in her life she wished she could forget. And searching for her place in the world alone had only made it harder to fit in.

She wiggled the blood back into her fingers, flexing and stretching them until the urge subsided. The undeniable itch to move things jabbed at her insides like a pitchfork that had been sitting in a pile of hot embers. Her telekinesis has been tucked away for far too long. It surged in her veins and pounded at the edges of her skull, threatening to come out in front of this parking lot full of people. But she couldn't allow that to happen.

She closed the car door and shimmied between the brick wall and the dumpster. He wouldn't see her there. He hadn't left her thoughts since that day she watched him carry boxes into the apartment next door, muscles flexing, with the swagger of a god.

Taming Fury / Ellen Cummins

Shaking hands with her new neighbor and then leaving. It was unlike Holly to act desperate when it came to a stranger, or anything for that matter, but that day she'd frantically scrambled for the pencil in her desk and jotted his license plate number on her wooden windowsill as he drove away.

The next day she watched out the window, checked her mail incessantly, and sat on her porch with her coffee in hopes he would drop back by. She hid her face beneath her dark curtain of hair, blending in with the backdrop as she liked it. Finally, he drove up and parked across the street. She watched him carefully, studying his every move. His long legs, muscular thighs beneath his jeans—business attire from the waist up. She hunched behind the post on her porch so he wouldn't see her.

She listened for the knock on the door and the sound of it opening, the greeting, and then the door closing. She dashed to her car and waited, pathetically thrumming her fingers against the steering wheel. Impatient. She'd never been this interested in a man before, because she knew how it would go. But this one had kind eyes from a distance, and the most lusciously fit body she'd ever laid eyes on. And there was no wedding ring on his finger.

A half hour later, he stepped out onto his friend's porch, shook hands with him and walked back to his car. She let him get two blocks away before she pulled out behind him.

Taming Fury / Ellen Cummins

She followed him here to this shopping center, parked next to the most inconspicuous bright yellow dumpster in the lot, and slid behind it to watch him. He stepped out of his shiny silver Volvo, keys in hand, cellphone to his ear, speaking gently as if responding to a feminine influence on the other end.

Who was the enchantress? Had he been claimed by some amazingly stunning woman? It was highly possible. Probably someone perfect—no extra chromosomes, no missing pieces. No psychic abilities. No birth defects at all. A perfect size five, blonde-haired, rosebud-lipped flawless princess type. A girl who didn't scorch flesh when she touched it.

He laughed into the phone, and a huge smile lit up his face. His designer jeans hid delicious secrets as he walked toward the row of buildings.

Holly deflated. Of course she could never know him. Her life was nearly that of a hermit's. Her neighbors didn't talk to her, not even the new, nice-looking guy next door, but he did smile at her at the mailbox. People couldn't stand to be near her because the static electricity she emitted was just too strong, so she didn't allow them to get close, speaking to no one and rarely making eye contact. Thank God she was able to build a small home-based medical billing service, or she and her cat Jasmine would starve to death.

Even her own mother shrugged away from her painful

hugs—and she didn't understand her own daughter either. Holly knew nothing of love really, except for the occasional visit to her parents' house that always had her crying in her car by the end of the afternoon. Physical intimacy was never an option, and because of it, the emotional part never had the chance.

"Can I help you?" A voice from above startled her.

She twisted around to see a young boy sitting on the edge of the brick wall, his grimy sneakers bouncing and splattering mud on her. He slapped his hands on his knees that poked through the shredded holes of his jeans and eyed her through greasy bangs. Clearly, he was homeless.

"Um...no," she said embarrassed. "I was looking for something...in the dumpster."

"Or at that guy getting out of his car." He snickered.

"Mind your own business," she groaned, wiping the mud off her face with her wrist. "And get outta here before somebody sees me."

"This dumpster *is* my business. Don't you see the bag of hamburgers in there?" He jumped down off the wall and then lifted a leg over the edge of the bin and slipped inside it. "See?" He stood up and dangled the crumpled, soggy bag in his hand. "You're not here to steal my Double Beefy, are you?"

"Not in a million years. Can you *please* go?" She peeked out and sighed. The man was gone.

"He works there, in that building." The kid unwrapped his half-eaten burger and took a bite. He took several steps backward inside the bin.

"Who?"

"The guy you're spying on."

Holly glared at him, unsure whether she should explain herself or scold him for calling her a spy. His matted blond hair was now standing on end.

"Feels like lightning is coming." He stared at the sky and climbed out of the bin, clutching his bag to his chest. "I'm getting out of here, and so should you."

He was up over the wall and gone in a flash.

The rain began to come down harder and she unwrapped her hoodie from around her waist and put it on. She flipped her hood up over her head and peeked out again.

The sign above the building read *Personal Fitness*. She scowled and grabbed her belly, pinching the skin that was coming out over her jeans. Then she smiled. She considered her full figure a blessing—stick figures were for cartoon characters. Her voluminous curves were sexy, but it would make for a great reason to inquire about some fitness training.

She marched toward the door, her head held high, shoulders back, determined. Ignoring the people who were wondering why she'd just emerged from behind a dumpster. If she could get inside the door for just a minute, maybe she could get one more up-close look at him to hold her over. A piece of him she could take with her.

More steam rose from her cheeks as she moved faster, weaving around a mother and son leaving the dry cleaners with their garment bags. Her eyes were dead-set on the building in front of her. *Please don't feel my heat. The kid from the dumpster didn't feel it.* At least, not at first. She just wanted to quietly blend in with everybody else.

She clenched her fists tighter. *Damn it.* If she didn't use her powers soon, she could possibly lose control of them in front of him. Hot emotions were her worst enemy.

Still walking forward, she closed her eyes and reached for the damp motes of dust from the earth, gathering them in her fist while static electricity buzzed inside her gut. A tiny electric current snaked the length of her arm, starting from the back of her neck. The tug rolled from her fingers to the empty beer can on the ground near a small garbage can on the sidewalk. *Up*, she willed. Reaching, she willed it to rise, sure that no one would see this small thing. It slowly lifted a few inches above the ground and hovered. She swished her hand, slamming the aluminum can into the trash. Her mind was a powerful thing. And this one tiny action would suffice for now.

She burst through the door of the building, adrenaline

fueling her courage. Mr. Perfect snapped his head up from his paperwork at the sound of the door slamming against the wall.

"Hi." He swallowed, taking her curves in with his eyes. "How may I help you?"

The urge to surge had subsided. But the need to know this man had not. She stared at his chiseled cheekbones, strong jaw, and molten brown eyes from across the room. If she got too close, he'd be repelled by her like the opposite end of a magnet. To push this perfect stranger away would kill her. But the loneliness had to stop.

"My name is Holly. And you are..." She waited, pursing her lips together to hold back the thoughts that wanted to tumble out of her mouth. *Please don't run from me.*

"I'm Jacob." He smiled and started toward her with his hand out to shake hers.

"Stop," she ordered.

He stopped. Confused, his brows lifted.

"Please don't come any closer." She placed her hand on her throat. "I have a little virus…nothing too terrible, but I may be contagious." She removed her hood and adjusted her collar that was beginning to cut off her air supply. "How do I go about signing up for some personal training?"

"Well, Holly." He smiled widely. "Personal training requires some up-close and personal contact, and if I have to stay seven arms' lengths away..." He took another step toward her. "May I? I'm not afraid of a few germs."

She cringed and stepped back. Her courage was fading fast. Jacob's cellphone rang in his pocket and he pulled it out, clicking the *ON* button. He put it to his ear.

"Hello?" His eyes darted back to Holly's. "I'm with a client right now, can I call you back?"

He should banish the princess to the black forest, but at least he was shrugging her off. This was a very good sign.

Holly glanced away when he smiled at her, waiting for him to disconnect the call, but the princess kept talking on the other end. Holly held her disguise—someone brave. Regrouping with the strong girl that lived inside her somewhere. The suffering couldn't show.

She fidgeted with her hair, brushing the wet chestnut strands away from her cheeks, trying to look and feel human. God had given her a gift that she hated, forced her into seclusion. At the age of twenty-five it was time to take her life back. It was time to make love happen.

"Okay then." Jacob tucked the phone back into his pocket. "That grandmother of mine always has so much to say." He gave her a wide smile. "How about that handshake? Honestly, I have a pretty strong immune system."

Her face flushed hot. Hotter than usual. Her shoulders

relaxed then tightened. This was *the* moment. He'd either scream in pain and retract or... Well, there hadn't ever been any other reaction. She willed her legs to move toward him, tracing the shape of his shoulders with her eyes, memorizing his scent. As he got closer, she confirmed that he was indeed everything she'd ever wished for physically, and she hoped he was kind as well. When his eyes met hers up close, there was an unexpected connection that swept through her. Like this might be the guy she'd been searching for.

Here goes. Their hands clasped.

His soft squeeze took her by surprise, and his hand lingered for a moment. He let go and wiggled his fingers, but there had been no mind-blowing electrocution. Her eyes went wide, and he smiled gently at her astonishment.

"Now that wasn't so terrible, was it? You have a mighty firm grip, but I like it. It says a lot about a person."

Her feet were glued to the floor. Had he felt it and was just pretending? That was some serious strength.

He walked over to a drawer behind the desk and pulled out a piece of paper. "Here's the contract, and here are the terms. What exactly are your goals? Weight loss, firming and toning? Or just a healthy lifestyle and maybe some self-defense training?"

His gaze drifted over her face and then over her curves

again.

"If you don't mind my saying so, I think you're perfect just the way you are. I'm the owner. Tim, the guy who does the actual personal training, is on a snowboarding vacation. I'm a bit short-handed today. I had to fire my lead PT a few weeks ago. Finn was a beast—I had to change the locks and get restraining orders to keep him and his family from hassling me. Ridiculous. We had some personal differences to say the least." He bit his lip. "TMI, right? Sorry. I hope that didn't freak you out too much. We can get you scheduled as soon as Tim gets back next week. That is, if I didn't make you want to run out of here screaming."

"Actually..." She shifted from one foot to the other. "I really came here to meet you."

Taming Fury / Ellen Cummins

Chapter 2

    Holly squirmed in her car seat on the way back to her apartment. Jacob had taken her number and would call her later that evening to come over for drinks. Or so he said.

    Her car screeched to a halt in her driveway and she speed-walked up the sidewalk, crammed her key into the keyhole, and nearly broke her neck hustling inside by tripping over the threshold. Immediately, she started lifting items with her mind—the cups into the sink, the magazines into a neat stack. She'd never had a man—or anyone—in her apartment before, and it had to look perfect.

    She hurried into the bathroom and started the shower. Peeling out of her jeans and hoodie, she stepped into the hot water, allowing it to wash away any self-doubt for a few moments. She poured the liquid soap onto her body sponge and let it lather up, rolling it over her breasts, her belly, her sweet spot. What would it feel like to have Jacob touch her, his hands in her hair? Pulling it back…

    Lost inside her fantasy, the steam began building, fogging up the tempered glass—a new heat scorching every atom in her body, emotions rising with growing hope. She rubbed the sponge up and down the length of her body, swirling it over her hips and below, suddenly enraptured by thoughts of Jacob on top of her. Underneath her. His lips all over her. Him thrusting inside her. Her lust arcing, her pleasure building—her back pressed against the fiberglass wall. She writhed until she couldn't hold it in anymore. She climaxed with a scream.

The glass shattered around her.

Sated and exhausted, her body glowed. She sighed as she wrapped up in her towel and tiptoed carefully over the shards at her feet. "This is getting to be out of control."

* * * *

Holly sat on the couch, her hands folded in her lap, staring at the phone. It didn't ring. Her hair was curled, her makeup perfect. Two glasses set on the table along with a bottle of Chardonnay chilling in a bucket of ice. A vanilla candle burned on the stove.

Did she really think a man like Jacob would be interested in her? He was just trying to be polite. Of course he'd felt her hideous electric shock when he shook her hand.

He probably really did have a serious girlfriend—the princess of normal-land. Her royal highness probably had him by the balls. Holly in her sexiest black dress and heels couldn't compete.

She flicked a finger at the flame burning just a few feet away and it snuffed out in a spark.

Taming Fury / Ellen Cummins

* * * *

This time Holly parked next to an empty delivery truck and peeked through its windows, watching for Jacob to pull into the parking lot. Far enough away but close enough to spy. She was being ridiculous, and she had the dark glasses and huge scarf to prove it. She waited for an hour.

He never came. The door of the gym remained locked while patrons came and went, peering into the window and then leaving with a shrug.

By the time Holly pulled back into her driveway it was noon. Her new neighbor might know something—this was a risk she'd have to take. Her face flushed hot as she headed toward his porch with her purse slung over her shoulder and holding her keys so tightly they stabbed into her palm. These up-close encounters terrified her.

She fluffed her hair and smoothed over her silk blouse, fidgeting with her fingers on his doorstep. *If you don't try, you'll never know.* She knocked on the door and stepped back.

A handsome brown-haired man in his thirties answered the door.

"Hi." He smiled slightly, his hand clutching his cellphone. "I know you. Next door, right?"

"Yes." She took another step backward, her heart in her throat, stomach twisting. She was the girl nobody knew. "Have you heard from Jacob?"

"My brother Jacob?" His brows stitched together curiously. "Funny thing you should ask." He held up his phone. "Just called him. Something's going on. The answering machine at the gym is full and nobody's picking up the phone. His cell goes straight to voice mail. How do you know him?"

"Well…" She hesitated. She barely knew him enough to go inquiring about his whereabouts but the truth would have to do. "He and I had a date, and he didn't show up, so I went to the gym, and it was locked up tighter than a nun's nightdress."

"A date?"

"Is that unusual? Is he *married*?" she squeaked.

"No." He laughed. "He's completely single. After his last relationship went south he vowed to focus on work instead of women. He'd been ready to settle down for a long time, but Bridgette took him for a crazy ride straight to hell, and that was it. And I mean crazy in the worst sense of the word—a box of Cracker Jacks with extra nuts. After he was finally rid of her, it's been straight to the gym every day, and straight home afterward. No more clubs. No more drama. Just time at the cabin. I'm sorry—how rude am I? What is your name?" He reached a hand out and stepped forward.

"I—I don't shake hands. It's this thing I have about germs." She stepped back, nearly stumbling over the edge of the walkway. Keeping the perfect distance was the key. "I'm Holly. It's nice to meet you." She gave him a limp wave.

"I'm Justin Jennings." He gave an awkward wave back. "Our parents have a weird thing about 'J' names." He thought for a moment, and then his eyes lit up. "He's got to be at the family cabin in the mountains. Sometimes, like when he and Bridgette broke up, he'd go up there to think…and to get away from her." He laughed. "But to leave his business high and dry? I'd better try to get a hold of Tim and see if he can get the doors open. Somebody's got to run the place while we try and figure out what's going on. And unfortunately, there's no landline at the cabin. I'd drive up there, but I have to pick up my son from school in thirty minutes."

"I can go check the cabin for you if that's all right. Give me the address, and I'll pull it up on the web. I can leave right now."

He sized her up and then looked toward her apartment. He knew where she lived. "All right. 347 Rustic Burl Road. Up near Jamison. What's your number?"

She gave him her number, and he entered it into his contacts, and she did the same.

Holly ran inside her apartment and began tossing things into an overnight bag just in case. She welcomed winter because she was always warm, but she wasn't a huge fan of driving in the snow. She packed a flashlight—even though she had her own built-in source of light—a blanket, and her bag of emergency roadside tools. Sweeping over the room one last time, she stuffed some lady essentials in her makeup bag. You never knew when you might need some all-entrancing perfume and silk undies.

Please be okay. Had she done something to him when they shook hands? She hadn't touched another human being since her last visit to her parents' house in June. She'd sent her brother Andrew to the hospital with third degree burns to the shoulder when she accidentally landed on him during a pillow fight. Flesh on flesh always ended up badly. Until Jacob. Her overactive brain tried to make sense of why he hadn't reacted like everybody else at her touch. And now he was a possible missing person.

As she drove to the cabin her mind was a blur of possibilities, her stomach a bundle of nerves. Did he actually *want* to date her after pledging to stay single like his brother said? Unsettled, and unsure, she pressed down hard on the accelerator. She needed to get to the cabin to find out if he was there so she could get some answers. According to Justin it wasn't like him to not pick up his phone and leave his business unattended.

She turned on her blinker, shifted into fourth gear, and passed the Winnebago that was puttering along at forty-five miles an hour. *Out of my way, gramps.* The higher she climbed, the whiter the pines became—winter wonderland be damned.

She wiped the tiny beads of sweat from her lip as she passed one car after another. She didn't know Jacob well enough to be feeling so many things at once. The way he looked at her, the wide smile, and eagerness to get her phone number caught her off guard, and she hoped she didn't look desperate when she gave it away so freely. One man in her life handled her touch for the first time. But did it change him?

She exited onto Dusty Bend Road, shifting down as she approached the sharp turn that curved around by the river. The gravel road was dusted with snow. She turned onto Rustic Burl, a tiny road with only three cabins, two of which looked unoccupied for the winter. The Jennings family cabin had one light burning in the second floor window and a silver Volvo parked in the drive.

Jacob was inside.

This was crazy—her showing up here unannounced and practically a total stranger. She parked, turned off the car, and stared out at the wooden shutters and redwood deck equipped with a set of old metal chairs and a picnic table. A pair of sneakers were drying on the welcome mat in front of the door. The snow had melted near the path, but the ground still looked slushy. Snow surrounded everything else and the river had iced over. Holly climbed out of her car and headed for the door, pushing all thoughts out of her mind. It was the only way.

She banged on the screen door. "Jacob, it's Holly."

The door swung open and Jacob appeared behind the screen. His sandy brown hair was a mess, his stern face pale, his jaw ticking. "Please step away from the door, Holly. You have to leave. You can't be here."

His words cut her. Reflexively, her hand went to her neck. It was coming to the surface. Cruel taunts, people squirming at her presence. Rejection. This was why she shut everybody out. Her chest heaved.

"What do you mean? Is something wrong? You never called me," she said, her feeble voice quivering.

"What I'm saying is…it's not safe here. You need to go back down the hill."

She couldn't read his expression to see if he really meant it—she didn't know him well enough. *Don't push me away.*

He put his hand against the screen, this time telling her a story without words. It was bandaged in white gauze up to the elbow.

Her hands flew to her mouth. "No," she cried.

"Something terrible is happening to me, and I don't want it to happen to you. You have to get in your car and *go*."

His angry tone pushed her buttons. Something clicked, and she took a step forward.

Taming Fury / Ellen Cummins

"I won't. Not until you tell me what the hell is going on. Did *I* do that to your hand? When we shook? I warned you. I've got a condition." She made quotation marks in the air with her fingers. "I have abilities. And they can be dangerous if I don't control them. It was selfish of me to allow you to touch me, but I just really wanted to meet you in the way everybody else gets to meet someone. Just wanted to feel human for once in my damned life. It was careless and risky of me, but you didn't act like I jolted you." She studied his face and took another step forward.

"Don't come any closer."

"You won't hurt me. I have tough skin and a strong mind that collects energy from particles in the air. I use it to move things. Fire is the easiest to manipulate, and if I unintentionally burned you..." She placed her hand over her heart and sucked in a heavy breath. "Let me see your hand."

She took another step then reached for the screen door handle, but he quickly flipped the lock shut, wincing in pain.

She cocked her head sideways, a half-smile at the tips of her lips. Locks couldn't keep her out—nothing could. She snapped two fingers together, casting a spark at the lock. It fell apart, pieces of metal clinking to the hardwood floor at his feet. She swished her hand and the screen door fell off its hinges, teetering and then falling flat as she stepped aside.

Taming Fury / Ellen Cummins

"If this is my fault, then I will make it right. Until then, I'm here to help you forget about your pain."

Chapter 3

Jacob backed up as Holly stepped inside the cabin, closing the door behind her. She circled him, matching his steps as he tried to avoid her.

"You can't burn me," she said.

She pulled her phone out of her purse and dialed.

"Justin, it's Holly. He's here at the cabin." She smiled at Jacob. "He's fine. He said he just needed to get away, but he wanted to thank you for your concern and he'll handle everything. He'll give you a call in a couple of days." She nodded, said "uh-huh" and "I will" a few times and hung up the phone.

She approached him, and he stumbled backward and landed on the couch.

"Let me see your hand," she said. "Can you feel static electricity buzzing through your shoulders right now? Do you hear a humming in your ears?"

He shook his head no, a bead of sweat forming at his temple. She moved closer, hovering over him, her heaving breasts draping nearer. Her buxom flesh grazing the air near his shoulder.

"Still nothing?" she asked.

Entranced by her, he gave a subtle shake of his head.

"Good," she said, calming him until he leaned, relaxed, against the cushion.

She sat down next to him, eye to eye. She trailed a finger over his shoulder and then down to his hand, circling it inside his open palm.

"You smell delicious." He breathed in her scent and exhaled quietly, squeezing his thighs together, eyeing her smile. "If you had any idea what happened last night when I got home..."

"If you had any idea what happened when I took a shower..." She smiled even more deviously. "Let's compare stories."

Jacob fidgeted. Like a schoolboy watching the sexiest, out-of-reach schoolgirl sashay by in her short skirt and clinging sweater. Wanting her.

"Tell me what happened to your hand, Jacob." She gingerly picked it up and cradled it in her hands, bringing it to her lips and kissing it softly.

"After we touched, my body began to feel like a force field of energy. Electrified." He watched her mouth closely as she kissed each finger one by one. "I drove home, made a sandwich, and sat down to pick up the phone to call you and get your address. All I needed to do was take a quick shower and change clothes, and then I'd be there. I looked forward to it so much—I needed it," he drifted and then came back. "Seriously, Holly, all I've ever wanted was a woman who didn't obsess over being bone thin and enjoyed my company for reasons other than what I could do for them. You are amazingly beautiful, and seem confident in who you are and what you want." He smiled. "That is so sexy."

* * * *

Holly's insecurities were slipping away with each word Jacob said.

"Get to the part about why you're wrapped up like Nefertiti." She giggled. "But thank you for the compliment."

"When I reached for the handset of my landline—you know, the phone plugged into the wall—a miniature thunderbolt of electricity blasted my hand. Then everything within a five foot radius of my hand that was plugged into an outlet started to spark, hop, or blaze red like it was ready to burst into flames. Until I wrapped my hand in gauze. Seems to be a barrier. The doctors at Urgent Care didn't know what to do with me because I was too nervous to let them take the bandage off. It was stupid of me, I know, but that place had machines plugged into every wall, and I couldn't risk the other patients' safety. I've become a fuse box without a ground wire. It scared the shit out of me, so I came here to think and try to make sense of it all."

Holly grimaced in pain. She didn't ever want to hurt him.

"This gift, or curse as I like to call it, has never been passed on to someone else through physical contact. It can't be 'caught' like a cold. It's a birthright...something that's in the makeup of our DNA. If I gave it to you by touching you, that's a first in telekinetic history. At least as far as I know." She squinted and pressed her lips together. "I'm sorry." She carefully took his bandaged hand again. "May I?"

"Go ahead. It doesn't hurt so much anymore now that you put that luscious mouth to my fingers. If I wasn't a gentleman, I'd beg for more."

"I'm just going to take a look. And the good news is, I'm touching you and it doesn't hurt, right?"

"Hurts so good." He winked. His eyes serious, lips parted just a tiny bit. Lusting at her touch.

Her belly clenched. Never had anything been so scrumptiously sweet. He watched her tenderly unwrap the bandage, unravelling another inch of her self-control with it. His woodsy scent hit her nose and she glanced up to catch his smile as if he knew. The color had returned to his face, and he brushed his other hand through his hair, his eyes begging her to kiss him. *Focus on the issue at hand.* The last twist of bandage came off.

"This doesn't look terrible," she said. "In fact, I think it's healing."

He looked at it and grunted, turning his hand this way and

that. "Astounding...everything about this day."

She stood up and put her finger to her lips—that legion of neurons hard at work again. "Now let's go have a lesson in the river on how to use this hot, newfound phenomenon."

* * * *

Holly locked the bathroom door and pulled her silk panties out of her bag. Stepping out of her comfort zone gave her a little adrenaline rush, and her heart pounded with excitement as she shimmied out of her cotton underwear and slipped into the sexy pair.

On her way to the house she'd noticed that the river had frozen over, but no worries. Their body temperatures combined would melt it and create a pleasant sauna in nature that nobody had ever witnessed. And teaching him about fireplay in the water was safer than sparking a fire near the cabin.

She adjusted her matching pink lace bra—a homespun bikini that normally she wouldn't let anybody else see. But Jacob appreciated curves. She had a few extra surprises up her non-existing sleeves as well. After inspecting herself one last time in the mirror, she stepped out of the bathroom and into the living room and waited for him by the window. Admiring the powdery, white landscape helped keep her nerves in check.

He emerged from the back bedroom in his running shorts, and his secrets were not hiding very well. His huge package was not to be taken lightly, and her pussy tightened at the thought of him slamming it into her—how the ache might send her over the edge. She forced herself to look up, and quickly became distracted by his knowing smile.

Jacob's gaze slid down her body, his eyes following her curves, then he smoldered at her. He blew out a breath and bit his lip. His worship weakened her. This next hour had to be strictly business, but after that...

Holly put her hands on her hips and smiled, retrieving her wits. "The best place to learn how to control fire is to be surrounded by its worst enemy. It's the safest way. My powers are mostly moving things with my mind, but I can control small sparks with it too. You, on the other hand, may have more than that. You've got to learn how to handle it if you want to get back to the real world."

"So who did the healing—you or me?"

"Not sure. Maybe it was a combination of both." She reached for his hand, and he stepped forward and took it in his, lacing his fingers through hers.

They walked together through the snow, half-naked, to the river's edge that was only a few yards through a grove of sweet-smelling pine trees. An unusual sight, but no one else was there to see it. Their combined heat melted the snow under each step, creating small trails of steam behind them, and Holly chuckled under her breath. How strange this must all seem to him.

"Watch this." A wicked grin rising, she stopped in her tracks. She narrowed her eyes and waved a finger daintily over a couple of pinecones on the ground, and they swirled up in front of them, dancing like two lovers in the night. "My gift can be a beautiful thing. Some days I feel worthy of something good, and then other days I understand why I'm not." She let go of Jacob's hand, clapped her hands together, and screamed. The pinecones exploded into bits. "I'm a mixed bag of perilous emotions."

"You're worth having a good life, and not one person on this earth doesn't have something they aren't proud of." Jacob stepped in front of her and cupped her cheeks in his warm hands. "We all have a little destruction inside us. Teach me how to be like you." His breath baked her cheeks, but she loved it. She could take it. She was made of fire.

"Okay, the ice is just about under our feet. Follow my lead."

Carefully, she stepped forward, studying the edges and listening to the flow of the water. She focused, trying to determine how deep it was, how fast the current was underneath. The snow was quickly turning to slush, and she slipped sideways a little but caught herself on a tree branch. She put her toe on the shore, tiptoeing closer to the water's edge as the ice cracked and liquefied under her feet.

"Here. This seems to be shallow enough. Does the current

run swiftly at this edge, or is there a calmer spot?" she asked.

He observed her, watching her intently. "My brother and I fly fish in this spot. It's pretty calm."

"First things first. Before you step onto the ice, try to set that dead branch over there on fire." She pointed to a large stick a few feet away.

"But it's not plugged into the wall." He smirked.

"Funny man." She smiled. "You have a current living inside you now. You should be able to channel it if my experienced calculations are correct."

"Talking like a mad scientist now, are we?"

"Concentrate. This is serious. Focus on the branch, and bunch up your hands like you're angry. Physically picture all of the energy inside your cells traveling to one part of your body. Could be your head, could be your hands. Put all other thoughts out of your mind. Think 'burn'. When you feel it coming, send the current to the branch, and once it's on fire, take it back."

"How do I take it back?"

"You'll know. You're in complete control of your powers, you just don't know it yet. Only you'll know how. That part I can't teach you."

He stepped aside and rubbed his palms together, glaring at the branch. He cracked his knuckles. Holly tried not to laugh.

His palm went up, a white blast shot out, and the stick burst into flames. The sizzling stream of electric light retracted back into his hand.

"Wow," she exhaled. "Surprise, surprise...you make me look like an amateur." She darted past him, stopped in front of the flame, and with one look created a swish of snow that snuffed it out.

When she turned around he was in front of her, red cheeked, eyes blazing, the heat from his chest electrifying her insides. She took one step back, not in fear but surprise at the way her pussy tightened and her stomach bottomed out. His eyes searched hers, then her lips. His hands reached for her hair.

"Maybe," he said, his voice low and sexy, "we're a mated match, and you were meant to hand this thing over to me so we could tear each other up without injury. Mind over matter. You're the mind, and I'm the matter. Do you like playing with fire?"

Holly's wall cracked—a fissure had started with his kindness and splintered all the way through her at the sound of his achingly sexy words. The pain of her lonely life washed away as her thoughts spilled out of her mouth. "I want you to fuck me."

He pulled her into his arms, gripping her hair, his cock already hard-pressed against her belly. She rolled her hands through his hair, mouth on his, tongues entangling. His lips searched hers, suckling and savoring. Two infernos stoking fast. He broke away and kissed her neck, then kneeled down to lick her breasts and belly. Peeling her panties down a bit, he rolled his tongue over the skin above.

She threw her head back and pressed her lips together, holding her squeal inside her tightly closed mouth. If she lost control, she could cause an avalanche or bring down a tree. The woodland creatures might be wise to take cover.

The perfect stranger was no longer a stranger. He had trusted her, even in fear of the unknown, and hadn't blamed her for handing him this burden. It was time to really let go. "Lay down, Jacob," she ordered with a wicked smile.

His face went serious, his grin replaced by a trace of vulnerability as he did exactly what she said, snow quickly melting beneath him. She knelt down, hovered over him for a moment, and then peeled away his shorts, gasping at his size. Exposed, he groaned in pleasure.

She wanted him in her mouth. She unhooked her bra, releasing her breasts, and her nipples immediately tightened in the cold air. All she had to do was look at his cock and he arched his back. Throwing currents wasn't just for beer cans. She pleasured him telekinetically, mind to flesh, and he thrashed—sounds causing pinecones to drop to the ground. The primal rumbles coming from his throat stirred her own desire. His cock pulsated harder with each charge she cast, and his groans were so intoxicating she had to end the game before she lost control and it became too dangerous.

She smiled, stopping the flow of electricity abruptly. "I'm about to make spring come early."

He smiled, clearly liking that idea. He ran his hands through his hair and reached for his shorts. He pulled out a condom, unwrapped it, and rolled it on.

She stood up and peeled off her panties and flung them aside. Being naked for the first time in front of him made her wet, and not from the melting snow that trickled under her feet. He smiled, his hands reaching out to touch her, his cock solid as steel. She straddled him and eased herself on. His hands on her waist moved down and gripped her hips. He rocked her and she rocked him, his thrusts cautious at first then urgent and furious. She fucked him hard, in control of her emotions for now, but his hands were all over her. His reverence fixing her broken life.

He flipped her onto her back and buried himself deep inside her, staring into her eyes as he slowed the momentum. Snow began to drop from the trees onto their bodies. Emotions growing from lust to something more. Love doesn't come this quick, but when he began whispering soft things into her ear, her heart delved into dangerous territory. "Thank you for teaching me how to let go," he said, his velvet voice sucking her down into that place where there was no way out but obliteration.

"Come with me now," he ordered. "Show me your love."

Her stomach buzzed, her pussy clenched, her mewls lilting. Her body would storm the gates and take no prisoners. He kissed her lips, his breath so sweet, his body moving in time with hers. She gripped his shoulders, following his muscular curves with her hands. The deep V of his back to his waist—his sweat trickling onto her chest. She loved his masculine scent. She rocked her hips and swirled them in ecstasy, arching and thrashing her head on the wet ground.

She came with a scream.

Birds left the trees and the earth shook. Jacob pumped her harder, kissing her still. He moaned, his girth sliding in and out faster, his body tense. He exploded in a guttural moan that echoed off the mountain.

Crackling sounds rang out, then there was a rush of water as the lake of ice shattered, and Holly slipped into the river. Water bubbled around her like a sauna. She gagged and spat, paddling and kicking to keep herself above water, but the current pulled her down and away from Jacob. She glimpsed him frantically running along the shore, screaming her name.

"Grab on to something—a log—anything! Stay above water, honey. I'm coming!" His image grew smaller, her eyes stinging and blinded.

Taming Fury / Ellen Cummins

Choking, she thrashed and kicked. She knew how to swim, but the current was strong—stronger than her. If she could scream, have an emotional outburst, maybe bring a tree down for her to grab...but she couldn't breathe.

This perfect day could not, would not, end in her tragic drowning. Her ears were full of water, sounds muting like the thumping of a broom beating the dust out of a blanket. Her mouth and lungs heavy, her arms even heavier. Sinking. Darkness. Cold seeped into her skin for the first time in her life. And only minutes after finding her reason to live.

Chapter 4

Holly's chest burned—air was being forced back into her lungs. A faraway voice faded in as she tried to pry her eyelids open, but they were frozen stuck. She coughed, her throat burning.

"Holly." The voice was louder. "Baby, wake up. You scared the shit out of me. Go on…let it out."

She turned her head and wretched. Blinking, she eyed Jacob who hovered over her, his eyes swollen and a new crease between his brows. Water dripped from his hair and face.

He wiped her bangs out of her eyes and pulled her into a hug. "You're as cold as ice, let's get you inside."

Half an hour later Holly shivered on the couch, holding the blanket tight to her chin, straining to keep it there. Her legs were tucked up against her chest in a ball. Jacob came into the living room with a hot bowl of something and a spoon leaning on the inside edge. A towel was draped over his shoulder.

"You need another blanket." He carefully helped move her legs and set the towel on her lap and then the bowl, and fluffed the pillow behind her head. "I think we have one of Gigi's quilts in with the linens." He took a few steps to the closet, opened the door, and rooted through the sheets.

Taming Fury / Ellen Cummins

"What the hell is happening to me, Jacob? I'm *freezing*. And weak. I don't even know what to think—I've never really known cold." She poked two fingers out, concentrating on the copy of *The Outdoorsman* on the coffee table, and squeezed her eyes shut. She willed it to move, but nothing happened. She groaned. "I can't lift *anything*. Not even a damned scrap of paper!"

"Maybe this is the answer to your prayers." He shrugged and smiled cautiously, unfolding a hand-sewn quilt. "You wanted to feel human. Freezing is a very human thing to feel. You were in that icy water for almost six minutes, and your heart nearly stopped. You're lucky your toes are still attached."

He sat next to her and placed the quilt over her legs, tucking it underneath her.

"I'd underestimated the strength of the current at that spot, but I was able to snag you near the bend just as you went under. I'm so sorry." He shook his head. "I'll hand-feed you to get you to warm up if you want me to. Anything to help you feel better." He began tucking a napkin under her chin.

"Damn it, Jacob, be serious. I'm not hungry."

"I am serious. I'll do it. Feed you, dress you, wipe your nose."

"Please," she snapped. "I'm not a child or an invalid. I'm fine."

"Wow." He shrugged, balling the napkin in his hand, his eyes pained. "I'll be in the bedroom if you need me."

He left the room quietly, leaving her alone to stew, and she pouted for an hour. He didn't deserve the way she'd spoken to him. Maybe he was right, maybe this *was* what she needed. Normalcy. The word bouncing off the inside of her skull didn't sound as good as she thought it might. Had she handed him her gift and then the icy river had shocked her—all systems down? Diffused her circuits? Snuffed her out? She'd liked being an untamed Fury more than she knew.

She cupped her mug with both hands and took a sip of her coffee. It was cold. She frowned and set it down. She already missed being able to do little things like warm up her cup with her palms. Focusing on the candle burning across the room on the cedar bookshelf full of classics, she snapped her fingers at it in an attempt to snuff it out. Nothing. She stuck her hand out toward it, drawing from it to snatch the flame. Still nothing.

Her lungs burned, and her heart ached. She set the bowl of soup on the table, flipped the blankets off her, and wiggled her toes. It was time to go. She bobbled into the kitchen.

She fumbled through the drawer and found a notepad and pen and scratched a few words out, leaving it next to the coffee pot.

Taming Fury / Ellen Cummins

Jacob,

This was the best day of my life. I'm sorry I barked at you. You're incredible—sexy and amazingly kind—everything I need and want. Please call me in a couple of days, and hopefully I'll have this thing sorted out.

Holly

* * * *

She struggled with the seat belt, her hands shaky and bumbling. Any other day buckling in would be a simple task, but her wires were crossed and her brain couldn't seem to send the signals to the right places. Driving would be risky too, but just like Jacob, she was running away to find answers. To process. She needed to understand.

She revved the car and pulled out onto the road, feeling imperfectly human when her gears ground and the car lurched violently forward. She missed the switch to turn on the heater, but after blowing out a hard steamy breath, she steadied her hand and was able to make the connection and cranked the heat to high.

Her head was fuzzy, her vision dusted in some sort of haze. Her tough-girl façade dwindled away as the moonlit countryside whizzed past her in the bug-dotted windshield. Before she snuck out, she'd lingered momentarily, propped in the doorway of

Jacob's bedroom, observing and listening to him saw logs like a lumberjack. He was tucked inside his grandmother's patchwork quilt. He had a family that cared—the kind that looked after one another. Hers stayed distant. Maybe this new change was her ticket back into her family's good graces.

Headlights in her rearview mirror suddenly blinded her, so she adjusted it away. Soon the entire inside of her car was lit up like Christmas.

"Get off my tail." She groaned. But it might be Jacob. She eased her foot off the accelerator and coasted a bit, squinting into the mirror. Only a faded silhouette of the driver could be seen. High beams flashed her. "Damn it, Jacob." She flicked her blinker on. "You don't need to worry about me." She coasted to the side of the road and put the car in park, idling to keep the heater going. She rolled down her window.

A behemoth man climbed into the passenger side, shut the door, and locked it. She gasped. Her heart in her throat, she scratched for her door handle and pulled it, but a woman was standing there holding it shut. The woman's blonde hair was pulled into such a tight ponytail that her high cheekbones seemed ready to break through the flesh.

A blinding force to the back of her head resulted in shooting pain to her face. Then darkness.

Chapter 5

Jacob hadn't slept that deeply in weeks. His body felt brand new. Holly's love had fed his starved loins and driven his psyche crazy. She was strong, lusciously curvy, and sensual. Adrenaline zipped through his veins—electrically charged.

He stretched and adjusted his raging hard-on beneath the seam of his boxer-briefs and yawned. Holly was only a few steps away in the other room, and he shamefully hadn't checked on her all night. But when his head hit the pillow, that was it. And she did need some time alone.

He brought his hands up close to his face and flexed his palms. Smiling wide, he reached for the alarm clock radio and threw a small jarring current that flipped the *ON* switch and dialed the tuner to a slow, easy song.

His cock twitched at the thought of Holly's plump lips, those hips. Her legs locked around his. Hopefully, she was feeling better. It was time to wake her up.

When he entered the living room and saw the blankets folded in the corner and her purse and keys gone, his heart dropped to his toes. Why would she leave without saying goodbye? *Fuck.* He went for his cellphone that was charging on the kitchen counter.

Taming Fury / Ellen Cummins

He reached for it then retracted his arm. *Control it.* He had to be careful not to set the house on fire, because the walls were practically made of kindling. The tips of his fingers hummed, ready to spit fire, but Holly had said he knew how to use it, possess it. He'd done all right with the alarm clock, but that was before his emotions were stirred up. He closed his eyes and calmed his heartbeat, but something wasn't right.

For the first time in his life, his intuition about a woman spoke to his softer side. Holly wasn't the type to run off—she was a go-getter, a fighter, fiercely determined. Someone who faced her problems head-on. She cared for him, but this new change had rocked her world. Depleted her of her powers she thought were a curse, but in reality had set her apart from everyone else and made her special. So special. Now she was gone, and he wondered if she thought maybe she wouldn't be good enough for him anymore. Well, she was wrong.

He grabbed the phone, but before he could dial he saw the note out of the corner of his eye. He put the phone down, picked up the note, and read it.

He relaxed his shoulders and blew out a breath. A couple of days would feel like forever, but she was worth the wait. No amount of time would keep him from her.

* * * *

Jacob wanted to throw his cellphone. Two and a half days

had passed—no word, no answer. He ran his hands through his hair and then dialed Justin, who picked up right away.

"Hey, bro," Justin said. "Glad to see you're all right. Have fun with my neighbor? She's quite the looker. She's got one helluva body."

"Your neighbor's name is Holly." He bit the inside of his cheek. He didn't expect that twinge of jealousy that rocked him and made him scowl into the phone. "Have you seen her?"

"Nope, not even at the mailbox. She's pretty good about checking that. And she's not sitting on her porch drinking coffee either. Is something wrong? Want me to check on her?"

"Please."

Jacob waited. His stomach growled, but food would not be an option until he knew she was okay.

"Bro..." Justin was back on the line, his voice concerned. "Three newspapers on her porch. A hungry cat too."

"Shit." Jacob hung the phone up, stuffed it into his jeans' pocket, and grabbed his keys. He locked the cabin up tight then jumped into his car, gunning the motor to life.

Holly's bright smile came into his mind as he drove his Volvo down the hill, going way too fast for his own good. The whites in her eyes shone like no star in the sky ever could, the way she put herself out there for him when they'd made love. The way she fucked him harder than any woman ever had, but was still sweet and soft like a vulnerable rose.

His thoughts went sideways, thinking about what had gone wrong. Where was she? Why hadn't she answered his incessant phone calls?

He should have gone after her the first day instead of playing with his newfound powers in the snow. Melting snowdrifts, turning rocks to cinder. Commanding the earth to be his new playground. Selfish, like a child.

His cellphone rang inside his pocket. He pressed the handheld enable button on the car's console. "Hello?"

"Jacob?" a woman's voice said.

"Holly?"

"Sorry. No," she replied, annoyed.

"Who is this?" Silence. Jacob's foot pressed harder on the accelerator, acid rising in his stomach. "*Hello?*"

"I knew you couldn't stay alone for very long." The woman's voice began to sound familiar, and he grimaced when the realization of who it was slammed into him.

"Damn it, Bridgette, I told you not to call me anymore. What do you need?"

"Nothing. Everything. But I have something *you* claim to need."

"What are you talking about? What do you have? I'm busy. I can't talk right now. Stop with your cryptic games and get to the point. And don't forget about the no-contact order. You shouldn't even be calling me." He pressed down harder on the pedal.

"I have Holly."

He lifted his foot off the pedal and the car coasted down the hill. The trees, the yellow lines on the pavement, and the world fell away.

"You have her? What do you mean, Bridgette? Don't fuck with me!"

The silence coming from the other end struck him, hurt him to the bare core of his soul. It undid him.

"Hello? Bridgette!"

Silence.

He slammed his fist on the steering wheel and tiny pieces of lightning spouted out of his fingers and into his clenched fists. He swerved the car to the side of the road and idled with his head in his hands. His complicated life had just gotten a whole lot more complicated. And the fire that lived inside him was going to be harder than ever to contain.

He checked his caller ID on his phone and found the call had come from his gym. He'd changed the locks. It was Sunday, and his small gym was closed on Sundays so his employees could spend the day with their families. He punched the accelerator, shred gravel, and within seconds his speedometer read ninety as he sped straight in the direction of the gym.

* * * *

Holly's belly rumbled and her face ached. Had it really come to this? Locked inside a room full of weights, treadmills, and those giant exercise balls? The irony of it made Holly groan. She hated traditional exercise. She loved long walks and bike rides though. She particularly liked *not* being hijacked by crazy ex-girlfriends and disgruntled employees of the man she'd come to love. She paused at the word. Was she in love with him? She barely knew him, but there was definitely a connection. And if she were given the opportunity to know him better, there was more than a strong possibility it could grow into something that might just change her life.

Her head pounded, and she reached around to rub the giant goose egg on the back of it—it had gone down since yesterday. The son-of-a-bitch had cracked her a good one. She scanned the room and tried to stand, but her equilibrium was off. There were no windows in this room. Screaming seemed like a good idea, but she wasn't sure if it would bring her perpetrators back into the room that much more quickly.

Think. A glass case with work-out gloves, fitness gear, handheld weights, protein packets, and water bottles hung behind a desk. How crazy was the chick really? And this guy Finn was huge. She wondered if she should arm herself with a dumbbell, but that would require breaking the glass and making noise. *Stay calm.* She prayed, steadying herself up onto her knees and then rising to her feet. Slowly, she tested her equilibrium, looking from left to right, up then down. She seemed to be steady enough to stand.

The door opened, and Bridgette stepped inside, closing and locking the door behind her. Holly had to get a good look at the woman she assumed was one of the reasons for Jacob's restraining order. She was tall and very thin, just as Holly had imagined, but definitely not the princess type. There was nothing demure about her. Nothing even slightly regal. Her perfect features worked together though, as would a model's face doctored in makeup and photoshop. Wide exotic eyes, big mouth with perfect teeth. Long, natural lashes. She was dressed in a tight blazer and stiletto heels.

Holly smoothed her top down and sucked in her tummy, allowing her sick insecurities to creep back in. Then she remembered how Jacob's breathing had quickened when he'd seen her standing naked in front of him, admiring and appreciating what God had given her, and her blood began to boil. Her wall had fallen down so easily for that man. Bridgette wasn't going to win this one.

"Get away from me." Holly straightened her posture, balled her fist, and hissed through her teeth. "You wacky bitch."

"Listen, honey...don't get your plus-sized granny panties in a bunch." She approached her, gliding confidently in her too-high-for-a-Sunday heels. "I want you to know this is nothing against you personally...well, maybe just a little." She twirled the ring on her finger. "As I already told you when you woke from your stupor yesterday, my brother and I have a few things to talk to Jacob about. Some of which are extremely personal. He doesn't really care about you, so don't get your sad little hopes up. Jacob doesn't always know what he wants. One minute it's marriage and kids, and the next minute he's changed his mind. Wants to be single, wants to think about his future. Can't handle it when the slightest complication or hiccup comes along. How am I supposed to act when all these women flirt with him every day? Women who come in here in their tight clothes, getting all sweaty, sticking their tits in his face like he's an available bachelor. Nope, I don't like it—didn't like it—but he felt I was too jealous. Didn't like when I'd show up here to take him to lunch and didn't like it when I'd get angry because he couldn't go."

She paused and hugged herself, seeming to be lost in a memory, her empty gaze darting around the room vacantly.

After a long silence, she continued. "So I broke a few things, made a few threats. I didn't think it would make him cancel the wedding. His scratches healed up nicely. And then

Taming Fury / Ellen Cummins

when I saw your car parked in front of his family cabin, the place he'd never take me—I hate fishing, hate the snow—I needed to know more about you. So Finn met me there and we followed you. Should I have asked you to tea instead?"

"Yeah." Holly glared. "It would have been a little more hospitable than clunking me over the head and knocking my face into the steering wheel. Why are we here? If you want to know about me, you could have simply asked. Are we here for some Chinese water torture? Cigarette burns or hot pokers to my eye? Jesus."

"My brother has a score to settle with Jacob, as do I."

"Well, I think you've both gone a little overboard. Don't you think so? I mean seriously, are we filming a made-for-TV movie here or what?"

"This isn't something we planned. It just kind of fell into place. This way we can get Jacob to finally talk to us...well, me. Although Finn wants to talk to Jacob too. Now that he knows you're here with us, maybe he'll blow in the door, wielding his sword to save his damsel."

"Let's act like grown-ups, shall we? I suppose Finn wants to talk with his fists."

"Jacob doesn't always reason well with words. As I'm sure you've learned. He's a man of few words, but speaks volumes with his cock. His generous endowments can make the tightest-lipped secret agent talk." Bridgette's face grew darker, the veins at her temples bulging. Her voice grew louder. "Did you two have a nice conversation?"

Holly's head spun as she stared at the bag of crazy standing before her. Finn planned to beat Jacob down, and who knew what their plans were for her? She was bait, that was for sure. There was no way in hell she was going to let them get to Jacob, although he was more than equipped to protect himself. She felt responsible for everything.

"Yes, we did have a lovely conversation as a matter of fact. Quite deep—and personal. But he said he wasn't ready for a serious relationship—was still trying to get over you." A not-so-well-thought-out plan began to develop as she watched Bridgette's demeanor soften.

"He's not over me?" she asked.

"No. Not that I didn't try to change his mind, but I understand love and the foolishness of the way one's mind works when things aren't easy." A lie. She understood nothing about relationships. "But love will always find a way." The truth.

"Okay." Bridgette traced her chin with her finger, thinking again. "Maybe he wants me back?" Another twirl of the ring. "He's on his way here, I'm sure of it—he'll check his caller ID. He wants to talk to me!"

Just then the door opened, and Finn stood in the doorway,

his frame filling the opening. He had no neck, his arms were logs, and the lines on his forehead gathered together into a nasty scowl. Even the veins on his oversized biceps seemed angry. *Steroids.* Holly squirmed when she thought of what she'd heard about men who took performance enhancers. Bad tempers and penises that shrank away to nothing.

    Finn looked from Bridgette to Holly, then back to Bridgette.

    "What are you so happy about? You two fucking besties now or what?" He scowled.

    "Listen," Bridgette said, holding her hands out to him. "I think Jacob wants me back. Maybe you should leave and let me talk to him alone. I could convince him to hire you back. Hopefully he didn't call the cops on us for being here, but if I know him, he didn't. He likes to keep things quiet so it doesn't freak out his clients. I mean, Tim *did* give us the spare key before he went on vacation. It's all legit. You just needed to get the stuff you left in your locker and that's it. We're lucky he hadn't changed the alarm code yet."

    "Have you lost your mind?"

    Bridgette and Holly both flinched. His booming voice thundered through to her bones. This one wouldn't be as easy to convince.

    "No, your sister's right." Another lie. "He said he needed you back, regretted his decision to let you go." Holly put on her most convincing smile. "Said you were his best personal trainer."

He considered her words for a moment, then his face turn tomato red and so did his eyes. He charged past Bridgette and smacked Holly in the mouth, knocking her against the wall. She crumpled into a heap on the floor. Stunned, she palmed the blood off her lip.

"*Really, Finn?*" Bridgette crossed her arms. "Was that necessary? You seriously don't need another battery charge against a woman on your record. Do you think Jacob's going to take you back when he sees *this*?"

"She's lying through her teeth. Just trying to make us let her go."

"This is kidnapping, Finn. Think about it—jail time will become prison time. And over a stupid job? I just want to make him talk to me...just the two of us. Just like before. We won't ever be apart again. Unless..." She turned around to face Holly who was still lying on the floor, gathering her wits. "Are you lying to me?"

She shook her head no and wiped a tear. Finn waved them off and stepped out of the room, slamming the door behind him so hard that the trophies lining the wall teetered.

"Because if you are..." Bridgette squatted down and sat on her heels in front of her. "I don't tolerate liars." She stood up, pulled a key from her cleavage, then walked to the desk and stuck it in the lock. She hesitated before turning it, tipping her head to the side and glaring at her. "No Chinese water torture here, but I do have something I want to share with you." She twisted the key and pulled the drawer open. Reaching inside, she took out a Taser.

Being a former Fury, Holly knew what this might mean if she still had her powers, but they'd been squelched in the river. Her face grew hot as reality set in. Regretfully now, she was just plain old ordinary Holly—nothing special, no secret weapons. Just Holly. And that was good enough. It had to be.

She sprang from the floor, and with two sweeping steps launched onto the desk, snatching the Taser out of Bridgette's hand and pointing it at her. Holly heard noises from outside the door—voices, yelling, things slamming against the walls. The hair on her neck bristled. Jacob burst through the door.

"Holly!" he screamed. "You okay, honey?" His nose was bleeding, a knot growing on his cheekbone, his college sweatshirt torn at the neckline. The smell of sulfur hung in the air.

She gasped and nodded yes. "Call the police, Jacob."

"I already did."

Bridgette stepped in between them, her perfect ponytail not so perfect anymore. "Honey? You call her 'honey'?" she panted.

"But what about us?"

"Us is over—it's been over. There is no us." He swept Holly into his arms and gave her a quick kiss. She winced, and then he noticed her busted lip. His eyes flamed crimson.

Holly heard a scream and the sound of shattering glass. Bridgette came at them fast with something silver raised above her head. Without warning, Holly's fire reclaimed her as she watched Jacob redirect the electrodes from the Taser in her hand straight to Bridgette's heart, stopping her, dropping her to her knees, giant barbell and all. Holly threw her head back as fifty thousand volts fired through her body, amping her, no darts necessary. They only needed to connect with the motes in the air to create electrified trails of light. All she'd needed was a little jump start.

Faint sounds of sirens in the distance gradually grew louder as they approached.

Jacob checked Bridgette's heart to make sure it was still beating. He dragged her stunned body through the door and out into the hall, shutting and locking the door behind him. The knot on his cheek was beginning to recede, and Holly checked her lip with her tongue.

"Before the police get here," he said, his body smoldering, "and since your lip is healing, I'm aching to taste you again."

He nipped at her chin and then, with the tip of his tongue,

coaxed her mouth open. She wrapped her trembling fingers in his hair, intoxicated by his kiss again. She couldn't wait to go home with him.

* * * *

Sitting in Jacob's bathtub built for two, with bubbles up to her chin, Holly rested with her back against Jacob's chest. She glanced over at his bathroom sink and grimaced at the brown towels and matching toothbrush holder that rested next to the faucet. His apartment definitely could use a woman's touch.

The past few hours had been rough, recounting the events to the police while they hauled Finn off in handcuffs and Bridgette off in an ambulance. The last two days had been the scariest of Holly's life. But the images quickly faded when Jacob moved her hair aside with his fingers and trailed his tongue along her earlobe, gently teasing her with his breathy moan against her temple.

"You've been through so much—no more loneliness," he said. "You're safe here with me." His arms wrapped around her, pulling her closer, and he rolled his soapy palms gently over her nipples, which pebbled at his touch. His huge cock pushed against her back and everything inside her went soft again. "Unleash some of that fury on me," he whispered in that all-encompassing, rugged voice that made her ache for his touch.

She turned and straddled him, easing herself down on his

cock and taking his mouth with hers. He grabbed her hips while their tongues delved deliciously together, and the lavender scented water began to sizzle and splash as their rocking became furious enough to empty the tub.

She slowed to trace his collarbone with her finger and then licked the hollow of his neck, exploring his skin with her tongue. She could see his strong heartbeat in his throat and she kissed it too. He lifted her face and moved a wet strand of hair away from it. He seemed to look right through her, reading her thoughts as if he had gained another superpower. "I'm all yours," he assured her.

He smiled and kissed her deeply, bringing the momentous rhythm up two notches with some quick but cautious thrusts. His cock was huge, but she could handle it. It was the emotions that came with the orgasm she had to learn to regulate. They could both learn together.

Holly gasped when Jacob lifted her out of the tub. He carried her to the bed and laid her down. He crawled on the bed and parted her legs, shifting on his knees to get in between them. She worshipped his body momentarily, eyeing his strong jawline and glistening skin that was still speckled with bubbles. At the sight of his throbbing cock she lifted her hips and squirmed impatiently. Electric waves of lust flooded through her, burning from her chest all the way to her fingertips.

"Put your hands on me," she begged.

He trailed his fingers from her lips down to her soaked pussy, rolling them down to her moist folds where he lingered momentarily to circle the flesh just above. He slid his finger inside and she arched. A burst of clarity came to her when she reached for him, whispering his name, panting and begging for him to take her. He was her own piece of the burning sun.

As he took her hips and slid her closer, she opened herself up wide. He claimed her, she was all his, and his magnetic lure had him holding her so tight she thought he might break her, but she was stronger than that. When he lifted away an inch to look into her eyes, she yanked him back hard and slammed her hips against him in a heated frenzy to fuck him back as hard as he was her. The headboard creaked, an unlit candle began to liquefy next to the bed, and the glass in the window bowed.

"Baby," he warned, placing his hand gently over her mouth and smiling. "Don't scream."

He was so many things to her. Their powers together meant infinite nights like this one, as long as they could keep the apartment in one piece.

Her shriek lilted, her pleasure building. His steel cock had her clenching to hold it together. He buried his face in her hair and slammed against her over and over, bringing her to the very brink of detonation. There was no stopping it.

One final thrust and they exploded in a tidal wave of thrashings and guttural screams. The curtains blew into a frenzied knot, but the window didn't break. The candle only puddled and dripped onto the hardwood floor. Controlling it had surprisingly gotten easier.

Holly ran her fingers through her wild hair. She burst into an almost diabolical laugh when she saw that only the candle had been ruined and nobody had gotten blown out the window by the surge, although the smell of sulfur lingered in the room. She'd definitely found her match.

Taming Fury / Ellen Cummins

About Ellen Cummins

Ellen Cummins was born and raised in Modesto California, surrounded by healthy orchards and thick valley air, spending her childhood summers swimming and climbing trees. Her favorite thing to do has always been to escape inside an adventure, be it traipsing through the desert, digging in her garden, going to rock concerts, or taking in the latest thriller at the theater. (She was stricken with Monster Mania at a very young age.) To her, there's no other feeling like being taken by surprise, or having her breath taken away by an unexpected twist. An avid reader of ghost, vampire, and other paranormal stories, she one day had an idea of her own and wrote it down. Soon she'd created new worlds from thin air and fell madly in love with her characters. A new obsession was born.

A manicurist by day and jewelry associate by night, she spends her in-between time caring for her gorgeous daughters and her amazingly bright and facetious son. Robby, her husband of nineteen years, has been an unexplainable force of encouragement. She loves to write about remarkable people with extraordinary gifts, and her greatest pleasure in life is to give them a voice.

Taming Fury / Ellen Cummins

Ellen's Website:

www.ellencummins.wordpress.com

Reader eMail:

ellierobby@att.net

CPSIA information can be obtained at www.ICGtesting.com
Printed in the USA
LVOW06s1328081215

PP10312300001B/3/P

9 781944 270032